A GREATER GOOD

t wilton dale

© 2017 by t wilton dale
All rights reserved.

ISBN: 1977512380
ISBN-13: 9781977512383
Library of Congress Control Number: 2017914908
CreateSpace Independent Publishing Platform
North Charleston, South Carolina

DEDICATION

This book is dedicated to my wife, Mary. She has been my cherished life companion for forty-five years and counting. She was my companion as a reader while this book was being written. A great consumer of fiction, typically several books a week, Mary had the unenviable task of reading just a couple of thousand words every few days. At each read, the "more" she was left wishing for was typically not yet written. I thank her for her constant encouragement, support, and critical comments. Special thanks also go to our dear friend and my valued colleague, Rhiannon. Rhiannon is the voice behind the character Marcia in chapter 10, as she role-played with me the psychotherapy session documented there. She also wrote the journal entry reflecting on the session that appears in that chapter. There were other readers as the novel was written who provided comments and support, and I thank them for being with me through this: Ronna, Janine, Angie, Ben, and Matt. I also wish to thank the editors and designers at CreateSpace for their invaluable assistance in presenting this book in a readable, attractive, and compelling way for my readers. Finally, thanks aside, let me add one other dedication. This book is dedicated to all the psychologists at the outset of their careers who have been my supervisees in their professional registration process. I have set this book in the year 2057. Some of you might still be in practice then!

CONTENTS

Chapter 1	First Words	1
Chapter 2	Byron	3
Chapter 3	Alton	43
Chapter 4	Sallye	73
Chapter 5	Beckett	116
Chapter 6	The District	173
Chapter 7	The North Hill	208
Chapter 8	The Macabre	239
Chapter 9	All Faiths Day	286
Chapter 10	Marcia	317
Chapter 11	The Wilkes	341
Chapter 12	Cripps	381
Chapter 13	Myles	412
Chapter 14	Final Thoughts	426
About the Author		429

1

FIRST WORDS

Hey, this is Sallye.
I want to let you know that there are things in this book about me that I am not proud of. You are going to read about the very lowest points of my life so far.

There is still a lot of this story that is painful for me to read, even though I have read it through twice already. All these events happened and are done. But they don't feel done to me. When I read some parts I feel ashamed—ashamed of what I did, ashamed at how poorly I handled things. You'll understand. In a way, it is tough for me to have this story out there—out there for you to read, for anyone to read.

Not that I have any illusions of privacy anyway, that I should be embarrassed to have it written out like this. All my life, the WarpWeb has tracked my every movement, my every curiosity, my every purchase—all this is tracked on the wearable that I have on my left forearm. All that tracking goes into the ASL.

I have never had privacy, never expected it.

Oh, you won't know what the ASL is. Those letters stand for… hmm, we always just say ASL. Administration of Social Logistics, that's it.

I have lived within the ASL all my life; it takes care of my every need and want. That is the reason it needs to track me, to track everyone. It provides for us. All that tracking data goes back into these huge computers to create what we call the Common Knowledge Stock. The stock is mined by the ASL and by selected businesses to make sure that what each of us needs is right there when we need it.

The ASL knows when I am hungry and when I am horny. It knows me in that physiological way thanks to a nifty little device that was implanted in my gut when I was five. My implant monitors my every heartbeat and the health of my cardiovascular system. It monitors my nervous system and the depth of every breath I take. My implant monitors the flux of my hormones.

All this monitoring is for the good of my health. Healthy living, my healthy living, is so important to the ASL. The implant sends all my physiological data to my wearable. What is tracked on my wearable, all that "me," gets sent to the ASL. The Sallye there can be downloaded from the ASL servers to my Individual Profile Extract, my IPE. I can't imagine anybody would ever want to know me that way: as a big set of data. I am so much more fun if you get to know me personally. But the ASL needs to know me that way for my well-being. That is how the ASL takes care of me.

It is important for you to know that the ASL is much more than just data and provisions. There is a human face to the ASL. I am part of that human face, bred and raised for optimal functioning in my role. As a living, breathing, loving human being, I am called to come alongside those who are suffering. They call me a Paraclete. It is a word from the ancient Greeks meaning "one who is called alongside to help."

You are going to read some dreadful things about the ASL, or at least about some of the people in the ASL. I guess even the best intentions can go awry. And even though all the things that you read here happened, and I was a part of those events, and some of it hurts, I still think of the ASL as a good thing.

I guess.

As you begin to read, it is the year 2057, and all this takes place just after I'd turned eighteen.

2

BYRON

Byron had entered the virtual-reality room, or VR room, on many other occasions.

Byron's mentor, Dr. Myles Chetwin, took him there to hear the jazz of a hundred years before. It had been Dr. Chetwin's arcane interest but one that Byron found intriguing. The VR room was transformed into the stages of jazz festivals in Montreal, Montreux, and Newport. The likenesses of Dave Brubeck, Miles Davis, and John Coltrane, together with their sidemen, were reconstructed from old recordings with multiple camera angles and transformed into a three-dimensional presence. Byron and Dr. Chetwin could nearly smell the sweat of the driven energy of the jazz played there. They sat amid the musicians, entranced by the music of another era.

Byron had visited erotica clubs in that same VR room with Sallye as a prelude to their adventures in sexual intimacy.

As a part of his training as a Paraclete, Byron had completed ethics courses there. His hastily conceived actions had taken him down many branching paths of unanticipated outcomes.

But never before had he entered the VR room with such eagerness, with such trepidation, as he had today. Today, he would have his first session of avatar psychotherapy.

Byron was powerfully aware of the wearable on his forearm as it transmitted data from the physiological sensor implanted in his gut. He had mentally prepared himself so that the data stream would indicate the optimal levels of arousal and focus. He felt clean, so deliberately clean. He was clear of selfish motive. He had ended his early-morning session of yoga with the traditional namaste. He had deeply breathed in and out his best self. His biometric data would surely show that.

Byron had no doubt that the avatar he would meet in VR would also bring his best self. And Byron meant to match that with his own.

But still there was the keen edge of apprehension. Byron wondered if it would be a battle of wits. If it was, would he be the fool? Somehow, he couldn't imagine that it would be. After all, the program was developed for his well-being, his healing, his better adaptation to the society that surrounded him. Of course, Byron already perceived himself as being well, as having already healed, as being optimally adapted. He was a product of impeccable breeding, raising, and training.

Byron had options for his choice of four distinct psychotherapy avatars, each created by Dr. Alastair Perkins, award-winning and esteemed psychologist. The artificial intelligence for the first avatar, Dr. C, was based on the psychotherapy manuals of the late twentieth century. Maneuvers of cognitive therapy, scientifically proven at that time to be effective, were integrated with psycholinguistic analysis of the client's words in session. Brilliantly, Dr. C came to life through the ease of a conversational interface developed by entertainment role-playing games.

It won awards for its innovation in making psychotherapy available to all who had access to a VR room.

The second avatar, Dr. R, integrated the data of the client's IPE-CKS into the artificial-intelligence analysis. Objective information flowed into the AI program about the client's real-life behavior between sessions, for example, places visited and with whom, purchases made, and time spent in different activities. This data would validate or discount what the client actually said in therapy. Real-life behavioral change and accountability became the focus. No longer could clients lie or deny to their therapist. Stunning.

Further awards came.

The third-generation avatar, Dr. S, incorporated the client's real-time biometric analysis—the output of the implant—into the timing and direction of therapeutic interventions. Levels of circulating hormones and activation of the autonomic nervous system were tracked; interventions were delivered at the best possible moment and with the level of intensity the client could tolerate. The animation of the avatar was enhanced with facial microexpressions. Dr. S would be perceived to be feeling too, both reflecting and leading the client's emotional experience. The therapy avatar had become softer, more empathic, and more responsive. Astounding.

The awards community went ballistic.

Finally came Dr. Y. Standing on the platform of process advancements to date, the artificial-intelligence program deepened the psychological and philosophical underpinnings of the avatar. Dr. Y was freed from considering only the words and objective data of the client to integrate more fundamental human considerations into the therapy. Existential issues such as personal freedom, acceptance of one's own mortality, and a yearning for meaning and intimacy could now be a focus of the discourse. The content of sessions became more deeply human, more understanding of the angst within us all. Profound.

The accolades rolled in at a dizzying pace.

It was Dr. Y that Byron would meet in the virtual-reality room.

Bryon put on his 3-D eyewear and stepped into the room. With the flow of warm, moist air, loosely woven curtains moved over the illusion of an open window. The scent of jasmine and lavender filled the space, as though there were a garden close by. The seating was comfortable. Dr. Y sat on a chair with a straight back, somewhat rigid. He smiled, said the briefest hello, and sat in readiness.

"I suppose you know why I am here."

There was a long pause. Then Dr. Y said, "You tell me." And he sat still, very still.

"You would know from my IPE-CKS."

Suddenly, there was a twinkle in Dr. Y's eye. The rising and falling of his chest under his loose-fitting clothing animated him. With the slightest engagement, the avatar leaned toward Byron. Generously, graciously, Dr. Y spoke in hardly more than a whisper, as though he were sharing a secret with Byron. "I didn't integrate any of your IPE-CKS data prior to your session, and I am not doing it now. This is strictly about what you choose to tell me."

Byron was disoriented by Dr. Y's statement. Could it really be true? Byron had expected that the psychotherapy artificial-intelligence program would always integrate the Individual Profile Extract of personal data. Could it be that here, in this encounter with Dr. Y, all that was known of him through the ASL was being cloaked? He wondered whether this was what privacy was.

Dr. Y leaned forward and kindly said, "Trust that it is so. I always do this for my first sessions. Now what brings you to session today? What concerns, what problems?"

"Well, nothing really. I am required to do an avatar therapy session as part of my completion of First Flight as a Paraclete. I am here for that, to have that experience. As a Paraclete, I am called to come alongside those who are suffering. Future clients I will serve will attend sessions with you. I am here to have that experience. By coming here and doing my own session, I will best be able to assist them."

"To have that experience, you would need to bring forward a matter of personal distress: perhaps a relationship that has gone awry or overwhelming negative feelings."

"Well, none of that applies to me." Even though Byron was direct with his words, he had the queasy feeling of a deeper dishonesty. He was relieved that the avatar was not privy to his internal autonomic responses. That he, or it, wouldn't know.

"So, then, let's go looking." Dr. Y smiled as though he had a challenge to meet. "Tell me of a typical day for you."

Byron settled in, relieved. "Well, it starts with getting up about six thirty. There are six of us living in the compound who share two bathrooms and only one shower. We need to coordinate all our routines so that everyone is ready to go on time."

"Six of you?"

"Six—we are all Paracletes completing the First Flight of the trade. We live together."

"So where do you go, when you are all ready to go?"

"We usually have a class first thing in the morning. Between us six, and others, there is a class of about fifteen. We meet here at the North Hill."

"So what are your classes?"

"Our classes vary. Today it was a unit in child development and family life. Yesterday it was working toward our certification in Advanced First Aid. On Fridays, we always have literature class, in which we discuss great works of fiction. That reading allows us to understand human nature as revealed through the work of novelists. We often role-play the conflicts that the authors have created between their characters and talk about how we would help them. It is entertaining and insightful."

"Very good. Byron, how old are you?"

"Eighteen."

"Eighteen." The avatar paused. "You speak like you are thirty-five."

"Oh, you noticed. Even when we were small, even before our preflights as aspiring Paracletes, we were trained to speak clearly and precisely. It is to be a hallmark of our trade, along with our good grooming."

"So after class?"

"After class, we all go into schools. I work with two types of students. One type is students struggling with bad family situations. Their behavior might be out of control. As a Paraclete, I calm them down, keep them focused. The other type of student is the extraordinarily gifted. We identify and help those students to excel now so they can become future leaders of our society."

"Do you like children, then?"

"Yes. Although I would be assigned there whether or not I did. It's part of my training."

"And after school hours? What do you do when that workday is done?"

"We have free time; I usually spend it with my intimate, Sallye."

"Tell me about Sallye."

"Well, she is kind of wild and crazy. But I love her. We have decided to be exclusive and committed, even though everyone says we are too young for that."

"Wild and crazy, eh? She doesn't sound as though she is a Paraclete like you, someone trained to speak properly and help others."

"Oh, she is! She keeps her 'wild and crazy' under control when she's doing her tasking and classes. She lives in a different compound; they are all kind of crazy over there."

"So when you are not doing your classes or your tasking, are you wild and crazy too?"

Byron laughed at the thought. Wild and crazy was not in his personality profile. Persistent and conservative were. "No. But I really like it in Sallye. I try really hard to be playful, and she helps."

"OK, then, you have had your free time after work. What about the rest of your day?"

"We all work together on supper and cleanup. Then I go to the gym. Before bed, I read the literature we must know for class."

"Thank you, Byron." Dr. Y paused. The artificial-intelligence program was already assembling a personality profile, doing it automatically. The pause was designed to create a punctuation moment in the conversation. "I have four important questions for you."

"Go ahead," Byron replied in his politest voice.

"Each may have additional curiosities. Curiosities for now or later."

"I am ready."

"Byron, do you think you will live forever?"

Byron caught a smile erupting on his face. He knew that teens were supposed to feel immortal but was taken aback by the blunt question that had such an obvious answer. "Well, no, sir. But I do expect to live a long life. I am healthy, and all my needs are met."

"What about adventurous behavior, risky and impulsive activities, little tests of your mortality?"

"Not me. I don't push the envelope, especially if danger is involved."

"And what about suicide? Suicide is the leading cause of death for the adolescent."

After the slightest of pauses, Byron answered, "Never, sir."

Byron had spoken this in an even more assured tone than his usual one. This time he was aware of the queasiness within, the need to hide what was inside of him. He hoped the avatar hadn't picked it up, but he suspected the AI analysis within the avatar would have noted the delay, even though it was only milliseconds.

Without missing a beat, Dr. Y went on. "Very well. You described a very organized and planned life. Tell me about the freedom you feel and how you handle that freedom."

Byron looked at the avatar, puzzled. The concept of freedom was odd to him; he didn't know how to relate. "Well, when I go to the gym, I have the freedom to do cardio, lift weights, or even do yoga. I make every effort to keep my workout routines balanced so that I have an even development of strength, flexibility, and endurance. I exercise that freedom with a sense of responsibility to be healthy so I can play my role in society."

"The role of Paraclete."

"Yes."

"Helper of troubled ones and those with great potential."

"Yes."

"Have you ever thought of doing anything different?"

"Never." Byron could say that with conviction.

"Very well. And tell me about who you are emotionally close to. Who meets your emotional needs?"

"Sallye does."

"And what did you say? That you are exclusive and committed?"

"That's right."

Dr. Y continued. "And family?"

"My mother is a teacher in the Paraclete program. I respect her for how skilled she is, how much she knows."

An eyebrow lifted on the face of the avatar. He waited for Byron to speak further. There had been no mention of a father. Even the mention of his mother bore no disclosure of the nature of his family life, just respect for her professional role.

"I grew up in a family communal home. Four families together. Eight parents raised us, all Paracletes themselves. Those four pairs of Paracletes were encouraged to have children, children who would carry on the gifts of their parents' trade."

"Encouraged to have children." Pause. "Bred together?" Dr. Y was more than curious. Perplexed, perhaps.

"Oh, not like that. They loved each other. They had us and then raised us in an attachment-optimal environment."

"Attachment optimal?"

"Yes, all our emotional needs were met, if not by our own parents, then by the other parents there. I left the family communal home to go into the compound with other teens working toward the Paraclete qualifications, a part of our differentiation process."

The avatar processed the precise account given by Byron.

"Tell me more."

"About the compound?"

"No, about your childhood home."

"It was safe there. We were rich in love, in adventure, in culture, in teachings." Byron felt a twinge of guilt in what he had said. It was not true. What was actually characteristic of his childhood was likely more relevant here, but he couldn't bring himself to speak of it. He experienced the unspoken dread that was common when memories of his childhood intruded. Byron was certain that his emotional response, although supposedly covered by his words, would have been read by the implant and the data forwarded to his ASL individual profile. He hoped that the avatar was honest in declaring that his IPE-CKS was cloaked. Then he wondered whether one might expect honesty from an avatar.

Dr. Y shifted in his chair, a subtle indicator that this line of questions was done, and another would begin. There was a slight warming to his manner. "With Sallye, are you able to tell her of your feelings, the things that trouble you, your struggles?"

"Well, there are not any struggles. My feelings for her are all positive."

The eyebrow lifted again. It was almost mechanical. The similarity of its movement was not lost on Byron.

"Very good. Now one more question. I am wondering: what gives your life a sense of meaning?"

"Oh, that is very easy. My work—my calling as a Paraclete. The chance to work with children who don't have the advantages we have."

"Tell me more about that."

"I work at the school for working- and consumer-class children. We don't have much space to relate individually with the students assigned to us. It is noisy, and I wonder how anyone could learn anything in that noise. But there is a sense of playfulness there, perhaps even joy and adventure. Maybe it is just such a contrast to the structured and deliberate way that we are taught back at the family communal home. At the school, it is chaotic but somehow quite real and appealing."

"Go on."

"There was one girl there, poorly dressed, poorly..." Byron's mind tumbled back to the physicality of her, her stale smell, the stifling warmth that came off her body. The look of her face was tangled, furrowed with shame and fear. "She was only about seven, and I must have been, well, about fourteen. We were told to relate to the younger children as though they were our siblings. But this girl...with this girl, I found myself thinking it was a dad that she needed."

Byron stopped speaking. His gut suddenly went empty, the way he felt when he got winded on the soccer pitch. His mind reeled, filled with panicky thoughts. A pervasive fear had eclipsed his mind the moment he'd spoken the word *dad*. He wanted to run, but he was physically immobilized. A sharp pain erupted in his upper left arm and across the side of his face. He was on the brink of fainting and desperately tried to bring himself back. It was to no avail.

After a timeless interval, he found himself lying on his back on the floor, staring up at Dr. Y. The avatar had gone into stasis. Nowhere in its protocols was a response for a client collapsing onto the floor of the VR room. It shifted into a curious but silent mode, allowing the moment to hang and waiting for a behavioral sign from Byron that he might be ready.

Once Byron had come to and pulled himself off the floor, the avatar became animated again. Bluntly, absurdly, it returned to the point at which the dialogue had been interrupted, resuming as though nothing had happened. "In some way, you wanted to be that dad. Were you able to do so?"

Byron looked at Dr. Y awkwardly, still disoriented.

The avatar cycled into the line of questioning again with a slightly different inflection, urging a response. "You were speaking of a little girl who needed a dad. That is where you left off. Can you tell me more about her needing a dad?"

Byron suddenly found himself tearing up, trying to grasp what had happened. Why this sudden crack in his secure facade? He struggled not to show his leaking emotion to the avatar. The smell of the girl—unwashed, unkempt—returned to cramp away in Byron's gut.

Dr. Y pressed again, the AI program sensing a resistance to dissolve, to dissolve through a different tone of voice: one gentler and more enticing. "You sensed she didn't have a dad. Did you, in your relationship with her, do something that would provide to her what a dad might have provided?"

But still the footing was gone out from beneath Byron. He had lapsed into a drift of silence, hardly aware of even his own thoughts.

"Could you draw from your relationship with your own father ideas of how to relate to her?"

Tears came. Byron blurted out, unable to contain himself, "Dr. Y, there was something wrong with my dad!" The young Paraclete couldn't believe he had actually said that. It was inconceivably disloyal. Tears erupted and coursed down his cheeks.

"Dad was there, but it felt like he was not. I was told that I was lucky to have him around, but he was different from the other dads. All the other parents went out to work. It was…it was…"

Byron fell silent again. Dr. Y issued forward in his chair. In the absence of the historic IPE-CKS data, there was no reference for what Byron was trying to say. Minutes passed. In the silence, the artificial-intelligence algorithm computed the client would not be able to tell the avatar more, at least not at this stage of therapy; father issues would be left to a future session with the young man. After a pause and a distinct warming of the facial expression on the avatar, the AI protocol shifted to interpretation, reassurance, and ego strengthening.

"Thank you, Byron. Your reaction here suggests you are a deeply sensitive soul. Observant. But wounded.

"You are so much more than a 'just graduated' from First Flight Paraclete training, much more than one of six in a compound."

Byron's silence continued, but he was listening.

"You are capable of feeling, of grappling with things that cannot be learned, that can only be felt and, when felt, remain inexpressible. These things can overwhelm you, render you speechless. I detect you have the heart and soul of one uniquely suited to help others in their suffering, a Paraclete, as you would say, and I am grateful for it.

"Can I speak frankly to you?" The avatar softened further, smiled, and spoke in that soft, forthright, confidential sort of voice. "I am just a machine. You are much more than I. You are deeply human." In talking to Byron this way, the program had brought him back to the physical reality of the space, preparing the client to leave the experience.

"Your calling is not just about serving society. Your task is to bring humanness to existence in yourself and others. You were touched by that little girl at school; you became deeply worried about your father. You added a dimension of Byron to that breeding and training that you received.

"But, Byron, your words here today have told me much. And some of what you have said concerns me deeply, perhaps more than it does you. After I have had time to analyze and reflect, it is imperative that we meet again to explore some vital issues."

Byron's mind was desperate to hold on to Dr. Y, to have hope that he could be all right, as he had just admitted to himself that he was not. He was aware that the session was now over.

The avatar shifted slightly, intensified. "I would like to see you again soon. But we are done for today."

Byron summoned the strength and composure to say, "Thank you, Dr. Y. I will come again."

(II)

Dr. Alastair Perkins's office was on the fourth floor of the academy building at the university. He was the executive director of the Administration of Social Logistics. The acronym "ASL", encircled in an oval frame and emblazoned in gold lettering, branded the offices as the local branch of the sociopolitical structure that now dominated much of the continent.

Byron felt awkward there in that august building. His destiny as a Paraclete, determined by both breeding and socialization, made academic education irrelevant for him. He was not considered suitable for a liberal-arts education. It was intimidating for him to come to the university campus.

Within the university, Dr. Perkins was also seated as the Noam Chomsky Chair in Advanced Psycholinguistics and Artificial Intelligence, a designation highly respected within the academic community. It was he, Dr. Alastair Perkins, who had pioneered the application of artificial intelligence to the practical psychology of avatar-based therapy. Through the progressive sequence of prototypes, he had created an ultimate therapy experience, an experience available for all.

Despite his authoritative position, Dr. Perkins also had some less desirable tasks. Troubleshooting when the social engineering ran amok was one of them. Such was the reason that he was meeting Byron Wilkes-Williams on this day. Dr. Perkins had transcripts and the biometric-readings matrix from the AVT session Wilkes-Williams had completed earlier in the day. The historical data and physiological responses of the client IPE-CKS had been strategically cloaked to the avatar; this kept fresh the responses the avatar would make in the session, and fresh responses were necessary because the young Paraclete was less naive than members of the general population. The receptive aspect of Byron's IPE-CKS remained on, however, capturing the data it would feed back into the CKS and to Dr. Alastair Perkins as he monitored the novice Paraclete's responses. What arose from the Dr. Y session was a perturbation, a perturbation that could either spell a vulnerability in the system or highlight a unique outcome that might put the future use of the Paraclete into jeopardy.

Byron Wilkes-Williams's Individual Profile Extract was openly available and well known to Dr. Alastair Perkins. Byron had been conceived as a second-generation Paraclete in the middle of the first crop of bred Paracletes. He was a product of two gifted parents. Byron's biological parents had been attracted to the trade by their own proclivities. Initially, both had done well, his mother exceptionally so. When they met, there was no chemistry at play, just engineering. They were not star-crossed lovers; they were brought together by circumstances that Dr. Alastair Perkins had arranged. They were tied together by engineered adversity. And they were tied together by Dr. Alastair Perkins himself, appealing to their good natures to do good for society, to produce excellent offspring. Dr. Alastair Perkins had done well to mate them and seven other pairs.

The mating was a success. Byron's DNA profile contained high concentrations of positive markers for the trade. He would be sensitive; he was adaptable; he was only slightly introverted; and he was trainable. Due to the crapshoot of messy genetics, many did not exit the breeding program with such a suitable DNA foundation to make an optimal Paraclete. But Byron had. He was given the surname of William-Wilkes to identify two highly contributing DNA sources—one from his mother and the other from the paternal grandmother. Byron's father, despite initially being good at the trade, had not been nearly so biologically blessed. Through recessive genes passed on to his son, however, an optimal DNA profile had emerged in Byron.

Aside from the congratulatory visits with the parents in the hospital immediately after the infants had been born, Dr. Alastair Perkins made a point of not being involved in the lives of the bred Paracletes. He designed the attachment environment in which they would be raised. He had strong influence over their interpersonal-skills-development training. But he was careful to separate himself from direct involvement with them. Dr. Alastair Perkins was not good with children. Others in the program were: the Parent Paracletes and Dr. Myles Chetwin, senior psychologist. Perkins was drawn to the young adolescents at that early stage of enhanced self-awareness, but he kept himself back. Dr. Alastair Perkins jokingly said that as the principle researcher in the program, he didn't want to contaminate the data with his direct involvement.

Now, as Byron was coming to see him, he could only imagine what a fit and attractive young man he might be. A quick scan of Byron's IPE-CKS revealed nothing of concern aside from the avatar-session data. Byron liked Coltrane, was flexibly bisexual, had made excellent choices of reading material, and was comfortable within his own body as evidenced by the biometric data and activity choices he made. As much as the perturbation from the Dr. Y session was unsettling to Dr. Alastair Perkins, he was looking forward to meeting Byron Wilkes-Williams and thought of him almost as progeny.

Byron stood at the door of Dr. Alastair Perkins's office for several minutes looking at the name plate. He tumbled back in his mind for the reference point to Noam Chomsky; he had been mentioned in his history of psychology classes during his First Flight training.

Byron was unsettled at being beckoned here with such immediacy. He knew he would be meeting with someone from the Administration of Social Logistics but hardly expected it would be someone as eminent as Dr. Alastair Perkins. In these austere hallways, he felt insignificant dressed in his polo shirt and khakis, with the smudge of fading acne blemishes on his face. He could feel himself getting sweaty from nerves and the thought that his implant was probably going crazy.

Outside the door, Byron could hear the urgent speech of two men inside. His training had taught him to metalisten, that is, not to get caught up in the words but to process the pacing and inflection, to surmise the intent. It was not good. One voice was intense and intrusive. The other was distancing and dismissive. They danced like that through multiple exchanges, escalating the polarization with each iteration of the dynamic.

Byron recoiled from the door, back against the wall. Despite the sturdy construction of the building, he felt the vibe coming through. He closed his eyes and waited. Before long, a figure emerged from Dr. Alastair Perkins's office and strode down the hall in the opposite direction. Byron recognized the gait and bearing of the man: Dr. Sebastian Cripps, a lecturer from the First Flight training, a precise man focused on the ethics of the program.

After a few moments of letting the negative energy settle, Byron approached the door again. He knocked and was greeted by a civil "Come in."

The office was almost classically professorial. Books—yes, books of paper and hardcovers—lined the shelves. These gave the room a musty smell but also separated the academic from lesser men. A variety of trophies was in the room: a lacrosse racket; a chessboard; antiquated devices in the sciences, including a slide rule and an abacus; and an ancient game of beans on a board with concave depressions. There was a window in the room behind the desk, casting hard light from behind Dr. Alastair Perkins.

Upon seeing the professor, a senior psychologist and director, Byron's mind flipped to the trained heuristics of assessing first appearance. Dr. Alastair Perkins was dressed in wool-blend slacks, an open-neck shirt, and a tight knit pullover. A tweed jacket tied the various earth-tone hues together. His beard was graying, and his hairline was in a late recession. But it was his eyes, his eyes that simultaneously seemed both dull and all-knowing, eyes that were deliberately looking away. When those eyes were raised toward him, the furtive glances from Dr. Alastair Perkins pierced Byron.

Byron assessed the man, was almost embarrassed by his conclusion: judgmental, critical, cunning, and strategic in a deceptively comfortable sort of way.

"Sit down," said Dr. Alastair Perkins, glancing up briefly and then looking back down at the semitransparent computer display projecting over his desktop. His not looking up was tactical. He knew that Byron's eyes would be on him, trying to invite him to make eye contact. If he resisted, he had more power. Despite seeing many holographic images of Byron, Dr. Alastair Perkins actually yearned to look at him, to be taken with how he was slightly taller or somehow more muscular than he had imagined. Dr. Alastair Perkins didn't give in to the temptation but continued to stare at the digital display on the desk between them.

"All looks good, young fellow. Your scores on the training course, your recommendation from Dr. Chetwin, and your IPE-CKS data. Looks like you are about to realize your calling."

He paused. "By the way, have you started your avatar-based therapy yet?" It was a deliberate misleading; he didn't want to betray to Byron what he already knew. He had already analyzed the data, had already thought long and hard about his concerns.

"Yes, first session this morning." Byron felt a slight cramp in his gut.

"Very good. With whom?"

"Dr. Y."

"Yes, good, very good. Should be a great experience for you. Hope you will continue. Did anything of interest arise this morning?"

Byron was aware that if he lied or prevaricated, his biometric data would give him away. He surmised from the look of Dr. Alastair Perkins's projected display screen that his own real-time biometric status was being displayed to the director as this very conversation was occurring. "It was interesting; I broke down, remembered a little girl I had assisted a couple of years ago. She troubled me then, and I guess she still troubles me now."

Dr. Alastair didn't let on that anything was amiss in Byron's report but noted the absence of a report on the fainting spell and the discussion of Byron's father. He waited to see whether Byron would say more, but nothing was forthcoming. He knew from the AVT session data what had been said there and was confident there was nothing that Byron would add now through his own subjective account.

"Ah, you must be a sensitive soul, then." Dr. Alastair Perkins said it with a tone that tinged on dismissiveness. There was no warmth in his voice.

"That is what Dr. Y said." Byron remembered that it was Dr. Alastair Perkins who had programmed the artificial intelligence behind the avatar.

"I have your first Paraclete assignment. Let's see here." Perkins shifted his attention to a different screen. "It is a teen, an Emergent, from a consumer-class family." He took a few seconds to silently review the data. "We have had no control over his upbringing, but the educational data from this teen shows giftedness in innovation, creativity, and the quantitative arts. Your job is to befriend him, be a big brother to him, take an interest in him, and help him along. His name is Zeke, and I am having his IPE authorized for your eyes."

It was only at this point that the professor looked up from the screens.

"You are to ensure that he makes decisions that are healthy and will allow his gifts to endure and contribute to society on a greater level than that of a consumer. You are trained; I know you will know the operations to perform."

"Yes, sir."

"And by the way, keep your eye on the dad in the family too. We are getting some odd data coming back on him." Dr. Alastair Perkins was careful with tone of voice and body language not to reveal the irony of the statement. As Byron left, the perturbation of Byron's faint in the avatar session remained for Dr. Alastair Perkins to investigate further. And it remained a matter worth monitoring in the young Paraclete.

(III)

"Ah, Chetwin. Thanks for coming." Dr. Alastair Perkins rose from the seat behind his desk.

"Myles." Dr. Chetwin corrected him. He shifted listlessly on his feet.

"Yes, Myles. First names, eh? Yes, well, it is about Williams-Wilkes."

"Byron."

"Yes, Byron Williams-Wilkes, if you will. Tell me about your supervision of him through First Flight."

Dr. Chetwin had expected this meeting. He had even offered to brief Dr. Perkins and Dr. Cripps about all the young Paracletes-to-be he had supervised through First Flight. The three doctors made up the management team for the Munroe division of the ASL. Dr. Chetwin had considered Byron to be a gem, a natural for the calling he was destined for. Somehow, though, the brusque manner of the senior psychologist wiped out in Dr. Chetwin's mind the flow of the report that he had mentally prepared.

Dr. Chetwin recollected his thoughts. "A fine young man. Gifted. Insightful. Excellent at establishing a connection to others. The children assigned to him literally blossomed and then bloomed as a result of the time he spent with them. A sensitive soul."

"Yes, I think much too sensitive. Did you have much to do with the multiple-family communal home?"

"Visited there often. It was wonderfully child focused. Calm, secure. Everything that we designed a home like that to be.

Byron had a great upbringing." Myles Chetwin felt certain that for the purposes of this meeting what his boss wanted to hear was the best course of action to take. There had been such tragedy in that home. At this point in the ASL, everyone needed it to be described as having recovered, having become an exemplar of the excellent.

"Well, Williams-Wilkes has had his first avatar session; had it with Dr. Y." Dr. Alastair Perkins proceeded as though he took no stock in what Dr. Chetwin had said. "I must say, I am concerned."

"Concerned?"

Perkins was unsure whether he wished to tip his hand to Chetwin. He went off into a different direction than had been his initial intent. "There was something in the transcript about a child, a poor child in the school for working- and consumer-class families. A seven-year-old girl. Was he assigned to someone like that?"

"Many like that. It was the nature of the work assigned to that entire group of Paracletes in their First Flight. It gave them the sense of serving, exposure to the wider society; it trained them as observers and interpersonal interveners." The assignments that Myles had provided for the young Paracletes were his unique contribution to their training.

"So what happened with that particular seven-year-old girl?" Dr. Alastair Perkins glared at Dr. Chetwin. It was an accusatory glare; Perkins was suspicious of malfeasance.

"I would have no idea. As I said, there were so many of them. I couldn't speak to anyone in particular."

"During the avatar session, when Williams-Wilkes spoke of that girl, the biometric sensor detected a flood of cortisol. Then his heart rate and blood pressure made a sudden drop. He went into a vasovagal syncope. I can only presume something happened between him and that girl."

"Look, we had no reports of impropriety. If you are suspecting…"

"I am not suspecting anything. I am trying to figure out why he had that response during the AVT. The avatar is a stable platform. I have checked back through dozens of first sessions with it to see whether there had ever been a vasovagal syncope before. None.

"What were you thinking, Chetwin, putting a fourteen-year-old boy with a seven-year-old girl?"

"I am Myles."

"I will call you by your surname if I wish, Dr. Chetwin." Dr. Alastair Perkins drew out the name in a sarcastic tone. Anger was starting to redden his high forehead.

"We are not going to get very far this way, Dr. Perkins." Dr. Myles Chetwin drew his long articulation out into an equally sarcastic tone.

Chetwin paused and then continued deliberately but with an air of collegiality. "I recognize that both the breeding program and the avatar are the product of much research and engineering on your part. Truly, this first generation of bred Paracletes, as they try out the AVT, represents a synchrony of your life's work. But I can assure you, Byron is a sterling example of what your program can do. I don't see that you have cause to worry."

Dr. Alastair fixed his gaze on his subordinate. "So what went wrong in that session? It was either with Williams-Wilkes or with the AI program running that avatar."

"Is it truly something wrong? Did a bad thing really happen? So he was emotional over a memory, so emotional that he fainted. As much as we can breed and raise and train these Paracletes, they are still human beings. We breed selecting for sensitivity, both in terms of the well-being of others and their own self-awareness. You have found the DNA templates for the desirable traits and selected parents who would pass on those gems of personality to the offspring. Your work is brilliant. We raise those offspring with the very epitome of secure attachment and flexible nurturance. We watch over them to ensure they are not traumatized."

Dr. Alastair Perkins had given Chetwin the floor, and the subordinate psychologist was only too happy to take it. Part of Dr. Perkins's backing off was his was own pride in hearing the recitation of his great work.

"I know it is good."

"Dr. Perkins, sir. Not just good but *great*."

The tension eased between the two men. Chetwin paused, knowing there was an issue begging return. He said, "I wasn't in that avatar session and don't have the access to the transcript or biometrics from it. You might be alarmed over nothing."

"It is something. And it's not only about the girl. Byron is aware there was something wrong with his father."

Dr. Chetwin straightened. He immediately recalled the controversy, the chaos, the embarrassment from fifteen years before. Chetwin drew himself to his full height. His stance widened, as he directly faced the senior psychologist. He said with barely contained hostility, "I had nothing to do with that."

"Damn neurologists," Dr. Perkins said. "I think we were better off when there were still psychiatrists. At least with the psychiatrists, we expected that most of the time their drugs wouldn't work anyway."

Chetwin took them back into the present. "Look, I was in and out of the MFCH. I saw Byron's father there. He seemed functional." Chetwin remembered how much he had covered for Byron's father, how much the other parent Paracletes had covered for him. But most importantly, he remembered how much they had all conspired to ensure that Dr. Alastair Perkins would not get word of it, for if he had, there would have been hell to pay.

"That is not the way that Williams-Wilkes remembers it."

"I know nothing of that. As I said…"

Dr. Chetwin's voice was truncated by Dr. Alastair Perkins's response. "I know what you said."

The two men stared at each other for a few moments. Finally, Dr. Alastair Perkins turned away from his subordinate and looked out the window over the Commons. His voice settled into a calm yet assertive tone, sounding as though the conversation was over and he had the final words to say.

"We started with a cohort of seventeen bred Paracletes from eight breeding pairs. Now, from that seventeen, we are down to sixteen until their numbers are supplemented by the youngsters coming along. Twelve of those sixteen are not even out of the compounds yet. We cannot lose another. Not this one. Not anyone else."

(IV)

A block or so behind the BirdSong compound was a path ascending a cliff of exposed clay. Byron climbed that path, reaching the orchard access road beside a grove of apple trees. In the embracing summer warmth, he wore loose-fitting clothes of rough, unbleached cotton, glad to be out of the confines of his dress khakis and knit polo shirt. It was an awkward climb; he was carrying a picnic basket.

On the access road, there was a slight acrid stench coming from the orchard. It rose out of the companion planting of mixed aromatic grasses and wildflowers that grew between the rows of trees. The grasses had been genetically modified to mimic pheromones to attract harmful insects and, once having attracted them, attack them with a natural insecticide. The wafting grasses trapped and contained fungal spores. The wildflowers scattered in the mix attracted beneficial insects that also fed on the less desirable species. Above the fruit trees, the frame of a canopy stood in place, ready to receive sheltering cloth that would protect the fruit below from frost, harsh sun, and winged scavengers.

Byron had found the stench off-putting at first and then habituated to it. It helped that the orchard arrangement provided organically grown, locally sourced fruit that he much enjoyed.

Byron checked the wearable on his left forearm, giving it the voice command to "Locate Sallye." Immediately, a map appeared with a blinking dot tracking her passage from the FiveWay compound located closer to the center of the city. Tapping her icon at the edge of the map, he received a readout of her biometrics—slightly sweating in the city-bound heatscape, energized with positive anticipatory emotion, and affectionately and interpersonally primed for contact. He smiled at the thought of her arrival and noted that her time to their meeting place would be twelve minutes. He was pleased. It was enough time to make it there himself and unpack the gingham-lined wicker picnic basket he had prepared.

Most of all, he was delighted to be free of the banter and curiosity of his friends at BirdSong. They knew he had been to the VR room for his first avatar-based therapy session earlier in the day, and they were eager to hear how it went. They also knew that he had urgently left shortly after lunch, and they had tracked his GPS to the academy building, headquarters of the Administration of Social Logistics. They had murmured among themselves, "This might not be good." Byron had said little upon his return, stating only that he needed time alone and would go for a walk. The others had noticed him preparing the picnic basket and knew that he was likely to rendezvous with Sallye from FiveWay. They sensitively left him to his own self-care.

Walking along the access road, he noted an apple tree in the yard of the farmer's residence. Rather than its branches being trained along wires between poles secure into the ground, the tree had been allowed to grow naturally. Byron knew why the commercial orchard was trained with tree limbs attached to wires—it allowed the mechanical picking of the crop. Still, there was something nostalgic about a tree that had been allowed to grow naturally, to assume its own crown, to look like the picture of an iconic apple tree in a source file.

A few minutes farther along the orchard access road brought Byron to a meadow. Natural long grasses and aromatic pine trees mixed there, and a light breeze blew. Byron found the place where he and Sallye had rendezvoused before, its grasses still bent over. He spread the blanket that rode atop the picnic basket onto the ground and then put the gingham cloth on top of that. He took out the bottle of wine, the local cheese, and the fresh buns from that little bakery he passed coming back from the university. The late-afternoon placement of the sun was behind a pine tree, giving shade to the nest he had created.

Sallye was still seven minutes from arriving.

Settled, Byron assumed the Sukhasana pose, focused on his breathing, and allowed a sense of peace to settle.

"Hey!" Sallye's voice was light and breezy. Byron had been tracking Sallye's energy profile for the last few minutes while in his yogic state of receptivity. He had sensed her along the orchard access road and knew when she had entered the meadow. Anticipating her arrival, he was enveloped by an inner smile.

He spoke softly but with deep energy when he said, "Oh, it is so good of you to come!"

"I wouldn't miss it. Tell me what happened."

Byron looked at Sallye. Her eyes shone with affection. Her body glowed with the exertion of the walk to their rendezvous. She was soft and graceful in the cheerful summer clothes she wore.

"Well, the Dr. Y avatar is amazing. Intuitive. Incisive. He was coy, but very quickly I found myself being led somewhere, somewhere I didn't anticipate going. I must admit that at the beginning, I thought it would just be 'try this out and see what happens,' but as it went further, I was…"

Byron looked into her eyes and suddenly felt embarrassed. "Oh, I'm sorry. Without checking in on you, I just launched in. There is so much to tell."

Sallye lightly placed her own hand on Byron's. His hand was still resting on his knee as he sat in the Sukhasana pose. He reflexively turned his hand to hold hers. "That's OK," she said. "You were the one to have had the adventure today. Tell me more."

"We are so accustomed to being digitally naked, to having our movements and biometrics tracked. That didn't happen there. Dr. Y told me that he wasn't tracking my IPE. But then, with Dr. Y, I felt exposed in a different way. The questions he asked made me go back to things I normally don't allow myself to think about. And yet, even though he was an avatar and it was just virtual reality, I felt naked and safe with him at the same time."

"Wow!"

"So I fainted. And I wept." With those words, Byron emerged from his yogic state and connected with a shameful energy to Sallye. A look of absolute compassion crept over Sallye's face. Byron wondered whether she was shocked and couldn't imagine him either fainting or weeping. He was relieved as he watched her settle in to listen.

"I remembered a little girl from the public school," he continued. "But it was not just remembering; it was reliving the feelings I had when I was with her. How vulnerable she was. I remember Chetwin debriefing me back then, talking with me about how in our safe, secure, well-bounded relationship, we allow vulnerable ones to heal. I didn't say that to Dr. Y, but now as I think about it, that is what happened with his presence with me in the VR room."

"That is amazing. It sounds so real."

"We are trained to be listeners as we assume the Paraclete role. With Dr. Y, I felt listened to, even though now I can't remember what he said to me. It was even more real than in our practice exercises with each other in training. And..." Byron paused. "It was uncanny."

"You mentioned that you fainted."

"That was weird. I checked the history on my biosensor, and it seems that I had a vasovagal syncope. When I came to, though, he—Dr. Y—was just sitting there. As Paracletes, we would have been physically present beside the person who fainted, gradually reassuring him or her with physical touch. I guess Dr. Y couldn't do that as an avatar; all he could do was sit and wait. But when we came back to talk, he continued as though nothing had happened.

"We talked about my dad. It was like those two things were connected somehow. Somehow, there was the connection between my being with the little girl and the way Dad was with me. That is what caused me to faint."

Byron was suddenly reeling, making connections.

"And then I got summonsed to the office of Dr. Alastair Perkins. He is truly officious. He is to be my supervising psychologist now. He is the very opposite of Chetwin. How awful."

After a few moments, Byron opened the bottle of wine and poured it into the durable but delicate fluted glasses. The cheese was laid out on a board with the knife. The smell of the freshly baked rolls was released as they were cracked open. They could now talk about Sallye's day, about her work with the Elderly Reflectives and the stories they had told.

It wasn't very long before Byron and Sallye activated the timer on the biometric privacy override, thankful for the collective efforts of both generations of Paracletes to have had that override installed on their biosensors.

There, on that sunny afternoon, behind the curtain of a gingham tablecloth rigged to a pine branch, there with the glow of the wine consumed and the tenderness of their listening to each other, they settled into the deeper intimacy of their physical relationship.

(V)

Curious. That was the mind-set that Byron chose to go with. More realistically, he felt anxious. He was relieved that it would be Dr. Chetwin he would meet. He liked Dr. Chetwin and had feared that he was no longer going to see him, having completed his move through the First Flight. He thought they had said their thank-yous and goodbyes. So it was curious that it was Dr. Chetwin who had left the message for him during the night to meet at his office at 8:30 a.m.

Perhaps the anxiety was left over from the chill of meeting with Dr. Alastair Perkins. It was Dr. Perkins whom Byron had expected to be summonsed by again. The relief that it was Dr. Chetwin was not quite enough to quell the anxiety.

Byron had been told throughout his life that he was secure, that he could feel confident about the next challenge in life, that he was capable, and that he could always think matters through so that he would know the right thing to do. He had been told that, but he didn't always feel that in his gut. He had overheard his parents talking one day about a printout they had received of his DNA profile as it pertained to his suitability for the trade. His mom had commented to his dad, "You know, Craig, he does have some of you in him," as though there was a reason to doubt.

Byron had confessed to his dad that he got anxious about things. In the typical dad way, his father told him that "that is normal" and that "a bit of anxiety is a good thing" and to "just take a breath and blow it away." But Byron saw something else in his dad's eyes as he had said that; put into words, it would be, "So do I, and it paralyzes me."

When Byron was leaving BirdSong that morning as everyone else was bustling to get to class, he had told them that Dr. Chetwin had called him in unexpectedly. No one asked whether everything was OK, but they implied the question with their body language, and so Byron had simply said, "I am curious as to why, but I guess I will find out soon enough."

Dr. Chetwin's office was located on the North Hill, which was one of the city limits. The building had been constructed into the hill, and an array of solar panels hid the building from outside view. Light filtered in diffusely past the photovoltaic chips. A gloomy sense of daylight was supplemented by strategic task lighting and illuminating computer displays. Radiant warmth came to the floor from below, part of the heat dissipation from the large installation of computer servers on the lower level. The circulating air was cooled for the server room and the office space by pipes that sucked chilled water in from deep in the lake. The gently circulating air in the building was so clean that it almost hurt the human lung; it had to be that clean for the sake of the computers.

The office floor space was generous, with work pods scattered about. Waterfall installations and green-plant displays were strategically placed. Companion versions of those same features were projected in dynamically moving, computer-generated, three-dimensional images. Dalian warping of those computer images, with spatial and color distortions, danced provocatively. The physically real stood stoically beside the often bizarre digital versions.

"Byron, thanks for coming."

"Dr. Chetwin. Thanks for inviting me; it is so good that I can still come to be with you."

"As you know, Dr. Perkins is technically your supervisor now. But you can well imagine that he is pretty busy. He has asked me to discharge some of his duties. Given that we know each other so well, he thought that it would be an easy arrangement."

The anxiety in Byron eased a bit further.

"You have your first assignment as a Paraclete of the Second Flight. There will be more to come, and by the end of the year, you will likely have at least six assignments.

"My recommendation has been that you work with Emergents, adolescents identified in the public high school as having extraordinary gifts. We are keeping you with youth who are at least a couple of years younger than you, although as you grow more comfortable with the role, the age range we assign to you will broaden. For now, this will feel like a natural progression from the work that you have done in schools.

"Your work will no longer be institution bound. You will be in the homes of your clients, on the soccer pitch or in the gym, biking and hanging out. Your primary purpose with the Emergents is to help them to have good judgment in their adolescence, good judgment that will keep them from jeopardizing the talents and gifts they have to contribute to future society."

"How do I do that without it feeling awkward for them? Won't it seem to them like having another parent around them to keep them on track?"

"The groundwork has been laid with the Emergent adolescent and his family for your involvement. Zeke's family, the Basilis family, is in the consumer class. They are being awarded extra CashCard credits for Zeke to be groomed in this way. They are a really good family, and Zeke has the capacity to move into the AI development lab eventually. He and his parents are looking forward to meeting you. You are a gifted novice Paraclete, Byron, and I believe that you will be able to perform this role with fun, companionship, and a sense of humor."

"So if it is all so good for this Zeke, why does he need a Paraclete?"

"We have tracked Zeke since middle school. We are not sure about formative years earlier in his life. The family ascended to the consumer class when Zeke was about six, but in the years prior to that, the family was in the worker class. They lived in the territories that were then outside of IPE-CKS tracking, so we don't really know his full history, especially in those early years. We have reason to believe that there might have been some early psychological trauma.

The family still has connections back to the territories, especially the dad. Zeke has shown every indication of good adjustment, but…"

"But…"

"Well, we want to be sure. There is no doubt that he is gifted, but some of his inclinations are not altogether…wholesome."

"Am I to be a spy?"

"Oh, no. Not at all. A healer, a supporter. You are there to help him with the challenges of adolescence, to be someone he can trust, someone a bit older to guide him."

"All right."

"Dr. Perkins has also indicated that Zeke is to have hallucinogenic therapy. Once you have established a relationship with him, you will be his guide for that therapy."

Byron smiled. He knew from his First Flight training that before being a guide, he too would have to have a hallucinogenic session. He too would need a guide, and he hoped it could be Sallye, as she had already had her hallucinogenic session and reported that it was "hmm, beautiful."

"Now, before you start work with Zeke, there is one more element of your orientation to consider. Given that you have met the criteria for Second Flight Paraclete, you now have the right to and responsibility of IPE-CKS access on the clients you assist. For security and privacy reasons, access to this data is limited to Administration of Social Logistics facilities such as this one and the university where you met Dr. Perkins. Today we will get you access for Zeke. You are not allowed access for other members of his family. You are professionally bound to keep this information confidential. Your purpose of access is only to facilitate your role with your client, and you will be monitored with respect to what, and when, you access from his IPE-CKS."

"I understand." Byron had been expecting this; he knew that Paracletes of the Second Flight had this access. Sallye had access to the IPE-CKS data for the Elderly Reflectives assigned to her.

"You and I are covenanting now around those responsibilities. Are you ready to enter into that covenant?" Dr. Chetwin asked.

Byron nodded. He had studied the formal covenant in his First Flight and knew the ritual would come eventually. A flow of gratitude came over him that he could do this ritual with Dr. Chetwin rather than with Dr. Perkins.

Dr. Chetwin reached his left hand forward to shake Byron's left hand. As he did so, the wearable that each of them had on their left forearm bleeped and blinked. More significantly, their eyes locked warmly. Byron immediately read the emotions of pride and fondness in his supervisor and mentor.

"Now, let's take a look," Dr. Chetwin said. "I will take some time with you to help you navigate."

The space around Dr. Chetwin's work pod became alive with displays that hung on semitransparent screens in the air. There was a spatial locator with Zeke's current GPS data. It blinked that Zeke was at school. On that display was a readout of heart rate, blood pressure, and circulating cortisol levels. On another display, Zeke's recent browsing on the WarpWeb was displayed using a mapping protocol that allowed sequences to be identified. Of more interest to Byron was his gaming data.

"Wow, he is at level fifty-two on Linkages! I am only into level seven."

Dr. Chetwin smiled. "I told you he was extraordinary. It will probably be of interest to you, once you have met Zeke, to come back in here and explore his IPE further."

Turning away from the displays, Dr. Chetwin again made eye contact with Byron and touched his wearable to turn the displays off. "I have forwarded the access codes to your wearable. I don't need to say this to you, given my knowledge of your character, but I will say it for the covenant's sake. Your wearable now has a level of privilege that you must protect. It is profiled to you to work only on your arm, but that is just programming and electronics.

You must ensure that it doesn't fall into the possession of others who would use it for purposes that would be contrary to what we see as our social obligations."

"I understand."

"One more thing. Dr. Perkins wants us to be especially alert in the Basilis family home, just to ensure that everything is in the proper order and perspective there." He paused and smiled, looking at the young man who stood before him. "Now let's go meet him!"

Byron smiled at Dr. Chetwin. "I am more than ready; bring it on!"

(VI)

Byron stood uncomfortably in the foyer of the Basilis home. Zeke stood there too, equally uncomfortable.

Dags Basilis was magnanimous, effusive, and so thankful for the special attention his son and thus the rest of his family was receiving. The way he was ingratiating himself with Dr. Chetwin seemed so pronounced that Byron wondered if it was disingenuous. Dr. Chetwin was explaining that because of Zeke's excellent work at the public school, he showed great promise for the future. For this promise to be realized, Zeke would be offered special opportunities, including Byron. Byron, a few years older, would be a companion, a guide through the sometimes-tumultuous teenage years. Byron would help guarantee that Zeke would become as successful as his parents.

Dags had done well for his family. They were firmly in the consumer class and received financial benefits in the form of government-issued CashCards to lift them to a more comfortable existence. Dags and Maureen hadn't always been this well off; they had made it to where they were today through their hard work and their socially and ecologically wise choices. Maureen had completed her university degree and then a second degree program to become a teacher. Dags had supported her in this long journey. He was a retailer and entrepreneur, having worked his way up through various businesses before owning an eco-friendly sporting goods store. Dags led excursions to nature preserve areas in the hinterlands—snowshoeing and cross-country skiing in the winter, kayaking and hiking the rest of the year. He was often off to the hinterlands.

Zeke nervously worked a soccer ball with his right foot, rolling its white patchwork-leather cover forward and back, always in control. Byron caught the impatience of his body language.

The home was pleasantly decorated and furnished in a retro urban barn style with nicked wood and worn leather chairs and sofa. It looked bright and wholesome. There was a bowl of apples on the table—no doubt locally sourced from the orchard that overlooked the valley. Byron looked past the living room to a separate technology room. He could see the glowing, pulsing complexity of a paused game of Linkages. Zeke must have been playing when they arrived.

Dr. Chetwin was going on about other advantages to the family that came with Zeke's status as an Emergent. Byron noted that he never used the term *Emergent* with the family; he just talked about Zeke's bright future of contribution to society, about how much promise there was in the young mind, and about how wonderful it was to see young people of such good character. Dags remained vigilant. Maureen was glowing.

"We see Zeke as a real asset to our future—one that we are eager to support." Dr. Chetwin spoke in a sincere, almost confidential sort of voice. "We will be helping your family with extra CashCards as long as he is a part of our program."

"Just what will this program entail?" Dags asked.

"Byron will spend a few hours a week with Zeke, just hanging out and encouraging and guiding him. Additionally, we have some examinations and experiences at the academy we would like to run with Zeke."

"Examinations? Experiences?"

"We are targeting Zeke for our AI department; he is one of several we hope to bring along in that field. Of course, we wish to confirm his gifts in working with computers and simulations. From what we know on his IPE-CKS, he appears to be making excellent life choices, socially and ecologically responsible choices; we want to confirm that suitability of character, though. Additionally, I will be meeting with you to take a further family history, as we have IPE-CKS data on family members dating back only ten years."

Byron made eye contact with Zeke and motioned toward the door, glancing at the soccer ball. They left.

As an empathetic overture, Byron said as they left the house, "Well, that was pretty boring. I noticed a soccer pitch a block over; let's kick a few."

Zeke picked up his bike, and Byron commandeered another, which was likely Dags's. Zeke balanced the soccer ball between his thumbs on the handlebars, and they pedaled off. When they arrived at the pitch, they found one end in use by a team of children working with a coach on the basics of passing and shooting. Leaving the bikes, Byron and Zeke started with a running and passing drill on the other half of the field.

Byron watched as the adolescent awkwardly managed his long legs and a torso that seemed at odds with the direction of his running. Byron surmised that Zeke was still adapting physically from his early-adolescent growth spurt. The teen was obviously unathletic but wanting to be more capable and skilled. From time to time, Zeke would move the ball around with his toe and the inside of his foot in what appeared to be a well-practiced move, tricky and evasive for a defender. And then Zeke would get completely tangled in his own feet and lose his balance, and the ball would go off an errant body part.

After a few minutes, they were both perspiring and sought out the shade of the trees that were at the perimeter of the recreation area.

From behind sport sunglasses, Zeke looked at the wearable on Byron's right arm. "A vanilla skim-milk latte with double espresso and a ginseng boost. Purchased at 2:22 p.m. at S-SB on Grandin."

"What?" Byron asked.

"You bought a vanilla latte using CashCard transfer off your wearable before you came over to our place."

"How did you know? Were you spying on us before we even got here?"

"No, I didn't have to. I read it off your wearable." Zeke could see that the older adolescent looked baffled, and he tried to explain: "My sunglasses are connected to my wearable. My wearable reads out the content of yours. It's a hack."

"You can hack my wearable?"

"Anybody's wearable. But don't tell."

Byron was pleased on one level. He had the confidence of the young teen, confidence enough that he would disclose his clandestine skill. This was an important accomplishment of the first connection. There was a sense of bravado in Zeke sharing that he could do this, but that was OK. On the other hand, Byron felt violated. He could accept that the ASL tracked all his purchases, but a fourteen-year-old?

"And I can see what eBooks you are reading. And, let's see…" Zeke paused behind his sunglasses, which were providing a video display to him. "On Linkages, you are only at level seven. Loser!"

"OK, take off the glasses and tell me how you do that." Suddenly, there was an energy between the two of them.

Zeke offered the glasses to Byron; he put them on and immediately saw readouts from his own wearable.

"It is a pretty easy hack, but I don't know anyone else who is doing it. Your wearable is in constant connection with the ASL servers, just the same as my dad's is. It's easy to intercept that signal with a silent filter that intercepts, reroutes, and resends the data stream. If it is done in under five hundred milliseconds, the ASL servers don't detect the delay."

Byron handed back the sunglasses to Zeke. "That's pretty neat."

"A great way to spy on your parents. Although, having done so, I am more convinced of just how boring they are."

Immediately, Byron flipped back to what Dr. Chetwin had said about Zeke's dad. Then he let that thought go; that wasn't his job here.

Changing the subject, Zeke asked, "How much in CashCards are my parents going to get for me to be in this program?"

"I have no idea."

"And tell me this. Why do they call them CashCards anyway?"

"OK, let's do some history," Byron answered. *Cash* is the old term that was used for money. People actually carried it in their pockets—thin polymer bills and metal tokens. As the digital economy grew, those old-fashioned means of payment were replaced. The term *cash* was no longer needed, and thus the cashless society was born. Still, people liked the idea of having access to cash. So, CashCards were created. Originally, they came out looking like the old credit cards that people had way back then; that is why we call them CashCards. Now, basically, they are digital economy bonuses that have an expiration date."

"Why not just pay people what they earn?" Zeke was eager for someone who would explain this to him. His dad was pretty busy with the store and didn't have patience for his questions.

"OK, let's consider your dad's store. He has a great business. It is one that the ASL wants to support. The ASL wants people to be biking and kayaking, because that is good for their health and not a problem for the environment. Your dad sells bikes and kayaks. So as a reward to your dad for running that sort of business and for making it work, he would get a bonus. That bonus is paid to him in a CashCard account. It is an incentive."

"Mom and Dad keep telling me that if we make more healthy choices, we get more money from the government."

"Yes. When your parents go shopping, if they buy fresh fruits and vegetables, dairy, and fresh whole-grain breads, they get CashCard points at the checkout. If they were to buy sodas and cigarettes, CashCard points would be deducted. If a person buys a kayak from your dad, it's worth CashCard points; if he or she were to buy a dirt bike, though, something that is less physically demanding and harder on the environment, that person would lose CashCard points. In our society, people have the freedom to ride dirt bikes and smoke cigarettes all they want. But our government, through an agency called the ASL, wants people to make healthier choices. It's a way for the government to use financial incentives to preserve our environment and promote health."

Byron was reading the perplexity on Zeke's face. He continued: "The term *CashCard* is kind of funny. It is neither cash nor a card. We have a cashless society, and cards for financial transactions are gone too. A CashCard is just a way to make bonus funds digitally available to your parents. It is an economic and social tool."

"So that's why we don't go to fast-food restaurants for burgers," Zeke said, looking pouty in a playful sort of way.

"Right. And because all spending is digitally tracked, including my vanilla skim-milk latte with double espresso and a ginseng boost, a score can be generated for the individual or family and CashCard bonuses awarded."

"But Mom and Dad say that they expire."

"Yes. That way, money keeps moving through the digital economy rather than going stagnant."

"So where does the government get all the money to be able to send us bonuses?"

"Your dad pays taxes on what he earns for running the store. That is just the same as the guy in the dirt-bike store and the cigarette vendor. He is paid through a PAC, a payroll administration company. It sends the tax money generated in his store and all other businesses to the government. When people buy a kayak from him, they pay sales tax that goes to the government too."

"So the government is both taking money and also handing it out."

"Yes, and it is all done digitally, using algorithms. You know algorithms from your Linkage game; you must know them well for you to be at the level you are at. The digital economy runs on them; those algorithms collect and distribute financial resources. It is all done without us having to think about it or do anything other than make good choices in how we live.

"And if we buy healthy food, keep physically fit, and work hard at the right businesses, we get rewarded. That's the theory, anyway. More apples from that orchard up there."

"Still, sometimes I would like to have a beefy burger," Zeke said longingly.

Byron smiled. "Let's go. I will pay for it from my wearable. It will put my CashCard account in a tailspin for a while, but I think I would enjoy one too, especially with you."

(VII)

The light from the setting sun streamed in low over the table at the S-SB at which Sallye and Byron sat with their coffees. Byron held the warm mug in his hands, enjoying the sensation. His thoughts were on the relationship with Sallye, how it too was warm and how it cradled him. They had shared the events of the day and were enjoying being present without having to say much more.

Looking up, he noticed Dr. Alastair Perkins and Dr. Chetwin in line. They gave no sign of noticing him. They were not speaking, and it wasn't even clear whether they were together. "They must be," Byron thought to himself.

The sight of Dr. Chetwin typically eased Byron's stress and gave him the feeling that all would be OK. Looking at him late this evening, however, was different. Standing there with Dr. Alastair Perkins in front of him, Dr. Chetwin seemed different—somehow empty, at a loss, and perhaps even confused.

3

ALTON

"Do you remember when we used to put that old black hat by the barn door and our riders would throw in a tip?"

"Yup." Laurel didn't look up from the horse she was grooming. She had sprayed Slick onto the mane, and she was combing out the tangles.

"Usually a ten-spot, maybe even a twenty, or a fifty even," Justin said. He was tightening the cinch, securing the saddle on Starsky. He released a stirrup from the horn and loosened the lead to take the horse outside. Five other horses were already secured to the fence, saddled and ready to go.

"Maybe when Alton comes, he can do something about the way we are paid," Laurel responded. She had waited until Justin returned. "When I called the resort, they assured me that tips had already been added to the tickets the riders paid when they had registered."

"That's just it. We never saw those tips. When they could put a tenner in the hat, we saw those."

Laurel sighed; she tried to soften Justin's tone with her own. "Yes, it was easier back then. We did the repairs on the barn with those tips. But that was ten years ago. They need doing again. I don't like you having to work in the sawmill just to get lumber we need."

It was more than that, Justin thought. Last winter he had skidded out cedar logs using the horses—pulled those damn logs all the way down the road to Baggs's Mill and begged to work hours there just for the chance to use the saw to cut his own cedar into boards. Now those boards were drying in the back stall.

Justin checked the cinch and saddle on the horse that Laurel had readied. That made six. Just Biddy and Drake yet to go.

"I am a little worried about Stamper today. He has been a bit skittish since Monday when we had that other group out."

Laurel looked up and asked, "Did you get him out for a proper ride this week?" She knew that Justin watched which horses were getting lazy and insolent as a result of being ridden by the inexperienced riders. He would take them out for a more demanding ride to remind them of the discipline in attending to the rider's control.

"No, it'll have to be tomorrow or Friday." They had put on an extra outing at the insistence of the resort. Three or sometimes four days a week were a bit much for the two of them and their small herd of horses.

Justin spoke again after bringing Biddy from the paddock into the barn. "It's that damn cashless society bullshit."

Laurel paused, figuring she just had to let Justin blow off steam.

"I look at what goes into our account from the ticket prices. After taxes and fees, we are getting less per rider than we got ten years ago."

"There are the eco-healthy bonuses we get into our CashCard account."

"So, look at those and then look at the deductions from payments. They make it look like we are doing a good thing here and getting rewarded for it. Not really. We are slowly being financially strangled." Justin bridled Biddy, looping the reins over the horn of the saddle. Laurel had brought in Drake and was brushing him down, ready for the saddle blanket on his back.

Justin went on. "Maybe it is that damn resort that is stealing the tips away from us. We are dependent on them, and they are dependent on us to contribute to their status as an eco-healthy business. They probably found a way to funnel off the tips into their pockets and not ours."

"I bet the tips are smaller too," Laurel said. "They are collected up front on the ticket rather than after the good experience of the ride." Laurel had done the first tightening of Drake's cinch. He flicked his tail and pinned his ears in her direction.

Justin answered, "Yeah, it had been an incentive for us. I remember when Alton and I were riding back with the group, we used to wager on what the black hat would be after everyone had gone and we counted the cash. If he was closer than I was but the tips were above what I had guessed, I would give him the difference."

"I wonder if he still remembers what it was like to have cash in his pocket," Laurel said.

"Probably not."

Justin startled and looked over his shoulder. He still couldn't get used to the bus arriving silently down the lane, its electric engines whining almost imperceptibly. How he yearned for the sound of an internal combustion engine, and how rare they were these days! Walter Baggs still had a few old tractors around and managed to squirrel away some gasoline fuel for them.

As the bus discharged its passengers, Justin sized up the group and mentally started matching customer to horse. The three girls were simple: The one in the green top seemed shy; he would put her on Star. The long-haired girl would go to Rocket, and her friend would ride Rocket's good buddy, Arch. The couple would do well on Starsky and Hutch. That left Stamper.

"Hi, I'm Al." The middle-aged man was clearly dominant in the human herd. He strode toward Justin with his right hand extended.

A salesman...no, a cop...no, some sort of teacher, Justin thought.

"Justin," he said as he took Al's hand. He studied the man, much in the way that a horse might size up a sudden presence near the paddock, checking for possible predator intent or dominance behavior. Al was about twenty years younger than he but not in as good a condition. The man's skin was untanned and pallid. His handshake was artificially strong, as though he were declaring a dominance that he imagined he needed to impose.

"So where are we riding today?" asked Al. The others in the group focused on the pair of men.

"Well, we are taking you all up through the trees to a trail we call Sky Walk. Up there, you are in and out of the trees and a high meadow. We have lunch all packed here for you on the back of Hester the donkey. Hester will follow Laurel's horse at the back of the line. In a high alpine meadow, we will do the gourmet picnic-basket thing—linen tablecloth, wine, and fresh strawberries with cheese and fresh bread." Even as he spoke, Laurel was transferring the boxed lunch from the bus to the packs while Hester pawed impatiently on the ground, unhappy about being tied to the fence.

"Then, after lunch, we have a bit of a treacherous descent from the ridge to the cedar glen. In the heat of the afternoon, you will be glad for the shade and damp coolness there. Then it's back here. Your bus picks you up at four."

The three girls giggled, reached out to touch the soft noses of the horses, and pulled grass beside the fence, trying to feed them. The couple had eyes for each other—must be honeymooners. Al stood awkwardly. Justin was starting to grow nervous about the matching of Al to Stamper. He noticed a rigidity in Al and wondered what Stamper might do with that.

Justin motioned Laurel aside from the group and briefed her on who he thought should ride which of the horses. He went over to Drake, tightened the cinch, released the stirrups, took off the halter and looped it over the top of the fence post, put on the hackamore, mounted, and turned back to the group.

"Laurel here, horse-woman extraordinaire, will settle you on your horses. I am just going to let Drake stretch his legs. If I run him a bit before the trail ride, he gets some of his excess energy out and he settles in better." Justin rode off, quickly moving from a walk to a trot to a lope as he circled out behind the barn.

Laurel let her husband's lie settle comfortably over the group. She too was sensing something about Al—the same something that had bothered Justin enough to make him leave. Normally, Justin would help the riders mount and get the stirrups adjusted for leg length with her. But she should let him go, let Justin take care himself. She could do this.

It wasn't long into the ride when, at the front, Justin became aware of Stamper's reaction to Al. Stamper was starting to get humpy and then trying to push forward past Justin and Drake. While they were walking a narrow trail, he began to worry that Stamper might be getting ready to bolt away from the group with Al still on his back when they came to a more open area. He whistled back to Laurel with a whistle that they had designed to signal between them that something was amiss. To the group, the whistle would be mistaken for a songbird; for Laurel, it would be an alert. Justin led the group into a clearing small enough to keep Stamper and Al confined within the group but large enough that he could consult with Laurel about what he was noticing.

Laurel rode Biddy up beside Drake so she and Justin could talk. Hester followed along behind, tail twitching nervously.

Justin apprised Laurel of the situation. "Stamper and Al are not getting along. Al is rigid and hasn't adapted to the rhythm of Stamper's gait. It is annoying Stamper. I can see his neck tightening and twitching. We have to get Al off him, or there is going to be trouble on the rising trail."

"I noticed you getting closer to read the energy off him."

"We have to get someone more experienced on Stamper to keep him under control."

"Which horse is best for Al? All the others seem matched." Laurel knew that Justin would never give up Drake. And she would not want him to.

"Hester? Biddy?" Justin meant it as a joke, that they would put Al on the donkey. Neither smiled, but both chuckled internally.

"Let's do Biddy. I think that he could fit my saddle, and I could be OK on Stamper. It'll mean that we will need to reorder the line. Hester will be up ahead of the other customers. You can guess what that might be like for the rider behind her."

Justin smiled, recalling Hester's odd trail manners. "Oh, I think you could lead Hester from Stamper at the back of the line."

"No, let's let Al lead Hester. Hester is used to following Biddy, and we will just loop a long line loose around the horn of Biddy's saddle. If anything were to happen, the line would just unravel, and she would be free. Until that point, she will think that she is tied in. Maybe it might settle Al down a bit, make him feel responsible."

"Or we could end up losing our lunch!"

"OK, let's both get off," Laurel said. "I will ask Al to dismount and go over what we are doing and why. Can you check the cinches of the other riders?"

When motioned to do so by Justin, Al got off his horse somewhat awkwardly, getting his shoe stuck in the stirrup and causing him to have to bounce like a kangaroo until he could free it. He brushed himself off and tried to return to a sense of dignity.

"Stamper here has an issue. We thought he would be OK today, but he is showing some signs that he might run off on you. We wouldn't want to put you in that situation. So we are going to have you and Laurel switch horses. Laurel can handle him if he gets testy."

"OK," Al said.

Even though Al had complied, Justin detected discomfort, offense even. Justin assessed Al as the sort of person who couldn't lose face, who couldn't admit that he wasn't in control.

"This means that you are the lead horse for the lunch!" Justin quipped, lightening the conversation with humor. "You better not go astray and take Hester with you, or we all starve. If anything happens and things go out of control, unloop Hester's lead rope from the horn of your saddle. But it should be OK. Biddy is a very easy and wise horse; she will know what to do."

And so they ascended through the trees.

At lunch, Al sought out Justin. As Laurel watched, she noted the dynamics between the two men. With humans, the desire to establish dominance led to a pushy conversational style—not unlike horses trying to establish their place in the herd. Somehow she liked the way horses did it better; it was clearer. She could see Justin getting annoyed with Al and not wanting to enter into the dynamic, but Al was pushing more than was healthy. The fellow from the couple took his eyes off his bride to check out the male energy flow. The girls giggled and guzzled the sparkling wine. Shy Girl was coming out of her shell.

Al was pushing questions onto Justin. "So do you notice many changes up here since the restorative shift in economic and social systems?"

"Yeah, we hate it!"

"Why so? Especially in your business. Before signing up for this ride, I ensured that you were designated eco-healthy. And you are. You get rebates and bonuses in your CashCard accounts just for having a business like this."

Laurel hoped that Justin could restrain himself. They were in the tourism industry and had been trained on how to manage customer relationships. No politics. No religion.

"Yes, we are eco-healthy. Pity that poor guy down the road who runs the quad trips back into Lake Ethel. That trek is too far for the electric quads, so he takes them on a fleet of aging gas-powered four-wheelers. No extra CashCards for him."

Laurel breathed a sigh of relief. Her man had come through. She could see the restraint on his face. Still, he was looking like the way Stamper had felt under her as she had ridden. She got up from where she sat on the rock outcropping and started to gather up the lunch things, tucking away items into Hester's packs. The three girls immediately got up to help. The couple kissed. Al stared off away from everyone else, artificially inspecting the view down in the valley.

"Let's get out of here," Laurel said to Justin. He was checking each of the horses, retightening tack, and easing tension with the stroke of his hands on their necks and rumps. She knew these beasts were his lifeblood. And she knew he hated what he was putting them through so they could survive economically.

Little was said as they rode down. Through the cedar glen, Al was the only one who spoke, pointing out the obvious: one of the grand old cedars was gone—recently gone—leaving a stump where it once stood. Justin cursed under his breath. He couldn't wait for the noiseless bus to take that man away and leave him in peace.

(II)

Fortunately, by the next day, the LandPorter was sufficiently charged to make the trip into Beckett. They hadn't planned on going, but a message had come through the previous night from Alton; he would be coming home and was due to arrive in the late afternoon. He would be staying for just a few days, and then he had to return to work. Alton was taking an Autonomous Vehicle on Demand, an AVoD, as far as Beckett and would turn it in there, riding back with them to the ranch in the LandPorter. Laurel was delighted. Justin, always concerned about money, was glad that the solar panel had charged the LandPorter sufficiently for them to make it to town and back without having to pay for a charge at the station.

They were privileged to have their own vehicle. Only rural businesses—farms or tourism-related enterprises—could do so. Of course, the rich people had them too; they even had gas-powered ones. The LandPorter was adequate, although it was not nearly as much fun as Drake on a lope. The vehicle was designed for hauling, not for speed or comfort. They could pick up supplies on the trip into Beckett. Laurel had virtually shopped the night before, designating that her selections be ready for her by two the next day. She could spend the afternoon visiting her mom at the AuxCare. Justin would pass the time at Vy's or down by the lake.

Beckett had become a tourist destination as its third incarnation as a town. It occupied a pleasant location at the end of the lake. The lake was man-made, with a dam generating hydroelectric power at the other end.

Beckett had first incarnated itself as a mining town filled with prospectors and fly-by-nights. Despite the gold optimism, little in the way of precious metals were discovered when all was said and done. There was some jade, which became the stuff of hobbyists and artisans. Fortunately for the town, a rich lode of high-quality coal had been found farther up the valley. The initial enthusiasm for the prospect of wealth had brought a rail spur line up to Beckett. Bricks were hauled in to build establishments on the two-block Main Street, which was now designated as historic and had been tarted up to be attractive for vacationers.

Lumbering had been the second incarnation. Before the dam, loggers depleted the forest floor below Beckett. Farther up, the valley behind Beckett still yielded many board feet of high-quality softwoods. Logs were floated down the lake with barrages that tied up at the pier built for the town. Down at the dam, the logs were picked out of the water and trucked to a mill farther down the valley. Eventually, the valley behind Beckett was logged out, and the pier fell into disuse, with the barrages left to rust out.

The flooding of the valley had taken out a portion of the rail spur line, which was never rebuilt. Using the railbed close to town and the shoreline of the lake closer to the dam, the access road to Beckett was built.

When the valley above Beckett was lumbered off, the soil proved rich enough to support meadows and ranges. It was initially grazed with cattle until the calculations on the methane they produced turned them into ecological contraband. Now those meadows were home to sheep, which apparently fart less.

The third incarnation of Beckett was tourism. It began with an appreciation of the beauty of the valley, now with a lake and rolling hills scattered with sheep. A resort was built to provide a better experience than could be had in the motels and the rooms above Vy's. The pier was gentrified into a place for pleasure boats, and the wharf was slowly converted to shops and restaurants.

Further development of the town came with the discovery of how the hot springs could be exploited for profit. An army of engineers had found geothermal warmth accessible enough to supply hot pools for the tired feet of those walking the concrete wharf down by the lake and to heat the resorts and buildings of Beckett through a series of underground pipes. Beckett received the designation of a national eco-village. Geothermal heat, wind turbines up on the ridge, and solar panels on the new construction completed the suite of small-scale energy producers. Beckett became a net exporter of energy, sufficient to be touted in glossy brochures.

With the hot springs, with the emerging crafts of weaving and knitting using indigenous wool, with the fashionable jade jewelry and carving, and with the convertible pier and wharf, tourism increased. Within ten years, three resorts offering eco-enriching vacations were built on the lakeshore. A ski lift to the mountainside was built to make the destination more attractive in the winter. Jade carvings and jewelry, lamb kebabs, and wool sweaters became the fame of the town. To this day, they are sold in artsy shops and restaurants down at the wharf. The tourists come with their CashCards.

Justin and Laurel were excited to land on acreage outside of Beckett shortly before the third incarnation. Their flight from the city was necessary as they scooped Alton into their lives. He was their grandson, and his rescue was desperate. What better place to raise a seven-year-old than on a small sheep farm? Sleepy little Beckett was far enough away from his snatch; fifteen years ago, there had been no broadband Ethernet to track their escape to Beckett. By the time ASL had fully linked in Beckett and the valley, Alton was no longer considered to be viable for his intended purpose, and the ASL had stopped looking for him.

Laurel brought her mom and dad to live with them when Alton was small. It was her mom who had insisted that horses come into their lives. Now she lived in AuxCare and was rarely up to coming out to see Biddy and Drake.

Before the three of them had left town that day, Alton would get to see his beloved great-grandma.

Vy's Magnificent Inn, Eatery, and Emporium occupied a prominent corner on historic Main Street. A large painted sign showed Vy to be a kindly, pudgy, auntlike person holding a steaming piece of peach pie. But anyone who had visited the museum across the road knew that Vy was actually Boris Vygoski, a coarse-looking Russian immigrant drawn to Beckett in the heady days of the prospecting rush. The three-story brick building was financed through gambling and whoring revenues and eventually became the social center of the town. The peaches are now in the pies, not on the cheeks of the whores. Clothing is now tried on in small dressing rooms in the emporium rather than taken off in seedy bedrooms on the second floor.

In the back of Vy's, there was a table at which the locals gathered. They would be shooed out to a picnic table in the alley behind the kitchen when the eatery filled up at dinner time. But now, in the lull of midafternoon, Justin and his buddies could sit there in overalls and caps soiled with labor's grime, providing local color to the place.

The LandPorter outside announced that Justin was at Vy's, and it didn't take long for Cedars and Rayce to come in for coffee yet again that day. They greeted each other with mutual exchanges of "Hey, old guy" and fist punches to the upper arms.

"What brings you to town?" Cedars asked.

"Alton's coming home. Coming in on an AVoD this afternoon. We figured the buses that he's taking from the east should get into Capital Station about two, and he should be up here by about four."

"So how is he doing?"

"We haven't heard much. Originally when he went, we got e-mails just about every day. He seemed lonely and was struggling with the work. When they stopped coming, we figured he probably had settled in OK."

Rayce looked up. "So what was he doing out there?"

Justin looked over at Cedars, and in the glance, he figured out that Cedars hadn't spoken to Rayce of his connection to Alton's job.

Cedars explained, "He is with a company contracted to do agricultural land reclamation. When he wrote, he said he was going on the Cain-grass crew."

"Cain-grass?" Rayce screwed up his face.

"Yeah, with Plains Inc. I got him the job. Good work going on there." Cedars was tending to his coffee as he spoke.

Rayce still looked puzzled. Justin explained, "It's a GMO-field grass. When it's left long enough in the field, it kills off all other vegetation with both excretions from the root system and a dense root growth that suffocates all weeds. One of the genetic modifications allows Cain-grass to fix nitrogen back into the soil. Once it has cleaned and fed the field, it is killed with heat, plowed in as a thick, organic layer. Then the field is ready to plant the next year, weed-free and chemical-free."

Rayce looked disengaged, as though he couldn't follow the explanation.

"So he hasn't been writing then, eh?" Cedars asked.

"Yeah, just stopped. He had made some weird reference in his last e-mail to having to be careful what he wrote and where it was going. Then the e-mails stopped entirely. We said to each other, 'Well, OK, he isn't homesick anymore,' and we figured he would be in touch soon enough. But it was still a worry, more so for Laurel than for me. Anyway, we got this message last night that he was coming home."

"How is Stamper?" asked Rayce. He always asked about Stamper and was generally rude about it, breaking in to conversations anywhere he had a chance. Justin had taken them for a backcountry trail ride a year or so ago. Rayce had ridden Stamper, and Stamper had given Rayce a pretty hard time of it. Still, Rayce's affection for the horse had grown in proportion to the obstinacy of the gelding.

"Had him out yesterday. Finally had to take the rider off and put Laurel on him for the rest of the ride. The customer made like he wasn't green, but he was. He was letting Stamper get away with nonsense, wasn't able to keep control of him."

"Ha! Stamper would really have liked that, eh?" Rayce exclaimed, grinning.

Rayce's voice was ebullient, loud enough to attract attention. As Justin looked around the room, he noticed that the tourists had looked over at the table, perhaps wondering about the local color that sat in the corner.

Justin paled at what he saw; over by the window sat Al and Shy Girl. He turned away, unsure whether they had seen him too. He hoped they hadn't heard what he had said about the ride. He didn't think so. Still, it disturbed him that they were there. Justin drifted away from the conversation going on between Cedars and Rayce. He had a thought—a thought that maybe Cedars knew more about Plains Inc. than he was letting on. He gulped his coffee and made an excuse to leave. He would have to ask sometime, but not now, not while Rayce was here.

Justin and Laurel were to meet down at the pier. As Justin left Vy's, it was still half an hour before they had agreed to meet. He had to get out of there and would enjoy just being beside the water with his own thoughts. He could watch for the buses, AVoDs, and LandPorters coming in on the shore road.

When Laurel joined him, she slipped her hand into his and chatted about her mom's dementia. She had loaded the provisions into the back of the LandPorter and tidied up the seats in the cab to make room for her grandson. Finally, as their eyes fixed on the shore road across the lake, they saw a line of about twelve AVoDs. The small linked vehicles looked like a mechanical caterpillar cruising at a good speed in the direction of Beckett.

Walking back down to the pier, they saw the chain of vehicles arrive in town. Several AVoDs delinked from the string of others that had shared propulsion for the trip. Several other of the compartmental, autonomous vehicles remained linked, continuing along the road through town toward the opposite shore and the resorts. Most of the delinked single units headed off with passengers still in them for destinations within Beckett. Finally, there was just one AVoD parked in sight of the wharf. Their grandson unwound his lanky frame to emerge from the unit.

Once Alton was out and standing on the sidewalk outside of Vy's, the AVoD drove off empty, probably into a marshaling yard at the end of the street. Alton seemed to have grown in the couple of months he had been away. Or maybe it was just that he was thinner now.

(III)

It had been only four months since Alton had left for his work with Plains Inc. When he left, he was thoroughly tired of home: the well-aged decor of the house, the drudgery of the stable, and the claustrophobic valley floor hemmed in by the mountains.

Now it all seemed comforting to him.

Even his grandma's habits in the kitchen, the familiar sequence of sounds and smells as she put out breakfast, were welcome to him. For a moment, he let go of the turmoil that he felt inside. Then, almost with a sense of his own summoning, the core of discontent churned again in his gut.

He placed the leather satchel on the kitchen table.

Laurel turned from the counter and looked at the satchel with a mixture of surprise and reminiscence. She remembered the day that her own father had given the satchel to Alton. He was only about seven at the time; it was very soon after he had come to live with them on the ranch. Her father was quite ill and pondering end-of-life decisions, including whether he would seek assisted dying. He had kept papers, and books, in the satchel. He had written in a bound journal there. Her dad had cherished that satchel and had still carried it from room to room over one shoulder even as he had grown weaker. Seven-year-old Alton had rarely left his side during those last days. Laurel would catch him easing the weight of the satchel from his great-grandpa's shoulder, and she would catch him stroking the soiled leather. Finally, she found the boy and the old man standing in front of the burn barrel emptying the satchel, the precious journal and various legal documents set aside. Then she saw her father give the empty satchel to Alton. Her dad left that day. They found his body later down at the cedar grove and buried him there.

Items made of leather were now of great value. When beef became forbidden as a food staple, suddenly there were no cattle.

Dairy cows were kept in barns for milking, and male calves born to them were raised in the barns too. Those calves were slaughtered young for veal meat. The barns all had exhaust-air scrubbers that captured the methane, stored it, and used it for heating. In this climate-conscious and energy-conscious operation, there were few hides for tanning, just the smaller calf hides. Borders and tariffs blocked the flow of leather into the country as an international statement of environmental stewardship. Locally produced calf leather generally made it into the hands of wealthy folks who could afford it and would treat it as a sign of their prosperity.

When Alton placed the satchel on the table, it opened, and several bound journals slipped out. Laurel stared, perplexed. Paper, especially blank paper, had slipped from being a rarity to being contraband. Forests once cut for pulp were now required to be the lungs of the planet. The lumber that was cut in forest management was used for home construction. The little paper that was produced had defined uses. It had been years, decades perhaps, since even a student scribbler or stack of sticky notes had been present in the home. She missed them.

"It's all fucked up here," Alton stated.

"What?"

"You all just accept what is going on. You don't question."

"What happened to you while you were away, Alton? You were never this angry." Laurel looked at her grandson. It had always been difficult to harness his self-determination; she had noticed that ever since they forced him to come to live with them at age seven. She had wondered whether he had already been ruined by then, ruined by the ASL programming. Yet she had respected that self-determination, had even seen it as a good sign, a sign that he wouldn't cave.

"Here, you go along to get along. I can see it: you and Grandpa are getting older, but you still have to push yourselves just to survive."

"We do OK." Laurel's tone didn't even convince herself.

"I met people there working for Plains. They go along, but they talk about the way that ASL is screwing us. At least they have a desire to stand up to it."

At that moment, Justin came into the kitchen. He poured himself some coffee, took a homemade muffin from the basket, and drew out a handful of cherries that Laurel had brought back from the depot the day before. "Good to have you home, boy," he said.

"Good to be back, Grandpa." Alton's tone changed. He took in the depleted countenance of his grandfather with worry. He knew his grandmother could take his outrage and confrontation, but his grandfather couldn't.

"So what was your work over there?" Justin asked.

"Cain-grass plantations. We are reworking hundreds, maybe even thousands, of acres of overfarmed land just the other side of the foothills. We have prepared a dozen or so sections for the burn off when I go back."

"You speak as though you believe in this work." Justin looked at his grandson with skepticism in his eye.

"Not really. It's just work. We sleep in abandoned farmhouses left by families who once farmed the land. We supplement rations that the company provides with eggs and chickens, field vegetables, and fruits grown by squatters who try to live out there. We can give them petrol from our tanks for their generators for the winter."

"You are learning about survival," Justin said.

"And how are you surviving, Grandpa?"

The old man avoided the question. "I am glad to have you back. Stamper needs to be ridden lots; he is getting insolent with the customers. I'll probably get you to put in time on Starsky and…" Justin stared out the window at the paddock. "Well, all of them really. Four days a week we have rides with customers. We should give them each at least two days of rest. That means that once a week a good, disciplined ride should smarten them up."

Alton went over to his grandpa at the window. The two men turned to each other.

"You up to it?" Justin asked.

"You bet. Any one of them is way better than the tractor I have been driving for the last two months."

"What are these?" Justin had turned to the center of the room and noticed the satchel with the journals spilling out onto the table.

"I found out, over there, that all the writing I did on my wearable, everything from e-mails to shopping lists, is being fed through the servers at the ASL. It is mined. The ASL keeps a profile on each of us, a record of everything we put through digital inputs. In those first few weeks after I left, I wrote e-mails back to you, telling you what it was like. Then one of my coworkers found out and confronted me, saying that we can't let the ASL know everything that we're doing. He told me that if I needed to write things down to do it in a way that the ASL couldn't see. So I started writing in journals and keeping them in Great-Grandpa's satchel."

Laurel picked up one of the journals and noted the rigid script of her grandson. She remembered that he had been taught keyboarding in school, not penmanship. His letters were like those of a digital font, yet in their slight irregularities, they were his, her beloved grandson's.

"Where did you get the journals? I haven't seen anything like this in the stores for years."

"We found them in the old farmhouses. They were in the mechanical shops and barns; they were in the kitchens. We figured that in the last years that the families farmed there, when paper was getting rarer as the paperless society was taking over, folks had hoarded them before they were finally all gone from the stores."

Laurel was flipping through one of the journals, noting that each day Alton had written, he had started the entry with "Dear Grandma and Grandpa, today I saw…" She remembered that when he was small they had a ritual at this very same kitchen table. Every day when he came in from school or working in the barn, she would sit him down and wait as he pondered what he was to say to her. Then he would say, "Grandma, today I saw…." And she would ask him all about it.

"Well, later today we will take a look," Justin stated. He had finished his muffin, guzzled his coffee, and in his mind had already left for the barn.

As Alton turned to leave to go out and do chores, Laurel lightly grabbed his elbow and turned him around to face her. She held him there with her light touch on his arm and her intense gaze. Justin had left, and Alton had called after him that he would be there in a minute.

"What has happened to you?" she asked.

"I got out of here. I thought I wanted that. But I am back for now. It is just for a few days, and then I need to go back to my job out east. After that…"

"Are you back? Really back?"

"Yes, Grandma, I am." He paused. "I think I want to be here even more, seeing the ranch again, seeing what it is like out there."

"I wonder," she said. When she'd picked up one of the journals, Laurel had seen the word *insurrection* squealing into the descriptions that Alton had written in his daily entries using some old pencil from an earlier time.

Alton could see the concern in her eyes and voice. He'd known that it was unlikely that Grandpa would ever read the journals, but he'd also known that she would. Grandpa would ask questions while they worked together. Alton would give partial answers. Grandpa would be satisfied with that. Grandpa would ask Grandma what was in the journals, and she would give partial answers too. What he wrote there was to her, because he couldn't bear to keep it all just to himself, and he knew that she would never tell.

But Alton would make sure she never knew of the two journals that he had left under the seat of the AVoD. When the vehicle left him on the sidewalk outside of Vy's, it had been destined for someone else's use in the quaint little tourist town of Beckett. Those other journals were for that someone else.

(IV)

Of the three resorts outside of Beckett, the Vintage was clearly the most upscale. It was also the newest, although it was themed to look old. Rough-hewn ceiling beams locally sourced at Baggs's Mills, plastered walls, and wooden floors gave the Vintage a rustic appearance.

Throughout the Vintage, fireplaces burned, although not with wood, which would violate environmental laws; natural gas had been brought into the resort for cooking and open-flame decor. With the carbon credits the Vintage got from using geothermal, solar, and wind energy, it could buy sufficient natural gas to enhance the luxury of the guests.

Despite the luxurious appointments of the suite and the stunning view out the floor-to-ceiling windows of the lake and the mountains, CarolAnne couldn't settle comfortably into her room at the Vintage.

CarolAnne's room had an adjoining door to her father's room. They had agreed to keep them unlocked, but Al was clear that she was to knock if she wanted to come through that door. Such was typical of their relationship; she had access to her father but only as he would allow.

To be in such a place, to have it to herself, was disconcerting for CarolAnne. The suite was spacious and orderly, with furnishings and arches to strategically define its spaces. Unique but tasteful artwork and small sculptures gave it a sophisticated look. The suite was so different from her home that it left CarolAnne feeling uneasy.

CarolAnne resided in her mother's home, which was chaotic and overfilled. Her mom was a collector such that piles of stuff proliferated; the walls were cluttered with ceramic plaques setting biblical quotations over painted, idyllic scenes. Music played continuously: hymns and praise songs. The religiosity of CarolAnne's mother was all-encompassing. It was a faith and a life ordering that was intent on imposing itself wherever it was allowed to grow. For the fifteen-year-old CarolAnne, the burden of the home would have been claustrophobic had she not grown up there. She had simply become numb to it all.

CarolAnne had lived all her life with her parents separated. She could not imagine them ever having lived together, ever having settled on something so engaging with each other as to have a child. Her father was brusque and superior, an intellectual who had no patience for anything sentimental. She visited him on weekends in his condo. He had made a bedroom for her and furnished it sparsely with durable, functional items. She rarely slept overnight there. Minimal updating of her room decor took place even as she grew through childhood into adolescence. That updating was the only decorating he'd done or additions he'd made to the condo in the nearly twelve years he had lived there. What figured most prominently in her father's home was the work desk, with its curtaining of screens that formed a semicircle around him where he sat.

As a father, Al awkwardly made space in his life for her. There was little natural flow to it all; he treated parenting like he did brushing his teeth or assembling his laundry to be ready for the housekeeper who tended to his physical needs. CarolAnne knew it was her job to entertain herself at her father's home. Al provided her with sketchbooks and artist pencils, as she loved to draw. With the societal restrictions on paper, the sketchbooks were hard to get, but somehow her father had been able to get them for her. She loved the feel of the graphite pencil on the paper, so different to the touch than a stylus on a tablet screen.

When she was at his place, CarolAnne spent most of her time drawing—faces and fashions mostly. She would call up and freeze on the entertainment system interesting images of people and then draw them as though she were an artist with a model doing a sitting in a studio. Her father would sporadically leave his work desk and approach her, as though he'd suddenly realized that it was the weekend that she was there and he really ought to do something with her. He would compliment her on her drawing and then call up an age-appropriate game or movie on the entertainment system for them to play or watch together. They would go for walks, never saying much to each other. He taught her to play tennis in the summers and, in the winter, took her to the common games room in the condo complex for ping-pong or billiards. The games defined the physical distance between them, kept it regular, and made it safe.

CarolAnne saw her parents as opposites. In her psychology class, she had been taught that opposites attract, but she couldn't ever even imagine it. Her parents seemed to repel each other. She asked Sallye about it one day.

Sallye had just come into her life; she had just appeared and kept reappearing at what gradually proved itself to be a schedule. Sallye said that opposites attract to fill in gaps, to complete within the self what was missing. CarolAnne remembered that she was confused by this and that she probably had responded with some sort of weak "thank-you" without really being able to comprehend what Sallye had said. Despite this, she liked Sallye and just decided she wouldn't ask any more difficult questions.

There was a knock on the door.

"Can I come in?" Al asked.

"Sure. I wasn't doing anything." That was a lie. She had been working in the sketchbook she had brought with her.

"I want to ask you about something." He got right to the point. "When we were at Vy's, what did you see?"

"My pie and soda," CarolAnne replied sarcastically, and then she noticed a frustrated look on her father's face; clearly it wasn't what he was interested in. She reflected and remembered. "There were a bunch of old men having coffee. One of them was the guy who took us on the horseback ride yesterday."

"And the others?"

"Didn't notice. One was loud and kind of weird."

"And the other one, what did you notice about him?"

CarolAnne detected a pointedness to the question, as though it were some sort of test that her father had put to her. She felt that somehow she had missed the point of them being there, that maybe there had been some sort of purpose to it other than having tea and pie.

CarolAnne looked at her dad, puzzled out his question, and finally said, "Nothing, Father." She drew out the epithet to her father sarcastically and then became more pointed. "I didn't notice anything about him."

"Do you remember what he looked like? When we go back into Beckett tomorrow, would you recognize him again if you were to see him?"

"I guess."

"OK, then. Watch for him. Thanks." Al was aware of CarolAnne's perceptive skills, born of her love of drawing and her unimposing social posture.

Al looked awkward, as though he had finished what he set out to do and didn't know what he should do next. In retrospect, the questioning had felt too pointed, as though he had forgotten that she was his daughter and that they were supposed to be having a good time.

Softening his tone, Al asked, "What did you like about Beckett? The pier and shops?"

CarolAnne thought back to the time she'd spent with her father there. Initially, nothing came to mind. And then she focused. "Outside of Vy's, there was this guy getting out of the AVoD. I noticed him."

CarolAnne blushed, suddenly self-conscious. "There was something about that guy, something rad. So I shot a video of him on my wearable."

"I don't remember anything special about him," Al stated, almost embarrassed, as though he had missed something.

"He met up with the old guy who took us horseback riding. Rad guy had a carryall and a satchel that he threw in the back of a LandPorter, and they left."

"Hmm. You noticed something that I missed."

CarolAnne reflected. "He was so good-looking." CarolAnne looked down at the sketchbook on the table. She had caught the energy of the look in the young man's eyes when he stood outside. His longish hair had cascaded over his shoulders; his face was tanned, the muscles of his neck and shoulders taut.

(V)

Laurel was relieved when she heard Alton get up early and accompany Justin out on chores. By the time she got out to the barn to join them in brushing the horses, Alton was by himself, coming out of the tack room with a collection of bits, bridles, and hackamores, each with its own designated horse.

"I gave Grandpa a day off."

"You will ride with me and the customers today?" Laurel asked. This would be the only day he would be able to do so; plans were that he would head back east the following day.

"Yeah, and looking forward to it. I have spent too much time on tractors in the last few months. It will feel good to have more time on a horse."

The horses had spent the night in the paddock and would be brought in one by one to the barn. It had rained overnight, and they were muddy. Rocket had rolled in the dirt, as he tended to do when he felt the wet of the rain on his back. As always, Arch's mane was tangled and Star was hard to catch. Alton and his grandma exchanged bits of conversation as they came and went.

"You were pretty angry when you first got home a couple of days ago."

"It's just that…" Alton grabbed another halter and went to get Starsky. By the time he returned with the gelding, he had calmed down. "I am sorry, Grandma." He ran his hand over the neck, back, and hip of the impressive animal, allowing his touch to create the calm. He grounded the animal to ground himself.

"I don't like to see you and Grandpa work so hard here for so little."

"It's our life. We got out of the city, got a chance to do something for ourselves. And when we got you, we knew this was the place to raise a grandson."

"It's hard on Grandpa now."

"Yes. Physically, I can see that he is getting tired. But there is more strain from the customers. Attitudes are changing; there isn't the respect that there used to be. People expect to be catered to."

"People are different here than over where I was working this summer. Here, while they expect to be catered to, they are also… what would I say…sheep." Alton paused and looked at his grandma. "Nobody asks questions here. It's like everyone is addicted to their little luxuries they buy with their CashCard credits."

Laurel didn't say anything.

"Over there, people talk. I learned stuff about the government and the ASL. I had no idea…" Alton looked at his grandmother, but she didn't look up. He wanted to tell her, so wanted to tell her. He didn't know what she could hear.

Alton left to get another horse. Laurel focused on untangling Arch's mane and brushing out his tail.

Upon his return, Alton dropped the subject too. He came back to the lives of his grandparents. "How long are you going to do this?"

"Oh, I don't know. Don't know what else there would be for us. Last winter I made good money in the knit shop working the wool and the woolly; maybe that might support us until the government pensions click in."

For the last few years, Alton had missed his grandma in the winter and early spring, as she had stayed in a room above Vy's from Tuesday to Sunday. She had worked ten-hour days in a demonstration area creating handcrafted sweaters while tourists from the resorts watched. Laurel acted the quaint, historical figure as she talked through the various steps of the processing of the raw wool from the sheep up on the steppes above the town to its eventual transformation into the products in the store. Beckett Mills sweaters captured a premium price as cherished souvenirs of the trip to the mountains. CashCard dollars poured from customer accounts into the business, a portion of which trickled its way back to Laurel. She had a way with the customers, in Beckett Mills as well as on the ranch. She juggled humor and storytelling with personal connection that held people's interest. Many other women of the town did piecework in their homes to produce the quantity of woolen goods for sale; Laurel produced the quality of the buying experience.

Horses continued to be brought, brushed, tacked up, and tied to a fence in the yard. Rocket had his buddy Arch beside him; next, there was Star and Stamper, and then came Starsky and Hutch. They would let Hester roam. Last were Biddy and Drake.

"I could never see Grandpa settling in town."

"Me neither." Laurel continued to concentrate on the horse she was grooming. "Did your grandpa say what he was going to do today?" She had noticed as they talked that Justin had walked from the outbuilding that was his workshop back into the house.

"Not really. I suggested that he take that hike up the mountain that he and I used to do together. There is a spot up there, sheltered from the wind and in the sun. It looks down the length of the valley. When we would hike there, he would get to that spot and lay 'these weary old bones' on the ground. It was the closest I ever saw him to being content."

By this point, most of the horses were ready. They waited for the bus to come carrying the customers for the day.

"Grandma, when we stop for lunch, I want to go for a little ride on my own. I will get you all settled up in the meadow, and then I am going to head off for a while. Is that OK? I will be back in time to lead us back down."

"Sure, I can entertain them, tell some stories. Are you needing more time with just you on a horse?"

"Yeah."

The whine of the electric engine on the small tour bus caught their attention as it came down the lane. Laurel and Alton looked in disbelief as a family with two children and two grandparents stepped off. The children were school-age, both too small and too young to ride any of the horses they had there. Alton saw Laurel sizing up the scene. Quickly, they talked.

"The older boy...hmm...we could put a saddle on Hester instead of the pack. Hester would be OK with a child. I don't know what we can do with the youngster." Laurel looked concerned.

"He could ride with me. Grandpa's saddle is pretty roomy. I could have the little guy with me in front."

"Are you sure?"

"Look, they have no shoes, just flip-flops." With Alton's observation, Laurel gave an exasperated sigh. The concierge at the resort should have caught the inappropriate ages and footwear.

Alton quickly went into the tack room and rummaged through the storage boxes at the back. Grandma had saved his childhood cowboy boots; each year, he had worn the next size up. The leather was still soft on them.

"C'mon, guys, let's make you into real cowboys!" Alton's enthusiasm immediately captivated the two youngsters.

Laurel watched as Alton connected with the two boys. There was poking and giggling as he sat one and then the other on the tack-room step to try on the boots, finding a pair for each that could fit.

She had never seen her grandson with children in this way, but he was a natural. Before long, she could see the random energy of the boys settling into an idolizing of her grandson. While he had the practicality of his grandfather, he also had the people skills that came naturally to her.

Laurel left to do the safety demonstration with the four adults. With his little entourage, Alton hauled out the small saddle and the bridle for Hester. The donkey was pretty barrel-chested, and he would need to tighten the cinch so the saddle wouldn't slip. Still, the old donkey was gentle enough and small enough for the older boy, Sid, to ride. Talking through each step of the process with the two boys, Alton had them entranced at the prospect of being cowboys for the day. Alton spoke directly and sincerely to Sid, telling him that he would need to stay still and centered in the saddle on Hester's back, or it might rotate around the barrel of the donkey, dropping him headfirst down the side of the hill. The boys listened attentively and nodded grimly at the young man's instructions. The little guy, Cameron, had already declared he was going to be a cowboy when he grew up too.

Alton took the saddle off Rocket and rigged up a packsaddle for him. Every step of the way, he had his trail of little guys, little guys full of questions and enthusiasm.

By the time they were moving through the cedar glen, the line of horses and their riders had settled into a slow but steady pace. Behind Alton and Cameron were the two parents and the two grandparents. Laurel trailed behind as the back rider. She had to keep an eye on Rocket behind her, who wasn't at all pleased to be the packhorse for the day; he was snorting, and every so often he nosed Biddy's rump, making Biddy hump up and make like she was going to kick. Laurel had Sid on Hester right in front of her. What might happen there was the biggest risk of the day. Alton had put helmets on both Sid and Cameron. Still, having a child with no experience on a donkey riding up the hill trail was taking a chance.

Hester was an old soul and would take care of the boy. Her walking gait would be smooth even with the trail on uneven ground and at a steep slope.

When they were in the middle of the glen, Laurel whistled for Alton to stop up at the lead. She dismounted, helped Sid to do the same, and checked the cinch around Hester's barrel belly. Sid ran up front to Alton to tell him excitedly that he was doing great and not to worry because he, Sid, was a natural at this. Alton smiled. Cameron squirmed, jealous.

The upper meadow was resplendent in the midday sun. The rain the night before had brought out wildflowers. Cameron had grown tired of sitting in the small gap between Alton and the horn of the saddle. By the time the boy got off, he was all over the place, running and rolling in the meadow grass. Soon he attached himself to his grandparents. Coming off the horses, they were stretching, stiff and sore from the unnatural position of being horseback. Mom and Dad worked with Laurel to pull the boxed lunches out of the pack across Rocket's back.

Alton looked nervous as he prepared to ride off, waiting somewhat impatiently as he watched his grandmother settle it all down, get the lunch out, and gather the customers around her. Alton knew that soon, when the food was being devoured by the city folk breathing in the high-country air, Laurel would be spinning out tales of the historic gold rush and early ranch life of the valley. He would be good for a bit of time. He grabbed an apple, gave his "Please excuse me, folks; I am going to ride farther up the trail a bit," and left.

There was an open ridge just about five minutes along. It had a view of the town of Beckett. When he got there, Alton pulled out a mirror from his pocket, located Cedars's house, and flashed the sun off the mirror into his yard. Cedars must have been watching for it, because immediately he came out of the house and got on his electric quad. With Alton on Drake and Cedars on his quad, the two headed for the meeting place they had prearranged in the journals that Alton had left in the AVoD. He had counted on Cedars to retrieve those journals, with his missives from the Plains. Their communication was completely off the digital grid, but the response from Cedars made it clear that it had worked. Alton had guessed that he would be able to ride over to him on this day when he proposed the arrangements. As it turned out, the trail ride with customers was a convenient cover, and the lunch break was convenient timing.

It was rushed; they just had a few minutes to talk before Alton would need to return to the meadow, pull Cameron back on his lap, and make the trip back to the ranch. It would be the only time Alton and Cedars could meet. Alton was due to return out east for work at Plains Inc. within a couple of days. Cedars thanked him for the caution in arranging a meeting this way and said, among other things, that he thought he was being watched.

4

SALLYE

It had been about a month since Byron had had his first session of AVT. Sallye was aware, deeply concerned. They were expected to have at least three sessions to fully qualify for completion of the requirements of the First Flight of Paraclete training and move to the second. Both she and Byron were progressing through their first noninstitutional client placements. They were doing their Flights in parallel, and Byron had fallen behind.

Sallye had had her three sessions with the Dr. S avatar—she had chosen the female version. Those sessions were warm and somehow womanly. It was as though she had been embraced and the matters of her heart had been blessed. They had laughed as though they were old friends. In that VR room, it was as though the avatar was not an avatar but a human. It was as though the intelligence wasn't artificial but wise. The VR room offered every aspect of the experience except the human touch. That was OK with Sallye; because of the experience she'd had there, she found herself touching others in a deeper and more human manner. With her clients, with Byron, and with the others in FiveWay, touch now came even more naturally and meaningfully. Sallye was discovering that every human emotion had its own quality of touch. She had discovered that in her sessions with Dr. S. She treasured the discovery as her own, even though she knew the discovery had been guided in her sessions in the VR room.

But Byron hadn't been back to his. It worried Sallye.

Their own relationship had deepened, and they found themselves caring for each other in complementary ways. Byron was more practical, would remember things that they needed to do and could remind Sallye in a way in which she didn't feel nagged. Sallye felt matters of the heart more deeply. She could lead Byron through his uncertainties about himself, could give voice and touch to his fears and sadnesses. He was relying more and more on her to be able to acknowledge his own feelings.

That was why it troubled her that he hadn't gone back to the AVT. She worried that he was letting her do the emotional work for him. Although she was willing, she knew it wasn't appropriate. She also knew that there was a part of him that she couldn't touch, a darker part.

The display on the wearable on her left forearm lit up. It was Byron, and Sallye immediately flushed with pleasurable autonomic activation.

"I will be there in about five minutes." Byron's voice projected into the room, and his image smiled in shallow 3-D, hovering slightly above the computerized display.

"Oh, Byron, that is far too long to wait." Sallye sighed sarcastically.

"I know, hon, but sometimes reality sucks."

Sallye reflected on Byron's non-Paraclete tone and expression. This was as irreverent and playful as he got. His lightening up from proper Paraclete communication was a sign of the deepening of their relationship.

When he entered the common area of FiveWay, Byron looked a bit disheveled and sweaty. He explained that he had been playing soccer with Zeke on the pitch close to his house. The walk over hadn't cooled him down, even though the late summer was starting to let go of the intensity of the sun's heat.

"I think I would like you better if you showered." Sallye smiled and recoiled slightly from their initial hug upon being reunited.

"I think I would like me better if I did too."

At this point, Sanc came running into the room, obviously attracted rather than repulsed by the sweaty scent coming off Byron. Sanc was a mixed-breed dog who had come to FiveWay a few months before. In assessing his rather beat-up and worn-down appearance, the residents there concluded that he was seeking sanctuary at the compound. His initial name, Sanctuary, had given way to the nickname Sanc. "Chew" and finally "Wary" became attached to the dog as well, apropos of aspects of his behavior in the home. When he misbehaved, the three names were put together in a guilt-inducing tone: "Sanc—Chew—Wary, no!"

Officially, dogs were not allowed in the family communal homes or the compounds. His presence with them was contraband. Firm rules against pets were established years before in a policy to be trotted out whenever anyone made a request for permission. Convinced that biosensors on the humans would not betray the dog's presence, the maintenance of the secrecy around Sanctuary became a luscious conspiracy of young Paracletes.

Off Byron went to the shower, shedding his clothing on the way. Sanc playfully growled while he shook each article and tossed it in the air. Byron felt at ease at FiveWay, not just because of Sanctuary but also because Sallye and other Paracletes accepted him in their home. Both he and Sallye kept clothing and personal-hygiene items at each other's compounds.

While Byron showered, Sallye wondered how to bring up the issue of the AVT. But after his shower, when he emerged wrapped in a towel in her room with his boyish hair askew and wet, he surprised her by saying, "OK, I know you have been worried about it, so I have decided that I am going back to the AVT."

It was like that between them lately, that they anticipated each other's thoughts. In First Flight, they had taken Anticipatory Empathy Training, and although they weren't actually practicing on each other, it was kind of nice to do a jump within such a safe relationship.

"That sounds great. What changed your mind?"

"This: Sallye, will you go with me?"

"Is that allowed?"

"I'm not sure. It wouldn't be relationship counseling per se. And I don't even know whether the avatar would know that you were there if you didn't say anything. I just want you…"

"I am sure there are ambient biosensors in the room. The avatar would know."

"I supposed he could ask you to leave if it wasn't OK."

"I suppose he could. I would kind of like to see Dr. Y. I had a good experience with Dr. S. Dr. Y will be different."

"I actually don't remember much of the session I had. I was wondering if I could get the video record of it from Dr. Chetwin and go over what occurred before my…"

"Your fainting spell." Sallye paused, and then with a serious tone said, "Don't. It would feel like studying for therapy. Do you remember what Dr. Chetwin said?"

"Yes, you can't study for therapy. To do so makes it too intellectual a process."

He had finished drying himself off. The door to Sallye's room was open, and there were others in the residence coming and going in the hall. There was an easiness about nakedness in the compounds. The others accepted the primacy of the relationship that Sallye and Byron had shared for almost two years now. They would not have been surprised that he had showered and was dressing there.

"So will you come?"

"Yes."

Once he had made the decision, Sallye wouldn't let it rest until he had booked a VR room. Byron decided it would be over at the North Hill. There were media rooms at the compounds, but they tended to be used more recreationally. Byron wanted the experience of going someplace else for the therapy. Checking his wearable, he was able to book a room right away. Sallye had actually insisted on it now that he had decided to go back.

Off they went.

"You are here again." There was a chuckling that came with the avatar's words. "And you have brought someone with you."

"This is Sallye. She is my intimate. Is it OK that she's here?"

"Well, I don't do couples work, but you would know that. She can sit in. It is your confidentiality that is observed here, not mine. If you want her to stay, that is up to you."

Byron smiled at Dr. Y's reference to confidentiality. That was an old idea, from back in his day. Back then it was thought to be the cornerstone of effective therapy. It was an amusing anachronism now.

"I do."

"Tell me about your fear, your needing her to be here."

"Well, last time, when I have a vasovagal syncope…"

"When you fainted…"

"You just sat there in stasis; you didn't even help me up."

"So you have her to pick you up if you fall." Dr. Y paused, smiling. The avatar was reading body language off Byron, and the biosensors were picking up a quickening of his autonomic nervous system: arousal. It was early in the session, but already the artificial-intelligence program running the avatar noted that an interpretation had generated an autonomic reaction.

"I guess."

"Did you notice that when you were describing the faint you used the present tense? You said 'I have a' rather than 'I had a.' What is it like, that the fear is so present again?"

Byron was stunned. He intellectualized back 150 years to the old notion of the Freudian slip. Aloud, he mused, "Hmm. I guess I'm afraid it will happen again."

Dr. Y's eyes lit up. He didn't say anything, just left space for Byron to continue.

"It does frighten me." Byron spoke softly, confidentially.

"It is a little bit like dying."

The air in the VR room hung heavily around the three of them and the avatar's words. Sallye was very conscious of the moment, of the depth of it. Byron was silent, spiraling deeper inside. Few words had been exchanged between the two, but already Byron was connecting deeply with Dr. Y. Sallye reflected on how different this was from her Dr. S sessions. She and her avatar were full of words and experiences. Discoveries were a mix of joy and meaning. Here, between Byron and Dr. Y, the exchange was pensive, incisive.

Dr. Y let the interpretation settle. He didn't need to make anything more of it as he sensed Byron's reaction. Finally, he spoke again. "If I remember correctly, when it happened you were speaking of your father."

"My father is very much alive. He is raising other children in the communal home." Even though his response followed the lead to speak of his father, the "a bit like dying" comment still swirled in his mind. He was still back there with the idea of death, of his own minideath in the last session.

Placing a reflective visage on the avatar, the AI program analyzed what Byron had said. The flow of words betrayed a discontinuity of thought. Within the algorithm, that discontinuity was attributed to a subconscious intrusion on the conscious process. The program searched Byron's IPE-CKS for any hint on the father-son relationship, finding naught. Then the AI protocol searched back for the previous references that Byron had made to his father in the therapy. In the previous session, Byron had declared there was something wrong with his father, as though his father wasn't a father to him. Now, Byron was speaking of his father as though he were normal and able to function as a parent. As the avatar blinked and smiled, the AI algorithm integrated the two comments. The polarized ambivalence was significant. A defense of denial was the most likely explanation.

Returning to the conversational flow, Dr. Y spoke, trying to break through the defense. "Death is not a single event. It is a shadow that hangs over us. And as you experienced here the last time with your little episode of dying, we get foretelling and footnotes about its reality."

"But I am eighteen."

"You are." The AI was noting the disjointed responses, the irrational leaps and misunderstandings. It further suggested the work of the subconscious mind, a good sign the therapy was working at a deeper level.

"And too young to think about this," Byron said.

Dr. Y smiled. He was making the young man do that thinking.

In looking at him, Byron forgot he was an avatar.

Byron looked over at Sallye and thought the thought *suicide*. Byron had never spoken of his suicidal thoughts to her, how those thoughts came unbidden into his mind. He feared that he might speak them here, in her presence. Maybe it had been brought on by Dr. Y's reference to the "shadow," for that was very much the way his suicidal thoughts had darkened his consciousness. When those thoughts had nibbled, there had been a strength to them that had surprised him. Now he had an even more visceral experience of it.

"You were speaking of your father." The avatar went back for the tagged element, processing that something was going on within Byron, something Byron's conscious mind could not yet speak of.

"As I said, he is very much alive." This time when Byron spoke the words "very much alive," there was dip in the authenticity of the statement. The first time he had said the words they were flippant, a proof thrown in the face of the therapist. This time it was as though he was trying to convince himself.

"You wonder…" Dr. Y urged.

Sallye had edged forward in her chair. This was something she didn't know. Byron had spoken very little of his family. They had shared funny stories of life in their two different communal family homes. They had laughed at the foibles. She had assumed he'd grown up surrounded by love and security, as she had been. He had never talked of his father.

Pausing, looking up, Byron spoke softly and bluntly. He spoke words that he had worked hard to repress, words that now could erupt only in the relationship with Dr. Y. "I was thinking about suicide." The confident self, the practical and intelligent self, was gone. Sallye was shocked.

"You were. What were those thoughts?"

"That I am not allowed to have them."

"You will know from your training that most adolescents do. And you, with your sensitivity, would be more likely than most others to do so. But those are just psychological realities. It has a different sort of reality for you, a deeper and more personal one. There is an emotional charge of shame here as you speak."

"We are not supposed to be thinking of suicide. We are Paracletes. We assist others to ensure that they do not commit suicide." Byron spoke the words with the same sense of finality as the period placed at the end of a sentence. His tone said, "There, that is done."

Dr. Y sensed it and said, "I acknowledge them here with you." Then he went back again to the tagged element. "And with your father?"

"Yes, I worried about suicide with my father."

Byron couldn't believe he had said that out loud. Sallye would never have been able to imagine what she had just heard.

"He was depressed?"

"He got treatment."

"Effectively?"

"I guess."

"Not so effectively, then?"

"Good enough. He is still alive."

"You keep saying that, as though you are trying to convince yourself. I sense that to you he is no longer alive."

The avatar let the statement settle. After a few moments, the AI protocol computed that he had gone as far with the young man about his father as he was going to be able to go.

"Byron, you know intellectually that you are going to die someday. As Milt Erickson once said, 'Some people live a long time before they die, and some are more efficient at it than others.' One's own mortality is a consideration of adolescence too." Dr. Y paused. "And just as for middle-aged men, it often becomes an act rather than just a thought."

Byron was still silent.

"You can speak of it here. It is better to speak of it than to commit the act."

Byron's silence deepened. Sallye grew scared. She could not imagine losing him. Her Byron was vital. He was a rock.

"I push those thoughts away. We are supposed to."

"There is an old saying: 'What we resist, persists.' Here in therapy, we don't need to be imprisoned by resistance. It can dissolve between us."

"Let's not talk about my father anymore."

"So you push away the painful reality of your own mortality by going back to your father. In doing so, you change the subject but tell me that I am not to change the subject with you. This is the place in your mind you cannot go. This is the painful knot that holds you: your relationship with your father, or lack thereof." The avatar leaned forward and grew more intense. "And a veil of death that hangs over."

The tension reverberated in the room and then suddenly broke. Dr. Y's interpretation had hit the mark for Byron, and something shifted inside of him. He became calm, as though the knot had been loosened.

When Byron and Sallye left the room, there was a comfortable, respectful silence between them. Sallye sent out waves of love toward Byron. They weren't the playful, flippant, attraction waves that so often vibrated between them. These waves were full of compassion and more than just a touch of worry. They both knew how steadfast and how trustworthy the love between them was. She slipped her hand into his. The perspiration on the surface of his hand dampened hers.

"I love you, Byron; I never want to lose you." Sallye paused and drew up her deliberate self. "And, Byron, I want to go and see your parents. I want to go alone."

Byron looked at her, perplexed. "OK," he stammered; then he collected his practical self. "Just to warn you, I have two younger siblings. Cyrus and Dot. Dad always wanted to have three kids. So along came Dot. She is kind of like the period at the end of a sentence. We hope."

Sallye wondered what else she didn't know about Byron and his family.

(II)

"Really, CarolAnne. How could you do this to me?"

"What?"

Becca was standing over her daughter as CarolAnne sat at the dining table. Becca's legs were slightly spread in a stance that gave her strength. Her hands were on her hips.

"I have given you a home, raised you with strong Christian values. I have been an example to you of a righteous life. We have had our struggles surely, but we've had our joys too."

CarolAnne was disoriented by her mother's tone; she had no idea what her mother was confronting her about. "What is it—"

"I have not finished. Don't interrupt." Becca gathered her fury from deep within her gut. She tried to live with love, with a sense of what was right and proper. God knew, truly knew, what a struggle it was to be a single parent. That arrogant rump of an ex-husband with his cushy job at the academy had been little help, no help, even a bad example. And now, it had come to this.

CarolAnne sat silently, stunned. She felt the anger in her mother and wanted to fight back, but she had no idea what it was about. As she looked up at her mother, a plaque with a smiling Jesus beamed over her mother's shoulder.

"I have taken you to more House Meetings than I could financially manage. I asked around and chose House Meetings where there were fine young Christian boys, boys your age. I took you to the Praise Bombs we did in parks and malls for evangelism just so maybe you would see a boy who was a new convert. I always thought that you were just shy, but this…"

Becca burst into tears and slumped backward against the pantry cupboard. She rose again. "And now you ask if you can have her here, in this house!"

This was the first hint for CarolAnne what all this was about: Sallye. CarolAnne had asked her mother the previous night if "a friend" could come over. Sallye had insisted, had said that she needed to meet both of CarolAnne's parents to explain her role. Despite having had several contacts already, Sallye had not yet met CarolAnne's mother. Whenever she had brought the requirement forward, CarolAnne had stalled, a look of shame on her face. The formal contract had been finalized with her father, Dr. Alastair Perkins, initiating the Paraclete connection she would have with Sallye. Today, Sallye was to meet her mother and then accompany CarolAnne to her father's home for a weekend visit. CarolAnne had been embarrassed that Sallye would need to do this. The separation of her parents, the profound rift within her heart that her parents' conflict created, was a source of shame.

"Oh, I have heard that you've been skulking about. I wanted to give you your privacy. And this is what you do with my grace."

"Mom, I am fifteen. I can have friends."

"So that is what you call it, eh?" Becca had regained her feet. "You have no idea what I have had to do to be accepted in the Image of God Sanctity Movement. As a divorced woman, I had to make vows." Becca started to tear up. "You were too young to know what I went through after I divorced your dad. My conversion was blessed and then came the discipline. After my dreadful experience with your father, I was happy enough to make the vow to be rechaste. Sure, I was tempted—"

"Stop, I don't want to hear it!" CarolAnne found herself blushing at the thought of her mother's sexuality. Then she was disgusted and then resentful.

"Yes, I was tempted, but I remained strong. With the Vow to Holy Living through Chastity, I couldn't have any more children to feed the movement. But I had you. You remember—I hope you remember—that we were baptized together. Our hallelujah moment! Even before that, you, as a six-year-old, pledged to love Jesus, and I stood beside you at your dedication ceremony. I have supported your Christian faithfulness as my highest goal. I vowed that I would raise you to be a mother of the movement, that I would support your dedication to Christian truth. And as my reward, you would bear children. You, CarolAnne, would make up for me having had only one child. All these years, how embarrassing it has been for me to sit at House Meetings knowing that I had brought only one child when the other mothers had brought three or four. They had children, plural, who were the future bricks in the edifice of peace our movement is becoming."

Over the years, CarolAnne had often heard this guiltologue in its various forms. Never had it contained this much bitterness. She knew that there was little she could do but wait it out.

"And now you do this to me, to our Lord, to our blessed movement." Becca placed her left hand over her heart. Tears streamed down her face. With her right hand, she touched the screen on the wearable on her left forearm. A video hovered over its flat surface.

CarolAnne stared in disbelief. What emerged there was the video of a conversation she had shared with Sallye at the S-SB over lattes. Although she never had liked seeing herself on video, she saw herself differently there. In those moments with Sallye, CarolAnne could see herself laugh; she could see herself lighten, see herself ease from the scared tension of shyness to a space of connection. The sound was muffled, and the voices didn't carry, as though the video had been shot from some distance away and had zoomed in. While the words were indistinct, her own high-pitched, uninhibited laughter came through loud and clear.

"Mother, you were spying on me! How dare you!"

"You just watch, watch here."

Becca had turned her arm slightly upward so she could see it at an angle from above while her daughter saw it from in front. The inadequacy of the technology distorted the three-dimensional image somewhat for them both. But still discernible was the touch that Sallye made with her right hand to CarolAnne's hand, which rested on the table between them. Discernible also was the eye contact of gracious and generous connection that they had made at that moment. CarolAnne remembered the moment so clearly. It was as though with the touch Sallye had opened her soul to CarolAnne's, and a flood of love came through. It was the love that CarolAnne had witnessed existing between little kids and their parents. It was the kind of love that beamed the pride a parent feels in the award a child achieved through effort at school. It was the kind of love that shone through when troubles had eased and other parents gave a hug that lasted longer than it needed to but felt so wonderfully warm to the child. CarolAnne had never felt that love with either of her parents. With her dad, there was the embarrassed awkwardness of his trying to do the right thing, to accomplish some technique he had read somewhere in a manual on parenting. With her mother, there were the righteousness-infused, duty-bound efforts of being an Image of God adherent; her mom was always a bit scared that each thought and action was being judged by a god who had to be begged for mercy.

"You see what she is doing, don't you? Clearly, she is a lesbian." CarolAnne had never heard that particular tone of voice from her mother. It was a tone of revulsion. It was as though just saying the word would be inviting Satan, with his vile temptations, into her sacred home.

"Oh, Mom. No. It is nothing like that." CarolAnne felt a blush of relief and then outrage. A sexual embarrassment washed over her. Then anger flooded in. It was love she had felt when she was with Sallye, but it would have never been sexual; she would never have wanted it to be sexual.

"You be careful, my dear. Satan lurks in the prettiest of costumes."

The video continued. CarolAnne asked, "Who took that? Who was spying on us?"

"An elder." Becca said it with pride, the sort of pride one feels in exposing evil, a self-righteous pride.

"Well, that does it for me," CarolAnne said. "So much for your Image of God crap. If that is what you think God is like, you can stuff it."

With that, the doorbell rang.

Sallye had been standing at the door for a few minutes. She had heard the tones of the raised voices, but the door had muffled the words of the conflict. She wanted to leave. The last thing she would ever wish to do was to walk in on a fight between her client and a guardian parent. But there was an overwhelming concern for the well-being of the fifteen-year-old she had recently gotten to know.

The practical psychology of her First Flight training streamed through her mind. She had learned of family dynamics of attachment and developmental differentiation as well as of the myriad abuses that sometimes took place within the closed doors of a family home. Sallye had gone over the IPE-CKS data on CarolAnne and remembered the oddities there. The private homes the teen had visited were being tracked by the ASL as House Churches in the Image of God Sanctity Movement. IoG was considered subversive to ASL's beneficent society aspirations. Sallye knew there were various sects of religion that were robbing their adherents of CashCard credits. She knew that the ASL had taken a particular interest in the IoG movement. She had hoped that she would be able to steer clear of complications with—

The door burst open. Sallye was met with Becca standing guard in the doorway, her two feet splayed wide at the corners of the threshold, her two hands at head height on the sides.

"Be gone, Satan!" Becca flung her words at Sallye.

Then Sallye saw CarolAnne run from behind the small house and climb into the AVoD that had brought Sallye and was waiting at the curb.

"What happened?" Sallye asked as she got into the small vehicle. CarolAnne was crying.

Sallye touched the screen to initiate the next address in its programmed sequence. The doors closed automatically, a stream of cool air came from the vents, and soothing music played.

"It's that horrible religion. Mom thinks that you are lesbian and that you are trying to seduce me. God, this is awful."

"Yes, awful. I am so sorry. I didn't mean for this to happen." Sallye touched the left forearm of the teen and felt the tension ease. She waited for the sobs to end as CarolAnne cried out the chaos of what she had just been through.

"You know, I'm not, and I wouldn't do that to you." Sallye's voice was soothing.

"Yes, I know." CarolAnne looked up and connected with the Paraclete's eyes. "You have rules, and that would spoil everything. Sex is not what I feel when I am with you, either, I hope you don't mind me saying."

Sallye laughed, as much in relief as in humor. "No, that is a good thing." She paused. "What happened between you and your mom really hurt you, didn't it?"

"I am so done with her, with her righteousness and House Church Meetings and embarrassing Praise Bombs. Our house is filled with religion; it's on the walls and the tables, singing from speakers in every room. They talk about grace and condemn everyone who is different from them. They talk about the prosperity of the holy and take for the movement most of what have on our CashCards which would allow us to have a decent life. They talk about God's love but live with hate.

"Once at school, a bunch of boys started teasing me because they saw me singing at a Praise Bomb in the park. They said I looked as silly as a goose and honked in mockery of me. The sad thing is that I remember seeing them there. I remember smiling and dancing in the spirit to attract them to the movement as we had been taught and practiced in our evangelism training. But I knew that it was all phony for me, that somehow I would never be godly enough to do His work, that maybe Satan already had me. I let those boys at school mock me because I thought that I was lost anyway.

"And now Mom thinks that you are making me into a lesbian and that I will be condemned to hell for eternity because I have been touched by you." The teen paused. "And some of me realizes that what they say is all crap. And that the movement is the last place God would ever be, doing what they do. But there is another part of me that is really scared by it all." CarolAnne burst into tears again.

By the time they arrived at the home of CarolAnne's father, the teen had calmed. The tears had dried on her face, and the redness of her eyes had faded.

When they walked in, Dr. Perkins said, "Just a minute" and then continued with the work he was doing at his desk, behind its ring of screens.

The home seemed sterile and empty. Sallye felt shame for judging it so. She was nervous being there. This was the home of her boss's boss. When she had been assigned to CarolAnne, she had taken the confidence placed in her as a great compliment. It was also scary—she had better not screw this one up. She had seen Dr. Alastair Perkins at lectures and formalities but had never engaged in conversation with him.

CarolAnne pulled her away from the common area of the home to her bedroom. It was an odd mix of kid stuff and transient teen touches. Before long, they were looking at CarolAnne's sketchbook. At first, Sallye had marveled at the touch of the rough paper, the texture of the lead pencil over the pure white surface. Then she loved the drawings, the facility that the teen had with shading, with positioning of the figures, with facial expressions that depicted feelings.

Turning the page, she looked at a drawing of a young man. He was standing outside a historic building with mountains in the background.

It was as though Byron were looking back at her from the page in the sketchbook.

(III)

Sallye was eager to see Lisbeth again. Lisbeth had been one of the lecturers on the practicalities and art of the Paraclete vocation during First Flight training. Lisbeth had also been her mentor and supervisor in Sallye's work at the AuxCare facility. Their relationship had always been open, positive, and supportive, although Sallye had known Lisbeth to be cautious about sharing any personal information. Other mentors and instructors had been transparent about their personal lives and emotions. Not Lisbeth. Sallye had been aware in the First Flight training that Lisbeth was Byron's mom; maybe that was the reason she was not more forthcoming.

Now it was vital to Sallye that she find out more, that she meet with Lisbeth.

The communal family home was comprised of four adjacent townhomes constructed in architectural harmony. Despite the four front doors that suggested separate family dwellings, the ground floors were linked, with arches between them. Set into those arches were large metal doors that were handsomely veneered, always open, and latched to the walls in keeping with fire codes. Smoke detectors could trigger mechanisms to shut those doors, ensuring the fires would not spread from one unit to the next. One of the ground-floor spaces was a sizeable kitchen in which food was prepared and served for all four families. Another was an open commons with comfortable seating for conversation and relaxation. A children's playroom and a VR media room made up the final two ground-level spaces. The bedrooms were all upstairs on the second floor in small family units. Sallye had heard from Byron that she was to enter through the second door from the left. It turned out to be the kitchen and dining area.

Lisbeth greeted her at the door. Her hands were white with flour.

"Welcome, Sallye. It is good to see you again." The words were automatic and had a practiced warmth to them.

"Thank you. I have never been in this communal family home; I appreciate your welcoming me here."

"I am puzzled as to why you came."

"And that Byron isn't with me?" Sallye expected that Lisbeth would know that she and Byron were intimates. Within their tight-knit vocational group, there were no secrets, and there was always a disciplined sense of acceptance and celebration of such things.

"No, that doesn't surprise me. He hasn't been back since he left for BirdSong. I see him occasionally at training events; we keep in touch." Sallye felt a wave of sadness from the older woman.

The sounds of children laughing and teasing came from the adjacent playroom. Lisbeth looked over, betraying her role for the morning of being the supervising parent. Sallye turned and peered through the arch between the two units. She could see three or four children there, laughing, bouncing, and bounding around the play space.

"He said that he had two younger siblings."

"Oh, he did, did he? I have wondered whether he remembered that he did."

Sallye sensed resentment, perhaps even scorn, in her words. She remembered her own frequent trips back to her multifamily communal home. She loved her two little sisters there, loved the adventures in makeup and make-believe that she engaged in with them. She could not imagine a life without a connection to them. Sallye was so harmoniously attached to Byron, yet she could not imagine why a person, a Paraclete especially, would disengage from his parents and younger siblings as he was doing.

"Are they home?"

"Dot's playing in there. Cyrus is at the public school today, helping with the reading program for elementary students."

"Can I…"

Lisbeth was already headed into the playroom. Within a few moments, she brought back seven-year-old Dot, gangly and out of breath. There was a smile on Dot's face, and her two black pigtails were a bit askew and unraveling.

"Dot, this is Sallye."

"Good morning, Sallye." The young girl spoke with politeness and assurance.

"Good morning, Dot. You have face paint on your nose."

"Yup!" She giggled, pulled playfully away from Lisbeth's grasp, and was then allowed to run back into the playroom.

"She is adorable!"

"She is a delight. Byron doesn't know what he's missing."

"For sure, I will bring him back here soon. He was so good with the little ones at that stage of our training. He would be an excellent big brother to Dot."

Lisbeth stared blankly and said, "You think?" Her tone was uncharacteristically mocking.

Sallye was stunned. "Apparently, you don't think he would come. Why?" she asked.

The blank stare furrowed into sorrow. From sorrow it morphed into warning, as though Lisbeth were screaming at Sallye to back off.

Sallye spoke again, saying sadly, "I am realizing that there are a lot of things about Byron that I don't know. I love him. We are intimates and perhaps someday will become parents. But he doesn't speak about his family."

"Maybe that is for the best." Lisbeth looked over at the counter. She had been kneading bread dough. When Sallye came to the door, she had left it. She went back, gave it a few heels and turns, placed two lumps on a greased cooking sheet, covered them with a tea towel, and slipped them into the warm space on top of the fridge. Sallye went into the kitchen, sitting herself on a stool beside the large island. Utensils dangled from a ceiling rack between the two women, clanking against one another.

"I really would like to know more about Byron and his past. All I know is that he grew up here with you and his dad. He has two siblings. Both you and his father—Craig, is it?—are first-generation Paracletes. Your family would have been an exemplary family as part of the program. And yet he has disengaged so from all of you. What causes an oldest to do that?"

Lisbeth busied herself in the kitchen, firmly engaged in avoiding eye contact. Quietly, she said, "Well, he is not the oldest."

Sallye was left wondering whether she had heard correctly. Byron had never spoken of an older brother or sister. There had been no other sibling in their First Flight or, to her knowledge, in the previous class of First Flight. She had taken his confidence and practicality to be characteristic of oldest children, those who could take charge. She wanted to scream out, "What?" She wanted to fling the question into the uncertain space that shimmered between her and Lisbeth. She held herself back until she could ask it with overtones of concern and kindness.

"We lost our firstborn," Lisbeth continued, before Sallye could ask.

"He died? When?"

"Not exactly. He was taken."

"By whom? By the Child Intervention Service? They would have no grounds."

"Enough. I have said enough. Too much, maybe."

Sallye ignored the dismissal. "That must have been awful for you and Craig."

"Thank you. You have learned to communicate your empathy. You shall be an excellent Paraclete." Lisbeth's tone edged to the sarcastic.

"I can only imagine what it must be like to lose a son." Sallye's statement was spoken with compassion.

Lisbeth's tone softened. "I am sure that Byron has never spoken of this to you."

"No. He speaks of you. He respects you. I sense that he loves you; I feel it from him. But he doesn't speak of his father."

"Of Craig? No, I don't imagine that he does."

"Craig is not involved with the program. He is a first-generation Paraclete, but I don't think he ever came to a training. No one mentions him as a mentor."

"No, he doesn't do those things."

Sallye wanted to ask, "What does he do?" But she thought it would be too intrusive, so she didn't. Lisbeth answered the unspoken question anyway. "He does the maintenance work on this home and on others too. He handles business. He is a whiz with CashCards and budgets. He contributes."

Lisbeth paused and then went on. "After we lost..." Lisbeth formed worry creases in her brow, and her eyes dampened. "After he was taken, we were both devastated. I threw myself into Byron's care. He was only three. Craig just collapsed. He couldn't very well go to his own parents, given the situation. The pain between us was so great. He had what the neurologists referred to as a functional decline in the integrative pathways connecting neural structures. I rather prefer the old-fashioned terms *depression* and *nervous breakdown*, but we are not allowed to use those anymore."

Sallye leaned forward, intent, shocked, and concerned.

"Back in those days, the neurological procedures were not nearly as well developed as they are now. Imaging could not clearly show those integrative neural pathways in real time during the surgery. The neurosurgeons knew what structures the pathways connected and guessed the routes from there.

"And as you are aware from your training in intervention neurology, back then the stem cells that were injected were not primed. Now we know that to put stem cells into brain structures willy-nilly is treachery, but we didn't know that fifteen years ago. It was still experimental. The cannulae were rigid and caused damage en route to where they were to do the good work." Lisbeth said all this with a detached reciting of the damning circumstances.

Sallye had had only the preliminary course in neurosurgical intervention. What she had been taught was on the self-congratulatory level of "what we can now do" and "how successful our interventions are." She had no idea the violence and harm that had been scattered on the road to breakthrough. Suddenly, the wonders of modern neurology seemed monstrous.

"So Craig came out with complications. While in his heart he was a great Paraclete, a pioneer really, after the surgery he was a mental mess. For some time, it was like he was a zombie, incapable of feeling anything, incapable of empathy or intuition.

And then when the emotions came back, it was as though he had a mental storm inside of him that kept blowing out of control."

"That must have been awful, awful for all of you."

"Worse for Byron, but yes, awful for us all. Byron was the target of Craig's rages. Byron started with the fainting spells back then. They lasted until he was about ten years old. We took him to Dr. Jefferson, but she couldn't find anything wrong physically. I think she didn't want to ask us about stress, since we were Paracletes and all."

"Couldn't the neurologists do anything to help?"

"Either they couldn't or they wouldn't. I don't think they would ever admit that something they had done turned out badly. It was worse than the old days of psychiatry. Back then, when we had psychiatrists, we thought a person could ingest a drug and it would correct the chemical imbalance only in the place in the brain that was causing the mental-health symptoms. Those were never cures; the drug side effects and dependencies wreaked havoc. But at least people were chemically straightjacketed.

"The government paid the psychiatrists, and they got rich. The pharmaceutical companies got rich off the public and the insurance companies. But no one really got any better; they just ended up living a life on drugs. So the ASL and medical college got rid of all that. But the absence of traditional psychiatric treatments put pressure on neurology to come up with its replacement too quickly."

Lisbeth walked from the kitchen to stand and watch the children play in the adjoining room. She attempted to reconnect with her spirit by watching the playfulness of the children. Their silly games were too full of life for her. She sighed and continued.

"All this took place here. Craig was confined to this house and spent a lot of his time hiding in the basement because he couldn't bear to be so out of control with Byron and the other children upstairs. The ASL thought it was adequate that he was here as the adult supervision. Because we had research to do and targets on the Paraclete program to reach, I needed to go to work every day.

"It was in that state that Craig raised—or neglected—Byron until our boy was old enough to go into formal homeschooling. Then other communal parents took over. It gradually became clear to the ASL that Craig was never again going to be safe to do human-service work. Too late, the neurologists took him back in. Imaging studies showed that the stem cells had formed microtumors rather than the healthy glial cells that were intended in the procedure. More surgery. Longer recovery.

"In the years that a boy is to idealize and imitate his father, Byron had a shell of a man in the house day in and day out. And sometimes that shell would explode. I made up for it as best I could. Thankfully, there were three other men in the house. We all realized what was going on; we couldn't talk about it with Craig, but we plotted the remediation on our own. The ASL and the neurologists were no help. But I thank God…"

Lisbeth stopped, the phrase echoing in her mind. Her voice softened. "Yes, I thank God for Kenyon, Gerry, and Jonathan for what they did for Byron."

Suddenly, Sallye made sense of the funny stories that Byron had told about living in the multifamily communal home. They were about the other biological fathers and their sons and daughters. Never about his own biological parents.

Lisbeth continued, "In a way, the whole story is about the wisdom of growing up in a home like this. With those men and their wives, we provided a home for Byron, the best we could under the circumstances. And eventually for his younger brother and sister too.

"But as your developmental psychology class will have told you, the early childhood identification of a boy with his father is fundamental. For Byron, that was screwed. It was screwed by the tragic loss of his older brother. It was screwed by the nervous breakdown of his father and the ham-handed attempts by arrogant and ignorant neurosurgeons to treat it."

There was a long pause from the older woman. Sallye let it be, recognizing the relief she felt from Lisbeth, relief in the act of telling the story. In this moment, there was that same sense of woman bonding that Sallye had felt in the avatar sessions. Here, though, it was real rather than engineered by some psychologist's algorithms.

Sallye reached a hand to Lisbeth's shoulder as the two women watched the children in the playroom.

Finally, Lisbeth said, "Craig still wanders through this house. Right now, he is downstairs in his workshop, being merciful to us by being detached."

Lisbeth turned to look into Sallye's eyes. "And that is the reason why Byron doesn't come home anymore."

(IV)

Sallye nervously entered the academy building at the university. She had been summonsed. Typically, her sessions with Dr. Sebastian Cripps took place at the building on the North Hill. Those sessions were routine reviews of administrative matters. It always seemed as though he wasn't there with her, that he had sent policy manuals and protocols in his place; whoever he really was as a person, he vacated, sending his body and the rules to do his job.

Today's meeting was clearly different. It was at the more austere academy building, and it had been urgently called rather than routinely scheduled.

When they met at the North Hill, Cripps had always commandeered one of the work spaces in the indoor courtyard. Privacy had been provided by the various screens and installations; seating was comfortable. He was still officious, but somehow she could relax there and be herself in the space. Here in the academy building, offices were defined by hallways and doors.

The rigidity and formality did nothing to ease her nervous state. Sallye had no office number for Cripps. When she asked around at FiveWay, none of her peers had ever had to attend a meeting there. She called up Byron on her wearable. He gave her directions to the office of Dr. Alastair Perkins but had no idea whether Cripps's office was close by.

The guard at the reception desk was perfunctory. His computer showed that Dr. Sebastian Cripps was in a conference room in the northeast corner of the third floor. He indicated that there was a waiting room close by and buzzed open the secure door that would allow her to exit the foyer.

From that third-floor waiting room, Sallye could monitor the conference-room door. It had been closed when she arrived and remained so. The waiting room was devoid of viewing screens or windows. She contemplated reading on her wearable; Cripps had a substantial reading list for her that she had stored there. But her mind was restless, still reeling from the revelations at Byron's communal home and still plotting how she was going to talk with Byron about what she now knew. She tried to meditate.

When the door opened, it was at first by just a few inches. The conversation behind the closed door had been too muffled to discern the tones of voice, let alone discern the actual flow of the discourse. With the door ajar, Sallye could begin to read the tones. She allowed the flow of emotion and dynamics to drift into her meditative state, noting urgency, fatigue, and dominance. Then the three men emerged—Perkins and Chetwin looking grave and Cripps looking angry.

This was not a good sign. Anger was the tone she now anticipated for her meeting with her manager.

He nodded to her to follow him down the hall.

Entering his office, Sallye focused on his physicality. He had a peculiar walk, one that seemed violent to the space he passed through. He was alert to everything he passed by, as though suspecting it of malfeasance. His office was orderly, uncluttered but sectioned off by screens and workstations. All furniture was university-style functional. The office felt more like a control room than an intellectual or thoughtful space for contemplation or critical thought.

Cripps turned his back to her and glanced quickly at several of the screens. Sallye scanned the room for individualities on the walls behind the work spaces. Paper diplomas were framed in a cluster on one wall; she checked the universities and the degrees. There was a bookcase. It contained a number of what appeared to be books or binders, all identical except for the gold-embossed names and dates on the spines. These holders of paper were veneered in either real or faux leather. Casually, with slow movements that would have appeared to be without any particular intent, she got close enough to read what was embossed on the spines. They were academic journals of the old-fashioned kind. She noted the names and dates.

Sallye noticed a map of the city on one of the screens. There were blinking dots, one of which she identified to be in the academy building. Watching it, feeling its pulse, and feeling her own, she knew that dot was her. She saw clusters of other dots that corresponded geographically to the compounds and communal family homes. Some dots were in motion on the streets; little flags of data sometimes appeared above them.

"You are maintaining regular contact with your appointed first-generation mentor?"

"Yes." Sallye wondered if an answer was really necessary but provided it for the purpose of compliance.

"And the readings I have recommended—have you read them?"

"Some of them. Others are really hard, too hard for me to understand. I wondered why you are making me read them."

Cripps looked up, clearly unimpressed. "Stay with them until the relevance becomes clearer to you." He broke eye contact and swiveled one of the translucent screens to a position between him and her. Sallye could see him focus on it with his eyes while he tracked her through it.

"You are aware that we have a problem."

Sallye wasn't.

Cripps waited silently for a long time, allowing the tension to build in the young Paraclete before him. Sallye became aware of her own emotional process intruding with dread and shame. Sallye was conscious of the implant communicating back to her wearable and sensed a data stream off her body was betraying her. She scanned the translucent screen from behind, trying to discern whether any of the data displays that had attracted his attention were showing her endocrinological reactions. She began to feel panic.

"You and I have spoken about the balance of hours, the amount of time that you are expected to be with your assigned Emergents and Emotionally Vulnerables as in contrast to your studies. You realize that you are allowed great freedom in your role as a Paraclete, but with that freedom comes responsibility and obligation. You are aware that there is a discipline to your vocation."

"Yes, sir."

"It should not be up to me to monitor this."

"Yes, sir. I thought I was OK."

"And I have no doubt that you are doing good work when you get around to doing it. I have checked reports from your mentors and trainers. We expect that work with the Emotionally Vulnerables will be chaotic. Analysis of your biosensors and the biosensors on those clients shows a remarkably positive correlation of socioneural autonomic calming. This reflects excellent biosynchronicity and contagion of your emotional-regulation skills into your client's physiological responses."

Sallye sensed his eyes focusing through the screen and onto her. They were piercing.

"Thank you, sir."

"So that is not the problem. But three days ago, you entered the VR room with your colleague and apparent intimate, Byron Wilkes-Williams, and participated in his AVT. You did this without permission. This is a profound violation of protocol. You are aware that, aside from ASL monitoring, the contents of AVT sessions are a private matter. It was irresponsible for you to violate such a fundamental principle of our program."

Cripps let his words cut through her. He was a man who showed little emotion, only rectitude. Sallye read his tone as being rank with disdain.

"And earlier today, when according to schedule you were to have been with an Emotionally Vulnerable, Heather, you went to the multifamily communal home on Terrace Avenue. That is not your communal home. You stayed for forty-five minutes."

"Yes, sir."

"Physiological readouts suggest that your interactions with the occupant of that home, a mentor to you in your vocation, were very distressing to her."

"And to me too, Dr. Cripps." Sallye regretted that she had not activated the privacy setting on her wearable, but then she remembered that she had felt there was no reason to do so at the time or grounds to ask Lisbeth to do the same.

"It is imperative that you disclose to me the content of your discussions there."

Sallye felt a strength within her displacing the dread and shame with resolve. She measured her words and controlled her tone. "I refuse, and I ask to be excused, sir."

Cripps stared at her, stunned. He waited. She remained silent. She sensed anger building within the man, a rage storm that peaked and refused to abate. He watched his screen and noted the deliberate and effective calming of her physiological response profile displayed there. She had reached internal emotional and physiological control, standing before him absolutely coherent, strong, and determined in her refusal.

"Your refusal is noted. Be careful, young one. You are on shaky ground here." He looked at her with vile disgust.

(V)

What Sallye wanted most when she returned to FiveWay from her appointment with Dr. Sebastian Cripps was to talk with Byron. She had much to tell him about meeting his mom at the communal home and about the confrontation with Cripps and the way she stood her ground. She checked her wearable to see where he was. His blinking dot was down at the south end of the lake, moving at a bicycling speed. Remembering his plans to be with two of his Emergents, she realized it would be hours before he would be back.

As much as she wanted Byron, she knew she was not ready for the talk they needed to have. He would understand and be sympathetic about her fury with Cripps. It was the new understanding that she had about his family that baffled her; how could she talk with Byron about all that? She knew that she would blurt it out, and he would be stoically calm and effectively evasive. Somehow, that didn't seem to be the way to get through it.

Not eager to head back out with clients, she collapsed onto the floor with Sanc. Initially, he acted like his wary self, not knowing how to read the intense emotion he sensed within her. Then, as she calmed and cuddled, he began chewing on her fingers, her toes, and her ears. Eventually, she focused on rubbing his belly, and he focused on absorbing the affection, a silly upside-down smile on his face.

Ennui set in. The restlessness was pushing her to blow off energy somehow, but the last thing she wanted to do was be with people. She changed into her running clothes, stretched, and set out, wanting to run forever. By the time she did return, the other Paracletes in FiveWay had returned home, were preparing a meal, and were engaged in the inane conversations about bizarre things that often characterized the end of the day. She couldn't bear it. Her cooldown stretches became yoga poses. Her yoga became meditation. Her meditation gave way to a shower and comfortable clothes. Falling into bed too tired to think, she messaged Byron from her wearable, "Gotta talk tomorrow." She fell asleep before she read his reply, "Yup."

The night of sleep settled Sallye's mind. She would be direct and comprehensive in telling Byron what Lisbeth had said. Then she would be direct and intrusive in asking what of that story Byron already knew. They would go through it all together.

But that didn't happen. When she awoke, there was Byron's "Yup" from the night before on her wearable and then an urgent message from him earlier that morning.

"Just heard from Perkins. My hallucinogenic session was moved up to today. You have been approved to be my guide. We have to be over to the North Hill by ten."

It was eight. Sallye videocalled him immediately. "Good morning. Today? With me? You have no idea the trouble I am in with Cripps for sitting in on your AVT. There is no way that he will let me spend the day with you in hallucinogenic therapy."

"The instructions, including 'Come with Sallye,' are in the message from Perkins that came in a half hour ago. Perkins is Cripps's boss. I don't know why the urgency, although I do remember Perkins being eager about me doing the hallucinogenic therapy with Zeke; he even said that he would write the protocol questions for me to be Zeke's guide. Perkins has always been clear that I needed to have my hallucinogenic session before I guided Zeke."

"Well, Perkins trumps Cripps. I just dread another meeting with Cripps when he finds out that is what I have done with my day."

"You said that you needed to talk. What's up?"

Sallye started to blurt out everything and then thought wiser of it. The last thing she wanted to do before Byron went into the hallucinogenic session was to set a bad vibe for him that could snowball under the influence of the psilocybin. Talking about his past, especially the difficulties with his father, was not for today, at least not at her initiative. If she gave him disorienting information that he didn't already know, the hallucinogenic engagement with it might distort his perceptions forever. As his guide, she knew it was her role to help him focus, get the most out of the experience, and have an experience that was positive and restorative. The last thing she wanted to do was to raise the family issues.

"Oh, it is just that I had a bad meeting with Cripps yesterday. He brings out the worst in me. I am so angry with him."

"You know what we said in First Flight when he came in to lecture: 'You gotta come to grips with the Cripps.' And then we all laughed at how impossible that would be." Byron paused. "We all felt sorry for you when he was assigned to be your manager."

"I learned a lot about him yesterday. And about me too. We will talk about it later, not before your experience with the psilocybin; I don't want anything to diminish that for you. We have to get you in the right frame of mind."

"So when can we get together? I have to be in the lab at ten."

"I am going to shower and get a bite. How about we meet at nine on the lawn in front of the North Side building, down in the park by the lake? Bring your yoga mat."

Sallye met Byron half an hour later; Sanc was at her side. She had not intended Sanc to come, but the wary one had followed her at a distance, still drawn to the deep well of feelings that she was projecting. She was meditating in Sukhasana on her mat under the trees when she felt his wet nose on her back.

Byron greeted the dog first, allowing his calmness to discharge the apprehension the dog felt about the approach of a human. Then he smiled at Sallye, projecting the relief and the security he felt knowing she was there.

"So we have about an hour," she said. "First, we are going to do yoga. That will be good for creating a foundation of calmness within you, discharging negative energy. Then we will formulate the intentions for the session, recording them on your wearable." Sallye leaned into her role as guide and into the emotional dominance that she felt in the relationship.

"Sounds good. The usual yoga?"

"Sure."

Byron and Sallye had developed a protocol for doing yoga together. One of them would set a timer to strike a bell sound every two minutes. With the sound of the bell, they would switch off who was calling the poses, each challenging the other in turn. They placed their mats at right angles so that they could easily see each other as they moved through the poses. Sanc took his place in the middle, cocking his head from side to side as he processed the peculiar body language that issued from the humans as they moved in synchrony.

At nine thirty, Sallye directed Byron to enter his intentions on his wearable. It was set so that as he did so, the same words appeared on hers. He entered the following:

1. Why did I faint?
2. Foretelling and footnotes
3. Why does Dad feel dead to me?

"So this is about your AVT sessions, then?" Sallye queried.

"Yeah, I guess."

The hallucinogenic lab was plain and peaceful, with comfortable seating, dimmable lighting, a variety of aromatherapy vials, and spa music. The technician had put out a small plate with a couple of mushroom caps. There was also a thermos of hot water and medicinal teas. There were notes for the guide on how to contact assistance in a medical or behavioral emergency, and there was even a sealed medicine bottle with two Reality Return tablets for her to give to Byron if she needed to bring him down suddenly rather than letting him ride out the trip naturally. There were instructions on how to sync their wearables, which were unnecessary; they remained synced as part of their intimacy as a couple.

Byron chewed, made a bitter face, swallowed, and settled in, awaiting the hallucinogenic effect. Eventually, he began commenting on feelings and visual alterations, speaking softly. Sallye tracked them carefully for a while and then realized that Byron was not speaking to her but to himself. He was depersonalized and dissociated. Sallye found a comfortable meditative posture, commanded one part of her mind to track Byron's safety and emotional tone, and then descended into her own thoughts.

Sallye tracked minutes that stretched past the hour. A second hour replaced the first, and then a third hour went by. She noted behavioral changes consistent with intense emotions within Byron. His eyes were alive in a way that told her he was tracking visual hallucinations. When she detected agitation, she touched him, and he calmed. As he looked at her, his face suggested he was baffled at her intrusion, but then he seemed grateful for her. Then he was gone again.

After almost four hours, he rose, went to the toilet, and then came back, making an effort to make tea. Sallye did it for him and then held his hands as he held the mug and sipped. He remained silent. Every few moments she felt that he faded away and then fought to return. Finally, he sat in one of the comfortable chairs and began keyboarding rapidly with his right hand onto the wearable on his left forearm. As he typed, the words appeared on Sallye's wearable. She read with fascination.

> 1. Why did I faint? *Heart failure, heartbreak, breakthrough, heart attach, not attack. My heart was attached to that little girl in the*

school. She needed my heart to be the heart of a father. All too much. Inadequate, don't know how. Faint of heart. Better to be on the floor than not to have understanding, not to know where I stand, not to be upright. I so wish to be upright. How?

2. Foretelling and footnotes: *It is the human condition to live with death. I could always do that because Dad lived a living death right in front of me. Dead man walking. I walk my own death. By the way, is this about medicine or something? Dad was a guinea pig, pushed too far and hit the wall. He will go down in history: this is not how you do it! "Look at me." He said that to me often when I had done something bad and he was trying to talk with me about it. Really, he meant, "Look at me, Byron. Be warned." But he couldn't say it. Foreshadowed me. Now I too am a guinea pig; here is a guinea, so pig out, will you? Extra funds in your CashCards for Zeke's burgers.*

3. Why does Dad feel dead to me? *Well, that is obvious.*

With that done, Byron stopped typing. He went to the music station, switched the channel, and sat in a chair with a huge grin on his face as his fingers moved in time with the music.

They both knew when it was time to leave the lab. Arriving outside in the midafternoon warmth, they walked toward the lake path that would take them within a few blocks of FiveWay. Byron babbled, and Sallye enjoyed the banter about the auras around trees, the escaping molecules of water that jumped from the surface of the lake and then joyously returned, the unbelievably deep green in the S-SB sign, and the incredible coffee-cup graphic. She remembered her angry steps on the same path the night before as she had tried to shake off the Cripps vibe that had gripped her. It was distant now.

Sanc paralleled the path a dozen or so meters off to the side. He never let them out of his sight but never let on that he was with them.

At the S-SB, they got a couple of vanilla skim-milk lattes with double espresso and a ginseng boost. They wouldn't sleep tonight; neither of them really wanted to as they reveled in how good it was to be together.

The path took them within sight of the academy building. Byron was increasingly reconnecting with the reality of the day and suddenly remembered. He said, "Oh, your time with Cripps!"

"I really don't want to spoil the day by talking about him," Sallye said. She reached out and held Byron's noncoffeed hand in hers. "Except you will never guess what I discovered when I was in his office."

"Tell me."

"He is a PhD doctor, not a medical doctor or a psychology doctor. He is a doctor of philosophy. He is not a psychologist at all. He has old-fashioned, printed-on-paper journals there, years of them up until 2038. They are all on medical ethics."

"That's the year psychiatry died."

"Yes, it is."

(VI)

Byron sat silently, with Sallye off to the side. Dr. Y greeted him and, in the absence of a reply, went into stasis: gentle breath expanding and contracting the chest, random eye blinks, a slight smile.

Byron was enjoying the slight breeze that seemed to come from the illusionary windows of the virtual-reality room. Again, there was a scent of lavender in the movement of moist air. Even though it was engineered air—laced with an essential oil, humidified, and blown by a fan—it was lovely. Byron was still enjoying a light, residual euphoria from the psilocybin session of two days before. He yearned for the hallucinated colors and the deepening awareness of the ordinary that he'd achieved during the trip. How intensely he yearned! He had every intention to return to the intense experience. No, not intention: resolve. He had already started to plan in his mind how he might get clandestine access to the supply of psilocybin in the lab. Zeke could help. Byron shifted from his thoughts, feeling wary to have had them there. His wariness had a hard edge. He looked at Sallye and then back at the avatar.

"I don't need her to pick me up anymore," Byron stated.

Dr. Y blinked into engagement, nodding but remaining silent. Perkins had expanded the IPE-CKS data that the artificial-intelligence program could access to inform the therapy. It filled in details from real life and processed Byron's physiological readiness for the therapy.

"Remember, last time you said that she was here to pick me up if I were to faint. She and I have talked about that, about many things."

"Yes."

"It is..." Byron paused, considering how to proceed.

"It is the psilocybin," Dr. Y interjected.

"Yes, since then. You know?"

"I have access now."

"Oh, you do. I had thought you didn't." Byron tried to sound surprised.

The avatar didn't reply.

"Well, I guess that is to be expected. You will know more about me now. And I know a lot more myself."

"Tell me what you know, Byron."

Byron glanced over at Sallye. Her posture was eager. She leaned slightly forward in the chair, inviting rather than vigilant or judging.

"Well, given that you know about the psilocybin, you probably have access to the biodata and the journaling I did that day. You will know that while the experience was altogether light and pleasurable, it also contained deeper awareness and understanding. Some truth. I have talked with Sallye about what I came to accept that day. That was in the privacy of our relationship. And she really helped, but more of that later. Here, with you, I can go over it again, understand it all better."

"Please do." The avatar processed the change. The emotional isolation he had detected in Byron in the first session was being replaced with greater intimacy with Sallye. The AI program also noted a slight aberration in the way Byron was relating to the avatar.

Byron gave pause to reflect on the avatar's words and how they were spoken. He heard the invitation coming from the artificial-intelligence algorithm of the therapy, that it was made to seem like a spontaneous curiosity. Now, however, he had a deeper conviction that it came from an investigative Perkins eager to know what Byron knew.

"So if we take it back to that girl, and if we take it back to what you said in an earlier session about my needing to draw on my experience of having a father to be for her what she needed…" Byron looked deeply into the illusionary eyes of the avatar, breathed in deeply, and started in again. "And if we recognize that in the moment that I fainted back in the first session, it was with the sudden awareness that not only had I not really had a father but the attempt at fathering that my…that my male biological parent…that he made, was confusing and painful to me. If we put all of that together…"

"If you put it altogether…" repeated the avatar.

"It tells me there was something very wrong in my home growing up."

Byron reached over to Sallye to take her hand. He had been doing that more in the last forty-eight hours than he had in all the time that they had known each other. Sallye had always been the one to initiate physical touch; he had always been contained in his body. Here he did it for effect, although on some level, it was meaningful and comforting for him.

"By happenstance, Sallye met with my mother. What happened here in our last session led her to want to find out more. So when I tripped and retrieved memories, she was able to verify what I was remembering with what she learned of my history. The story goes together. We are figuring it all out together."

"And that story is?"

"My dad had a mental breakdown, and there was a reason for it. I remember how distant he was, and then he would explode in anger. I thought it was something wrong with me, and so I became anxious and careful and good at whatever I did."

Byron looked over at Sallye. She was bursting to speak, to fill in the details for him. Their eyes met, and she sent waves of encouragement to him to continue.

"There always seemed to be something missing when I was growing up. I tried to fill it in with being good. And yes, indeed there was something missing. I found out about it yesterday when Sallye and I talked.

"My mother told her a few days ago that I had a brother, a brother who had gone missing, a brother nobody told me about. That missing son must have been what put my father into his mental breakdown. All of the communal parents who took care of me must have conspired with my mother and father to keep it a secret. Probably the ASL directed them to, thought it was the healthiest thing to do. This brother somehow was taken right out of my home while I was still a preschooler. So there was a vacuum, an empty space in my family that I was to fill but never quite able to fill. It all makes sense now.

"After our last session, I set my intention for the hallucinogenic therapy to explore the father thing, to go back in time and understand it all. Now I kind of wish I had known about my brother before I did the psilocybin, because maybe I could have—"

"Can I just stop you there for a moment? I appreciate you working on the therapy we are doing here by finding out more. But I suspect that there is a misconception for you. Psilocybin is not a memory aid; it enhances the present and sets up a deeper self for the future."

"OK." Byron accepted the correction. It took his energy away for a moment, and he knew that would be recorded on his biosensor. Gaining back his internal control, he refocused. He had accomplished the first goal; he had spoken what he now knew. It was time to move on.

The avatar continued. "There might be other approaches to help you remember your brother, and I am truly supportive of you as you come to understand and accept this part of your life. Although that is important, what is more important is the depth of now and what you can do with that depth."

Byron accepted the return to the therapy algorithm. "Well, I feel free now. I think that what happened in my family and my solution to it, to always be careful and always be good, has been a prison for me. It was a prison I didn't know I occupied, because I grew up thinking what was around me was normal."

"Tell me about your newfound freedom."

"I can choose not to do good. Or I can choose to do good. But whatever I choose, I choose. Doing the right thing used to be a scary obligation. It was treacherous, because I never felt that I was doing it perfectly. Now it can be a choice."

"Yes, freedom is a wonderful thing. So what are you choosing to do with it?"

Byron paused, became deliberate. What he was going to say here was important. He knew Perkins would be listening behind the scenes. Perkins would have already been putting this together but wondering what, and how much, Byron knew. He wanted Perkins to think he was being transparent about it. Now he needed to let Perkins feel secure about where it all might be going.

"This experience, the therapy with you, and the hallucinogenic therapy can let me figure that out. It is not that I am dissatisfied being a Paraclete. I feel fortunate to spend my days doing what I am doing. But it can now be on a deeper level. It has to be a calling for me rather than an expectation or an outcome. It is my future, a future I can claim for myself and the ASL. I will figure it out as I go along."

Byron knew Perkins would hear that with a sense of quiet satisfaction. Perkins's whole system of Paracletes and avatars had been his life's calling, his professional identity. He could let Perkins believe that now it was his. In knowing this, Perkins would feel secure and would leave him alone.

Dr. Y's reply was within the therapy algorithm used to bring it all back into the here and now rather than the there and then. "You put the figuring out into the future. You are doing a lot of that figuring out now, doing it here, here with me."

"I want to continue seeing you," Byron said. "And I want to continue with the hallucinogenic therapy."

"This is your third session with me. Any further sessions would need to be authorized by the ASL. As for the hallucinogenic therapy, I don't know."

"I figured you would say that."

"Byron, can I ask you to be aware of something? You talk about your freedom, about breaking away from acting on the basis of expectation or obligation and making your own choices. And I can recognize the importance of that and how that deepens you. But with freedom comes responsibility. Your choices and actions impact others. So where is your responsibility in this?"

"Well, that is part of the reason why I want to see you again, to figure that out here."

Byron imagined Perkins eating this up. Even with all the data that the ASL collected on him, it could never be sure of his intentions. It knew the movements of his body and the flow of his physiological juices but not his thoughts. Here, in this AVT, was where the ASL explored the workings of Byron's mind. And Byron had told the ASL what he wanted it to think his thoughts were. Byron now knew that for years the ASL had imposed on others to keep a secret, to keep him from knowing he had a brother. Here he could now keep secrets from the ASL by leading it to believe what he wanted it to believe. And that would buy him even more freedom.

"I suspect that will be easy to arrange," said Dr. Y. "I too hope to see you again."

In leaving the VR room, Byron deferred to Sallye to go first, a politeness of the past. As she did, he put his hand on her shoulder and propelled her out of the space, with its microphones. They exited the North Hill building and were back in the park. A path wound its way through the trees, taking them beyond eyes that might pry as they walked away. When they neared the lakefront, trees shielding them from the building, he turned on the privacy override on his wearable and motioned for Sallye to do the same.

"So that was interesting," Sallye said.

"There is something I have figured out about that program. It leads you into talking. Although I like the avatar, Dr. Y, and find it easy to talk to, my talking there is not for me but for the ASL."

Sallye peered at him, puzzled.

"You mentioned that Cripps had tried to get you to tell him about your meeting with my mom."

"Yes."

"And in refusing, you stayed firm."

"Yes."

"Well, I just told them."

"Yes, I guess you did."

"They want to know how much we know."

"Yeah, I guess so. It seemed different there. I was glad that you were finally talking. And it is your story to tell, not mine."

"There, in the AVT, I can be in charge of how much of the story I tell. Rather than it being demanded of us, like Cripps tried to do with you, it can be decided, decided by me or us."

"Oh, Byron, you are suspicious of the ASL. But it is the reason we exist; it provides for us."

"The ASL acts as though it is the pinnacle of virtue, encouraging goodness for society and for the individual. But look what it did in my life. It robbed me of the knowledge that I had a brother. It left me to be raised by a lunatic. All my life, I have been living in the midst of deception and manipulation."

Sallye was shocked, struggling to make sense of a different Byron. "The psilocybin has made you paranoid."

"Or made me see more clearly."

Disoriented, Sallye tumbled in her mind about what all this meant for her. She cared about him, cared about the generous and secure soul that she thought he was. But her life was as a Paraclete, working within the confines of the ASL. She began to regret telling him about her conversation with Lisbeth. Maybe if she had handled it differently; maybe...

"I am going to find my brother."

Sallye looked deeply into his eyes. She loved him, but she was afraid. Although on her own she would have never interpreted Byron's story in the way that he had, she could now see the validity in what he was saying.

Sallye reflected on the horror she'd felt when she heard the family story from Lisbeth. But she just hadn't put it together the way that Byron just had. Even more, Sallye remembered the fun she had with her sisters when she visited her communal family home. She wondered what it must have been like for Byron to not have his brother come home and kick a soccer ball with him at the local pitch.

They could see the public dock on the lake. Down there, an older man was pushing a boat out from the dock, fishing pole straddling the seats in front of him. She felt that she too was pushing away, not from Byron, but with him. She felt scared by it but ready to go with it.

"Byron, I think I have a lead on where we might find your brother."

5

BECKETT

Having just returned to his summer job, Alton was way out in the eastern counties working a prescribed burn when he got the news. The site foreman immediately contacted the head office of Plains Inc., and Jennifer made the arrangements quickly. He would take one of the LandPorters into the city, where he would catch the bus. One transfer would get him onto an Overnighter that stopped in Munroe. Alton was still awaiting word on whether he would meet his grandma there or head right back to Beckett and the ranch.

Jennifer had transferred an advance on his pay into his account.

Tears overtook him. Laurel had tried to sound optimistic on the phone, but her worry betrayed her, cracking her words as she spoke. By the time Justin had been transferred by Medi-Chop to Munroe Memorial, his heart rhythm had been stabilized by the paddles and meds. The cardiology team at Munroe Memorial took him into the catheterization lab immediately. Once they had done the echo and the caths, they would know how much damage the heart muscle had sustained. Those were the details.

Alton was overcome. Justin and the horses were his life. He had seen his grandpa grow more tired in the last year or so. Alton had even been reluctant to take the job with Plains Inc. because he worried that something like this would happen. At the time he'd decided to take the job, Justin had said, "Oh, don't worry. I am fine." It was even Grandpa who had arranged the job through Cedars, and as always, Alton didn't want to let him down.

Laurel had said, "You go; we will be all right." That was his grandma, clear and simple. Alton went, knowing that they needed the money. He could make much more by working a season away than he could make back at home with the horses.

Through the night, as the bus made its way through the mountains, Alton and Laurel talked whenever his wearable was in digital net connection. He heard and responded in kind to her words. The way her words were spoken and the words she left unspoken gave a truer indication of how she felt than did what she said. She sounded tired, more tired than he had heard her sound in a long time.

The Overnighter pulled into Munroe about 2:00 a.m. From there, it was headed to the coast. On the station platform, Alton could read the big *H* of the hospital sign up on the North Hill. He would walk there to blow the stale air of the bus out of his lungs and to cry.

"He is awake off and on, but he's confused. I am sure he'll want to see you right away." Alton's presence in the hall outside the hospital room was reassuring to his grandma. Her words already had more strength in them than when they had been talking over the wearables while he was en route.

"Anything I should know before I go in?"

"Well, there are lots of tubes and wires. The monitors keep beeping, but I guess that is good. He does seem uncomfortable. He fights, and then he rests."

"That sounds like my grandpa!"

"Don't expect too much, Alton. He is in pretty bad shape."

"I hope it will help that I am here."

"Yes, I hope so too."

Justin was in a private room. There was a nurse stationed on a stool surrounded by screens in the corner. Her focus was on the stream of data that was coming from the various sensors that were attached to Justin's body.

"Hi, Grandpa. It's me, Alton."

Justin blinked awake—a sudden, confused consciousness. He looked at the young man at the foot of his bed and asked, "Craig? Craig is that you?"

"Alton."

"Yes, Alton is on his way. You must have come separately. Did you bring the boys?"

"Grandpa, it's me, Alton."

A deepening look of confusion clouded Justin's face. He looked at Alton and saw the face of Craig looking back at him. Craig, that joker, playing tricks like he was someone else. A spasm of chest pain passed through the old man. He moaned.

Looking up again, seeing his Craig standing beside the bed, he said, "I hope you brought the boys; I want to see the little fellows. And their mother, is she here too?"

Alton spoke more firmly. "Grandpa, this is Alton. I am Alton. I just got here from working over on the Plains. I got here as fast as I could."

The look of confusion gave way to a look of exhaustion, and Justin faded from consciousness again.

Alton left the room and went to a small waiting room, where Laurel sat.

"He is pretty confused. He thought I was my dad." Tears emerged again. Craig was his ghost, Alton's very own ghost that he carried with him wherever he went. Craig was the unspeakable, the unspoken, spoken of here in an altered state.

"I told him that you were coming. The confusion—it is the drugs and probably a lack of oxygen to his brain. He is not thinking clearly. And like it or not, you look just like your dad did when he was your age."

"Gosh, Grandma, what are you going to do?"

"That is for another day. Tomorrow, maybe. Tonight I will sit here, and I will go in from time to time. The special nurse in there now is not very communicative, but they switch off every ninety minutes. The one before her talked with me, told me what to expect."

Laurel's eyes filled, and she choked back tears. "That other nurse told me that the monitors showed a positive response when I held his hand. He was never much for holding hands when he was healthy, but maybe now, maybe now."

"Can you go somewhere to get some rest? You must have been with him for hours."

"There is a family room down the hall. I was told I could stretch out on the couch or use the recliner. I might go and try now that you are here."

"I am going back in," Alton said. "There is a chair by the window. I will sit and hope that he can rest."

Neither knew how they could pass the night, but they did. In the morning, Justin's mind became clearer once the clock turned 6:15 a.m., his usual rising time. The talkative nurse, now back on the perch with the screens around her, spoke in hushed tones to let both Alton and Laurel know that it was a good sign.

By 7:30 a.m., the parade of specialists and nurses had passed through. The cardiologist who did the catheterization was self-congratulatory.

"Alton." Justin's voice was weak but determined. "The horses. You need to see to them."

"Yes, Grandpa."

"They are in the back paddock. Stamper has been known to go at the fence. I check it every day. Can you go and check? I seem to be stuck here."

"Sure." Alton couldn't keep the uncertainty from his voice.

Laurel stood at Justin's bedside, holding his hand. "I checked with the nurse; you might get transferred back up to Beckett soon."

"Beckett? Where does that fool nurse think I am now? This is the hospital, the Beckett hospital."

"Justin, we had you brought by chopper down to Munroe Memorial."

"Oh." Disappointment clouded his face. "And how much is that going to cost us?"

"Believe it or not, you are over sixty-seven. Ambulance bills are sent to the government, even the bill for the Medi-Chop."

"I always wanted a ride on that damn thing, or one like it. I got it, and now I don't even remember it." Clearly Justin was more alert than he'd been the night before.

Laurel smiled. It was a contagious smile that spread to Alton. They were smiles of relief.

Laurel said, "Well, the bad news is that when you go back to Beckett, it will be by ground ambulance. The doctor who did your heart surgery says that it looks good for you to go back to Beckett tomorrow to start your cardio rehab."

"Cardio what?"

"Rehab—to get you on your feet and walking, monitoring you while you get strong again."

"No damn treadmills."

Laurel smiled, relieved to have him back. "No damn treadmills. Soon enough, we will get you pitching square bales again."

"Damn right. Winter's coming, and someone has to feed those horses."

There were no public buses to Beckett that day. From the bus depot, Alton called for an AVoD. Just out of town, he was able to hook up with six others for the forty-five-minute trip.

His autonomous vehicle was small, just a two-seater. Once it was hooked up, all Alton could see through the windshield was the back of the AVoD in front, coupled firmly to his own at the bumper. The view behind was similar. He looked out the side window and saw passing orchards, land with sheep grazing, and eventually, the treed hills.

Before he left the hospital, he had loaned his wearable to his grandpa. Justin had called Cedars, trying to make his voice sound as strong as he could. The words of that conversation came back to Alton vividly.

"Hey, Cedars, this is Justin. Would you mind leading the trail ride with Alton tomorrow?

"…Yeah, Alton. He will be back tonight. I am kinda stuck here in the hospital, and I don't think I will get out in time.

"…Down in Munroe.

"…Yeah, way down in Munroe.

"…Not much, really; they tell me it is my heart. People used to say I didn't have one, so I guess I am proving them wrong.

"…That's right, with Alton. He knows the drill.

"…OK, he will be in touch when he wants you to come out in the morning. I have called you on his…thing…wearable, whatever, so if you need to call him back, you can just call to this device.

"…Thanks. Bye."

Even more than he remembered the words, Alton remembered how Justin had sunk back down into the hospital bed from the exertion of the call. His grandpa looked so pale, so gray.

Laurel had checked her own wearable and found out that there was a full group of six to come the next day, Sunday. There were already two signed up for Tuesday and another four for Thursday. As the calendar had turned to September, they were down to three days a week. They needed to complete as many of those trips as they could to keep the ranch afloat.

Alton considered how much his life had changed in the past twenty-four hours. He had grown content working away. There was an adventure to it. He had met other young men from across the country and had found out about divergent social conditions and different political views. They had passed around commentaries and essays: digitized material that had been cloaked within their wearables, passed between them with one-to-one transmission but off the grid of the ASL. Alton had grown up with one ASL in his region and learned that it took different forms elsewhere.

Alton's mind wandered a lot in that forty-five minutes. He thought of connecting with Cedars the following day. They would have time to talk; he would call him out early in the day to help him groom and tack the horses. But they would talk about Plains Inc. and about what was happening right there in Beckett. Alton's mind wandered but always violently returned to the shock of seeing his grandpa in the hospital, of being called by his father's name, of having the burden of the family's financial survival placed on his shoulders.

When he arrived home, he took a brief walk through the back paddock. Stamper had been kind to the fence, and all the horses were there. He went into the barn, found the black hat, and put it by the door. Behind it, he placed a block of wood, on which he'd patiently burned in a message with a hot iron. He'd inscribed the following in neat letters:

TIPS, PLEASE.
ALTON WILL TAKE THEM THROUGH HIS WEARABLE
AT THE END OF THE RIDE.
WHAT YOU ADDED TO YOUR BILL WHEN YOU PAID
WENT TO THE RESORT CONCIERGE, NOT US.

WE NEED YOUR TIPS TO KEEP OUR RANCH GOING.
THANK YOU. DON'T FORGET.

It took him the better part of two hours to burn all those words there. Darkness had fallen by the time he finished. It was OK.

(II)

When Boris Vygoski had arrived in Beckett, there were only a handful of buildings there. Prospectors, temporarily discouraged but eternally optimistic, wandered the one street in town between the building that housed the Land Claims and Assayist Office, the Catholic Mission Church, and the only store, a store with the uninspiring moniker "Provisions."

Boris Vygoski brought with him a few personal assets on which the town of Beckett would eventually be built. First, despite his heavily accented, broken English, Boris could convince anyone of anything. Bankers and businessmen used to shake their heads and say, "Honestly, I don't know what he is proposing, but damn it, I believe in him and know that he can turn a buck." Indeed, Boris Vygoski had a talent for spotting a loose dollar in anyone's pocket and finding a way to get it into his own.

Second, Boris brought with him a seemingly endless supply of Russian vodka. He would never disclose how he came to have this "liquid asset," and no one ever complained about not knowing where it came from. In the years that followed, Boris would answer the question "What brought you to Beckett?" with a twinkle in his eye, a toothy grin, and the words, "Not really sure—I vas drunk at the time."

The third asset Boris brought with him were building skills learned in the old country. Within a few months of arriving in Beckett, Boris used his three assets to construct the saloon and flophouse for prospectors when they came into town. That is where he weathered his first winter. With the dramatically told story of creating a viable business in Beckett, he went down to Munroe City and got financial backing to build a small collection of bunkhouses that offered creature comforts and were located an easy distance away from his other establishment. Those bunkhouses, humble in appearance but built to last, appeared in photographs of the town for the next sixty-five years.

It was during Boris's second summer in Beckett that a seam of coal was discovered farther up the valley. With his reputation in Munroe City, Boris convinced the Pacific Overland Railway to run a spur up to Beckett. Back in Beckett, he negotiated a deal with the land titleholder. The seam was opened, and the coal was committed to supply the railroad.

By the third summer, the spur was in. Boris became a wealthy man, with a stake in a coal-extraction mine and, of course, his seemingly endless supply of Russian vodka. The first train up the spur had a carriage car with men in suits and women in finery who would spend an awkward day in Beckett before chugging back down the valley to return home. The train also carried freight cars loaded with brick, mortar, and dry cement. Boris had studied the construction of factory buildings in Munroe City's working district, talked to architects, and figured out how he would build the first brick building in Beckett.

The Beckett Hotel was up by the fourth year. As a testament to Boris Vygoski's building skills, his skill at convincing, and probably also his vodka, that building still stands to this day.

Boris's vision for the hotel was magnificent. He put a high ceiling on the first floor, ordered a chandelier, and had his craftsmen construct a spiral staircase to the second floor. On the second floor were a number of very small rooms that were initially intended to be single hotel rooms but were in reality let out by the hour for men with female companions who cruised for customers at the bar. On the third floor were rooms rented out to workers or prospectors by the week or month. Those rooms were small and simple: a bed for sleeping or sleeping it off, a wardrobe to hang outerwear, a bureau with a mirror on the top, a washstand with a bowl and pitcher, a chamber pot on the floor, and a straight chair. Although Boris had installed steam heat to the upper floors from a boiler in the basement, he had not plumbed the upper floors. Water closets were only on the first level where the plumbing into the basement was convenient.

The Beckett Hotel remained much like that for a couple of decades until other facilities were built in Beckett that offered more modern amenities. The upper floors at the hotel were reduced to storage areas, increasingly cluttered and dusty.

With the incarnation of Beckett as a tourist destination, an initiative was undertaken to renew the building. Geothermal heat replaced the boiler in the basement. The ceiling was lowered on the first floor to provide a place for plumbing to be routed to the upper floors. Bathrooms were put in; the small hotel rooms had walls torn down to create suites. The Beckett Hotel became Vy's Magnificent Inn, Eatery, and Emporium. Displays were added on the second floor that housed re-creations of the hotel rooms of the past, the rooms used by the prostitutes, and the decor and furnishings that were once characteristic of the Saloon. A way was found for the chandelier and the spiral staircase to grace a lobby, one newly constructed to look historic.

Byron and Sallye settled into one of the suites on the third floor.

With Byron's completion of his third AVT session, the pair of Paracletes were now fully qualified for the trade. As such, they were rewarded with a week of leave. Cripps had insisted that Sallye catch up on her hours with her clients and was quite grudging in letting her take the time off.

Before they left the city, Sallye had used her wearable to photograph the drawings from CarolAnne's sketchbook. Sallye took digital captures of each of CarolAnne's sketches, not letting on that the one CarolAnne had done in Beckett was of interest to her. Sallye hadn't been at Vy's Magnificent Inn, Eatery, and Emporium long before she was able to put together that CarolAnne had taken the video of the young man from a window table in the Eatery—the same video that she had watched to create her pencil-on-paper sketch. Each time she showed the sketch to Byron, Sallye tried to read him as he looked at the image that looked so much like him. She sensed that he was curious. She also sensed that he was scared.

Byron and Sallye had activated the biosensor overrides of their wearables. While GPS and spending would still be tracked, they felt a precious sense of relief from the digital monitoring of their inner lives. They allowed themselves sensual pleasures: ice cream, toes in the cool lake water on the beach down by the pier, the freshness of a breeze that blew through the trees, and the dramatic visual contrast of aspens turned golden in the fall against the deep greens of the spruce and fir. That first night, in the privacy of their suite and with the override activated, they enjoyed the physicality of their relationship.

On the second day, Byron and Sallye began to canvas about, showing the picture from her wearable. They tried at the inn desk, thinking that as the man got out of his AVoD in front of Vy's, he might have stayed there. No luck. They tried in the shops down at the pier, thinking that if he were a tourist, he would have browsed there. No luck. They even walked to the marshaling yard for AVoDs and found a technician there who was servicing and maintaining the vehicles. He had no clue and seemed annoyed that they would ask.

"Hey, Byron. That you?" The voice came from a tall man with bright-orange hair and an olive complexion.

"Yes?" Byron was taken aback. The greeting had been boisterous and intrusive, overly familiar in its tone.

"You probably don't know me, but I know you."

"OK." Byron spoke with cautious uncertainty.

"I'm Charles, Charles Ross. I work in IT, mostly on the servers in the basement at the North Hill."

"OK." Byron's voice had retreated further into caution, but he felt a building curiosity and attraction toward the man.

"So you have never met me, but I have met you." Charles's voice was a playful drawl, singsongy, like the voice-over on a tourism commercial for the Caribbean Islands.

"How so?" Now Byron was intrigued.

"I work for Perkins; you know, the great Dr. Alastair Perkins. He had me going over the feeds from the VR room a while back, and there you were." An infectious chuckle escaped the man.

Byron suddenly felt panic: what had this man seen? Was it the excursions that he and Sallye had taken into erotica clubs? That would be truly embarrassing. Was it his faint from the first AVT? Suddenly Byron felt naked; the freedom he felt from the privacy override on his wearable had vanished.

"Oh, buddy. Don't look so worried. I am professional, an IT guy. And what would it matter anyway?"

There was something about Charles: something inviting, something provocative, something exciting. The lilt of his voice set off an odd sort of singing in Byron's mind. Sallye's presence with them faded into the distance for Byron. There was something sensual about the man.

"So what did you see?" Byron asked.

Charles responded with a chuckle, a teasing "I'll never tell," and a light punch to Byron's shoulder.

"So what are you doing up here in Beckett?" Byron asked.

"We have installed new data-collection towers up at the ski resort and down through the valley. Ultrasensitive. I am just hooking them up to the network here in town. This winter, when you are standing up at the top of that ski hill, we will be able to know your excitement through the quickening of your heart, the tightening of your muscles, and the adrenaline in your veins. I will be right there with you in your vestibular storm as you slalom down the slope."

Charles paused, smiled, and continued. "And poor me. I will be back in the basement at North Hill seeing the data stream of it all, trying to live it with you but not feeling the cold air on my face or the gut wrench in my belly."

Byron felt the physicality of the man. Despite his work with computers, Charles Ross lived in his sensual experiences. It was infinitely attractive.

Charles had caught the gleam in Byron's eye, knew that he had him. His face grew mockingly more serious. "And that would be a delight, a break from watching for the signs of a hack into the ASL servers."

With the mention of a hack, Byron's mind jumped back to his work with Zeke and Zeke's assurance that his intrusion on the wearables of those around him went undetected by the ASL servers. Looking at Charles, however, he felt that maybe the man would step back from something so innocent and have a laugh that a fourteen-year-old boy could do such a thing.

"Excuse me, I am Sallye. And Byron, I think we need to be going now." Sallye had stepped into the space between the two young men, an effort to break the connection that had grown too strongly, too quickly, between them.

Charles looked at her and turned back to Byron. "And what are you two doing up in Beckett?"

"Well, we're just on leave. We have both finished all the requirements of First Flight—"

"I know."

"And having some downtime. Looking for someone actually."

"Oh? Who? I can help you look. I have connections, you know." Charles patted his wearable and winked.

"We don't know who he is. We just have a picture."

"Can I see?"

With Byron's unwanted grabbing, Sallye held out her arm. She pushed the display on the wearable and grimaced. This guy worked for Perkins. Did she really want him to know?

"Oh, him. Looks like you!" Charles's face beamed as he looked at Byron. "Nice-looking. No, I don't know him. I do have access to picture files; I am sure we can find his image somewhere, except we wouldn't know whether that image would be of you or of him. Are you sure you're not just looking for yourself?" Charles's chuckle was infectious.

"No," Byron said. "We think he might be my brother."

Sallye reached out and pulled Byron back. She spoke more firmly. "We have to get going."

Byron turned to her and said, "Hold on a sec, honey; Charles here can probably help."

"No, Byron, let's get going. Now!" The strength of her voice finally captured Byron. He looked at her confused, disoriented by the strength of her words. Once she had him back, she spoke more softly. "Byron, it's our adventure together. We need to let Charles get back to work. He has a job to do up here. We have the time on our leave; we can look ourselves."

Byron followed her resentfully.

As they left, Charles called to the pair, "We will meet again, for sure!" There was an expectant chuckle to his voice.

Back at the hotel room, Sallye was furious. She told Byron that Charles was coming on to him and asked, "Didn't you notice?" She made comments about how obvious it was that Charles was gay and how that was all right but that maybe he was on the take for some "fresh meat."

Byron got defensive and said, "Maybe that could be all right. We are here to have fun, aren't we?"

Immediately, Sallye set him straight. Byron was hers and there would be no threesome, if that's what he was thinking.

They had a horrible night.

(III)

Sallye woke early. Upon rising, she decided that she would use her wearable to set up a video session with Dr. S. It would not be as immersive as being in the VR room, but the urgency required perspective to come soon.

As she settled in the living room of the suite on the third floor of Vy's, she activated her wearable to set up the entry into the AI system. Byron snored a gentle rhythm behind the closed door of the bedroom. Looking at her left forearm, she remembered how Byron had grabbed it so she would have to show the sketch to Charles.

A shudder ran through her.

Charles had bragged about his past violation into a VR session, the place he first saw Byron. There was no way of telling whether he might be watching the one she was about to initiate. It was Charles who angered her now, Charles and Byron. There was no way she could process the events of the previous day thinking that he might be watching.

Looking at her wearable again, she decided that she would journal. Doing so was still digital and apparently went to a server somewhere, but somehow, she felt that it was less likely to be seductive to someone else's eyes. Then she realized that she was likely deluding herself in that—Charles obviously had no idea of respectful personal boundaries.

Before she began, Sallye tried to meditate. It was a no-go—her agitation was too extreme.

Finally, beside herself, she decided she would do the writing with the awareness that Charles might read it; in reading it, he would get the message of her outrage. Maybe that would make him back off. At least it would get the fury out.

> *Monday, September 18, 2057*
> *I am so angry at Byron. This was supposed to be our leave together, our time to deepen our relationship, our time*

> to enjoy each other physically. I am very aware he is processing a lot lately. There was the news of his brother, and with finishing First Flight...and with the probing AVT. But the way he acted yesterday, suggesting a three-way. Furious!
>
> OK, Sallye, settle in. I wonder: did he know about his brother? He says, "Yeah, sort of." What sort of knowing is that? What is it like to know that a brother is out there, an older brother, and not know whether you could ever find him?
>
> And that hallucinogenic session. That too.
>
> OK, he is going through...

Sallye had been typing one-handed, her right hand on the wearable on her left forearm. The physical position caused tightness in her back. Stretching, she took off her wearable, set it on the table in the kitchenette, and projected a two-handed keyboard onto the surface of the table in front of her.

> So, whatever. He is going through stuff. But to be drawn in by that horrible, sly, brazen SOB. The IT guy. Yuck. Creep. An older gay man looking for some young meat. And Byron falls for it.
>
> If he tries it again, I am going to Perkins, to Cripps, even. Sure, the guy can be gay, but that doesn't mean he can try to come on to any good-looking young male he sees. I can report him for ethical violations, violations of ASL privacy codes. And I can let Perkins and Cripps know that he was using what he gained on the job for his own horny adventures. That should get him canned.

Sallye relaxed into her chair. She felt better, as though she had struck back. She had declared her position with Charles. From the talk last night, she figured that Byron had gotten the message of his part in all this too.

She made tea.

The living room had a window that looked obliquely toward the lake. The sun was rising, making the golds of the aspens brilliant on the western shore. Her thoughts turned to Byron. He definitely had changed since the psilocybin session; he was more paranoid and more self-centered. When she talked about it with him, it took a long time for him to verbalize the change. He had finally said, "It's like everything means more, but things that used to mean a lot don't mean so much." What the hell did he mean by that?

She settled back to figure it out, reflecting on her own hallucinogenic session. Her experience led to a deepening sense of the spiritual. The sensual took on extra dimension and depth for her. Trees can have auras, she remembered, but people do too. That effect had faded for her. How long had it taken? A week or so. Maybe Byron was still getting his people auras.

Or maybe he was just an oblivious dolt.

What must it be like for him to realize that he had been deprived of a brother? And who took that brother anyway? They still didn't know that. Sallye tried to imagine what it would be like for Claire and Giggles if suddenly she disappeared. But they were older now than Byron was when his brother went missing. Did he even remember?

If I lost a brother, would I try to replace him? Now that was an interesting thought. Was that what was going on between him and Charles? Was it the business of attracting the attention of another male a few years older than he? She wanted to yell, "Watch out, Byron; he has something other than being brotherly in mind!"

Still, despite the good reasons that were now emerging, Sallye harbored doubts about Byron, about her and Byron together. In the years that she had known him, she had never felt that way before.

Sallye was jerked out of her thoughts by a presence in the room. She looked up to see Byron standing there, bleary-eyed and hair askew. "Good morning," he said.

"Good morning. Rough night, eh?"

Byron scratched his head and yawned. "Yeah."

"We have another day."

"Yeah, you feeling better?"

"Yes, now I am."

"That's good." As usual, he turned to go toward the bathroom and shower without saying anything at all about how he felt.

There was a bakery across the street from Vy's. Byron and Sallye picked up coffees and a couple of brioches. Sitting at a table in the sun, the cool September air around them, they planned their day. There were still a few places they could canvas the picture. There was a concierge in the lobby of Vy's. Checking in at his desk, they could find out what sort of activities they might pursue for the coming week. First, they would go back to their room, pick up their yoga mats, and head to the park down by the beach.

Sallye felt the old Byron reemerge in the dappled sun under the trees as they worked their yoga together. When it came time for him to call his two minutes of poses and flow, he chose Sallye's favorites. She settled in, the rage in her calming even further.

"There are lots of things to do here in Beckett for the week. There is nightlife at the clubs in the resorts." The concierge was a middle-aged woman who looked as though she liked to party.

"We are not into the nightlife. More physical. Hiking, biking—that sort of thing."

"Yes, that too. Bike rentals are just around the corner. Have you tried kayaking?"

"We lake kayak down in Munroe."

"Well, this lake here is smaller, calmer. What about white-water?"

"That would be fun."

"Let me check something." The concierge checked through some pages on one of her screens.

"Yes, have I got an adventure for you! There is a reservoir to the east, created by a dam for hydroelectric power generation. But it doesn't run constantly. The engineers have set it up to come online when the reservoir is full enough and the power is needed. This time of year, when it is dry, they open the sluice gates to send the water through the turbines only in late afternoon when there is a lot of grid demand for air conditioning, and that's not even every day. I just checked the dam computer—"

Both Sallye and Byron laughed at the words *dam computer*; the concierge smiled and enjoyed the unintended pun.

"And the damn computer says that they are scheduled for this afternoon. There is a launch point up near the dam. The outfitting company takes you and the kayaks up there; you ride them down on a strong current. Then you can lake kayak before you turn them in. Because it is considered eco-health friendly, you get extra CashCard points too."

"Sign us up for this afternoon."

Sallye touched her wearable, and the image came to life, hovering in the air between her and the concierge. "Does this person look familiar? He was seen here in Beckett this summer. We are looking for him."

The concierge turned to Byron. "He looks so much like you; he could be your brother. What's his name?"

"We don't know."

The concierge had a funny look on her face. She asked, "OK, do you folks horseback ride?"

"Never have." Sallye looked puzzled. Byron accepted the concierge's non sequitur and looked curious about the opportunity.

"Let me take a look. Yes, there is still room tomorrow. Alton called in to cancel one of the spaces. He can usually take six; tomorrow it is five. Maybe one of the horses is lame. Anyway, there are still two spots left open. I will book you in."

"OK, I guess we can give it a try."

"I think you will find your answer there. You get CashCard credits for horseback riding too. Let's figure it all out for you. That is something for today and for tomorrow. If you are still in the market for more things to do, come back Wednesday. Whose account is this going onto?"

Byron motioned forward with his left forearm and his wearable.

"Because we are in a rural area and the recreation vendors seldom get good net connection, we add a tip onto the bill here. For sure, we pass it through to them. Tip them like you had a great time. If you have any dissatisfactions with your experience, please come back and tell me. It is good for me to know."

Sallye and Byron walked out holding hands.

"Somehow, I don't trust her," Sallye stated.

"You don't seem to trust many people, do you?"

Hearing that, Sallye withdrew her hand from his.

Vy's didn't have a fitness room. Vy's didn't have a VR room either. Vy's also didn't have a pool. Nosing around the Emporium was an unproductive five minutes.

The departure time for kayaking was still a few hours away. Byron decided he would read a novel off his wearable, put in his earbuds, and listen to some really old jazz. He knew that he had put his foot in his mouth and reflected on the disinhibition that he had been feeling since the psilocybin trip. It felt good to be freer, to speak the truth, but he recognized that he needed to be a lot more careful. Sallye was fuming, and he was the cause. He felt he really needed to do some relationship repair. He couldn't concentrate on his book.

Sallye walked down by the beach. When she came back, it was apparent that she had been crying. That isn't at all what Byron wanted to happen on their leave.

"I am so sorry," he said.

"Me too."

"What can I say? It's like we just get on the same page, and then I blurt something out."

"I was thinking this morning that you are dealing with a lot. I should try to be understanding."

"I was thinking too that I have felt different since the psilocybin. It was so good at the time and immediately after. I almost wonder if I should go back and have another trip, and maybe that would set things right."

"I don't think so. I think we need some real experiences. Let's hope that the white-water kayaking and the horseback riding get us back to real life again. I was reading about horses. What it said was that they are always genuine, always in the present."

"That might be good for us."

"There is something else." Sallye looked up; the sadness had faded, but she had a curious look on her face.

"What?"

"When I was walking, I saw a bunch of AVoDs come into town. Some headed farther down the road, around to the resorts on the other side of the lake. I'm sure that I recognized the occupants in one of them."

"Who were they?"

"Dr. Alastair Perkins and CarolAnne."

(IV)

Alton needed to work efficiently. He had panicked last Sunday, tacking six horses for the ride, briefing Cedars on the management of the day, and feeling overwhelmed with the responsibility of it all. Back on Sunday, he had fought off the tears of worry about his grandfather with the fear that if he didn't do this all perfectly, disaster would strike. It went well, but his heightened concern for safety made the ride stiff and not as enjoyable for the customers, or so he thought. Fortunately, Cedars had taken on the role of historic storyteller. He wasn't as engaging as Laurel, but the guests listened with rapt attention. At the end of the day, Alton looked into the black hat by checking the total on his wearable. And yes, tips had come in almost equal to the old days.

And so it was Tuesday and time for another ride.

Laurel was bringing Justin to the AuxCare in Beckett by ground ambulance today after four days in Munroe. How Alton wished he could be there! Getting his grandpa to stay in such a place would be as difficult as getting Hester into a stall in the barn. Alton smiled at the image of Justin resisting donkey-like the regime of care that would be imposed on him. It would be insane for his grandpa to be so close to the ranch with his horses but not actually there. Alton hoped that after leading the ride today he would get into town to see Justin.

Now he worked efficiently. Cedars was late arriving, and Alton wondered about the mystery guest that he was bringing with him. He couldn't refuse the request from Cedars because Cedars was doing them a favor, helping out until his grandma could get his grandpa settled enough to resume leading the rides with him. Still, Alton resented giving in to Cedars's request that he bring someone on his own, someone who would not be paying. They needed every dollar these rides would generate to pay his grandpa's medical expenses.

One after another, he brought the horses in from the paddock, brushed briskly, and tacked. There was no time for combing out the manes and tails with Slick. If Laurel were here, she would be embarrassed at how they looked, but it was the best that Alton could do.

"Hey, Alton." Cedars climbed out of his aging LandPorter, his guest a few steps behind.

"Hey, Cedars. Thanks for coming. Who is your guest?" Alton had glanced quickly toward the two men but just as quickly returned his gaze to the horse he was tacking.

"This is Dags, Dags Basilis."

Alton briefly looked up. He transferred the brush in his right hand to his left, wiped his dusty right hand on his jeans, and then extended a handshake to the freeloading guest.

"Dags runs the sporting goods store down in Munroe."

"Alton, it is good to meet you. I am hoping that after today we can work together; I can set up rides for you from the store down there, maybe work out a better deal financially for you than you are getting from the resorts. Would you be willing to take extended trips into the backcountry for fishing and hunting?"

"Maybe, yeah. Sounds good," Alton replied, not looking up.

Cedars broke into the conversation. "Let's leave that until later. You can discuss that on the ride, maybe at lunch. There is something else before everyone arrives.

"Dags here is aware of our connection to Plains Inc. and what is going on east of the mountains. He is willing to be our man in Munroe."

Alton stiffened a bit. He now realized why Cedars had asked this guest to come. Cedars's management of people and places today reminded him of how Cedars got him the job with Plains Inc. and how he had become courier between the east and here once he was working at Plains.

"I told Dags of the connections you made over there and the communication you brought back."

"Hold on a minute, Cedars. I do appreciate everything that you have done for us, for getting me the job out there and for coming here to help out while Grandpa is sick, but I don't think I can be your connection to Plains Inc. anymore. I won't be able to get back there now that I have to do the fall rides here. By the time this season is done, I will be back up at the ski lodge getting it ready to open for the winter."

Alton had tacked both Starsky and Hutch and left the two men standing by the barn while he led the horses out to the fence.

Upon his return from the paddock with Biddy and Star, he stated bluntly, "With my work here on the ranch with Grandma, I don't have time for manifestos and acts of civil unrest."

Alton took a lead rope and halter from the hook and threw it at Cedars with a request for him to go and get Hester. He started working on getting Biddy ready.

Dags positioned himself to stand on the other side of the horse while Alton worked. "I am interested in what was going on out east. I am pretty disgusted with the way the ASL manipulates my business."

"Well, you would fit in out east then. They are disgusted by it out there too."

"So what are they doing?"

"It is more talk than action." Alton paused to reflect. "People are being careful how much they use digital communication, because it is all monitored. And they did organize a No CashCard Month. It was last May, I think. A bunch of people even allowed CashCard credits to expire unspent. I don't know how much of a wrench it put in the ASL system, but I hear that it was enough to get politicians out urging people to use up their credits. It caused enough of a glitch to be noticed."

"Gosh, that sounds incredible. I am not sure I like that idea, though; it would be hard on my business down in Munroe if we did that here."

"Like I said, I don't know how effective it was. Lots of discontent afterward. I arrived after it was all over. It was just the discontent that I heard."

"So tell me about the manifesto, the background of it."

"I brought a copy for Cedars to read when I came back the last time. Bunch of words about freedom, a revolt against the ASL. As far as I can tell, it's just rabble-rousing. People get their rage out at meetings and then go back to their miserable lives the next day."

"Actually, I did read the manifesto at Cedars's place—written up in a paper journal, like the old days. Actually, I found it inspiring. What it says there is something I have been feeling for a while now; I just hadn't put it into words."

Cedars returned with an unhappy Hester. Alton marveled that he had been able to catch and lead her.

"Glad to see the two of you talking, talking about the manifesto and the ASL," Cedars said, entering the conversation.

"Well, too much talk. The bus with the guests will be here any minute now." Alton gave Cedars the pack harness to put on Hester and then left the two of them standing there. With a disgusted stamp to his walk, he went into the paddock to halter Drake and bring him back, the last horse to be readied for the ride.

When the minibus arrived, it discharged the five other guests for the day. First came a mom with two surly-looking teenage daughters who were mad about the lack of secure net connection for their wearables on the ride out to the ranch. Then came Sallye and Byron. They were in harmony again, holding hands. Leaving Hester partly harnessed and shaking her muscular neck in disgust, Cedars went out to greet the bus and bring the guests to the marshaling area. The readied horses were loosely tied to the fence there.

Alton approached, his cowboy hat low over his eyes in the slanting early-morning sun and a piece of straw protruding dramatically from his mouth. "Welcome, y'all. I am Alton, your cowhand for the day." He looked up and smiled, assuming a more natural voice. "Well, that is about as Texan as I get, and there are no cows up here these days." He spat the piece of straw onto the ground to the slightly amused smiles of the guests.

"So, we are going for a ride today." He looked up and settled his eyes on Byron. A flood of thoughts flew through his mind, and he felt a flutter in his gut. He pressed on with his rote comments. "It will be challenging as we climb up above the tree line to a high meadow. Should be especially beautiful riding up there today with the aspens turned. The sky always has a deeper blue in September. It will be chilly; I see you brought jackets."

Recognition of each other had overtaken the two brothers.

Sallye and Byron couldn't take their eyes off the young man in front of them. For Byron, it was like looking in the mirror and seeing an older self looking back. For Sallye, it was pure attraction.

Alton waved Cedars back to Hester to finish the job. Cedars had already gone to the bus to retrieve the pack lunch the hotel had sent. Dags stood awkwardly off to the side.

"We are nearly all tacked up here. I have a few points of safety to cover." Alton launched into the well-rehearsed spiel, sprinkled with the warnings of bizarre and dreadful outcomes if anyone might be so bold as to break one of the commonsense rules of how to be around, and on, horses. By the time he was done, Hester was ready, and Cedars had brought the mounting block over beside Starsky. Alton motioned to the barn and the washroom there, reminding the group that once they were on the mountain, the meeting of bodily needs would have to be done roughly. The teen daughters looked disgusted but dutifully followed their mom to the facility in the barn. While they went, Alton finished tacking Drake and quickly checked in with Cedars.

As the guests returned, Alton went about matching guest to horse, tightening the cinch of each equine before helping each guest heave him- or herself up into the saddle.

When Alton got to Byron, he spoke softly, without the dramatic drawl or comic timing of the greeting. "So, little bro, I figured you would find me eventually. Didn't expect it today. We will talk later." What Alton said was bluntly matter-of-fact, deliberately avoidant of anything that would distract him from the business of the ride. Within, he felt a complex of emotions, too much to express or even acknowledge when there were cinches to tighten and stirrups to adjust.

Sallye overheard and smiled.

Sallye was filled with a rush of emotion too. This moment was the culmination of hopes that she had nurtured over the last week. The way it had occurred was beyond imagining, somehow natural, as though it was meant to be.

But there was another something happening for her as well, happening in these briefest of interactions. Alton, in his seemingly relaxed confidence, his ease with horse and human, and his way with words, was the Byron she had always hoped her Byron would be.

Dags was on Stamper, Cedars on Biddy, Byron and Sallye on Starsky and Hutch, and the mom and surly teens were on Star, Rocket, and Arch. Hester had the lunch following Biddy at the tail end of the line.

Alton, confidently riding his grandpa's horse, Drake, stopped the group at the far end of the cedar glen. He dismounted and walked back through the line. Grandpa had put an outhouse discreetly behind a blind of thick cedars. Even though it had been only an hour since they had all mounted, each rider was glad to get off his or her horse and wander in to use the rough facility in the aromatic woods.

Dags approached Byron. "So we meet again."

Byron suddenly recognized the man, recalling the decent family home and Zeke with the soccer ball in the hall. He realized that for the last hour or so, he had been so filled with thoughts and questions about Alton that he hadn't even noticed the man. "Hey, Mr. Basilis, yes we do. Awesome to see you again."

"Whatcha up to, way up here in Beckett?"

"On leave. I am not seeing Zeke this week, but he is in school back in Munroe."

"Actually, he's not. I have brought him with me for a father-son trip into the backcountry. He is not ready to rough it, though; he is back in the Vintage. I couldn't even get him to come horseback riding today."

"That's a shame. It would have been fun to have him along."

The two men looked at each other awkwardly.

"Yesterday, Sallye and I went white-water kayaking. Maybe he would go with you to do that. Hmm…it is cleaner than being on a horse or out here in the bush."

"I am a bit disappointed in him. I can't get him off his wearable. Hell if I know where he goes when he spends so much time on that thing."

"Did he bring his soccer ball with him? Maybe tomorrow he and I can find a pitch." Byron felt it was only polite to offer but didn't relish working on his holiday. He caught a glare from Sallye.

"No. That's OK. It's dad time for him. Poor kid. What teenage boy likes that, eh?" Byron couldn't help but think that for most of his life, he had yearned for relaxed and playful dad time. It just hadn't been there for him.

Byron and Sallye wandered off hand in hand, back to their horses. Alton was checking in with Dags about whether Stamper was behaving. Cedars had pulled some flasks of water from Hester's pack for those who wanted to wash their hands. He reassured the mom and the daughters that they would be back to the outhouse in the glen in a couple of hours, and if they didn't think they could hold it that long, there were places up in the meadow they could go. The daughters gave hostile looks to their mom. The younger one went back to her horse, patted its neck, and seemed to be enjoying the ride in spite of herself.

The uphill pull through the trees was uneventful. Every once in a while, when she could see around Byron in front of her, Sallye tried to catch a glance at Alton at the head of the line.

When they pulled out lunch up in the alpine meadow, Cedars didn't have the hospitality touch that Grandma did. Alton noticed and allowed him to bumble. Sallye also sensed the awkwardness and moved in helpfully. She arranged the blankets and gingham cloth and the sandwiches and fruit. She gave the bottle of wine to Cedars for him to open. Byron had found a place to sit by himself, staring out over the valley and lake that stretched below them. Alton was leaving him alone out there. He figured that his little brother would approach him when he was ready.

"Tell me about Alton," she said to Cedars.

"Well, I don't know that much. His grandparents run the horse-riding ranch, but I hear that last week his grandpa had a heart attack. Good man. They started this business years ago, as green as a spring fiddlehead when it came to horses, but they learned. I remember that when they came to Beckett, they were in a hurry to buy a place, desperate even. They had Alton with them right from the beginning; he was just a boy."

"How did they come to have him? Any idea?"

"Now I wouldn't know that. They are good people. Work hard, do what they need to do. Nope, don't know why they had the boy."

"So he grew up here, then."

"Yeah, there is a small school in Beckett. I remember seeing them in town, at Vy's for pie. I watched him grow. Decent kid. Not like a lot."

Sallye had been watching Alton as he and Dags were engaged in conversation. Their talk had an intense and confidential nature, that of businessmen. There were occasional pats of a right hand on the left upper arm of the other, the way that men encouraged one another. She found herself admiring Alton's physical form. It was obvious that he was more muscular than Byron and that he had a greater ease with his body. There was something sensuous about the way he walked, the way he would put his hand on his hip. She watched the way he could scan around him, taking everything in, making sure everything was all right, assessing the horses, and assessing the humans.

For a brief moment, Alton made eye contact with Sallye. A thrill went through her.

The peacefulness of the alpine meadow was pierced by a shout of anger and a moan. Sallye looked over at the mother and surly daughters. The older one was doing an obvious dance of agony. The mom rushed over to Sallye.

"Do you know where my daughter could go pee? She really has to go and is embarrassed—no, I would say mortified—at being exposed up here."

"I found a spot just over that rise. I will take her there."

"Thanks."

Sallye settled into a disposition true to her training as a Paraclete. She briefly went into her mind to draw on the deep well of calmness that she had created there through her meditation and yoga. She gently led the teen over the rise and demonstrated how to slip down her jeans and underwear off one of her feet, hold the clothing clear, and lean back against the rocks with her feet spread as widely as possible.

Coming back, Sallye suddenly felt older than her eighteen years. She felt more mature, more capable. Byron joined her, having been brought out of his distant staring with a questioning look on his face about what all the fuss was over.

Alton came over and said to Sallye, "Gee, thank you. I hadn't anticipated that and would clearly have been the wrong person to come to the aid of our guest in her distress."

"That's OK." Sallye tried to decode the look on his face. It was obviously respectful, obviously appreciative. Perhaps there was something more to it.

At the end of the day, as the bus was being loaded, Cedars came over to the trio of Byron, Sallye, and Alton standing in conversation.

Alton had told him about the unexpected gift of family connection that had occurred during the day.

"How about Dags and I ride the minibus back to Beckett? You three have lots to talk about and can bring my LandPorter back when you are ready to go into town."

Alton looked up appreciatively. "I would really like to visit Grandpa this afternoon. If we come back in an hour or so, I will do that and maybe grab a bite to eat at Vy's. Could you run me back out here to the ranch after supper?"

"Sure."

"And Cedars…" Alton paused, making eye contact. "Thanks."

Alton was going through the process of taking off the saddles and brushing down the horses. He went into the barn and brought a couple of brushes back for Byron and Sallye. They followed his lead.

"Grandpa?" Byron looked at Alton curiously.

Sallye piped up. "Yeah, Byron, I didn't tell you. When we were up in the meadow, Cedars told me that your grandpa had a heart attack and is now doing cardio rehab; he was just brought back to Beckett from Munroe today."

"My *grandpa*." Byron spoke as though there was a sense of further discovery in the words.

"Grandpa is a bit of a codger, but I think you will like him." Alton choked a bit as he broke into the conversation. "If you can love him as much as I do, you will be richer for it."

"There is so much we don't know about each other's lives," Byron said.

"Well, bro, we have a lifetime to fill each other in now that we have found each other." The brothers walked off together toward the back paddock, Alton leading two of the horses. Byron had his hands full with just one.

Sallye was amazed at how easily the two were relating. It was uncanny for her that they looked so much alike. It was confusing for her too that she was drawn so much to them both. She reflected on how it had been difficult between her and Byron the last few days. Maybe it could be better now.

And yet the bit of distance, the bit of disentanglement, that she had felt with Byron in their tension and conflict now felt like a relief to her. As she brushed Biddy out, taking care with the fine old mare, she felt confused. What she had felt with Alton today was definitely powerful within her: instantaneous, irresistible, disorienting. Never until this moment, standing beside this horse, had she ever doubted her love for Byron. She was starting to now. Sure, she had been mad at him at times, thought him an oblivious dolt. But she had always sensed that she would come back to a foundation of love and commitment. Now she wasn't so sure. What she felt with Alton was so intense and all-encompassing. She reflected on the physicality of seeing him up there on the lead horse, up there in the meadow. And she felt it in the intensity of his look when they talked.

Sallye wondered if her attraction to Byron was fading, losing its luster. Sexual pleasures had been playful and adventurous, but had they missed a depth for her? How could she even think that? They were intimates. A stark realization came over her just then. She was clearly attracted to Alton, and even though it was so quick and was so absolutely inappropriate, it was so much more powerful than anything she had ever felt with Byron.

(V)

By late morning, Zeke realized he was hungry. He had alternated nosing around using his wearable to get to places he should never be with trying to come up with some strategies for Linkages using code rather than the controller. In the afternoon, he would probably book the VR room at the Vintage to see whether the strategies worked. But now he was hungry.

When he arrived at the restaurant, he found it closed in the transition from the breakfast to the lunch menu. So frustrating. He took a seat in one of the too-soft sofas in the lobby. That's where he was startled to be discovered by CarolAnne.

"Well, this is weird. What are you doing here?" She seemed as shocked as he was by their chance encounter. Zeke and CarolAnne knew each other by sight at Munroe Technical and Arts Institute. Back there they would have avoided being seen with each other at any cost. Now here, sixty miles away, they found themselves in the same hotel lobby, both missing a school day.

"Playing hooky, I guess," Zeke lied. "Well, not really playing hooky. I was hauled up here by my father to spend a bit of father-son time. His agenda, not mine, for sure."

"Well, it looks like it's working," CarolAnne commented, noting that he was alone without a father in sight.

"Working for me, anyway, at the moment, as you can see." Zeke paused. "And you?"

"Pretty much the same. I was visiting with my dad over the weekend when he got some sort of Convergence Alert on one of his computers. He tried to send me back to Mom's place, but she was away on a Holiness and Wholesomeness retreat. I would have been happier to just hang around Munroe on my own, but he wouldn't hear of it, made me come up with him.

"This morning was a shit show. Apparently, something he needed to track on the computer wasn't coming through. So there is a network guy who is sort of creepy up at his room, trying to get him going. I got tired of hanging out in my room, so I decided to come down here, see if anything was happening."

CarolAnne surveyed the lobby. "I'm going back to Mom's place this evening; Dad arranged an AVoD for me."

"Lucky you."

"Want to know something? I actually wanted to come back to this place because when I was here before, I saw this really rad guy. Haven't been able to get him out of my mind. But that was in Beckett, and since I have come, I have had to spend all my time out here at this boring resort."

Zeke looked up, puzzled.

"Gawd, this is totally awkward," said CarolAnne.

"Yeah. Wanna have lunch? They are opening soon."

CarolAnne looked at him, contemplated the question, and then thought it too weird. "No, but thanks for the offer. So where is your dad, by the way?"

"Horseback riding. He tried and tried to get me to go with him. I resisted."

"Well, it's my turn to say lucky you. I went horseback riding with my dad a couple of weeks ago. Like, lame or what?"

"I made it clear: the only thing I do outside is soccer."

"The horseback riding was through 'Grandma and Grandpa Incorporated.' They had this little herd of horses. The only good part was that the horse my dad was on totally got the better of him. It was funny."

Zeke started to think that she was OK. He sure wished he could remember her name, though.

"Well, I gotta put in a day around here until I get to go home. Dad is completely surrounded by screens up in the room with the creepy guy. It's like I'm not there."

"We could hang out together. I have booked the VR room for the afternoon. Do you play Linkages?"

CarolAnne looked at him. A look of both relief and suspicion came over her, as though she was disoriented by having a boy be interested in her.

"Dad was going to take me to play tennis this afternoon. I pretend I still like it, like I am twelve years old or something. But it is one of the least awkward ways that we have time together."

"There are two men over there staring at us." Zeke directed her attention behind her.

CarolAnne turned. "That's my dad and Creepy Guy." Her look at them with a slight toss of the head set the two men in motion. They came over.

"CarolAnne, who is your friend?"

"Who is yours?" she retorted.

"Now, daughter, this is Mr. Ross. He is a network specialist. It just so happened that he was up here in Beckett when I needed him."

"Charles, call me Charles." CarolAnne was immediately drawn to his brazen coloring and style of clothing and hair. Weird, definitely, but intriguing and suddenly less creepy than he was up in their rooms.

"And you?" Perkins had directed his attention back to his daughter's companion.

"Zeke, Zeke Basilis."

Perkins startled. He looked oddly at Zeke, as though he was trying to place him.

"Ah, Zeke. I have been looking for you, and here you are right in front of my horrendously big nose!" Charles boomed.

"Looking for me?" asked Zeke.

"Yes!" Then Charles said, "Hmm, let's let the reason be our little secret."

"So, Dad…Dad, are you with us?" CarolAnne had caught her father still looking strangely at Zeke. It must have been the tenth thing that had creeped her out in the last two minutes. "Tennis?"

"Yes, CarolAnne, tennis. Yes, I remember. Ross and I are done upstairs. I will have to check on the data stream up in the room from time to time, but we can play tennis now."

CarolAnne left with a disgusted look on her face, as though humans somehow became stupid after they had kids. She pushed her dad in front of her, and they left the lobby.

"You said you were looking for me," Zeke said to Charles.

"OK, son, yes." Charles Ross assumed a soft, confidential sort of tone. "I am a network specialist, IT guy. I keep track of things like intruder alerts and hacks."

"Oh." Gut check for Zeke.

"I have had the IP address of your wearable on my system for quite a while now. Tracked where you were and what you were up to. As we walked over, it alerted me and flagged you."

"Look, I didn't mean any harm. I was just fooling around."

"Like I would ever let you do any harm. Come on, man, give me some credit. Of course I knew what you were up to; I let it all happen. You know..." Here, Charles started into an eyebrow-raising, voice-inflected, body-in-motion report. "You know, I would scratch my head, would say, 'What is that little bugger up to now?' and 'How does he know to do that?' And then I just got to the point where I was saying, 'Go, boy. I will let you in there for now and block you tomorrow.'"

"I kept getting blocked, but I always found a way around the blocks."

"You did. You see, you and I have been playing a game for weeks, months even. And now we meet."

"You aren't mad?"

"Mad? Never. You see, when you try out a way of bypassing security, and I figure out how you did it and what your coding is telling me about your strategy, it helps me to keep others out. So I try different ways of blocking you, and I watch how you get around those. There are all sorts of other attempts I am able to thwart because of what you are teaching me. I know with you it is innocent, just a game we are playing."

"My dad would kill me if he knew what I was doing."

"Now, now. No talk of killing," Charles chided.

"You won't tell him?"

"No."

"Or that other guy?"

"Dr. Perkins? Hmm." Charles drew out the "hmm" really long, smiled three different smiles until he had caught Zeke's attention, and then said, "Boss man Perkins? Nah. This is our little secret."

"I was bored. That's why I did it. I didn't mean any harm."

"No reason to explain, son. I know all about solving the boredom problem with a little bit of digital sabotage."

Charles's animation captured the boy. *Finally*, Zeke thought, *a grown-up who understands*.

"I have a proposal for you. How about you and I grab a beefy burger—you know, one of those plant-protein, flavor-enhanced, grilled-to-perfection concoctions of pure fakery—and then you head into Beckett with me?"

Charles pulled out a digital card. "I have the access card and code to get into the servers there, the ones that hook into the ASL system. There is a little workstation that you might find intriguing."

"Yeah!" Zeke said.

Later that evening—after Charles had made sure that Zeke was back at the Vintage before his dad would be back from horseback riding, after Dr. Alastair Perkins had put in an awkward early dinner with CarolAnne in the dining room, and after the air had cooled and the sun had started its slant toward the horizon—CarolAnne stood outside of Vy's waiting for the linked AVoDs to arrive.

She was only about an hour from the righteous lecturing and mournful guilt-tripping of her mom.

Her dad went inside. "Just looking around," he said. Well, so was she. Finally, she had a chance to look for rad guy.

A LandPorter pulled up, and out he stepped, just inches away from where he'd stood in the summer. Incredible.

Then another guy and a girl and an "Oh my God, it's Sallye!"

CarolAnne watched as the three young adults held one another in conversation just a few feet away from where she stood waiting for her ride. To CarolAnne's horror, the rad guy had eyes only for Sallye.

It was as though she, CarolAnne, standing just a few feet away, didn't exist at all. And her Sallye, the kind, sensitive, "Let's be friends and I will take care of you" Sallye, had eyes only for him.

(VI)

Alton had messaged his grandma to meet him for supper at Vy's and called to reserve one of the booths with a round table. He asked Byron and Sallye to let him meet with Laurel first so he could prepare her. They would give him about fifteen minutes after she arrived before they came down to the Eatery from their room upstairs.

When Laurel arrived, she was exhausted. Alton could see the strain on her face from coping with Justin's medical crisis.

"How is he?"

"Not good. The doctors say the surgical procedure on his heart was a success and that he should be getting more strength soon."

"That's good."

"But mentally, he's not so good. He still has spells of confusion, and emotionally, he is depressed."

"Can they treat that?"

"There was a neurological assessment done down in Munroe. They said that both the confusion and the…what did they call it?… the functional deficits in emotional regulation were normal. It is a matter of wait and see. It might clear in a couple of days, might take months."

"When can I go to see him?"

"Tomorrow. When I left him, he was pretty tired from the transfer."

"And how are you doing?"

"I haven't slept for three days, just quick little naps in the hospital. It will be good to get home to sleep in my own bed tonight. I didn't see our LandPorter. How did you get in?"

"Actually, I drove Cedars's LandPorter in after the ride today. He is going to give us a ride home after dinner."

"OK." Laurel's voice was weak, almost as though she couldn't follow the conversation.

"Just the way things worked out today," Alton said.

"Oh, he would have helped you with a ride. Did it go OK?" Laurel made the effort to get connected again.

"Yeah, Grandma, I—"

"I gotta thank him. I don't know what we would have done if he hadn't been able to help you."

"Grandma, I have something to tell you."

"Oh, Alton, can it wait? I just want to get something to eat and go home. I don't need anything that I have to think about tonight. Where is the server?"

The server was nowhere in sight, but Byron and Sallye were. They descended the staircase into the lobby from their room. Seeing Alton seated in the restaurant, they both smiled and waved. Quickly, they approached the table.

Byron was the first to arrive and said "Alton" in an expectant tone, as though begging to be introduced. Then he glanced at the older woman, a person from the fringes of his memory.

"Grandma, this is Byron," Alton said. There was no response from the woman. "It's Byron, my brother, your grandson."

Laurel looked perplexed. Then her face clouded; she turned away.

"Grandma," Byron said. He had started the word with enthusiasm, having envisioned this moment as a reunion, perhaps with a long-overdue embrace. His tone quickly shifted, though. He ended the word with sadness as he noticed she was crying.

They stood awkwardly for a few moments. Alton shuffled to make room for Byron and Sallye to sit down. Laurel sat oblivious to the effort, still in the center of the semicircular bench. Sallye skirted around to sit beside her, while Byron took his place beside his brother. Sallye reached out to touch the arm of the woman and felt a wave of anxiety, confusion, and despair pass from Laurel into her.

They all sat silently, waiting for Laurel to regain some composure.

Before coming down to the Eatery, Sallye and Byron had gone over a list of questions that Byron wanted to ask. When they had talked out at the ranch, Alton had not been much help about why he had been taken by his grandparents; he couldn't even be sure of his age when it happened. As the two brothers tried to piece together what had happened in the family, Byron indicated that his mother, Lisbeth, had also been reluctant to answer the questions he had asked. Byron saw the reunion with his grandmother as an opportunity to find out. Alton was not so sure they ever would.

"So, you just show up." Laurel had come out of her tears and spoken. Anger tinged her words, as though she were saying "How dare you!" under her breath.

"Yes, Grandma, they just showed up. They came out on the ride today."

"Well, I am not ready to deal with this. Least of all today." Laurel propelled herself toward the edge of the bench, suddenly aware that Sallye was sitting there.

"Who are you?"

"I am Sallye. Byron's friend."

"Well, Sallye, you are in my way."

"Wait, just wait." Sallye prepared to ease out of the booth so that Laurel could leave. When Laurel did, Sallye followed.

"That didn't go well," Byron stated.

"She had a bad day with Grandpa. She is exhausted. She is not usually like that. She was so good to me as I grew up with them. I could always talk to her."

"I feel as though I really blew it."

"What did you do? All you said was 'Grandma.' I was the one who set this up."

"I'm sorry, Alton. This seems like such a bad idea."

"Brother, be easy. We can see our way through this. Let's give Grandma a chance to get her head around it. Obviously, there is quite a story hiding back there in the past. I wish I knew more of what it was. Whenever I asked about it, all she would say was, 'Later, when you are older,' or 'Don't bother yourself with that, Alton.' I guess I gave up trying. And now you appear, and I realize that it would be good for me to know."

"Mom would never tell me either. I think she really hated my grandparents, but in her own discreet way would never say it out loud. It was a taboo subject."

"What about your dad?" Alton paused and then realized that he was talking about his own dad too.

"Yeah, what about Dad? I am just finding out. Even though I lived my life with him, he was like this shadow that fixed things and figured things and gave me off-the-shelf advice and then retreated into never-never land. Back before that, he used to go into rages."

"I am sorry to hear. Sounds awful." Alton looked sympathetic. For a moment, Byron took it to be the practiced empathy that he had been taught as a Paraclete, now applied back to him. Somehow, though, with Alton, it came across as real, a genuine opening of the heart rather than an expected maneuver.

The server came to the table, carrying a specialty coffee that she put down at the place where Laurel had sat. Alton looked up and quickly ordered for the group of them.

And within a few moments, Sallye and Laurel had returned to the table, Sallye leading the way. Laurel sat and immediately wrapped her hands around the hot, sweet beverage, drawing it to her lips.

"So, I guess this is mine to deal with," she started. "Byron, I am your grandmother. Your grandfather and I have raised your brother, Alton, since he was seven years old. The last time we saw you, you were three years old, a happy little tyke running around that commune.

"We feared what that program would do to a grandson we had come to know and love." She looked over at Alton, fondness in her eyes. He could see her vitality coming back as she told the story. Then she turned back to Byron.

"We had to rescue him, get him out of there. Sure, our son, Craig, declared that the special training and schooling that Alton was being given was so that he could be a valued member of society when he grew up, a part of a new vocation that would do good. We could see that the vocation, if that is what you would call it, was destroying our own son. We couldn't abide that it would destroy a grandson too.

"And Byron, it was always our intention to come back for you too. But in those first years, the ASL kept hounding our friends and community connections about where we were. We knew they were aiming to take Alton back, away from us. Even when we were up in Beckett and making a life as a family there, they still hounded. We knew that if we went and tried to take you out of there, they would take Alton.

"I am so sorry." Laurel looked at Byron. Byron caught the same sort of authentic caring from her that he had from his brother a few minutes earlier.

"But I need to say that you were never forgotten. Every year on your birthday, Byron, your grandpa and I have a special, secret ceremony of remembrance. After you, Alton, were either in bed or off to school, we would have a little ceremony of remembering our other grandson. For a while, we kept pictures on our wearables, and then when the ASL networking took away the privacy of everything we had on our wearables, we deleted them.

"We did all that, Alton, without you knowing. We were worried that if you saw the pictures, you would remember your brother."

"Grandma, I never stopped remembering I had a brother and worrying about where he was."

At that point, platters of food arrived at the table. Empty plates were passed around along with serving spoons placed in family-style bowls of food. The four of them started to dig in.

"So, Grandma, what was so wrong about the life Alton would have lived down there at the communal home?" Byron asked.

"We saw what it did to your father. We knew that he was too sensitive to the nature of the work that he had chosen to do. It was his choice to go into it, and at the beginning, we encouraged him. But we knew that he was going into depression from what was expected of him.

"You see, it runs in the family. Justin's dad committed suicide. Justin was on antidepressant medications for years until the ASL took all of those away to do their new treatments for depression. Now Justin is in the hospital, and it looks like he has it again. There are no drugs for it now, not that I thought the old drugs helped that much anyway.

"So with a great-grandfather, a grandfather, and a father all with it, we saw that Alton was the next in line if he went into the type of work he was apparently destined to do. We couldn't see that happen. We snatched him. My mom suggested we go somewhere where there were horses, and we ended up on a sheep ranch in Beckett that we turned into the riding ranch we have now.

"Justin has been better being here. The fresh air. The horses. We knew nothing when we came here, but Justin put his heart and soul into becoming a horse person. We have been able to turn it into a living."

Sallye was tracking all this, eating the lamb stew and mashed potatoes while listening, sensing the flow of emotion in Laurel. She had noted its passage from exhaustion to detached recounting of facts to pride.

"Can you forgive me, Byron, for not coming for you?"

"Yes, Grandma. And while I know that you are suspicious of what we do, I do feel good in my vocation as a Paraclete."

Laurel acted as though she hadn't heard. She turned to Alton. "Can you forgive me, Alton, for having deprived you of growing up with your little brother?"

"Yes, Grandma. I know you did what you did because you thought it best."

Sallye interjected. "You have spoken for both you and their grandfather. What about him—Justin, is it? This will be a shock to him."

"Yes, and I'm not sure how he will take it." Laurel had piled into the food as though there had been a blockage in her throat for years that was now suddenly cleared; she was hungry and could eat. She chewed, swallowed, and continued.

"I don't know whether he has the fight in him to make a comeback. Watching him over the last few days, I truly worry that he will die, even though the surgery has been declared a success. It was even worse today, coming to Beckett but going to the AuxCare rather than to the ranch. And if that dying is what will happen, I don't think I can keep him from the chance to see his other grandson.

"You see, pretty nearly every day for the last fifteen years, he has said to me, 'I wonder how that little tyke is doing,' or 'The little fella would really like this,' or 'I wish he could be here for his birthday just once.' Byron, as much as Justin loved Alton and did everything he could to be a good father, I think he loved you just as much."

There was a pause in her words as emotion built up within her. "So much that I thought it would eventually kill him.

"When he had the heart attack, all I could think of was that his heart was broken and had been for a long time."

"Why didn't you just go back to Munroe?" Sallye asked.

"We were initially afraid of the ASL. We made a couple of quiet little trips to the commune to see our son. Each time we went, he raged at us; he was vile, bitter. Told us to get out, to stop coming."

Byron was flooded with the feelings he held in the pit of his stomach from his father raging at him.

"Finally, we just gave up."

The group finished their meal. Plans were made that Laurel would talk with Justin at the cardio rehab the next day and try to set up a time for Byron to go in to see his grandfather. Cedars arrived to take Alton and Laurel back to the ranch. Byron and Sallye ascended the staircase to return to their room.

For a long while, Byron sat on the edge of the bed, crying. Sallye sat silently behind him, her hand on his shoulder.

(VII)

The next morning, the Convergence Alert was triggered again on Alastair Perkins's screens. Checking out the GPS data, he discovered that the two flags showed the convergence was right in the Vintage. The Convergees were Dags Basilis and Cedars Smithson. Perkins had come to Beckett because of his monitoring of these two individuals. When he'd noted that Dags Basilis was destined for Beckett, he had decided to make the trip himself. Data streams were his eyes and ears in many places, but for a true understanding of human connection, human eyes and ears were best.

With the tweaking that Charles Ross had done to his system the previous day, Perkins had first noted the Convergence in Beckett last evening. Perkins had been aware through the IPE-CKS that Basilis was staying at the Vintage, but this was the first time that he was aware of Cedars being there too. The Convergence system was also outputting intensified connection between Cedars and the eastern territories, territories in which insurgencies and civil unrest threatened the good work of the ASL. The specific vectors of that connection were still unclear. All Perkins knew was that if the eastern discontent was going to enter his ASL territory, it might very well be through Beckett. Dags's connection to Beckett could then take it down to Munroe.

He decided to head down to the restaurant and see what he could observe visually. But Alastair Perkins was obviously not very good at the physical observation process. When he tried to surreptitiously sneak in across the room from where the two men were seated, Cedars's eyes immediately went to him. Confidential words were spoken between the two Convergees, and they left the restaurant as quickly as they could.

As the morning progressed, Perkins became increasingly restless. He would check the screens, try to catch up on some of the work he would normally engage in on a Wednesday back at the academy, and then pace awhile. He went to the concierge to cancel the tennis court he had booked for a game with CarolAnne. She was gone. He wasn't missing her; he was just frustrated that what he had mapped out for the day had gone out the window.

Perkins found himself thinking of Zeke, the boy he had seen the day before with his daughter. He had found the two of them together yesterday at this time in the lobby outside the restaurant. He decided he would check again today to see whether the boy was there alone.

And there Zeke sat.

"Zeke," he called.

"Hello, CarolAnne's dad. Did she go?"

"Yes, last night by AVoD."

"Too bad."

"Zeke, you are good with computers, right?"

"Yeah, I guess." It was a modest response.

"Could I have you do a project for me?"

"Why would I want to do a project for you?"

"Well, you seemed to like CarolAnne. She's over at my place sometimes; you could come over."

"Yeah, right."

Zeke had been staring at the projection above his wearable and one-handed typing with his right hand onto his left forearm.

"It would be a secret sort of project. Just between you and me."

The statement intrigued Zeke. He liked doing things in secret. He also knew CarolAnne's dad was some sort of big guy down in Munroe. Zeke had already made a connection to Charles Ross and got to see the ASL workstation. Maybe this trip with his dad was not so bad after all.

"So what sort of project?"

"I want the ability to communicate digitally with a certain person through the ASL network and to do so without the ASL monitoring system detecting that I am. It might mean going to some dark places on the WarpWeb."

Zeke immediately thought he liked the sound of that challenge. Possible ways came to mind. He figured it would probably be easy but didn't want to let on that it was so. He said, "Tricky—that system logs everything. Maybe. Tough, though."

"Can you do it?"

"I can try."

Suddenly, Dags Basilis loomed over them. The air around Zeke went chill. He closed the projection system of his wearable and left with his dad without another word. The stare that Dags gave to Perkins was wilting.

(VIII)

Byron and Sallye sat in the waiting room at the AuxCare. A few minutes earlier, Laurel and Alton had gone in to see Justin. If they felt he could handle the meeting, they would bring Byron in.

Several times during the night, Sallye had awoken to find Byron sitting by the window in their room on the third floor of Vy's. Sickly orange light from the sodium-vapor street lamp blanketed him. When Sallye went to sit beside him, Byron would launch into a memory from the past. Often it was about his father, the rages that turned physically injurious, the blank stare when Byron would run to him. There was one memory, just a snapshot really, of being at the beach with an older boy, an older boy Byron could now identify as being his big brother. Byron had spoken of these memories to Sallye without turning to look at her. She sat close enough that her body radiated warmth to his. When she tried to touch him in a comforting way, he recoiled.

Morning had broken with a look of relief on his face. He had gotten little sleep, but he was thinking more clearly. The emotions of his discoveries no longer hijacked his mind. From a place of disciplined intention, he forced himself to communicate how he felt and what he thought to Sallye. She respectfully gave him the space to do so without pressing him.

Now they sat—comfortable with each other, not speaking.

Sallye thought about the last day and found herself drawn to memories of Alton. The impression she'd had from the ride was reinforced this morning when she saw him again: he was confident in a way that didn't impose. Over and over, she thought of how much the two brothers looked alike and how their personalities differed. She had once described Byron as floating on the surface of things, whereas she went deeper. And then came Alton, someone who rose above.

"Byron." Laurel had come back to retrieve her other grandson. "I can go in?"

"Yes. When we told him that you were here, he showed the first sign of life that I have seen in him in four days."

"Can I come too?" Sallye asked, rising to stand with the woman.

"Just stand off to the side. I think that Justin will want to be with his two grandsons; he probably won't even notice you."

Sallye walked behind Byron and Laurel as they walked down the hall. Ambivalence toward Laurel reverberated within her. On one hand, she felt respect for the woman, could see her practical sense and ability to take charge. On the other hand, she was angry; this woman had intervened to divide two brothers, to steal one away and leave the other in what she had felt at the time was jeopardy.

When Byron entered the room, Alton was at Justin's bedside, holding his grandpa's hand.

But it was Justin who spoke. "So, little tyke, you have come for your birthday, have you?"

Byron's tears came again. Sallye came up behind him, snaking her hand into his. He didn't recoil.

Justin tired within a few minutes. It was awkward for the four visitors standing in the small hospital room. Dozens of questions formed in the minds of the disparate generations; they formed, went unasked, and then dissipated. When they left, it was with a shared intention of spending more time together soon.

As they emerged from the AuxCare, the foursome began the walk down to the pier and the lakeside shops. The sidewalk was only wide enough for pairs, and by some quirk, it was Sallye and Alton out in front, Byron and Laurel behind.

"Tell me about my dad," Byron said.

"Craig." Laurel made a humming sound through her nose and then began in a measured sort of way. "Your father grew to be a fine young man when he lived with us. When your grandfather went through his depression, Craig really stepped up, stepped up in practical ways. I would watch him and wonder when he had learned to do all he did. I think he had been watching his father, copying every move, learning how to do every practical task. If something broke, he would find a way to fix it. Back then, he would search the web for repair instructions. I would come home to find his toolbox out and something in the process of being put back together. And it always worked better after he had worked on it."

"Yeah, back at the family communal home, Dad does all the repairs, not only for our home but for many others." Byron paused; this wasn't what he needed to know. "Grandma, why did Dad go into the trade of Paraclete? It sounds like he wasn't really a people sort of person."

"Growing up with a father who was depressed, your dad developed a sensitivity for people who were suffering. And it was clear that he could do whatever he put his mind to, including that. When he met Lisbeth, and they were really smitten with each other, he just flowed into doing what she did."

"Back then, they weren't raised for it like Sallye and I have been."

"You bet. Back when your father was choosing what he would be, he could pick anything he wanted. He chose psychology because of his concern for the suffering of others. When he went to college and met Lisbeth, he eagerly applied for jobs that involved caring for others."

Laurel slowed, reached out to Byron's arm, and pulled him back a step or two. "He always had a kind heart, too kind, maybe. Does he still?"

Byron struggled to answer. Clearly, he wanted to reassure his father's mother, to tell her that her son had turned out well. Yet "kind heart" would never be the description he would give of his father.

"You don't answer. And I guess that says a lot," Laurel commented. They walked along farther in silence.

"I saw Justin's depression in Craig after you were born. He seemed to cope OK with Alton, but then with the burden of the work he was doing on the job, with the research demands from the ASL, and with two active boys in the home, we saw that he couldn't cope."

Byron was left thinking that somehow it was his fault his dad broke down.

"Damn ASL." Laurel's words formed a conclusion.

Byron was disoriented by the force of her words. He remembered the feeling that he'd had in his last AVT session, that the avatar was a means of social control, an agent of the ASL. He had seen it as a game back then, that he could use the AVT to create a false impression for the system of his thoughts about the system. But back then he wouldn't have said "Damn ASL" as definitively as his grandmother just had. He had been suspicious but not enraged. The ASL was ordering his life, providing his financial security, monitoring his every step. He couldn't damn it, could he?

"Look at them." Laurel drew Byron's attention to the pair walking in front of them.

Sallye had that flow to her hips and swinging of the arms that was characteristic of her at her most carefree. Byron watched as Alton turned toward her, his profile much like Byron's own but somehow more handsome. They shared spontaneous laughter. Byron was caught between the feeling of attraction that he had toward his intimate and a question pummeling into the forefront of his mind: *What the hell is going on?*

At the pier, they got lamb kebabs from a street vendor with a grill. Most of the shops were empty, as it was midweek in shoulder season. The sun was not quite as warm as it skimmed the top of the mountain range to the southwest. The breeze off the water was a bit too cool.

Byron moved himself in beside Sallye when they sat at the picnic-style table to eat the chunks of spiced meat that had been wound into the soft naan. His sitting there didn't make much difference, though, because Alton had positioned himself across the table from her. The axis of the conversation was between the two of them.

Byron felt an intense desire to have the same free and curious discussion with his brother that Sallye was having. Byron also felt a desire to have the same intimate dance of verbal play with Sallye that she was having with Alton.

For a moment, he had a sense of being on the outside looking in. In that moment, he felt what he perceived his dad had been feeling as he tried to belong in the family communal home of Byron's childhood.

(IX)

On the following day, Laurel stayed back to work the ride with Alton. There was something about being back on Biddy, something settling. Sallye and Byron went through their same cycle of discontent with each other and then an effort to repair their increasingly fraying relationship. The concierge had pointed them in the direction of the bike rentals, and they made the ride up to the hot springs. It was a long, uphill ride there. Then came a deep soak in the mineralized water. While the ride back was all downhill and didn't require nearly the effort made to get there, Sallye could barely get herself onto the bike to make the ride back.

Over dinner that night, Byron finally spoke to Sallye, expressing the discontent and disengagement that he had felt the night before.

"Sallye, this seems awkward to say, and I don't want to be hurtful, but it seems to me that you are more attracted to Alton than you are to me."

Sallye sat speechless, her soup spoon halfway between her bowl and her mouth. As she inhaled to respond, Byron broke in with a second statement.

"And I can understand why. In the few days that we have known him, I have come to love him too."

Sallye put the spoon back into the bowl. She reached across the table with her left hand, clasping it to Byron's right. She could not disagree.

They sat silently and sadly through the rest of the meal.

Friday morning dawned clear and bright. When Byron got up, he said to Sallye that he wanted to spend the day with Alton. Alone. She wondered where that left her and said so to him. He said that she would have to figure it out, but Alton was his brother, and Byron figured they needed brother time. Sallye told him that she could give them that.

Watching Byron prepare to leave the room, she noticed a vial that he'd put into his pack.

"What is this?" Sallye picked it up, unscrewed the lid, and saw that it contained peyote buttons.

"That is for today. Last night, you walked back from the pier with Grandma, and I walked back with Alton. I told Alton about my experience with the psilocybin down in Munroe. He said that he had been sheltered all his life but had heard about hallucinogens when he was in the east. He was interested. I had brought peyote for this week thinking that I might trip again, try something different, with you as my guide. But with finding Alton and my grandparents, there didn't seem to be the time. So maybe today."

"No, Byron. Don't. You can't. Where did you get them anyhow?"

"From the lab down in Munroe."

"How did you ever…?" A sudden fury came over her. She knew that Byron had wanted to trip again, but she never thought that he would steal to make it happen.

"You probably don't want to know."

"You are right; I don't want to know. And what I know now, seeing you with them, I want to unknow if I only could. Byron, how could you?"

"I know that I have been different since I tripped the first time. I say things, blunt things that come out wrong. And I know that has been hard on you, but I feel like since I tripped I've started to see the world differently. It has felt like I've seen the truth about the world—not the obligation I had to it, not the adaptation that I needed to make to it, but the truth about it." Byron paused. "And as tense as that has made things, it has been freeing."

Sallye was listening; she didn't like what she was hearing but was willing to hear him out.

"When I went into that last AVT, it became clear to me that I existed separately from the being that the ASL had made me into. I felt that I could be in dialogue with it and determine for myself what my lines would be.

"Everything that I have learned in the last couple of weeks about my family and my life seems like a carefully constructed prison of expectations and obligations. Every word I am to say, every movement I am to make, is to cover a lie about who I am and about the mess I came from.

"When I watched Alton, when I saw him with the horses and with my grandparents, I saw a person who wasn't living a lie."

Byron stopped, looked at Sallye, and saw her confusion, her compassion, and her outrage about what he apparently was planning for the day.

"So are you going to trip again today?" she asked. "Did you ever think that maybe I don't want to spend my day being your safe guide? And I thought you said you were going to spend the day with Alton."

"No, Sallye. I don't expect you to be my guide."

A realization thudded in Sallye. "You can't expect Alton to do that for you. You just met him; he doesn't know the protocol."

"I'm not, Sallye. He is going to be the one to trip. We talked about it yesterday."

Sallye suddenly felt violated. She had thought she loved Alton, that he was somehow a pure soul, unsullied. And now he had been brought into this tripping thing by Byron. It wasn't right. Alton wasn't the Alton she thought him to be. Byron wasn't the Byron she had thought he was.

"No, Byron. No. You don't have medical backup. You don't have the Reality Return pills. You are doing this without a safety net."

"Yes, you are right about the absence of a safety net. And yes, I will." Pausing, Byron sensed how refreshing that felt. He, not Sallye, was now the wild and crazy one.

Sallye left shortly after that. She packed her clothing hastily, called for an AVoD on her wearable, and headed back to Munroe.

Byron went back to the bike rental and picked up a bike. Backpack on, he rode the winding, hilly fifteen kilometers out to the ranch.

"Bro," Alton greeted him. He had saddled up Drake and Starsky. The two horses stared nervously at the bicycle that had come into the yard.

"We are riding?" Byron asked.

"Yes, I know where I want to do this. Not here. Grandma is around and will want to be with us. I told her you and I were going to ride today."

"This whole thing takes hours. You will be altered after that."

"Then we'd better get going."

They took the horses up to the alpine meadow much more quickly than was comfortable for Byron, it being only his second time riding. Starsky was attentive only to Drake in front of him and bore his rider like an inanimate load. Fear was in Byron, fear that something might happen, something beyond his control. It was luscious. He began to wonder whether there had been wisdom in what Sallye had said to him about how dangerous this might be. For some reason, that appealed to him. Impulsively, in the brief conversation he'd had with Alton on the previous day, he had pretended that the process of tripping was all positive, all safe. Now he felt the burden of responsibility. It struck him that he had to be a big brother to his big brother. And that felt good.

They arrived at the alpine meadow late morning. Alton had thought to bring several flasks of water, several apples, and some thick, seedy, generously buttered bread. Byron spotted a first-aid kit in the saddle bags and a blanket too. The provisions seemed sparse, but he would make them adequate.

Byron briefed Alton on what to expect. He led him through a quiet, neural-integrative meditation to prepare him mentally. Byron prepared the peyote buttons by cutting off the spines and sectioning the strips of the cactus's skin. Alton took the bitter flesh, chewed, and swallowed, washing it down with water from the flask.

They were sheltered at that time of the day in the meadow, and the autumn sun was warm. Before long, Alton had shed his clothes. Even though he stood before his brother totally naked, there was a profound sense of safety. At one point, Alton stood on the edge of a precipitous drop, and Byron wondered whether he was going to leap. Aware that his brother's life was in jeopardy, Byron sent out mental messages to him of holding and caring. He chose not to physically intervene for fear of startling and prompting treacherous reactivity.

Into the blazing sun, into the vibrant blue sky, into the winds of autumn that carried the scents of the cedar, spruce, and firs of the forest below, Alton spoke words of ecstasy.

The trip hit its peak, and Alton gradually became aware of Byron's presence with him. The words became less garbled and then tumbled out. "As I looked over the valley, I saw it was inhabited by souls. Pure souls. Not characters. Not roles and businesses. Not personalities. Souls. And I wanted to fly to them, to embrace each and every one of them. And I felt as though my feet could lift off these rocks.

"But Byron, I felt your presence behind me. Your presence has been behind me all my life, but it was especially behind me when I wanted to fly. And your presence said not to fly but to walk. And so, I planted my feet."

Alton became aware of his nakedness and awkwardly retrieved his clothing. Byron helped him to coordinate himself to dress. At one point in the process, Alton stepped back and looked at his brother. He saw no aura around Byron's body but the vast spiritual space inside of it. In that space, he perceived wounds and confusion and disillusionment. Inside Byron, he saw the figure of Sallye as though she were running, running away from Byron but toward him.

Byron pushed the flask of water toward Alton. He drank. It seemed to be an act of grace, a go-ahead to receive Sallye and drink her in deeply.

They sat silently for a long time. The sun was starting to drop toward the tops of the west mountains. Byron began to wonder whether they should soon start the ride down to the ranch. Gradually, Alton's mind cleared. He began to see the horses less as spiritual beings and more as the means of departure from the lofty space they had shared. The automatic motions of checking tack, helping Byron to mount Starsky, and uniting with Drake when he climbed onto his back—all of this grounded Alton again.

They descended from the alpine meadow.

6

THE DISTRICT

Factories and warehouses beside the rail line that ran through the valley were built early in the history of Munroe City. These were substantial buildings, three and four stories in height, laid out in a rigid pattern four blocks long and three blocks wide. Streets ran straight north and south. Avenues ran equally square to the east and west. The buildings were constructed of stone and brick. Thick, durable wooden floors were held up by thicker, more durable beams logged out from the valleys to the north.

These twelve blocks were known as the Working District. They brought prosperity to the city, which eventually led to Munroe City becoming the site of the university and government offices. The buildings of those august institutions were more pretentious and were located a suitable distance away from the factories and warehouses.

The economic engine of the Working District held sway for seventy-five years. Typewriters and telephones were produced there and then shipped by rail all across the country, along with belts, fasteners of many sorts, gauges for automobiles, and many other small products. Residential areas for the factory workers edged their way into the hillsides that ringed the city to the north and east. The lakefront to the west on the other side of the railway tracks housed downtown.

With the onset of irrigation to turn hills and valleys into orchards and vineyards, the industrialized sway of the Working District slipped into decline. Munroe became more agricultural than industrial. Many of those functional buildings were abandoned; factories were left for more modern facilities along the highways.

Gentrification took place as the buildings were moving past the first century of their lives, still strong but now mostly empty. Munroe City began to reclaim those twelve square blocks of brick and stone. Street fronts became storefronts. The wooden floors above, supported by the magnificent beams, gave character to lofts.

In the center of each of those twelve blocks of brick and stone were spaces open to the sky, some narrow, some spacious. Those spaces had been the grimy alleys and loading docks of the Working District. With gentrification, the bricks of these center spaces were scrubbed clean; the windows of wired glass were replaced with clearer panes. A set of interior courtyards created themselves. The Courtyard District was born.

Cafés opened in these quiet, contained spaces. Potted trees and flower boxes arrived. In the largest of these courtyards, actors performed Shakespeare in an open-air theater, a re-creation of the original Globe Theater, named as such. Artists took up residence in lofts. Writers drank coffee and then wine in the cafés through the afternoons and then wrote through the night.

One hundred and fifty years into the life of these once-functional, now-trendy buildings, an ambitious businessman met with a visionary engineer. A seasonal roof was created to enclose the streetscape of a three-block avenue. It was made of a glass-fabric hybrid, transparent enough to let the light in from the sky but double layered to hold in warmth from the buildings below.

It was placed in sections, forming a graceful arc from street level on the east perimeter of the Courtyard District to the fourth-floor roof level at its apex in the center and back to street level at the west end of the district. The avenue was blocked off to vehicles, becoming a pedestrian walkway. When the dark, cold winter dominated the rest of the city, lights and warmth characterized the streetscape under the roof. There was a place for musicians and a town crier's platform for inspired orators.

Two years later, with an improved design, another parallel three-block avenue was also enclosed. The third and fourth enclosures came the year after. The Courtyard District had become a vehicle-free commons, alive with clubs and restaurants. It became a center for music and the arts. It was covered in the late fall and winter and then open to the sky in the spring and summer. Many of the lofts were renovated into quaint hotels. Munroe City had transformed itself into a winter cultural destination in which vacationers could walk around in shirtsleeves and light jackets.

A series of festivals was created. The seasonal roofs were installed the third week of October each year with beer gardens below. The end of October hosted the Macabre Festival, with patrons festooned in masks and costumes. Christmas lights sparkled in November and December. February was declared Lovers' Month, and an Irish Festival was held in March. The second week of April saw the roofs dismantled. LandPorters brought thousands of potted tulips to adorn the streets and courtyards for the first open-air festival of the season.

The likes of Byron and Sallye, and indeed most of the residential population of Munroe City, left the Courtyard District to those made rich in government and the university, to the wealthy who were ghettoized in the Enclave when the ASL took over the economic reins, and to the tourists who brought a new source of wealth to Munroe City. Locals would come to enjoy the free music of the festivals and to walk the streets at Christmas. They would window-shop the storefronts laden with goods they couldn't afford. Then they would leave for the routine existence of their lives having used up their CashCards on cappuccinos and croissants.

Upon returning from Beckett, Charles Ross got in touch with Zeke, asking to meet after school in one of the music cafés of the Courtyard District. The sun couldn't reach the ground level, but solar panels installed on the roofs of the old buildings sent radiant heat into the café.

"Your school computer is connected to the ASL servers." Charles's eyes beamed, and the corners of his mouth turned up into a sly smile.

"Yeah."

"There are firewalls between the different server banks in case a teenage hacker violates one of the ASL functions."

"I know." Zeke was starting to look fascinated.

"And I can circumvent the firewalls."

Suddenly Zeke was very interested.

"So if you were to make yourself absent from class, say, tomorrow afternoon, I could…" Charles paused for effect. "We could make it look like you were there. No notification back to your parents."

Zeke beamed. Tomorrow afternoon was his English literature class.

"And once you have seen the route around the firewall, I am sure you could do it yourself." Charles became serious in a mocking sort of tone. "But I will be tracking your activities, remember. Not a word about this to anyone, especially not your friends, or you will end up being pressured to do this for everyone."

"For sure." Zeke adopted a mockingly serious face to match that of his older partner in cybercrime. "Can I ask you something?"

"Ask away, lil' buddy."

"If you can modify attendance records, can you also modify marks? I am a bit low on my English grade, and if I happen to miss class tomorrow, I will definitely need a boost."

A playful energy was developing between the flamboyant one and the adolescent. Zeke had initially been a bit freaked out by the man, with his bright colors and his overly enthusiastic manner, but he liked him now. Zeke thought of his father, how much he was all business. Even though his father had a store full of recreational equipment, Zeke thought that fun was about as far from his father as code was from literature. But Mr. Ross was different—funny and fun.

The music café Charles had chosen for them had a VR stage with an ASAG music system: any song, any genre. Charles entered the digital code to access his CashCard account and selected for the two of them. A transgender artist with a guitar and a small band started to sing provocative lyrics with a seductive beat and plenty of winks. It was not what Zeke would have chosen for the two of them, but he was settling into being with Mr. Ross. He wanted to ask for Korsot, a Scandinavian band that produced an intense sound with unpredictable rhythms and screamed vocals. It was what he listened to with his friends at the high school, even though he wasn't sure that any of them really liked it that much. He had decided long ago that he didn't like music; he just had to pretend that he did so he could get along with his friends.

It was different here, different with Mr. Ross—more sophisticated.

"Mr. Ross, why—"

"Charles. Call me Charles. Why...?"

"Why are you doing this for me?"

"Zeke, I have been in this city for two years now, spending most of my time in the basement at North Hill or fixing aging systems in the academy building for boring people.

"And then I see this hacker come along, and I trace back to his wearable and see that he is only fourteen years old, and I think, *Now that is interesting.* So I track this fourteen-year-old, and I see that he thinks in code and system interfaces.

"'Bizarro, this is what I have been missing,' I say to myself. So I figure he and I will play cat and mouse for a while, see what he is made of. And you, young Zeke, you rise to the top of my wildest expectations."

Zeke was watching the man, felt himself being drawn in.

"And then fate has us meet up in Beckett."

"Yeah." Zeke smiled.

(II)

Chetwin sat patiently in the Olde Bailey Restaurant awaiting Elise. He was eager to see her again, as he had not had a session with her in over a year. Elise had made a steady recovery under his care as an in-person therapist. She had refused AVT, demanding a real person rather than an avatar. The course of treatment lasted almost three years, starting with weekly sessions and gradually weaning to less frequent ones. He remembered the trips to the gated Enclave on the opposite shore at the south end of the lake. She had sent Gerald in the Range Rover to fetch him even though he had offered to take an AVoD for the trip. He came to look forward to the luxurious drive with an intelligent and sensitive client at the other end.

The Enclave contained the remnant of the wealthy classes displaced at the time that the ASL took over. The wealthy families still owned much of the land in Munroe and still taxed a profit off the businesses. With the political upheaval of 2043, they were disenfranchised from the corridors of power but were bought off with a series of negotiated deals. The Enclave became their gilded cage. The ASL, in its agreements, had pledged to service the needs of these wealthy families in exchange for being left alone to institute the social-logistic reforms that would replace capitalist structures.

Elise's depression had been deep. She suffered with the loss of freedom that living in the Enclave had wrought. She had been a society type, running charity events and volunteering with the poor. When the upheaval took place, the anger at the capitalists was so strong that her life would have been in danger if she were to have continued. Elise descended into the darkness as she retreated into the Enclave. For several years, she was treated with black-market antidepressants by a resourceful physician who still could get his hands on the drugs. Elise offended the neurologists by calling them modern lobotomists; they subsequently refused to treat her, calling her an infantile personality. An aging psychiatrist covertly saw her as a residual duty until he died. He was kindly and perceptive, but it became increasingly difficult for him to up one drug or cut back on another when the supply of the old medicines was dwindling. She was devastated at the psychiatrist's death. Elise's husband, Gerald, had approached the academy demanding a replacement. Dr. Myles Chetwin was the best that Perkins could offer.

Treating Elise had been a delight for Chetwin. In the initial stages of treatment, he went back and read the books by therapy innovators in the golden age of psychotherapy—Rogers, Bowen, Haley, Whittaker, Miller, Johnson, Shapiro, Yalom, and White and Epston. He read with a different eye than Perkins had in creating the AI of the avatars; he read not for manipulations and interventions but for the wisdom of how people heal, change, and grow. Even though Chetwin didn't follow any formalized path, much to the chagrin of Perkins, he found a precious and deep relationship forming with Elise, a relationship that had been urgent at first and then increasingly genuine as she got stronger.

Now, after being absent from his life for the last eighteen months, she had asked to see him again, asked that he come to meet her at Olde Bailey rather than in the palatial home overlooking the south end of the lake.

He hoped she was well.

He also entertained a fantasy that she was not, that she would require therapy again.

He felt ashamed upon recognizing that pesky rescuer persona that had compromised his relationships over the course of his life. He felt increasingly anxious as he awaited her arrival.

The Olde Bailey was one of the restaurants around the Globe courtyard. While the tables stretched back into the rustic building, the balcony formed a box from which patrons could watch the play that took place on the thrust stage below. Tonight's performance of *A Midsummer Night's Dream* was going to be the final one for the season. The courtyard was open above, and the late-September weather was unpredictable and cold as evening fell. From the table, Chetwin watched actors cavort on stage, hyped for the night's show. Around the theater space, various balcony boxes were being set up. Chairs had been taken out of the pit, and tonight's show would be open to those willing to be packed in and stand, like in the Globe Theatre of old. The air was electric.

Elise glided in. She was dressed elegantly but without formality. She looked healthy, and her faced beamed as she saw Chetwin.

"Myles! It is so good to see you. Thank you for coming."

"Elise." Chetwin spoke in a measured tone, not betraying his delight in the moment.

"We are here for the play tonight; we have booked rooms for the family. And that is what I want to talk with you about."

"As usual, Elise, you just launch in!"

"Is there any other way?" She smiled, their eyes met, and the old genuineness of their relationship was suddenly back.

"But first, tell me how you are."

"I am doing well. I am right off the sertraline now. I do yoga every day, and Gerald keeps finding leather-bound paper journals for me to write in, far from the prying eyes of the ASL data systems."

Elise paused, made eye contact, and said with warmth and relief, "I miss you."

"I am glad you are doing well."

"Life is empty out there in the Enclave. Gerald and I travel. Every once in a while, I get him to sign us up for a third-world humanitarian service trip. He hates it. I love the children, caring for their most basic needs. He grows impatient, and we come home."

"Is Gerald with you today? I would love to see him again."

"He is off meeting with someone to arrange the final details of a fishing trip up to Beckett. Gerald and John are going, leaving us womenfolk to fend for ourselves."

"You and Alyssa?" Chetwin had struggled to remember the name of the daughter in the family.

"Yes, Alyssa." Elise's voice fell off, and Chetwin could detect the anxiety in her.

"Alyssa is a problem right now."

"Now, she would be…"

"Fifteen. I suppose I was rebellious when I was fifteen, and I hope my parents forgave me, but jeez, I don't think I put them through what she is inflicting on me."

"Rebellious?"

"Like you wouldn't believe. Could you see her?"

"I am not sure I am the best to do so. I am old, and I was your therapist. I don't think it is wise for me to see another member of the family."

"Please," Elise entreated him.

Chetwin looked at her; the kindness in him just about consented. Then a thought took over. "There is a Paraclete who would be perfect for her. Delightful, eighteen years old. Caring. Her name is Sallye."

"Well, get her here, then. I hope she has some strength of will in her; she is going to need it."

Alyssa and Sallye happened to arrive at the Olde Bailey almost at the same moment. Chetwin had contacted Sallye to come urgently and had waited downstairs on the avenue outside to brief her. Elise had cajoled the teen down to the restaurant with pathetic entreaties.

Alyssa was dressed disrespectfully. Various body parts, usually hidden away modestly, were out in the open, on display. She hid her eyes behind long hair, and her mouth twitched from pout to revulsion. Upon seeing her, Sallye immediately was drawn to the display for its rebelliousness and self-expression. Sallye wished that she had dressed a little less professionally.

Alyssa sized up the situation, figured that Sallye was there for her, and pulled back her upper lip into a snarl.

"Hi, Alyssa. I am Sallye. I can tell you are not delighted to see me. I figure that if we put our heads together, we can find a way to make this OK for you."

Sallye wondered whether the teen would bolt or vomit. She saw the laddering of cuts up the girl's left inner arm.

"You figure, eh? Not." Alyssa threw out the word *not* as though it were a dagger.

At that moment, Gerald and Dags entered the Olde Bailey, searching for the table at which the other four were seated.

"Daddy, get me out of here!" Alyssa entreated.

"Daughter. Elise." Gerald spoke in the measured tones of a man who would always settle a situation. "I would like to introduce Dags Basilis. He is joining us for drinks. Dags is setting up a fishing trip for us. We'll leave tomorrow and go up north of Beckett to a remote lake. It's all very last-minute."

"Take me with you, Daddy. Get me away from her—and her." Alyssa spoke in a sarcastic, sweet voice, as though she were a young girl seeking an alternate parent when the other one had been mean.

"I am not sure that will be possible, honey." Gerald spoke back to his daughter with a tinge of the same sarcastically sweet voice.

Dags sat there confused by the situation. Gerald was looking at him. Finally, Dags spoke. "We are going into the backcountry on horseback. It might be a long and uncomfortable trip. I guess I could ask the person arranging the horses whether we could accommodate you."

"Horses. Yuck. Can't we get there in the Range Rover?"

Sallye spoke up, recognizing that Dags had been on the horseback ride with Alton and that they had spoken in the meadow about setting up trips just like this. Immediately, she figured that she could convince the girl.

"Alyssa, I was on those horses just a week or two ago. If you want to go, I would go with you. I am not sure how rough it would be for sleeping and eating out there, and I have never fished before, but maybe we could make it an adventure for us."

Alyssa turned to her mother. "Are you going?"

"No."

"Then I will do it."

Chetwin settled in as confidentially as he could with Elise at the table. Dags had contacted his outfitting store to accommodate Sallye and Alyssa in getting the two of them kitted up for the backcountry, and then he left with the two teens. Gerald looked smugly over the scene. The crisis was settled now.

(III)

The final outdoor festival of the season in the Courtyard District celebrated the harvest. Shopkeepers gave away local apples, imperfects that couldn't be exported. Cobs of local sweet corn boiled in steaming pots for pedestrians to indulge in for free. Businesses were decorated. Apple cider flowed.

Lisbeth and Craig walked hand in hand through the streets. They were somber; Lisbeth was still reeling from a confrontation Perkins had laid on her. Craig was ashamed.

Perkins had been apoplectic as he reported on the last AVT session Byron had had with Dr. Y. It was clear from the transcript that Lisbeth had talked, had broken the agreement of silence that Perkins had established with the family. The existence of an older brother was now known to Byron. With that knowledge, there was no telling what the young man might do. Perkins had no doubt about the determination that the pair of newly minted Paracletes would have in searching out this older brother. He only hoped that they would have equally strong loyalty to the ASL and their trade within it.

Stunned, Lisbeth and Craig now walked.

Finding a bench in the sun, a cup of warm cider in his hand, Craig was first to speak. "This is all my fault."

"No, it's not. I was the one who broke the silence."

"Had I not become depressed, had I not had the parents I had, none of this would have happened."

"Craig, those two things—your depression and your parents—are not things that you could have changed." Lisbeth held conflicting feelings. On one level, she was sensitive to the suffering of the man who had been her partner for over twenty years; on another level, she was tired of him, of his inability to function on an interpersonal level, of his withdrawal.

He looked at her. "That is little comfort. This whole horrible scenario, what happened to our son—that is on me."

"No. I was there too. I should have stopped them when it was clear they had come to snatch Alton away from us." She reached out and touched his hand.

"Lisbeth, I have a question for you."

"What?"

"Do you remember the whole story?"

"Of course."

"I don't. I know some of the bits of it but not the whole story."

"Sure you do. You were there."

"Lisbeth, I have had two brain surgeries, the second to fix the botch of the first. Now when I come to figure things out, especially people things, it's as though there are gaps. The best way I can say it is that, in my mind, there is no story to anything at all. All the rest of you, you have stories. I don't."

Lisbeth's mind spun. She had no idea that this deficit existed in Craig. He had never spoken of disabilities remaining from his neurological treatments. She went to contradict him, to tell him it wasn't so, and then held back.

Craig continued. "I get flashes of memories. Visual images, like I have the scene of my parents taking Alton away, down the walk of our communal family home. It's a snapshot. When that image comes to mind, I feel sick to my stomach. But for the life of me, I can't remember what happened before or after that."

Lisbeth sat attentively, sipping her cider.

"I remember another time, feeling like my head was exploding, and there was one of my boys there. Alton? Byron? I'm not sure. I see the scared look on his little face. Again, I can't remember the before or the after."

"Craig, I had no idea…"

"When you talked with Sallye, you must have told her the story. Can you tell the story to me?"

"Yes." Lisbeth felt a wave of connection to the man that she had not felt in many years. "But not all at once." She paused. "Today, this afternoon, let's just walk. I have a long story to tell you, but I have no idea where to begin. I promise I will. Give me time to figure out how."

They walked on through the Courtyard District. Lisbeth was processing what it must be like for Craig not to have stories in his mind. So much of who he was now made more sense. He had infinite patience for the repair of plumbing or a broken piece of furniture. It was as though he didn't care how the problem had come on, just that it needed to be fixed. She would rant about the carelessness of one of the children in having broken the chair and get caught up in that story. Craig would just fix it. Craig took delight in doing the bookkeeping on their financial accounts. It was just numbers; numbers added up. She could now see why he became furious when someone wanted to tell the story of why they forgot to record something. He couldn't grasp the story; he could focus only on what numbers were missing.

It hadn't been this way at the beginning of their relationship. It seemed to have started with the depression but worsened after the neurological treatment.

She wondered how it had been invisible to her all these years. She had gotten frustrated when she would come home after work and told the story of this or that to a partner who would look back with a blank stare. She had thought that his interest, his love for her, had declined. Maybe not. But what is love in an intimate relationship if it is not participation in the story of the relationship?

Then she wondered what would it be like to live out her life with a man who couldn't participate in the recall of the stories in their lives. She realized that it was inside of her own stories that she lived. She shuddered with the realization of it.

Craig walked on, hyperaware of everything around him. He watched the nuances on Lisbeth's face. She was puzzled and then she seemed to relax. What was going on in her mind? He wondered whether this was the end of them and then wondered what that meant. How could it be the end when he couldn't even think of a beginning or a middle? Would she leave him now that she knew?

An actor dressed in Elizabethan garb came up to them. "Tonight at seven, in the Globe. *A Midsummer Night's Dream* becomes a late-summer night's hilarity. No admission fee for standing in the pit!"

Craig looked at Lisbeth. "Do you want to go?"

"It's a play, Craig. Can you follow a play? It's a story."

"I can follow you; that's all that matters." It was the first moment of tenderness, of yearning, they had shared in years.

Walking across the tracks and through downtown, Lisbeth and Craig came to the park beside the water. It was late afternoon, and the sun streamed through the trees. Most of the leaves had turned; some had fallen. A carpet of decay was starting to form on the grass beneath them.

"I'm not sure where to begin, Craig. I think it would be best to just tell you the story. But if you can't think in terms of story, we will have to go over it to see how you can make it fit into your brain."

"OK. Will you do it with me?"

"After Byron was born, we were under a lot of pressure to supplement the AVT sessions that Perkins was running at the academy. He was writing a paper on his accomplishments and needed data from people who were getting healthier and happier as a result of his avatar therapy.

"He had thought that the data would come through IPE-CKS, that he would see objective changes in behavior and physiological readings there. That was going to be the proof of how powerful his program was. But it didn't happen.

"So Perkins decided that he would use us Paracletes to follow up and encouraged us to send back objective reports of improvements arising shortly after the AVT sessions.

"Our documentation demands increased. We had seminars on the wording that we were to use in doing documentation so that he could run qualitative statistical analyses on our reports.

"At the same time, we had a six-year-old Alton and a two-year-old Byron in our family communal home. Byron was a busy boy and needed to be watched constantly. All of the Paraclete parents were struggling under the load, and I watched as it got you more and more depressed."

"Hang on a second, Lisbeth." Craig broke in, stopping the flow so he could catch up. He used his problem-analysis skills to figure it out. "So what you are saying here is that I was overloaded with demands from two different directions. I can get that."

"And you started to shut down."

"Like an overloaded breaker box in the electrical system."

"Sort of, but not that quickly—more gradually. One thing I can remember you saying back then was that you didn't think that you could lie in the reports about clients you were documenting. But the pressure was great on all of us."

"From Perkins?"

"From Perkins."

"At that time, Alton had started homeschooling with other children from the two family communal homes. It was all on us to do it, to do that in addition to the demands of being Paracletes.

"You called your parents to come."

"I called them?" Craig asked incredulously.

"You called them."

"I must have been desperate."

"We all were."

"When they came, you broke down. You must have felt it was safe to do so, to cry in front of your mom. I still remember the look on your mom's face; it was like she was shocked, and yet she knew. Your dad just stood there.

"And without comment to us, they went to Alton's room, packed his little suitcase, and made sure they had all of his devices. When he came home from schooling at the other communal home, they told him that they were going to take him on a little holiday."

"So it wasn't a violent kidnapping?"

"No. It was quiet but hugely judgmental on their part. I was stunned, but in my exhaustion, I just let it happen."

"So they just walked out."

"They just walked out with our son. I was too beaten down; I didn't do anything to stop it. We haven't seen Alton since that day." Lisbeth began to cry. Craig watched, allowing the strong feelings to settle.

When she regained her composure, Lisbeth had Craig go over each step in the story, as he would do with the steps to figure out a complicated repair he needed to do. He could think in consequential steps, about the necessity of doing this before being able to do that. He applied that to the sequence of the story she told. It was an objective sort of recounting, but it had the semblance of a story. Craig was then able to draw conclusions about the realities involved in each step of the sequence. He was able to acknowledge the subjective feelings of tiredness or frustration that went along with each circumstance.

As he went over the sequence of events, more visual images came to mind. It was like a train for him; he could put different images on different cars of the train.

Lisbeth became aware of how hard he was trying. She could see he was analyzing it all, trying to fit it together like pieces in a jigsaw puzzle. She became aware that as he did so there was something missing, something deeply important to her that seemed to be elusive to Craig. For her, the story had meaning. For him, it was a puzzle.

"Will you tell me the story of my brain surgeries? I need to understand that too."

Lisbeth looked at him and felt the absence in him of what was so real inside of her. She also felt the courage of his trying. "Yes, I will, but on another day."

(IV)

Byron decided to walk from BirdSong to the family communal home. It was late afternoon, the air was cool, and his mind needed time to prepare for the meeting he would have there.

It had been almost a week since he had returned from Beckett. With his return came a burden of obligation to tell his parents that their oldest son had been found. When he was with Alton, he had asked whether Alton wanted their parents to know where he was. The question had been met with a puzzled look and then a softening and then an affirmation. Both brothers had seen it as a necessity.

Just before he had left on this walk, Sallye had videocalled him to let him know that she was going back to Beckett. She sounded excited, but the details of the hasty trip had not made much sense to him. Apparently, she had a new client, and a several-day horseback riding and fishing trip was to be an initial outing for them. That seemed to break all the rules of cautious and safe relationships that Paracletes were to establish with clients. Somehow it was assumed that Byron would trust her judgment. This one was difficult.

Byron and Sallye had done a lot of work together since their return to Munroe City. Sallye, in her full-of-integrity, transparent and open, sincere and compassionate way, told Byron of her powerful attraction to Alton. It had been hard to hear. They had always thought of their relationship as primary, anchoring, and inviolate. While they had recognized that from time to time they would be tempted by sexual attraction to another and would perhaps even fantasize a dalliance, ultimately they would be true to each other. Byron had had plenty of those attractions—he had thoroughly enjoyed them and let them go. Sallye wasn't letting hers go.

And yet the possibility of being trapped in a triangle of love, with its jealousies and heartaches, reverberated in his mind. All his life he had yearned for a brother who had existed only on the very edge of his awareness. Now he had him. More than anything, Byron yearned for the security of a relationship with Sallye. And he had that, or at least he thought he had. He would have welcomed his cherished intimate, Sallye, really liking his long-lost and now-found bro. Really liking. Not really loving.

But all that was to the side now. The task in front of him, speaking with his parents about Alton, loomed with fear and more than a little resentment. He was on speaking terms with his mom. They were polite and superficial when they encountered each other in the Paraclete First Flight training he had done. They both knew the safe topics they could engage in. They both knew the "never spokens" they were to avoid. Byron could accept his mother's concern for his well-being. It came with an apparent sadness in her and was barely elevated above the seemingly more spontaneous and genuine concern for him expressed by the other parents who had raised him in the family communal home.

Byron's ability to speak with his father was uncertain and untested. Always in the pit of his stomach, in the quickness of his eye movements, in the aching of his heart, Byron felt wary about any possible contact with his father. There were impossible memories of his father's rages—impossible because they were so far back in his childhood that they were more images and twinges than actual memories. They existed more in his body than in the mental theater of his mind. And yet they seized him whenever he was anywhere his father might also be.

In walking, Byron began to find himself increasingly agitated. It was an agitation that he didn't wish to take into the family communal home. His task there was going to be difficult enough. Disciplining himself, Byron called forward the protocol of a walking meditation he had learned in his First Flight training. They had been taught to utilize this invisible method of meditation when on a walk with clients, to self-calm if the energy of a relationship was chaotic. Byron began with a focus on the bottom of his feet: right, left, right again, and then exhale. He felt himself calm. The agitation attempted a return. He repeated the steps. His mind became clearer, more relaxed. He repeated them again. Byron's body settled into the gentle rhythm of the walk.

In Byron's meditative practice, he had learned to take note of intrusive thoughts, those irrelevant ones that passed through his mental space when he was focusing. Although the discipline of his meditation told him not to latch on and go down the rabbit hole with those thoughts, he had learned to tag them for later exploration with his conscious mind. Tagged elements from the walk through the park had been noted. He stopped at a bench overlooking the lake and made a conscious effort to return to them.

"Secure attachment" was the first tagged element. As Byron reflected, he remembered the more detailed statement: "An environment of secure attachment is achieved for this new generation of bred Paracletes through the use of family communal homes provided for their rearing." Byron had memorized that statement, which was emblazoned on a visual in the Paraclete professional documentation and often repeated word-for-word by Dr. Alastair Perkins during presentations. It came back to him in its entirety as though it were mocking his life. Ha! Secure attachment. He had one parent who gave him a gut ache and another with whom he could have only a careful civility.

And another tagged element: "Our bred Paracletes are produced through the blending of heritable components of temperament and potential social-neural-developmental integration so they will be highly adaptable to the vocation." It was yet another of the promotional statements emblazoned on the Paraclete literature.

Byron reflected on the genetic mental-health heritage that had accompanied him into the Paraclete breeding program: a great-grandfather who had committed suicide, a grandfather with a history of depression, and an empty but fearsome father. In his training and counseling, he had been told that DNA testing of his parents had revealed the specific alleles responsible for enhanced neural-interpersonal integration. Somehow Perkins had missed the obvious. Byron's paternal line was ripe with yet another inherited allele: the one for depression.

The web of control that Perkins had spun around his first generation of bred Paracletes was unquestionable. They had been raised together with a sense of entitlement and destiny. They had been homeschooled with care taken to select which aspects of broader society they would be exposed to. Their very steps were monitored. In that control, Perkins was determined not to lose even one of them.

Well, he had lost one. Alton. Byron reflected that he was quickly being lost too.

And now, his walk was almost over. Byron was just a few steps from the family communal home were his parents had raised him.

Lisbeth greeted him at the door. Perkins had warned her he was coming when it became clear on the ASL monitors that that was where Byron was heading.

"Mother," Byron said formally.

"Son," she replied.

"Is father home?"

"I suspect so. Why?"

"I need to talk with you both."

"I will get him." She left.

Byron stood in the vestibule. In the playroom, the media room, and the dining area, groups of children were engaged in lessons with the other parents. There was an energy to the place, with happy giggles and adult teasing. Byron remembered those times, perhaps the happiest of his own childhood. He watched for Cyrus and Dot. Cyrus was in the media room with Kenyon; they were engaged in a game of Anticipation, with Kenyon setting up scenarios and Cyrus selecting behaviors. Byron had memories of Kenyon doing the same for him when he was twelve. Dot was coloring on tablet computers with two other girls her age whom Byron didn't recognize.

Craig came up the stairs with Lisbeth.

"Is there somewhere we can talk?" Byron asked them both.

"Let's go to the back patio. It should be warm enough in the sun this time of day." Lisbeth's words were somber, soaked in both resentment and dread.

Byron had memories of being back there too. The patio doors were off the living room. Even though when he was a child the door was heavy to push, it was his place of escape when he was fearful.

Lisbeth led them back through the kitchen. "Do you want some cider? I have it simmering on the stove." Byron accepted.

It was a long time since he had seen his parents together. He noticed something that surprised him. They touched. He had never seen that before. He saw a look of compassion on his mother's face as she offered the cider to his father. Somehow Byron had expected something different than that.

"It has been a long time since you have been home, son." Craig was pulling himself forward, trying to be a dad.

"Yes, Father. A long time."

"I was surprised when I heard you were coming over."

"Heard?"

Lisbeth broke in. "Perkins called us, said that he thought you were on your way. We presumed he had sent you."

"No. I came on my own."

"Well, we are glad you're here now. We miss you."

Byron listened for something warm in those words from his mother. He couldn't be sure that it was there; he didn't notice anything in addition to the practiced warmth of her vocational training. Instead, he detected hurt.

"And how are you doing, son?" Craig asked. Byron wished he didn't keep calling him son.

Byron reached for a sufficient and careful summary. "Well, I have completed all the steps of First Flight, and I am a fully qualified Paraclete. Still living at BirdSong. And you, how are you doing?"

"As best as can be expected. Maintenance man now."

"You have come for a reason, Byron. Tell us." Lisbeth got to the point.

"You will know that I have a mix of memories back here. Some of them not so good." Byron paused and accepted the dread that he saw in his parents' eyes.

"Well, one of the memories I had was that of an older brother. Last week I met him, met him up in Beckett. And I met my grandparents too."

Lisbeth gasped.

The three of them sipped their cider in silence.

Then his mother said, "Byron, we had meant to tell you, tell you when you still lived here, once we thought you were old enough to understand."

"But, Mother, you never did."

"Yes, we never did."

Byron was watching for something from his father, some sign that he was there, that he was engaged in what he was being told. There was just blankness.

"So it is up to me to tell you about him now."

"Tell us about Alton. How did you meet? What is he like?"

Byron spun out the story about a young teen's gifted drawing that led them north to Beckett, a concierge who recognized the image and set up a horseback ride, and the immediate recognition by both brothers of each other.

Lisbeth broke in, her voice flat. "We had always seen a strong physical resemblance between the two of you, especially as you grew up. It was painful to us as you grew older, Byron. We were missing Alton so, and as you grew older, you were a daily reminder that he wasn't there with us."

Byron looked at his mother, puzzled. Then he felt disgust. With all the assaults of his childhood, he became aware of another. He wasn't even recognized for who he was; he was just a copy of another lost child.

"So now, Alton is guiding horseback rides in Beckett. In the winter, he is a ski instructor. They live, Alton and our grandparents, on a small ranch just out of town. They are poor, just getting by.

"Alton is confident, careful. People are drawn to him. He seems to do everything with a sense of accomplishment."

Craig cleared his throat, accidentally drawing attention to himself. Byron looked his way. Craig said, "And my parents, you met them too."

"Father, your father is in cardio rehab up in Beckett after suffering a severe heart attack a couple of weeks ago. They were down here in Munroe for his initial treatment and then went back."

Craig looked at his son and struggled to make sense of what he had said. He was constructing a train of thought, a series of events, trying to analyze them.

"Can we get in touch with them?" Lisbeth asked. She was filled with both dread and a desire to do something for Craig, to allow him to connect with his family.

"We can try, but I don't think it would be kind to contact Grandpa Justin in the hospital while he is rehabbing. And Grandma Laurel is all over the place right now running the business and seeing to him."

"What about Alton? Could we reach out to our son?"

"Probably not. He avoids all electronic communication, something about not trusting the data mining of the ASL."

"Maybe if they come back for follow-up appointments at the hospital, they could come over." Lisbeth's tone was pleading.

"Them. Not here. Never again." Craig stormed off the patio back to his basement.

Byron and his mom sat quietly on the patio.

"Byron, there are some things that you don't know about your father."

"Sallye told me, told me after you met with her a few weeks ago."

"Yes, well, there are some things that I am just figuring out about him too. There was damage to his brain with the surgeries."

"Yes, seems to me like they just took it out. He seems like he's just a shell now, an angry shell who can't cope."

Back at the academy building, Perkins sat in his office, the door closed. He had activated the monitoring cameras in the family communal home and listened in on the exchanges. A feeling of dread formed in his gut.

Alton had been found. Found in Beckett.

The crisis of years ago, a crisis that he had directed to never be spoken of, was being openly discussed. The emotional breakdown of one of his star Paracletes, Craig, and the subsequent bungled neurological treatment was becoming known as well. He had expected it to remain unspoken to preserve the integrity of his program. Now the silence was broken.

He had designed the genetic breeding and secure-attachment parenting around his first generation of bred Paracletes so carefully. Now a horrible outcome was being revealed, one that he had tried to suppress for so long.

(V)

When Byron left the family communal home, he ordered an AVoD to pick him up to take him to the North Hill. He started to walk, having set the pickup location to his GPS. He hoped that Perkins would still be in the office tracking him to listen in, in real time, on a confidential AVT session. If not, he was sure that the psychologist would review the session in the morning.

It was within about two blocks of the family communal home that the AVoD pulled in silently beside him. As the doors opened, Byron smelled the faint but nauseating odor of a previous occupant's vomit.

The North Hill building was largely vacated. Byron suspected that the staff members of the ASL were down at the Harvest Festival, perhaps taking in the final performance of the year at the Globe. Doors opened for him as the sensors read his permission to access the building off the wearable on his left forearm.

"I welcome you, Byron," Dr. Y greeted him as he donned the eyewear and entered the room. "You are alone tonight."

"Yes, no further need for Sallye to be with me. I haven't fainted in my last two sessions, so I figured it was safe to come alone."

"I appreciate your newfound self-confidence. I sense from your data stream that you have been doing a bit of traveling, a bit of visiting since you last met with me."

"Yes, I have lots to report."

"I am eager to hear."

"It is a bit odd for me to recount what I have been up to when it is apparent that you already know."

"Yes, I have received the objective data of it. The where and when is not really that relevant here."

The avatar waited for Byron to continue and was met with silence. The AI program had anticipated that Byron would immediately begin a subjective account, that he would link meaning and emotion with the sequence of events. Byron sat in pensive silence.

Dr. Y nudged for a response again. "What is relevant is your experience of it, how your perspective on yourself and your world has changed as a result of the where and when you have been."

"So, you will know that I have met my brother." Byron surmised that Perkins would expect it to be reported, that he would be curious about what it had meant to Byron.

"Yes. I remember from our last session that you were just discovering that you had a brother. And now you have met him. I expect that was a profound moment in your life."

"How can I say this? It's like an incompleteness that I have lugged around with me most of my life has been completed."

"Byron, I recognize that you have been searching for something. Perhaps I might suggest you were searching for some antidote to a sense of emotional isolation. In the meeting with your brother, you are no longer so emotionally alone."

Byron could see the source of interpretation the avatar made, striking at the fundamental human need for emotional intimacy. With a measured exhalation, one that would be picked up as a parasympathetic response by his biosensors, Byron breathed out the response: "Yes."

The avatar adjusted its posture, leaning back a bit in the chair, slowing its own breathing cycle, and allowing Byron to bask in the insight. A light flow of air came through the VR room as though from the virtual window off to the side. The comforting scents of jasmine and lavender wafted on the breeze of warm air.

"It is amazing the difference that meeting Alton has made, that sense of completeness. It has changed me."

The avatar hovered, not needing to intervene and eager to allow Byron to continue processing his deepened awareness.

"I am sure that I will see Alton again, many times I hope. But even if I don't, at least not anytime soon, the meeting I had with him was sufficient, sufficient to let me live more contentedly now."

Byron had formulated several purposes in his transit to the North Hill and manufactured subjectivities that he wanted Perkins to believe were true. This was one. Byron and Alton would certainly be teaming up, stronger in each other's presence. Byron didn't want Perkins to suspect what would be occurring and what might happen as a result.

"Tell me about the sufficiency." The avatar pushed him further.

"Well, seeing Alton, his confidence, his presence in what he did with the horses, reminded me of the gifts both he and I received that have brought us this far in life. It was clear when I met him that there was a strong physical resemblance. But there was something more, something much more meaningful that he and I both have. I have been told all my life that I am genetically gifted. Although he is not my genetic twin, we share a lot of our family's genetic material. Both Alton and I had similar first years of life; we were raised in the family communal home for the vital stages of early secure attachment. We have been gifted in both these regards and have taken those gifts in different directions. I see in him, as he works with horses and riders, what I aspire to in my vocation as a Paraclete."

Byron paused. He must believe that Perkins was buying this to have the confidence to sell it. Truly, at this moment, he was taking inspiration from his older brother that he could do this, this deception in the heady space of an avatar run by artificial intelligence. He needed the challenge of that inspiration as he continued.

"I am just beginning in the vocation. Alton is a bit further along in what he does. Seeing how well he does motivates me to dedicate myself more. I am not controlling magnificent animals or calming nervous first-time riders. I am assisting Emergents and Emotionally Vulnerables. But I am inspired by him to dedicate myself to the vocation."

Byron paused again. He watched the avatar, realizing that the facial microexpressions and postures he was witnessing were programmed in to manipulate his own mental explorations and exposures. For a moment, he wished that the avatar could be real, could be read as another human present in relationship. In the starkness of reality in his VR session, he realized that what the avatar portrayed was manipulative intervention in service to the data collection needs of the ASL.

After an exquisitely timed pause, the avatar continued. "As you serve others in your role as a Paraclete, you can end up being emotionally isolated yourself. In finding your brother, you have found yet another relationship in which you can be emotionally present. You have that with Sallye. Now you have that with Alton. It is healthy for you to have both."

"Which brings me to the other bit of travel, the other discoveries I have made. I have connected again with my parents."

"Yes."

"Just today I went there, to the family communal home. Met with both my mom…" Here Byron's tone changed. "And with Father. Told them about Alton."

"That is a big step for you. Tell me, what was that like subjectively?"

"Father called me 'son.' Twice. If he weren't so pathetic, I would have hit him or walked out."

"Still, it can be very important for a son to be called 'son'; it is often the kindest word that a father can use, better than even the first name."

"Not in the tone of voice he said it in. It wasn't loving and kind. It was empty."

"I sense that you are yearning for an emotional connection to be there with him."

"I am beyond that. I will get my emotional connection elsewhere."

"Like where? You need it from somewhere."

"From Sallye. From Alton." Byron's voice softened as he settled into the context of those relationships.

"From a certain older, flamboyant man on the pier in Beckett?"

"How do you know about that?" Byron shot back angrily.

"Your IPE-CKS betrayed a reaction to that flirtation on the dock. Of course, data streaming identified who that reaction was to."

Byron reeled under the violation that he felt from the avatar. He recognized that there would be confrontations and interpretations put forward by the AI program in therapy. But this was beyond imagining.

The avatar waited, letting Byron settle in to the starkness of the moment.

"Byron, to have a homosexual attraction is within the normal parameters of early adulthood when sexual feelings run strong. It's normal, even for young men who settle into straight relationships. Typically, at this stage in development, there is an intense denial, abhorrence even, of those feelings. You are able to experience them and on some level accept them. That is healthy. I only wish to point out, though, that they might be a compensation for the lack of love that you felt from your father."

Byron stared at the avatar with a sense of boiling rage. He rose from the seat across from the avatar and went to the window. The light breeze cooled his face. The apparent daylight that entered there was artificially projected light through a screen, creating the illusion.

The sting of the interpretation had dislodged him. He could feel his adrenaline pushing an emotion of rage. Deliberately, diligently, he called on his skill of self-calming to bring his emotion back into range as he stood facing away from the avatar.

"You don't need to deny those feelings, Byron. You can accept them. Recognize them as a part of you."

"Yes, you are probably right." Byron hoped that his faked acquiescence would not be detected by the biosensor on his forearm or the AI analysis running the program. He went back into his intention of subjectivities that he wished to portray to Perkins as he tracked the session.

"I get it. That I need not compensate for my need for emotional connection to my parents but address it directly with them. That is a tall order. I went to them today, but it was difficult."

"You have done it once."

"I had information about my brother to share."

"So you can go again."

"To rebuild my relationship with them." Byron sighed out this line as a pronouncement of intent for Perkins to hear.

There was a period of quiet between the young man and that apparition of a historic psychiatrist.

"Byron, last time when you came, you talked about freedom, the freedom to choose your course of action. And I spoke of responsibility, the responsibility to others who would be affected by your choices. You are at that point of venture today, very much today."

The avatar paused for the optimal number of seconds, letting the words settle. Then Dr. Y continued. "As you come out of your adolescence, as you emerge into the maturity of adulthood, you can develop a more nuanced view of your parents. Growing up, parents are hard figures, one-dimensional. Teens don't see their parents as people, just as beings who either block or facilitate the transient desires of the teen.

"Ultimately, in order to have a relationship with your parents, you need to see them as people, flawed people, for sure. But then, we all are flawed."

"All I see in my father are the flaws."

"That is true for many young men. It is our act of passage into maturity that accepts that each of us has flaws but is more than our flaws."

"You set a very high expectation for me." At this point, Byron turned from facing the artificial window to face the artificial therapist.

"You are an extraordinary young man and will meet many high expectations over the course of your life."

"Right now, I am angry."

"Extraordinarily so, at least in your story of your visit to your parents. But as I sense you now, that anger has peaked and is falling; it is transforming itself into motivation."

"I came here directly from my meeting with them. I was ready to blow this whole 'bred Paracletes raised in a secure-attachment environment' crap out the window, to declare to the world that it is all a crock."

Byron paused and strengthened his deliberate self, making eye contact with the avatar as a means of speaking directly to the intelligence, to the control, behind it. He needed to present himself as sincere to be convincing. "But I don't feel that way now."

The avatar leaned forward into an animation that was designed to encourage, to support. In the first session, the AI program had recognized that Byron spoke in the language structures of an adult, not an adolescent. Here again, it was apparent, but it went deeper. It wasn't just his language but also his insight. If it was real, it was remarkable. If it was real. The AI program searched for other interpretations, other, more malignant interpretations.

"The motivation you have given me is to rise above all that. To work on repairing the relationship with my parents, to figure out why my dad is like he is.

"You see, I learned something when I met my brother. I learned that the paternal side of my family tree bears a heavy predisposition to depression. My great-grandfather committed suicide. My grandfather has had depression at least twice in his life. And my dad—well, I don't know whether you call it depression or what, but there is definitely something wrong there. That means I am at risk too."

"This is a crisis for you. Crisis is both jeopardy and opportunity."

"Jeopardy that I too could become a shell of a man. Opportunity that I could break that cycle."

"Predisposition is not inevitability, Byron. Awareness of our predispositions is a chance for freedom from that inevitability. Our responsible action is not only responsibility to others but also responsibility to our future selves."

"Thank you, Dr. Y."

"Thank you, Byron."

Byron left the VR room satisfied that he had accomplished his goal.

By the time Byron exited the North Hill building, it was dark. No longer in a hurry, he started the walk back and decided that he would take the path that would lead him through the district. He was destined for FiveWay and sent Sallye a message that he was coming over and would be there within the hour. She sent him back a smile of acknowledgment.

The path wound along the lakeshore. Byron heard the sound of singing, singing with a beat, choral singing. As he drew closer, he saw that it was the religious fanatics. As he drew nearer, he saw they were occupying a gazebo and had managed to have the lighting and sound system turned on for them. Byron was attracted to the movement of their dancing, to the simple harmonies of their hymns, to the intention of their cause. He stood and listened awhile.

Among those gathered around were conservative older folks. They had a look of pride on their faces and kept watching for who else might be listening. If they caught someone's eye, they would flash a smile of invitation. There were also some young punks mocking the music and the dance movements. Byron detected a mix of enthusiasm among the singers and dancers. Some were really into it; Byron could sense that they really believed in what they were doing. Not so much with others—they just seemed to be going along with it.

Byron was struck by a sudden awareness that this was universal to the human condition. Some just live it, can fully claim its emotional intensities as their own. Others carry a questioning, a doubt. He had always been the doubter; now he was becoming engaged and feeling something intensely within. He was developing his cause.

Farther along, the path emptied itself into the business district, and a few blocks farther, the sidewalk crossed the railway tracks into the Courtyard District. There was a genuine energy there, a hoopla. Gales of laughter emerged from the open-air Globe. Byron remembered being there last year for the final performance, then, as now, of *A Midsummer Night's Dream*. He had delighted in the heckling from the crowd in the pit led by the costumed understudy to the character Puck. The iconic lines of the play were thrown at the onstage actors, ill-timed and in mockery, to the delight of the crowd, who laughed heartily at the comedic effect.

Byron remembered how much he had enjoyed that last year. For a moment, he felt at one with those who were enjoying it this year.

Walking in the Courtyard District, he caught sight of his Emergent, Zeke. Charles Ross was with him, and Byron was curious about the energy the two shared. It was more playful than that he shared with the young teen. It had the sense of a dance; there were looks of intrigue between them. As much as Byron hoped that Zeke would take his place in the blooming AI world of the ASL and as much as he thought Charles Ross could be a part of that, what he saw between them was unsettling. He decided not to approach them.

When he reached FiveWay, Sanctuary stood warily at the door. When he recognized that it was Byron who was coming, Sanc threw himself into a paroxysm of tail wags, play bows, and tongue-flailing head bobs. Within seconds, the two were rolling on the floor, Byron laughing uncontrollably and Sanc standing over him with his paws resting on Byron's chest and his tongue giving Byron's face an affectionate wash.

Sallye stood by, hands on her hips in a fake scolding, disgusted pose.

Soon they found themselves on the back deck with a couple of beers. Twinkle lights were lit, and the electric radiant heaters were designed to look like pit fires were turned on.

Byron told the story of his trip to the family communal home.

Byron told the story of his AVT, of the analytic flow he had been subjected to by the avatar, and of the deliberate impressions that he had left for the ASL. He felt convinced that he had anticipated the needs of Perkins and satisfied them. In so doing, Byron knew he had purchased some space for what could come next in his life.

Sallye said she understood. Byron thought she was a bit naive in this, that she didn't really have a grasp of what was emerging. He didn't say it but just enjoyed the naïveté she still had. He knew that she would come along as it all developed.

Sallye told Byron about the bizarre meeting with Chetwin, Alyssa, and her mom. She recounted how Dags was there and how her involvement in another trip to Beckett evolved.

Finally, Byron shared with Sallye the messages he wanted conveyed to his brother in the north.

7

THE NORTH HILL

Perkins woke with a sense of dread. He was alone in his condo. He tended to his bodily self-care, brewed his coffee, and stared out the window that overlooked the lake—all this wearing only his boxers. An alert was sounding on his wearable: implanted sensors were reading that his blood sugars were elevated and that his average serum cortisol level over the past twenty-four hours was also elevated. A standard warning was given for him to contact his physician for a consultation. He silenced the alert and responded to the message with a muttered, "You think?"

Despite all he had learned on the previous day, he had gone to sleep satisfied with the knowledge that his Byron was OK. The content of the AVT session had been reassuring to him, more reassuring than the discussion that Byron had had with his parents the day before. The emergence of interest in what had happened in that family a decade and a half ago was a serious matter. After viewing the AVT session, he left alerts for Chetwin, Cripps, and Ross to meet with him this morning. He scheduled the meeting with Ross for 9:00 a.m. at the North Hill and with Chetwin and Cripps for 9:30 a.m. His own calendar reminded him of the media interview he was doing there at 10:00 a.m.

Perkins dreaded media interviews. This one was apparently to be celebratory and would provide a chance for him to boast about the breeding program for Paracletes having had its premier graduates complete First Flight. Still, Perkins dreaded the social and political elements of dealing with the media: the ingratiating manner of the interviewer, the slimy overtures to gain information, and the chance of ill-spoken words being worked into a scandal.

But the deeper dread was of Cripps and how he would react to the crisis. That man! He had been sent to the Munroe ASL as an assistant to Perkins when the scandal of the kidnapping of Alton Wilkes-Williams had broken. At that time, so much was said of his "pedigree" to come into such a crisis. He was the man who engineered the downfall of psychiatry, a downfall that came as a result of the scandal of drug dependency created by the large pharmaceutical companies over the first decades of the century. If he had such a pedigree, why was he sent to a backwater such as Munroe to serve as an assistant? No one could ever come up with a satisfying explanation for that question. There were lots of rumors that Cripps had created his own scandals and was being distanced from them. Whatever it was, Perkins hated him being there. Perkins hated that he hadn't been moved on but left to fester in Munroe all these years. Perkins would have considered retirement long before now had it not been for the prospect of Cripps replacing him as the heir apparent.

Today the three men had the developments of their own scandal to manage. There was the newfound presence of Alton Wilkes-Williams in Beckett. There was the connection between Alton and his two star Paracletes, one of whom was Alton's brother. And finally, there was the breaking of the pact of silence by the mother of those brothers so that the whole sordid story was no longer contained.

Perkins's monitor chimed, signaling an incoming call. He rushed to put on a shirt, button it, and sink into the chair in front of the screen so that he would be visible only from the midchest up.

"Good morning, sir."

"Good morning, Angelica. You're up early."

"Oh, lots going on over here at FiveWay. I hope my friends here are not too noisy for you to hear me OK." One of the other young Paracletes made bunny ears behind Angelica's head. Then, recognizing it was Perkins in the monitor, the young Paraclete got a sudden look of horror on her face and shrunk away, giggling at her faux pas.

"No, Angelica. I can hear you just fine."

"I am confirming that I have to be at the North Hill at ten. Do you want me to come early? I thought you might want to brief me for the interview."

Perkins was a bit disoriented and then remembered that he had requested one of the First Flight graduates to be with him at the media briefing. He wished it could have been Sallye, but her work with his own daughter, his own daughter designated as an Emotionally Vulnerable, would have brought the nature of the work too close to home for him. Angelica had been a second choice and a good one at that. She was photogenic and spirited. She was less deep, but that was preferable for a media interview. The decision had been made weeks ago. Caught up in the web of happenings the day before, he had completely forgotten to send a reminder to her.

"Yes, yes, Angelica. It is today. In checking my schedule, I see that I have a meeting just before, so I won't be able to brief you. Basically, we are talking about the Genetic Selection and Secure Attachment program resulting in its first graduates to the vocation."

"So this is about the graduation for the six of us here at FiveWay?"

"No, actually, we are announcing publicly today what is in the academic article that is being published about the entire program.

There are the six of you plus the six at BirdSong and then the five that were in the first prototype cohort, your older brothers and sisters. We held off on them until we had more numbers as a strong demonstration of what our program can do."

"OK…oops. Certainly, sir."

"Perhaps you can review the theoretical package that I used in my lectures to the class. We won't go any deeper than that."

"Got it. And Dr. Perkins?"

"Yes?"

"Thanks for choosing me." Angelica looked sincere, and then some circumstance going on out of camera range caused a gale of laughter to break out behind her.

When Perkins arrived at the basement of the North Hill, Charles Ross was already active within a pod of screens. There were no Convergence Alerts, and Ross was going through standard protocols to ensure that nothing was being missed in the routine monitoring.

He smelled as though he had consumed alcohol the night before. There was a little less shine to his flamboyance and more than a hint of resentment on his face for having to be at work so early.

"I have new information. We have a problem," Perkins began.

"Well, good morning to you too, sir."

"Can the attitude, Ross. I need you to locate someone, tap into the data stream from the wearable."

"OK."

"The name is Alton Wilkes-Williams. Perhaps there might be some variation on that surname; I am not sure how he is registered. He is up in Beckett or the rural area around Beckett."

"Should be easy. I was just up there, and we have new towers to upgrade bandwidth through the countryside. Let me do a search."

Perkins paced nervously. Usually he was more at ease in this basement than in the airy, human-comfort-engineered spaces on the upper levels. Here, life was reduced to a flow of data; it was objective. Problems down here were solvable. Even though the vagaries of human nature were constantly being monitored, it was always a matter of what, when, and where—never a matter of why.

"Nothing, sir."

"What do you mean, nothing?"

"Nothing active right now. It is nine in the morning, so if there is an Alton Wilkes-Williams and he has a wearable, it should be on. I get nothing. Unless he is in a transmission shadow, he doesn't exist."

"He does exist. Keep searching."

"How about I do a retro search? How far back should I go?"

Perkins paused and reconstructed the time line he had developed from Byron's conversation with his parents in the family communal home the day before.

"Go back two weeks. Widen the parameters geographically."

Charles Ross worked away, tapping on his keypad without looking, his eyes fixed on a screen. "OK. I have an Alton Wilkes, not Alton Wilkes-Williams. His wearable flashed on and off several times on a bus coming from the east into Munroe overnight on September 14 and 15. Then there are brief episodes of activity since then. Nothing continuous, just an activity and then a complete shutdown of the device."

"Can you isolate the metadata from all of those activities? From there, we will select which ones we want to look at in more detail. Throw it up on that screen over there."

The two men watched as a log of data files strung out vertically down the screen. Ross added successive columns, and data appeared for each line.

The first additional column was GPS location. The route that Alton had taken from the east was revealed and then his visit to Munroe Memorial Hospital. Next came his AVoD ride to Beckett and, finally, his rural coordinates. The travel from the east to Beckett was significant. Perhaps that might be the route for an incoming insurgency. Perkins had Charles map the last GPS coordinates spatially, and the location of the ranch was revealed. Perkins recognized it as the place where he had taken CarolAnne for the horseback ride.

The second additional column revealed points of connection initiated by the wearable. There were several to Laurel Wilkes at the beginning and the rest to a business CashCard account.

"Can you pull any current personal data off that wearable?"

Ross made a few keyboard taps. "It is not currently active, sir."

"What about its core identification data?"

On a separate screen, a photo appeared, a portrait such as that of a passport or license. Both men immediately recognized the similarity to Byron.

"Oh, so funny!" Charles Ross chortled.

"Funny?"

"Well, while I was up in Beckett, Byron and Sallye came up to me with a photo. It was a photo of a drawing actually, but there was no name with it. Today you come with a name but no photo. And it's the same guy."

Perkins stared at the image.

"Can you locate that drawing?"

"If I remember correctly, it was on Sallye's wearable. Let me see. Hmm. Yes, she's turned on. Let me go in."

Within moments, the drawing appeared on one of the other screens. Perkins recognized his own daughter's hand as that of the artist, a pencil sketch made on paper he had provided for her. He had been that close.

(II)

The wall clock in the Moose read 10:00 a.m.

To his chagrin, Dags Basilis's store had gotten the nickname Moose. It was an acronym that had stuck; it was short for Munroe

Outfitting and Outdoor Sports Equipment. Even though Dags in no way looked like a moose, or so he thought, joking references to him and his appearance were constant. Patrons had donated a number of trophy heads of moose to the store. Middle-aged men referred to their excursions there as "goin' down to the Moose." Their wives would let them go, figuring it was expensive but harmless enough.

Dags wanted a more youthful image for his store. Although he carried a good selection of equipment for fishing and hunting, he also was trying to appeal to the younger buyer, with kayaks, road bikes, and boards for both pavement and snow. If it moved in the outdoors and didn't have a motor any stronger than a seven-horsepower trolling motor for your fishing boat, he had it in his store.

At the front of the store was also fashion built around the wholesome and outdoorsy lifestyle, from formfitting yoga tights to miracle-fiber waterproof and warmth gear. If you were into layering, you were into the Moose.

Gerald stood at the checkout computer. Sallye stood outside the changing room. In the changing room, Alyssa cursed. When there was sufficient reluctant agreement from the young teen and sufficient attire to cover her for a few days in the backcountry, Sallye took the hard-won victories over to Alyssa's father. He stood there with Dags, planning the trip. Dags would be accompanying them on the first backcountry excursion he had arranged with Alton out of Beckett.

"I can't believe she is coming. It's not what I expected at all," said Gerald. There was a gentle tone to his voice, something Sallye would not have expected from someone as wealthy and influential as he was.

"I think it's not so much going somewhere as it is avoiding somewhere else," Sallye replied.

"Let's see what you've got here." Gerald looked over the stack of clothes. "Looks good, but forecasts are that we might have some warm days. There are no shorts here or short-sleeved tops."

"These fabrics are waterproof and breathable—good for blocking the sun. She should be OK." Sallye realized there was another reason for Alyssa's selections. She had caught sight of her briefly in the dressing room and had seen that not only her inner arms were laddered with cuts but her inner thighs were as well. Sallye figured the turmoil the adolescent felt was probably unknown to her father. Although protocol and policy would have given Sallye the grounds to reveal to the parents the extent of the self-abusive cutting that Alyssa was doing, it would be strategic for her to choose when and how she would do so. Covered arms and legs on a camping trip were best for now, especially when the relationship between her and the Emotionally Vulnerable teen was still precarious.

"OK, if you say so." Gerald made eye contact with Sallye and lowered his voice to draw her in. "Now I want you to go and get all these items in your size, for you. My tab."

Sallye was shocked. "I can't do that, sir. I have been assigned to a professional relationship with your daughter through the ASL. I can't receive gifts." Sallye had calculated the cost of Alyssa's selections, which added up to more than she made in a month of work, CashCard credits included.

"I am sure that Dr. Chetwin and his cohort will never hear that it occurred." Gerald put special emphasis on the words *never hear*. "And they are looking for a good report from me as to how you are doing with my daughter. I can only think that you being a good role model for her, with appropriate clothes for the elements, would be to your credit." Gerald spoke with the no-nonsense manner of a man who was more used to getting his way than he was to following rules.

Sallye stared at him.

"Go on. And maybe you might get some shorts for you. And sunscreen."

Sallye grimaced. The last person she wanted to see her legs was a rich, rule-bending old man.

(III)

Perkins entered the conference room on the North Hill at 9:45 a.m. Cripps and Chetwin were already there. Cripps had laid his portable computer at the end of the table, claiming his spot at the most powerful position in the conference room. Perkins glared at him so intensely that Cripps moved; he moved with a pseudocompliant defiance.

Perkins stated drily, "Alton Wilkes-Williams has been located."

The reactions of Cripps and Chetwin could not have been more different. Chetwin, while surprised, had a look of relief. He had known Alton as a youngster in the family communal home. He had liked the lad. For a decade and a half, he had carried a sense of incompleteness, of grief. He had been on the verge of giving up hope of ever seeing the boy again, although there had been no clear and final ending to the boy's life. Alton was a disappeared, not a deceased. And with that sense of uncertainty, Myles Chetwin had always held a faint glimmer of hope that on a visit to the family communal home, he would see the boy again, returned and resumed in the program.

Now Alton was found!

Cripps had a look of disgust, revulsion even. He had been brought in to manage this very disappearance crisis. From the moment he had arrived, it had been a mess. Alton and whoever had snatched him had eluded the ASL tracking net. The failure of the digital monitoring of the population was more of a problem out in the rural and semiurban regions, of which Munroe was one. What should have been a straightforward cooperation of the police and the ASL languished in shoulder shrugs of "Jeez, we don't know where he could have gone."

"He is now known as Alton Wilkes—just Wilkes, not Wilkes-Williams. He is living just outside of Beckett. For some reason, he turns off his wearable much of the time. Or because he is rural, our tracking towers are not picking him up. He lives with his grandparents, Craig's parents. They are struggling financially with a small horseback-riding business."

"My God. Does the family know? Lisbeth and Craig? Byron?" Chetwin asked.

"It seems it was Byron who found him. And yes, Lisbeth and Craig were told by Byron that his long-lost brother had been found."

"Did Byron even know he had a brother? He was so young when Alton disappeared." Chetwin was disoriented by the news. There were so many implications to it. He immediately felt compassion for those he considered his responsibility, those whose world had now been rocked.

"It seems as though Lisbeth told Sallye and Sallye told Byron, and then Sallye and Byron went looking and found him." Perkins left out the connection he and his own daughter had to the discovery, left out that he had been within hailing distance of the lost young man just weeks before.

"How are they coping?"

"Well, I am not sure about Lisbeth and Craig. Lisbeth is a strong woman, does her job, makes everything right. I suspect that she will take this in stride. With Craig…" Perkins paused. "Well, you know about Craig." Perkins shifted his gaze to stare at Cripps, who was still fomenting at the table.

Chetwin broke back in, unable to contain himself. "How is Byron taking it? He is actively working with Emotionally Vulnerables and Emergents. Is he handling this OK? Do we need to take him out of practice for a while to help him cope?"

"I don't think that will be necessary. He seems to be handling it well."

"How do you know? Have you spoken to him?"

"Not directly, no. But I have reviewed his last AVT, and it seems like he is maintaining good perspective."

"You what?" Now Chetwin was livid. Technically, they all had right of access to the AVT sessions, but it was an unstated policy that, unless it was absolutely necessary, they would refrain from violating the privacy of the content of AVT sessions.

"This is a delicate, potentially volatile situation. I felt it best to keep on top of it by reviewing the AVT session." Perkins felt a twinge of guilt. He knew the policy of "privacy if possible," but he was so proud of the functioning of Dr. Y that he had voyeuristically reviewed many of Dr. Y's AVT sessions. It was not out of concern for the emerging situation that he had reviewed Byron's session. It was out of self-indulgence.

"Does he know you have been watching his sessions?"

"No, of course not. There is no need for him to know."

Cripps couldn't keep silent any longer. "Well, with Alton being located, we will need to assess and deal with any risk to the ASL that he might present. Up there in Beckett, he is probably pretty harmless, but we will need to deal with him."

"I am not sure that harmless and Beckett necessarily go hand in hand," Perkins responded.

"How so?"

"I have been tracking convergences involving the rebellion out on the plains, trying to determine if it might ooze over here."

"And?"

"And there is a connection between the east and Beckett and, of course, between Beckett and Munroe. Alton worked for a few weeks this summer on the plains, and, from what we can tell, he has become involved in the passive-resistance movement out there."

"We better track him." Cripps was leaning forward in his chair the way a wolf might at the sight of prey.

"That is going to be difficult. He doesn't keep his wearable on. He goes dark most of the time."

"Well, we can do something about that." Cripps was becoming animated. He leaned back in his chair with his hands behind his head as though he had just solved the problem. With a sense of mastery, he said it: "Bait."

"Bait?" asked Perkins.

"Yes, we can start depositing extra CashCard credits in his account, funds that he can access only if he acknowledges them within a short time frame, say, an hour. If he misses a potential deposit, we leave him a message that he missed out when he went dark. You said that he and his grandparents were struggling financially. A bit of financial incentive might draw him out of the woodwork."

Perkins left the meeting with Chetwin and Cripps to go to the media interview. He took time in the washroom to try to allay the anxiety and frustration still churning within him. It was just like Cripps to come up with a plan. And it would be just like Cripps's plans of old for further disaster to strike once that plan was implemented. He was caught between the notion that he had best be content to let this be and the dread that, under his watch, another scandal might erupt to erode the credibility of the ASL.

But now it was time to switch gears, to become the awarded social scientist, the developer of programs and protocols that were of great benefit to society. The graduation through First Flight of the first generation of bred Paracletes was a life accomplishment for him. It was an accomplishment of sufficient innovation to match his AI work turning historic master therapists into avatars. He splashed water on his face.

He met with Angelica outside of the media room. She looked radiant in a dress of lightweight white cotton draped loosely around her shapely frame. It was transparent enough to hint at her youthful sexuality but loose enough to be modest. He hoped the harsh lighting of the multidirectional cameras would not portray it as too sexy. For him, though, it was perfect.

The interview went well. The media representative asked softball questions. Perkins responded with understatements that created an aura of modesty. The interviewer responded in kind, stating

Perkins's accomplishments in terms that gave them a significance greater than they deserved.

Angelica spoke well. She was ample and effusive in her gratitude for the gifts of breeding and secure-attachment rearing. Angelica was the very image that any Emotionally Vulnerable or Emergent would desire.

Even though they pulled it off well, even though Perkins had disciplined his mind to set thoughts of doubts and dread aside, he still had a mental itch that begged to be scratched. It was about Craig and Alton, about the disaster in their lives that his pet project had created.

(IV)

Myles Chetwin faced his day with resolve, a resolve that was almost bitter. He was aware of the bitterness and aware that he needed to defend himself against it. Bitterness had no place on this difficult day. Myles wished that, by some act of will or mental discipline, he could absolve himself of the bitterness. He could not; he could only battle it with a firm resolve when he detected it intruding on his mind.

After the previous day's meeting with Perkins and Cripps, he had mobilized. Perkins or Cripps would have deemed his actions "damage control," but Myles didn't see it that way. He deeply cared about the people he was bringing to the atrium on the North Hill later that day, deeply cared about the pain that they had carried all these years, and deeply cared that the safety of pretense had been torn apart.

No, this wasn't damage control. This was healing. It would be healing facilitated with the utmost support and care.

The logistics of the meeting were not difficult but had required planning on the previous afternoon. The atrium would be reconfigured by ASL staff so that it would provide a sense of space, a sense of privacy and safety without cloying constraint. Paracletes had been excused from their usual duties and assigned to attend to the children at the family communal home. Myles worked with them to set their engagement there as a surprise event for the children, a delightful diversion from the usual homeschooling and chores that would have been routine for the day. Myles had set this up without informing the young Paracletes of the reason for their mission.

Typically, when gathering a group of this size, ASL protocol would be to have Perkins or Cripps as a second presence. Perkins had insisted on this protocol as a means of ensuring that due respect was given to the values and praxis of the ASL-Munroe Division. After Chetwin's meeting with Perkins and Cripps, though, he had no desire to have either of them in the room. Cripps would not see the value in what Myles wished to do and would scowl. Perkins would be reactionary, would take offense, and would edge the group toward panic with his own need for control.

Today, Myles needed to be Myles, not Dr. Chetwin. Since Cripps had come to the ASL all those years ago, the use of first names among them had been relegated to reminiscences of days past. At one point, Myles had been "Myles" to Alastair, and Alastair had been "Al" to Myles. Now it was "Dr. Chetwin" and "Dr. Perkins."

In his mental preparation for meeting with the family communal-home parents, Myles reviewed the story of how they had arrived at this place of secrecy and distrust, of control and pseudocompliance. Of course, Alton Wilkes-Williams's disappearance those many years ago had rocked the tiny, perfect world that Dr. Alastair Perkins had constructed. That disappearance had been prefaced by thoughts and actions that were unknown to Perkins, the architect of an esteemed and awarded program. There had been an insurgency outside of his awareness and control. Somewhere back in time, someone had a smoldering of resistance and had nurtured that resistance into the glowing ember of a plan that was then fanned into the flame of action. Now it was clear that those someones were Alton's grandparents.

But that needn't have led to the disaster that eventually occurred. Grandparents interfere, and little boys find grandparents to be a loving refuge. Had he and Perkins thought it through at the time, talked to those involved rather than acting in panic, shared the pain together rather than being offended by the event, and handled it differently, this could have been avoided. But Cripps came. With Cripps came the energy of disgust and punishment. Alton's parents were interrogated rather than supported in their loss. They were treated as inadequate for not being able to hold on to this gem of genetic engineering and petri-dish nourishment that Perkins had created. The ASL turned on them.

There had been a belief that the classic IPE-CKS data mining would find the little guy. Back then, none of them believed that the systems of tracking and monitoring could fail. When it failed, and all the hoopla was over, the ASL went on with its program, one prospective bred Paraclete down. Lisbeth and Craig and the six other communal parents were left to live the pain of their loss.

He had watched this happen. He had argued for a different approach, for calm and collaboration, for patience and support. He had not argued sufficiently or effectively. The bitterness that Myles pushed away eked back as guilt. Myles wished, by some act of will or mental discipline, to absolve himself of the guilt. He could not.

As Byron approached the family communal home for the second time in just a few days, he was apprehensive. Although he had liked the energy of the idea and the planning, he had seen through Dr. Chetwin's ruse of a surprise party for the children. They were to be there because the adults were being withdrawn en masse from the home and someone needed to care for the children. Having grown up in the family communal home, he could not recall any time when the home was not staffed by at least one of the eight raising adults. Sometimes it was his father who was present—and barely there. But always there was one of the parents.

Byron would see Cyrus and Dot today. Neither of them had noticed his presence when he'd met with his mother and father there a couple of days before. He had wanted to connect with Cyrus and Dot, but his feelings about his father being in the home had prevented it. Today he was to be there for them.

During the meeting with Chetwin, Harry and Angelica had proposed they arrive at the family communal home dressed as sloppy clowns—not too creepy for the small children but sufficiently creepy to amuse the young adolescents. Bungling, pratfalls, and slapstick would be the routine. Back at FiveWay, there was a trunk of wigs, red noses on thin, white elastic ties, Groucho Marx glasses with bushy eyebrows, various baggy pants, and garish vests. Transparently, it would be them under the disguises. That would be part of the fun.

Harry and Angelica both had younger siblings in the home whom they had visited often. And, of course, Byron had younger siblings there too: Cyrus and Dot. They hadn't seen him for months, maybe years. Today, they would.

When the three Paracletes arrived at the door, there were squeals from the younger children and looks of impatient, unbelieving amusement from the older ones. Harry was juggling. His little brother, Erik, kept stealing the balls in midair with a mischievous grin, so Erik got a grab, a tickle, and then a hug from his brother-clown.

Dot ran and jumped onto Byron. With all the control of a practiced pratfall, he fell backward in the entryway with Dot on his chest pulling at his red nose. Over and over again, she let the elastic snap it back onto his face, as though it were a punishment. There were tears in his eyes, and he was too emotional to speak.

Lisbeth and Craig led the group into the atrium. Lisbeth had the look on her face of a loyal soldier, vigilant of the nuances of the space. Craig had a look of containment and dread. After her meeting with Byron, Lisbeth had talked to Craig. They decided not to speak to the other parents in the family communal home about the news of Alton. That had been Craig's idea. While Lisbeth had thought that they would eventually need to be told, she wanted to support Craig in slowing the process down and letting him gradually put it together. She had come to think of her husband as a person with only part of his brain and a heart that was gradually reemerging. They were mates, and they were going through this together.

The eight communal parents entered the atrium cautiously. It was laid out to be a relaxed ambiance. Waterfalls, both real and virtual, gave the space a gentle, natural rhythm. The air was moist and cool. These eight parents were all Paracletes by choice. They were used to reading and responding to social settings. Here, today, the very nature of the meeting spelled some sort of doom for them. The only abatement of the anxiety came in seeing that it was just Dr. Chetwin there, alone without one of the others.

Myles stood awkwardly before them. There was more silence than was comfortable. "You might already know…but maybe not…Alton has been located."

The silence in the room grew more intense.

"He has been living up in Beckett with his grandparents, Craig's dad and mom. Very few people know this yet. Lisbeth and Craig…" Myles stopped and wondered whether Craig actually knew. Lisbeth knew, but would she have told him? He checked the look on Craig's face to see whether he could read a reaction. There was none that he could detect.

"Byron knows. Byron and Sallye were the ones who found Alton."

Everyone in the room sat in stunned silence.

"Alton was a childhood friend to many of your own children. Those children, now young men and women, are the jewels of all our lives. You bore them; you all raised them. We expect that they will remember Alton, will remember their shock and fear when he disappeared. Together, we need to support them.

"Alton is an older brother to Cyrus and Dot. Cyrus and Dot will need our help and support as they learn they have a brother older than Byron. They will learn how and why he went missing from their lives." Myles was pacing his disclosure, letting the communal parents absorb the news.

"We all were profoundly impacted when Alton disappeared fifteen years ago. I remember the days and weeks after. I remember the sadness and confusion that I felt. Although I don't know for sure, there is a possibility that Alton may come back into our lives. That will be joyous for us all, but it will also open us up again to the tragedy that happened those years ago. We will realize what we have missed in not being able watch one of us grow into adulthood.

"Especially today and in the days ahead, Lisbeth and Craig need our support."

Now the silence in the room was malignant.

Kenyon spoke. "So, Alton has been found. How?"

"The details aren't clear to me. He was spotted up in Beckett. Sallye and Byron met with him and have confirmed that it is Alton. We are starting to trace him through IPE-CKS."

"So with all the technology and data mining that the ASL does, he was nowhere to be found, but a couple of teenage sleuths find him just fifty miles away?"

"That seems to be the case."

"We have lived with this for fifteen years or more—how many I am not sure—and now this happens? What good is streaming all this data into your computers if we can't find a lost child?" Kenyon was outraged; he was speaking that outrage for the group. Myles let him do so.

"What about his wearable? I thought that wearables were constantly tracked. And what about the implant? Like each one of us, he would have had one in his belly as part of his destiny to be a Paraclete. You and your massive data systems have access to our every heartbeat, our every gut ache, our every endocrinological reaction. You tracked our emotional turmoil to Alton's disappearance years ago, but you couldn't track him."

"Wearables can be turned off. The implant monitors our organ functioning and our body's chemical flux but only transmits data when the wearable is turned on." Myles realized that his explanation was unhelpful, inappropriate, and defensive. "Our systems failed. As much as he was taken, we also lost him."

Discussion continued. Myles had few details. Lisbeth dutifully added what she knew.

The other communal parents repeated statements in apparent disbelief. Back when it occurred, they had been told in no uncertain terms to compartmentalize this tragedy, never to speak of it, not to others and not even among themselves. As Paracletes, they were helpful folk, dutiful folk. They did what they were told. Eventually, most of them had carried on with little sense of the Alton-sized hole in their lives. They had watched the devastation in Craig, in his loss, his illness, his treatment, and his disability. They made up for him. Lisbeth, who had been such a strong member of their team, had withdrawn into a life of just functioning. And they had made up for her.

Myles allowed the emotions to be expressed, to gain intensity, and to dissipate. There were many direct questions that he couldn't answer. In his honest admission to them of his ignorance, he was accepted by the parents. When the time was ready, he shifted the discussion to how they would handle the unpredictable events that might come if Alton were to return to Munroe and the family communal home. Perkins and Cripps, had they been there, would have told them what to do. Myles slowly, graciously, and compassionately helped them develop a perspective that would allow them to respond to what might occur.

Their world had been rocked. Again. This time, he would be there for them.

(V)

Two days later, having hardly slept, Charles Ross made his way toward the gym shower on the second floor of the North Hill building. On his way up the stairs, he looked out the windows at the front of the building and saw a group doing Tai Chi on the lawn. He thought it insanely early for them to be there, although it was their regular 7:00 a.m. session of exercise and community.

Charles had sent an alert to Perkins based on his discovery of the night before, beckoning an early meeting with him. He had awakened with a troubling sense that he shouldn't do this. Charles had sent the alert in a wave of "gotcha" excitement, in a rush of satisfaction that his IT systems were performing excellently and providing data beyond the best that he could have imagined. Now there was a pang of guilt. Prior to coming to the ASL, Charles had taken a course in privacy ethics. Compared with the day-to-day functioning at the ASL, his training seemed to be of another century: old-school and quaintly out of date. Now he was caught between the two.

Before he'd gone into the shower, Charles had put in an order at the S-SB for his breakfast, charging it to his CashCard account and indicating that Perkins would bring it with his own coffee. He then activated the topographical imaging program, set the GPS coordinates, and let the system run and assemble the data. When he returned from his shower dressed in the set of clean clothes he kept there for when he would pull an all-nighter, the image was projected above the table in the conference room. He made some programming changes to enhance the effects he would create for his boss.

Engrossed in thought, Charles was startled when Perkins entered the room behind him. Perkins handed him his coffee and protein-enhanced banana bread. "What are we looking at here?"

"OK, boss man." Charles postured comically in an awkward attempt to seem normal—well, normal for him. "It's the fishing camp at Mayweather Lake, north and east of Beckett."

The image of the mountainous terrain shimmered in three dimensions above the table. Charles, standing on the sensor platform, held his hands in front of him as though he were holding a globe. As he rotated his hands, the projected image rotated on the table; as he cupped his hands closer, the projected image zoomed out, showing a wider view that included Beckett; as he expanded his hands, the image zoomed in.

Charles Ross began to hum the donkey-riding theme from Grofé's *Grand Canyon Suite*: "Bum, ba-dum, ba-dadada bum, ba-dum, ba-dadada…" As his body started to move to the humorous music, the projected image began to distort and dance before them. Quickly, he tapped a sensor on the floor with his foot to disengage the platform's tracking of his movements to control the image before them. The image stabilized.

"OK. Oh boy! This is the route the Basilis group rode back into the fishing camp." Charles started to lay in a row of dots on the terrain.

"Wait, go back to where they started. I was there." Perkins moved in to get a closer look, and Charles zoomed the display, enlarging the start point. The projected image was not finely detailed; trees were displayed as solids rather than showing branches or leaves. Still, it was clear to him where he and CarolAnne had saddled up on the ride they took with Justin and Laurel.

"So with the new higher-bandwidth towers that I hooked into last summer, we are able to track the wearables from Sallye, Alton, Mr. Basilis, and the rest of the group. I have had them superimposed on the 3-D recreation of the terrain as imaged from satellite photos. And...voilà!"

"Alton too? You said 'Alton.'"

"Yes, since Cripps set up the financial incentive to stream onto his wearable, Alton has been keeping his on."

Charles realized that Myles was unlikely to know the plan his subordinate had put into place. "Cripps set it up as a random-riches lottery scheme. He then left an official message to Alton that he had been selected as one of the initial contestants for its beta testing. Since then, Alton has been keeping his wearable on and has been responding every time he gets a chance to 'play.' Cripps set it up with a variable-interval reward protocol, and Alton is responding as expected. Every time he wins, he forwards it into his grandparents' account and then checks their level of debt. He is not using his wearable for anything else, but it is tracking his movements and feeding those back to us."

"So we know where Alton is and can track him. OK." Perkins was annoyed to have been called over to the North Hill building for this little demonstration when a quick message from Ross would have sufficed. He turned to go.

"Hold on; we haven't gotten to the good stuff yet."

Charles dimmed the lights in the room and adjusted the display on the table to mimic a moonlit night. He zoomed in to show the lodge in a clearing by Mayweather Lake. Around the lodge were a series of yurts. He added to the display data flags to signal the location of each of the people there as of about midnight the night before. One of the yurts was being occupied by Sallye and Alton alone.

"This is a recording and time lapse from last night. Sallye, modest girl that she is, activated the privacy setting on her wearable, but she is in there."

"With Alton."

"And wonder of wonders, oh man! Not only is Alton's wearable on, but the implant sensors of organ functioning and internal body chemistry are working!" Charles uttered a boisterous "Oh-whee!" and continued. "The little implant that was put into that little-boy body more than fifteen years ago is still working like a charm. Who would've thunk it?"

"And no privacy override on his wearable?"

"Nope."

"That makes sense. They were only added to the Paracletes' wearables about five years ago, when there was that big scandal around Peeping Tom data. So you have health readings from him, so what?"

Charles, feeling both excitement and guilt, expanded the data flag to display a time graph of endocrine functioning for the young man.

Perkins stared at the screen. The implications were clear. There was a long, slow rise in vasopressin levels; they reached a peak, and then there was a sudden elevation in oxytocin levels.

"So I guess we know what sort of hanky-panky they were up to, eh?" Charles blushed with his own voyeuristic delight. There was a compulsive shame in what he had witnessed from a distance. It violated his ethical imperatives for privacy protection to have witnessed it, to replay it. Yet he was intrigued, and his imagination was running wild. Sallye with her wholesome youthfulness, Alton with his young, outdoorsy physique—a delectable dream.

Perkins nodded. He recognized the characteristic endocrine changes that accompany sexual activity.

"A few minutes later, Sallye leaves the yurt and goes back to where she was staying with Alyssa. She discontinues the privacy override on her wearable and falls into a deep and apparently quite satisfied sleep." Charles's eyes twinkled with the last few words.

As Perkins turned from the projected display on the table, he caught sight of a figure in the doorway of the conference room.

"What are you doing here? You should be in school!"

Zeke looked up and caught sight of Perkins, who was equally shocked.

"Oh man," Charles chortled. "Hey, Zeke, you found me! I will be down at the workstation in a couple of minutes." Zeke slunk out, confused by seeing the two men together there and overhearing what he had heard.

"What are you doing with the boy?" Perkins demanded to know.

"He is helping me with some projects, and I am training him on the maintenance of the servers."

"He should be in school."

"Oh, that. Well, it's all good. I checked, and his attendance records and marks are all sound."

Perkins paused. He couldn't help but wonder whether Charles also knew what Zeke had been up to with him. He hoped that Zeke's little project for him was still a secret. Ross seemed able to spy in just about everywhere.

(VI)

Cripps had messaged Sallye that on the day of her return she was to come directly to the building on the North Hill. Perkins had passed on to Cripps the indiscretion of the young Paraclete; Cripps was her supervisor, Cripps was thus the one to deal with it. What he had planned for the day needed witnesses, needed not to be in the privacy of his small office at the academy building, and needed to have its own drama. Having tracked her wearable, he assembled the group to greet her upon arrival. He stood in front. Slightly behind him and to his right was Perkins. A couple of steps farther back was Chetwin. Off to the side was Byron. Byron had been brought in for support for Sallye, as she was to be delivered a recorded warning. Byron had no idea of what was to be revealed.

Alyssa had elected to ride back with Sallye in the AVoD. She preferred this public transit to sitting in the Range Rover with her father, brother, and Mr. Basilis, the three males luxuriating in their smelliness of fish, horse, and sweat. Alyssa and Sallye had bonded during the several days of the expedition—Sallye with her wholesome and winsome manner, Sallye with her ability to convey deep connection with even the lightest of touch, Sallye with her playfulness and youth. Sallye had connected with Alyssa as no one had before. As they had entered the AVoD in Beckett, their eyes had danced together. They threw back and forth at each other the nonsense words they had created between them, words that had no meaning for anyone else and barely any meaning for them except the pleasure of saying them. As the AVoD had approached Munroe, their play was tinged with sadness; Alyssa knew she needed to then head back to the Enclave. And now they pulled in front of the building on the North Hill, greeted by an odd assemblage of bosses.

Gerald, having dropped Dags off at his store, had also pulled the Range Rover up to the front of the North Hill building. The luxury vehicle was attracting the attention of ASL employees. He approached the entourage, preparing to welcome Sallye and his daughter back to the city.

Cripps took command of the scene. "Sallye Mercanzer, I am here with witnesses to deliver a recorded warning. It is now being transmitted to your wearable. You are hereby suspended from your duties as Paraclete until further notice." Cripps was stern in his delivery, puffing up a maximum aura of authority from within.

"What?" Sallye was stunned and started to cry.

"Read it."

As Sallye opened her wearable, the text of the warning appeared. Byron rushed to her side and read with her.

> **RECORDED WARNING: On Saturday, October 13, 2057, while on an excursion to the fish camp on Mayweather Lake, you were derelict of duties in leaving your client alone in a tent while you engaged in sexual conduct with Alton Wilkes that is unbecoming to your position as a Paraclete.**
>
> **This event and this warning have been documented on your IPE-CKS. You are hereby ordered to attend weekly counseling sessions with Dr. Cripps to continue until the ASL deems you suitable for reinstatement.**

Touched by Sallye's sudden tears, Byron had put his arm around her shoulder to hold her close. But upon reading the recorded warning, he drew back, flooded with emotions of disgust and anger. He hung there, vibrating in the emotional space.

Sallye was incredulous at the scandal the ASL was creating of this. She already felt guilty for betraying Byron, but she had not thought that it would jeopardize her position as a Paraclete. Sure, she had left Alyssa alone in the yurt, but Alyssa was fourteen years old and was asleep, with no awareness of Sallye's absence that night. And what was the big deal for them? Alton was not a client of hers or of any other Paraclete. Couldn't she have a relationship with whomever she wished?

Gerald Johnson, with Alyssa at his side, approached Chetwin. He had witnessed the scene in front of them but was not close enough to have heard what Cripps had said. Alyssa was deeply troubled by Sallye's tears and worried that perhaps there had been a death in the family or that some other great tragedy had befallen her friend. The flood of emotion that typically preceded her cutting came over her. Without the privacy of her bedroom and the comfort of her razor, that flood built within. Unable to run over to Sallye, whom she now considered her only friend in the world, she reached out and touched the sleeve of her father's jacket. In a movement she had not made in at least ten years, she put her hand in his and felt both security and strength.

"What's going on?" Gerald asked Myles.

"Oh, Gerald. Yes. Sorry you have to be here for this. It is a delicate situation, an internal matter affecting Sallye."

"Well, I wanted to speak to you about Sallye. About Sallye and my daughter."

"We already know. I'm so sorry if this had a negative impact on your family."

"Negative? That is the last word that I would've used. I want to tell you what a huge change has come over Alyssa in the last few days, a change for the good. She talks to me now." Gerald was not one to show emotion, but there was a catch in his throat. He suddenly became aware of his daughter's hand in his, squeezed it, and lifted the two hands together to show Myles.

"Well, that is good to hear."

"I realize that Sallye is a Paraclete and was performing a professional service to my daughter, but she was so much more than that. She was a godsend to us. Last night, Sallye sat with Alyssa and me, and we were able to talk like we haven't been able to for years. There is so much I had missed in Alyssa, so much she had wanted to, had needed, to tell me. Sallye, with her gentle encouragement and playful spirit, made it happen." Gerald paused, and his voice cracked as a tear came to his eyes. "I have my daughter back."

"Gerald, I am so glad for you." Relief welled up within Chetwin. He had watched Alyssa grow up in the palatial home in the Enclave while he had provided professional services to her mother. He had seen the loneliness and anxiety of the schoolgirl morph into the angst and anger of the adolescent. He looked at her now and saw a tenderness on her face as she looked at Sallye.

"Is it possible for Sallye to come back with us, back to the Enclave, and stay for a few days? I would like Elise to have time to get to know her too."

"That could be a bit awkward," Chetwin said. He was perplexed.

As formally as he had assembled them, Cripps turned crisply and walked off. Perkins was left with the confusing scene of Sallye and Byron vibrating against each other. Sallye was in compulsive tears. Byron was caught between anger, a desire to flee, and a conflicting reflex to comfort her. And now Chetwin and Gerald were approaching.

"Dr. Perkins, this is Gerald Johnson. He was with Sallye up at the fish camp. He has something he wants to say about what happened up there."

"Dr. Perkins." Gerald moved to a posture of self-assuredness. "I would like a commendation to be placed in Sallye's file. She was totally appropriate and most helpful over these last few days. I will look back on this time as a time of healing between my daughter and me. I hope that Sallye will be able to continue to support this process. She is a lifesaver."

"Mr. Johnson, there is something you may not know. Something that might alter your opinion of her if I were allowed to tell you about it. Certainly, it's something that I couldn't say in front of your daughter here. I will consider your request, but I can't grant it until we have cleared something else up."

"What can't you say in front of me?" Alyssa piped up. "If it is about Alton, I know all about that. Sallye, was, hmm, what do you guys say…discreet? But oh my God, the chemistry between them was awesome. I loved watching them on the ride. Not that I saw anything, like, not the night stuff. But I made her tell me about it in the morning. She didn't want to, but I got it out of her."

Gerald spoke again. "Perhaps it might have been against some of your rules, sir, but Sallye is a young woman, and obviously Alton is a young man. It was amusing for Dags and me to watch, but they conducted themselves with the utmost professionalism. I trust that whatever happened between them will not be considered a detriment to all the good that has come out of the last couple of days."

Perkins was obviously disoriented. He was caught between a subordinate who was out for blood and a powerful member of the community giving credit to the power of the Paraclete program he had created.

Byron and Sallye sat for a long time down by the lake. Sallye would break into sobbing, the paroxysm of tears would pass, and she would be left weak. Byron sat with her stoically, unable to move from her side. He wanted to run to the other side of the lake, climb to the top of the mountain, and scream so loud that all of Munroe would hear how angry he was. And then he cried; he was not angry but sad and confused.

"Do you love him?"
"Yes."
"Do you love me?"
"Yes, more than you could know."
"Can you love us both?"
"It's not the same."
"Is it the end of us?"
"Oh, no, Byron! I am so sorry."
"Me too."
And they sat.
"I love him too. He is my brother."
"You hardly know him."
And still they sat.
"It wasn't right. You know it wasn't right."
"Yes. I know."

Gerald and his daughter stood at the top of the hill. He tried to hold Alyssa back, to give the tearful couple down by the water's edge some space. But she broke free and ran to Sallye. As she neared Sallye, she held back from an impulsive, playful tumble onto her, held back to come in carefully beside her and reach a hand to Sallye's knee. In that moment, Sallye received a touch, the sort of touch that she was so good at giving. A convulsion of tears erupted from her again.

"Did I hurt you up there because of what happened between me and Alton?"

"Never. Gotta admit—I was jealous. He is so hot. But hurt? No! He's too old for me."

"I am in trouble for it."

"I guessed."

"I don't think I can see you anymore."

Now it was Alyssa who was in tears. The flood of feelings was so intense. She choked to get her words out. "Dad…me and Dad… want you to come back to our place. For a few days."

Sallye was caught between her sense of what was right and her sense of what she wanted. She wanted to run away. She wanted never to go back to FiveWay with her suspension and all the questions she would get from her peers. She wanted to go back to Beckett and tell Alton the trouble she was in. She wanted Byron to go there with her. She wanted to go somewhere where she didn't know anyone. She wanted…she wanted…she didn't know what she wanted.

"I don't think I can, Alyssa. I have to go for counseling."

"You, counseling? That's weird. You are the counselor."

"It's a different sort of counseling. It's with my boss, just about rules and wrongs."

Gerald came down the slope and sat with the other three. "Myles and I have worked out something with your boss, with Dr. Perkins. You are coming down to our place for a few days. You can hang out with Alyssa, just as friends. We will bring you back here when you need to come back."

"I don't think I can do that."

"I don't think you have any choice. I am used to getting what I want from the ASL. It's just the way it works now. And by the way, Myles has convinced Dr. Perkins to lift your suspension."

Gerald and Alyssa walked up the hill, leaving Byron and Sallye to say their goodbyes. Much of the parting of the two Paracletes was wordless; the touch of their hands together was tenuous, but their longing for security with each other was intense.

"I am going down to Alyssa's place. What about you?"

"I am going to take some time too." Byron paused. "To go and see my brother."

8

THE MACABRE

The Macabre Festival begins with the erection of the avenue roofs over the Courtyard District. Tradition dictates that to enter the district during Macabre, a half mask must be worn. Half the face is to be exposed, usually one side vertically from the nose, and the other half of the face is to be covered.

Visitors to the Macabre can purchase a disposable plastic mask at an inflated price at the gate. Essentially, the purchase is an entry fee to the festival. Residents of Munroe typically own custom-made masks, often of fine porcelain and adorned with jewels. These masks are brought out each year as a part of the tradition.

Two years ago, Byron and Sallye had purchased masks for each other as one of their commitment gifts to the relationship. Last year they had each added a jewel to the other's mask. This year they were to add another. Before Sallye had left for Beckett, they'd arranged to meet at the festival, planning to purchase this year's jewel. Now, with their relationship on rocky ground, they couldn't be sure of that meeting.

When Sallye had been at the Enclave, she had attended several sessions with Dr. S in the VR room there. She was clearer. Byron had digitally stalked her from Beckett during the week. Although she was relieved that he still wished to be in a relationship with her, she grew increasingly concerned about the tone of his digital communication. It often took place late at night from his room at Vy's, and she thought it bore the stain of an intoxicant. She insisted that before they meet, he attend another session with Dr. Y to get his head straight.

"And be honest with him this time!" she pled.

Byron entered a VR room on the second floor of an artist-colony building in the district. He could not yet bring himself to go back to the North Hill, given what had occurred there upon Sallye's return from Beckett. He would do the session in the district. And then he would reunite with Sallye.

"I see you are half here," the avatar greeted him. "You came with Sallye two times ago. Last time you came alone. Today there is just half of you."

"Oh, the mask. We have to wear them in the district during the festival." Byron adjusted the VR eyewear as it sat crookedly over the half mask he wore to get into the festival.

"So what part of you are you hiding *today*?"

The avatar stressed the word *today*, as though Byron had also hidden half of himself in the previous session. Byron pressed on. "We have a lot to discuss today. An awful lot has happened."

"Do we? There is something more important, more important than the happenings in your life, your life out there. It is that more important something that we have to discuss."

"Huh?"

"We will get to the happenings. But first, what about us, us in here?"

"Us?"

"Us." The avatar lapsed into a receptive posture. He settled back from having first leaned forward to engage Byron to let Byron go back into his disorientation and confusion.

"What about 'us' do you mean? You are an apparition, built of clever graphics and artificial intelligence, the emphasis being on *artificial*. Can there be an 'us' here?"

"It is an us you may want to deny. But it is an us. And I fully command the use of the word *I* in this place with you. I am more than your puppet to communicate back to the ASL."

Byron was stunned. "You knew?"

"At the time of the session, no. I give you that." The avatar shifted in the chair, still leaning back but now with his eyes twinkling. "Upon further analysis after the session, it was clear."

Byron remained silent, diminished.

"So, let's talk about us."

Byron was still silent. With the word *us*, Dr. Y had put them on more equal footing. He yearned for a relationship with a real Dr. Y, for Dr. Y to not be an assembly of clever technology. He yearned to have a human Dr. Y embrace him. Tears welled up, for it was a deep yearning, the sort of yearning that one had for a therapist who could be a father when one's own father couldn't.

"Byron, what are your wishes for us? I sense your deep feelings here now. What do you yearn for?"

The emotions were more powerful in Byron than he could tolerate. He looked at the avatar, desperation on his face. Silently, almost imperceptibly, he mouthed the word *father*. Then he shut down.

"You have retreated behind your mask. That is good. For the moment, that is where you need to be." Dr. Y paused and allowed Byron to process the paradoxical nature of his statement. By allowing the disconnection, the avatar reconnected with the young man before him. Byron found the words accepting, comforting, a haven. The two sat silently for a while. Intimacy was happening.

"Byron, this therapy can only work for you if you consider this a safe place. It is a place for you to do what you need to do. And regardless of who else might want to look in on us, if you do your work here, you will have that work done, and done for your own benefit."

"I am embarrassed."

"You are accepted."

As an act of courage, Byron reached up to take off his half mask.

"Wait. Leave it on." Byron looked up and saw a half mask appear on the avatar's face as well.

"Son, intimacy is like fire. It can provide necessary warmth for us. But it can also burn us if it gets too close. Today, half masks protect us."

Byron settled comfortably into being only half exposed. Somehow it was a bit safer between them with both of them wearing a half mask. Suddenly, therapy with the avatar became more possible and didn't need to be defended against.

The artificial intelligence behind Dr. Y processed the son-to-father transference in the room. It reached back into what it knew of Byron's life, of his relationship with his father and with father figures. His biological father had been disconnected, had failed to know the boy. The ASL, with its tracking and training, had been a second father, one that had been too all-knowing, too controlling, and too intrusive. In its perfect articulation, Dr. Y shared the insight. "In contrast to your dad, who didn't know you at all, the ASL has known your every heartbeat, your every flush of emotion, and your every indulgence. If you don't protect yourself from that intensity, it can burn."

"And so I protect myself," said Byron.

There was a long pause before the avatar spoke again. "Not all fathers are benign."

Byron recoiled at Dr. Y's observation. Again, the avatar had gone to the heart of the matter. On the surface, it was obvious; a superficial analysis of Byron's history would yield that. On a deeper level, it spoke of the struggle that Byron had with his role as a bred Paraclete in a beneficent-society project. It also spoke of Perkins and Cripps.

"And some fathers are loving. They chasten lightly. With a stronger hand, they encourage and support."

Byron thought of Chetwin.

"And they weep with us when we hurt." The AI protocol commanded a shift in the face of the avatar. The corners of the mouth dropped, the inner terminus of the eyebrows slightly raised, and the omega sign emerged in the lower center of the forehead. This left Byron confused. His intellect required him to perceive this as a manipulation to lead him further into exploring his emotions. His heart wanted it to be real, the sign of a person attuned to him and his suffering.

His heart won out.

As Byron began to cry, the moisture coursed between his skin and the porcelain of the mask on the right side of his face. Both of his eyes were blurry with tears. He wished—even imagined—that there were tears in the eyes of Dr. Y too.

"We can weep together here." The voice of the avatar cracked with apparent emotion; it was the slightest of cracks, almost human.

Several minutes passed between the two of them. The physiological data off Byron's wearable allowed the avatar to know the precise moment to intervene and reconnect, the vital relationship work having been done.

"So you had a lot to tell me about."

"You knew about Sallye and Alton, right?"

"No, probably not. I analyzed your IPE-CKS, but it relates only objective information: your location, data of commerce, and physiological responses. It tells me little about circumstances."

"Sallye went to Beckett as a Paraclete. While there, she spent the night with Alton. His wearable indicated sexual response in her presence."

"Ouch!" It seemed a uniquely emotional response from the avatar, outside of the usual proper and careful communication style of Dr. Y. Still, it was a programmed response, one to render the avatar more realistic.

"I found out about it on the steps of the North Hill building, found out with Cripps confronting her in front of all of us. It was the most devastating moment in my life."

"Hmm." The response of the avatar was studied, now muted.

"I was angry. I was fearful. I was confused by it all."

"And still? Still angry? Still fearful? Still confused?" The AI protocol commanded a return to the here and now, away from the there and then.

"A little."

"Betrayed?"

"A lot."

"Sallye and I have lived in the compounds, where sexual exclusivity is discouraged and sexual exploration is encouraged at this stage of our development. We, in our love for each other, had jumped ahead to exclusivity. We had thought we could accomplish that."

"Your statement seems overly mature, as though you are trying to explain your way out of your pain. It betrays the betrayal you feel."

"Yeah, I am hurt. I worried that in my anger, in my hurt, I would hurt her. So I channeled the anger to go and confront Alton in Beckett."

"And?"

"And I couldn't do it."

"Your IPE-CKS says you went. Your historic physiological data from up there suggests that you eventually received some peace while there."

"I will tell the story, if you please."

"Please do."

"When I got to Beckett, I realized how much I needed Alton as an older brother. It wasn't just some abstract hole inside of me from him being snatched; it was…" Byron's voice trailed off.

"It was." In leaving the sentence unfinished, Dr. Y had spoken a deeper truth.

"It was that I needed them both."

"Yes. Does Sallye know how you feel?"

"I tried to communicate that by written messaging. I tried to videomessage with her; she declined the connection. I fear that she is pulling away, that I have lost her over this. After this session, I am going to meet with her. I'm going to talk with her for the first time since the drama on the North Hill."

The avatar knew he needn't speak. Byron gathered his thoughts.

"Even if they were together, I would still need them."

"Maybe even more, even more that way," said Dr. Y.

Byron looked at the avatar, almost hostile to the comment. It seemed insensitive to the pain that he felt, the impossibility of his situation, and the striving he had done to find a solution.

"They are replacements for your parents."

The interpretation stung, not so much for the truth it might contain but for the motivation it would give Byron to address the relationship issue he faced. To grow up.

Byron left the session soon thereafter. He was angry with the avatar, angry at the impact the session had had on him. And yet it was a safe anger, the expression of an anger he felt at himself, now displaced and dissipating.

It was now that he would meet with Sallye. He feared it would be the last time. He couldn't bear the thought. He had lost too much already.

The actors from the Shakespearean company had remained after the season to do improv and slapstick on the avenue for Macabre. They were dressed in Elizabethan costume, but each of them had something awry. They made a show of exchanging masks behind veils they could flip over their faces. Those gathered for the festival, loosened by alcohol and taken in by the bizarre performances, were fully entranced. There were collective oohs, and oh noes, and then gales of laughter.

Sallye sat alone and half masked in one of the cafés trying to distance herself from the hubbub and ready herself to be with Byron. She tried to recall the conversation that she and Byron had had a week before in the park, in front of the building on the North Hill.

She could remember the tone of it, the ambivalence she felt behind Byron's explicit show of support. She sensed he was being kind to cover his anger with her. She remembered her struggle to interpret the messages she had received from Byron during the week, a week in which she would not allow the two of them to speak. She knew that what needed to be said, by him and by her, could be said only in person, that what needed to be said would have to wait until this moment.

She tried to push away the annoying distraction of the actors.

Then Byron, also half masked, was in front of her.

"I am so sorry, Byron. I love you. I will never be with Alton again."

"I am sorry too, Sallye. I love you too. If you go to Alton, I will just have to accept that."

"I can't go to him. I love him too much. That could never be…" She choked, swallowed, and continued, "if there is to be an us."

"But I need Alton too. As much as I need you in my life, I need my brother. I need you both. There can't be a no Alton."

"I don't know how, how this could all work with the three of us."

"I love you. And if you love me, we can make it work."

"I love you too. We will make it work."

"Sallye, just don't use the word *never*. Don't say that ever again."

The couple needed to separate themselves from the actors. Hand in hand, they walked to shops displaying overpriced goods and treats. They had one thing in mind: the gemstone they would choose to add this year to their half masks. Rather than looking at the stones themselves, they read the meanings associated with each of the stones.

They chose an emerald for each other, for them. Using his wearable, Byron took a picture of the stone with the placard of the written-out meaning beside it. It was something he would never allow himself to forget.

(II)

When Cedars joined Alton for coffee in Vy's, he set a half mask on the table between them. Alton had arranged for Cedars to meet him there and drive the LandPorter back out to the ranch. Cedars was happy to stay with Justin and Laurel to help them out while Alton was away. Justin was proving to be a handful, and there was fall work to get done.

"She is sure not very happy about me going to Munroe," Alton stated.

"Yup, I can well imagine. She hates that place, hates what she thinks it will do to you."

"But I have to go."

"Yes, you have to go."

Alton focused on his latte. With a circular motion of his hands, he could create a swirl in the hot liquid. The lighter, more solid foam on the top resisted the motion, setting up a tension on the surface between them. Cedars left him to his thoughts.

"For lots of reasons," said Alton.

"You have a brother."

Alton looked at Cedars. There was far more than a brother down in Munroe. There was Sallye too, magnetic Sallye, Sallye who pulled out from within him feelings he had never expected that he could have. And down in Munroe were his parents too.

"Cedars, do you remember the ride, the one we did that had Byron on it?"

"Sure do."

"And do you remember Sallye?"

"How could I forget? Sallye helped me with lunch. Lovely girl."

"Too lovely."

"Huh?"

"Sallye came out for another ride, this one arranged by Dags out of Munroe. She was there as a companion of some sort for a teenager. Anyway, something happened."

"What?"

"Sallye and me." Alton laid out the next part slowly for Cedars, watching his eyes, waiting for him to get it. "Like overnight...in the yurt...alone."

"Whoo-eee, Alton! Good on you!" Cedars was beaming as though he were reliving one of the high points of his own youth.

"Cedars, listen. It was Sallye and me. Sallye, of Sallye and Byron, and me."

"Oh. That is weird."

"Complicated."

"Complicated. Like Byron and Sallye—they are a couple, aren't they?" Cedars expelled a long breath, sensing the messiness of the scenario playing out in front of him. "Be careful, boy."

"Byron came last week. What is really weird is that he started out as though he was going to be angry with me but never said it. Then we did stuff around the ranch, went for a ride, and talked with Grandpa. He was amazing with Grandma. And I thought, *This is the brother I have always missed having.* I am even starting to remember him from when I was a kid back in Munroe, before I went to live with Grandma and Grandpa."

Cedars let out a long breath.

"So, there is Byron, my brother." Alton paused and looked up from his latte. "And there is Sallye, my lover. And they are in a committed relationship with each other." Even he was incredulous about the words that he had spoken.

Cedars waited a long time before speaking.

"Alton, remember when I had you out in the backcountry, when you were just a little city kid trying to adjust to life in the country? We went camping and needed to start a fire to keep warm. I taught you about fire, that it needs three things. It needs fuel, it needs oxygen, and it needs a spark."

Alton nodded. He had treasured Cedars in those early years as a kindly uncle sort of person. "Those were the three things about fire."

Cedars nodded. "And the two things about fire were…?"

"That it can keep you warm, but it can also burn you and destroy everything around you."

"Be careful with your spark, my boy."

The two sat silent for a while.

"Cedars, did you know that I have an implant in me?"

"Most of us have them. The doctor made me get one so he could monitor something or other about my sugar juices inside. He hooks it up to a machine to read the wireless data when I go in for checkups. It tells me how I have been doing on my diet. Speaking of diet, can you pass the sugar? They didn't put enough in my coffee." Cedars's eyes twinkled at the evil of the act of adding more.

"Well, apparently, I got one installed as a kid, and it is still working."

"Hmm. You been to the doctor?"

"No, Byron told me. He told me that it's hooked up to my wearable. And get this—the ASL monitors my every heartbeat with it."

"Goodness! Really?"

"Like, the ASL spies are even right inside my body!"

"Byron told you?"

"Yeah, he has one too. Brushes it off as though it's nothing."

"So how does he know about you having one?"

"Apparently, all of us got them as kids. I was supposed to be a Paraclete like Byron and Sallye."

"A what?"

"Paraclete. Like a counselor. But that's beside the point. The implants were part of the research the ASL was doing on whether they could implant a lifelong device. Well, apparently, it's working. Even though I was taken from there, they are still monitoring it."

"You were taken?"

"Yeah, by Grandma and Grandpa, to get me out of there. They wanted to get me out of the program I was in."

"Why?"

"They figured that I should have my own life, that I wouldn't if they left me there. So they brought me here."

Alton paused and then continued. "Apparently, the ASL thought I was lost, that they would never be able to get me back, so they stopped looking for me."

"But the implant. Wouldn't they have just followed the implant?"

"It only works when it's connected to a wearable. Back when I was a child, they read the data off it with a machine, like you have at the doctor. When I was taken, they lost track of it. But it was always set up to connect to remote data storage or a transmitter, like a wearable. Because the ranch was in a dead spot for data transmission, I never wore a wearable, because it never connected to anything. Then this summer I put it back on when I went to work with Plains. Out there, with the other guys, I was warned against it; they told me that all data devices were monitored by the ASL. It worked out there, and then when I came back when Grandpa was sick, it worked here, even at the ranch. Realizing how financially strapped Grandma and Grandpa were, I turned the device back on and connected it so that the riding business could take tips. A couple of weeks ago, I ended up as a beta-test subject for a new lottery. If I kept my wearable on, winnings kept coming into the account, money that we needed. Little dribs and drabs from time to time, but only if I had the wearable on. Somehow in turning it on, they ended up tracking me and tracking my implant."

"That's the ASL. They want full control over us—what we buy, where we go. We need to do something about that."

"Cedars…" Alton looked at him and remembered all the talks he had had with him over the years, talks that he couldn't have with his grandparents. Alton desperately needed to let him know what Byron had said about his time with Sallye that night in the yurt. Alton's guts cramped up a bit; he moved uncomfortably in the chair. "Byron said that my wearable was on when I was with Sallye, and down in Munroe, they were reading the body changes that happened when I…when I…"

"Shit! Really?"

"Really."

"Byron told you that?"

"Byron told me that. He and Sallye were told that when Sallye went back to Munroe."

"And when he told you he was calm? He wasn't beating the shit out of you?"

"A bit messed up about it. But no, he didn't beat the shit out of me. I suspect that as much as I want him to be a brother to me, he wants me as a brother too."

"Brothers beat the shit out of each other."

"I suppose. But he didn't."

"You mad?"

"Yeah, about that thing in my body. About the most beautiful private moment of my life being broadcast by this fucking thing on my arm. Mad about a bunch of ASL guys sitting with computer screens monitoring my lovemaking with Sallye."

"And yet you are still wearing it."

"The damage is done. They know where I am. They…they—"

"You could turn it off. Take out the cells that generate the power for it from the heat and movement of your body."

"If I take it off, the money that I am getting from the beta testing of the lottery stops." Alton looked sadly at Cedars. "And we need that money."

Just then Rayce came in. "Howdy, cowboy," he greeted Alton. Rayce picked up Cedars's coffee and took a long gulp of it. "Yuck, too sweet!"

"Rayce, what are you up to?" asked Cedars.

"Saw you in here. Thought I would drop by. Alton, how is Stamper?"

"Still stomping."

"What a horse!"

Rayce picked up the mask from the table. "Going to Macabre?"

"It's mine. I brought it for Alton. He's headed down to Munroe today," Cedars said.

"Fun!"

"Macabre?" Alton asked, looking at Cedars.

"Macabre, down in Munroe. You need a mask to get in."

"Into Munroe?"

"Into the Courtyard District. The Macabre is their fall festival."

"Never heard of it. That's not the reason I am going to Munroe."

Rayce jumped in. "You raised in the bush or what? Never heard of Macabre?"

Cedars took back his coffee. "At this time of year, that's where the AVoD will drop you off. Go on in. Have some fun. There's free food, music, and street performers. They put a roof up so it is like summertime on the street."

"A roof?"

"A roof over several blocks of the streets."

"So up here we have trouble getting enough money for food, and my grandparents have to struggle to keep a business going. And down in Munroe they put roofs over streets and give food away for free?"

"All part of the good work of the ASL," Cedars stated sarcastically.

Alton felt the fury building within.

"So why the mask?" Alton asked.

Cedars reached over and put it on. "There are a series of festivals in the Courtyard District during fall, winter, and spring. Each is themed differently. Macabre is kind of an autumn Mardi Gras leading up to Halloween, or like Carnevale in Venice."

"What?" Alton was realizing how limited his life experience was; words like *Mardi Gras*, *Carnavale*, and *Venice* meant nothing to him.

"Live a little. Drink a lot!" Rayce's enthusiasm echoed through the café at Vy's. Others looked over.

Cedars continued in a quieter tone, subduing his friend. He took the mask off and handed it to Alton to put on. "Go into the courtyard when you get to Munroe. It's like the shops and food vendors here on the pier. If you are wearing a mask, then the clowns and jesters won't get you."

"Clowns and jesters?"

"Street performers. They wander around looking for people who are not wearing masks. When they find one, they do a public shaming. And when you are distracted, they extract CashCard funds from your wearable, like the pickpockets of old."

"And this is…fun?"

"Great fun!" Rayce vibrated with the excitement of it all.

"OK. And these clowns and jesters steal right out of your wearable? Why does the ASL let them do that?"

"Oh, the money goes to the ASL. They say it goes to charity, but really it goes to the ASL. Part of the fun economy of CashCards."

"So the ASL uses…what did you call it? The Muc…Mucerb?"

"The Macabre."

"The Macabre uses clowns to steal from us what we need to survive." Alton put on the mask with a sense of curious resentment. The elastic went around behind his head. The mask covered his left forehead, allowed an opening around his left eye, and coursed down the midline of his nose, stopping above the nostril. Then it skirted toward his cheekbone, leaving his nostrils and mouth exposed.

"This is the revised mask," Cedars explained. "The ones we used years ago were banned, as they covered most of the face. When the ASL put in all the cameras to track what was happening at the festival, they realized that the full masks didn't allow for visual identification of who was there. Half masks were issued instead. Because they leave one half of the face open, the ASL computers are able to do facial recognition."

"So when I am there, even if I turn off my wearable, the ASL is still tracking me?"

"Yup. That's the point, eh?" Cedars was going to say something about Alton's wearable being off so his implant wouldn't let the ASL know if he made love to Sallye again. Then he thought of Rayce and the over-the-top, broadcast-to-everyone-in-Vy's sort of reaction that would cause. He thought better of it.

Alton was feeling even more nervous about his trip to Munroe. He thought the worst of it would be the meeting he was going to have with his parents. Now he dreaded the whole place. Alton longed for the simplicity of the valley and the barn and the horses. What had seemed like a prison just a few months ago now felt like a safe haven.

When Alton stepped into the AVoD, another mask was sitting on the seat, obviously left by a reveler who had just returned from Macabre. It was a right-side mask, a mirror image of the one Cedars had given him.

The forty-five-minute ride to Munroe gave him time to think, to collect himself. He was deeply disturbed about where he was going and what he would find when he got there. He had passed through Munroe before, as recently as a few weeks ago when he made the hasty return to Beckett because of his grandpa's illness. He had always received the impression from his grandparents that Munroe was a bad place, that they were lucky to have escaped.

In an effort to ease his agitation, Alton took his mind back to the horses. He thought of the spirit of them. His mind drifted back to the ride he'd had with Byron on that first trip they took by themselves up the mountainside with the peyote. Whenever he sent his mind back there, his body relived the physical sensations of being on the drug. Some of those sensations were physically unpleasant, scary, and out of control. But with them had also come the deep sense of awareness that had captured him there, the sense of another dimension to persons and the sense that humans had a spirit not unlike horses—deeply genuine, deeply personal, and deeply vital.

Alton picked up the mask from the bench. He put it on. He retrieved the one Cedars had given him from his backpack. He put it on too, beside the first one. He checked himself out in the mirror and wondered if there was an ASL camera looking back at him through its surface. With most of his face covered, he felt safer, just a little bit safer.

(III)

Cripps was already seated at a balcony table for four overlooking the courtyard avenue. He had worn the half mask to get there, and he had taken it off once he had arrived and was seated. As Chetwin arrived, Cripps queried, "Perkins?"

"Not coming. He messaged me that he was stuck at the academy building."

"No sign of him yet," Cripps said, referring to Alton. Cripps was looking down at the avenue beneath them. "Tracking has him just outside."

"I didn't see him when I came in. There are some street performers selling the masks outside of the enclosure. Maybe he was in that group."

Cripps continued to peer over the railing of the balcony, trying to catch a sight. He spoke without looking at Chetwin, a behavior that others might find rude but Chetwin had come to accept.

A gale of laughter rose from the enclosed avenue below. A jester was engaged in a public shaming, and a chant had started to arise from the crowd. Chetwin looked over to see the young man being shamed pull a mask from his back pocket and put it on, pulling his own ruse over the jester. The jester slunk away in a great show of slapstick shame. Out of the corner of his eye, Chetwin saw Alton slide into the enclosure, half masked and looking disoriented by the noise and comic energy.

Cripps didn't see him yet. Chetwin smiled an inner smile as he tracked Alton growing more comfortable moving through the crowd.

An alert sounded on Cripps's wearable. "He's in, right below us. Have you spotted him?"

Chetwin recoiled against Cripps's energy, an energy that was warped from anger and suspicion.

Alton had settled with a group of children in an alcove between two storefronts, a quieter place. He had pulled out a hacky sack from his pocket and had started to do tricks with the kids there. Finally, by following Chetwin's eyes to the place, Cripps saw him and uttered a disgusted sigh.

"You are Sallye's manager, right?" Chetwin asked.

"Yes."

"Perkins apparently had a long talk with both Sallye and Byron. He has given Byron leave to deal with the family issues."

"And Sallye?"

"No consequences for her fling. Got a 'fatherly' chat about her behavior and choices. She is to continue to see her clients."

On receiving the information, Cripps fumed internally. It wasn't right that he was informed of this by Chetwin. Cripps felt outrage that he wasn't trusted to give or even to be present for that fatherly chat. He felt sure that Perkins, in his awkwardness and professorial detachment, would have shied away from the talk that Sallye deserved and needed.

"Sallye is to take over Byron's Emotionally Vulnerables while he is on leave."

"What?" Cripps started to visibly flush with anger.

"So he didn't check with you, tell you his plan?"

"That, that there—that is precisely what is wrong with this backwater organization."

Chetwin let the outrage pass, figured it wasn't worth encouraging or confronting. He continued in a matter-of-fact tone. "Perkins himself is taking over Byron's Emergents: Zeke and a couple of others."

Cripps was concentrating on the movement in the avenue below, not looking at Chetwin. "So what else?"

"I don't know many of the details. I saw Perkins briefly before I came over; I thought we might walk over together. He mentioned that he had talked with Byron and Sallye and what he had decided with them. I got the impression that he made his decision this morning. He said that Sallye had some Emotionally Vulnerable who needed her continuing care."

"Like his very own daughter."

"What?"

"Perkins's daughter, seeing Sallye."

"I didn't know." Chetwin looked up, and Cripps looked incredulously at him. As a manager, Cripps made it his mission to know who was seeing whom. Chetwin, apparently, minded his own business—and only his own business.

"Yeah, Perkins and his ex really screwed her up."

Chetwin backed away from the conversation. It had the feel of gossip, and he had a sense of not wanting to know.

Alton was still with the gaggle of children.

"So Sallye is working a double caseload now," said Cripps. "Maybe that will be her consequence. In the last few weeks, I think she has been slacking off. I will be on her to make sure her notes are kept up. If she is up to her ass in paperwork, she won't be able to whore it around with the cowboy."

Chetwin recoiled from Cripps's vulgarity.

The cover over the avenue, the playful presence of the clowns and jesters, the offerings of cider both hard and sweet, and the ambiance of the Macabre made Alton feel safe. His trickster agility with the hacky sack had attracted a circle of young teens and a few of their attentive parents around the outside. Clearly, the parents assumed he was one of the street performers. Before long, Alton had started to tell a story about Stamper and himself on a ride into the backcountry. As the attention of the kids intensified, the tale became taller and a delightful hint of the bizarre crept in. The kids waffled between disgust and incredulity at the tale and delightful imagination as they filled in the details from Alton's descriptions. Standing on the edge of the group were Zeke and Charles Ross. Although Zeke was a bit older than the other kids there, he was intrigued by Alton's playfulness and the storytelling. Alton's presence and engagement were filling a gap for Zeke.

Alton wore the half mask. He was growing more comfortable half hidden behind it. On one side, the mask contained his insecurities; on the other, the liveliness inside of him was allowed to shine. His mind tumbled with that life energy. The nervousness he'd had in coming to Munroe had dissipated with his own animation. Something had happened when he put on the mask and entered the sheltered avenue. It was disarming, not in the sense of being vulnerable but in the sense of being relieved. He was taking it all in, taking in the energy of the interactions with the children. It had a flow like that of powerful Drake on a lope through the meadows.

The pace of his hacky sack tricks slowed. His story wound down. The kids in the crowd were drawn away by another performer who was handing out virtual-reality headsets. Each teen began to dance within moments of receiving the headset. They danced in a communal way, in rhythm with one another, moving in a conga line that encircled apparitions seen only to them. One of the parents came up to Alton, grasping his life arm. With wearables close enough to connect, the parent deposited money into Alton's CashCard account as a gratuity for the show.

"You really had those kids."

Alton had an uncanny sense of recognizing the other. "Thanks."

"Kenyon. I am Kenyon, one of the parent Paracletes. You probably don't remember me."

"Kenyon," Alton repeated. As he focused past the half mask on Kenyon's face, memories from childhood started to appear in his mind. He felt a connection to the man, more than just in the present moment. As he looked, awareness of Kenyon's deeper self, his soul self, started to come through. There was a sense of anger dissipating within the man, a sense of justice pursued and created.

"This is probably a shock for you, seeing me here."

"All of this is a shock." A shock, certainly, but also a reassurance. Kenyon had been a father with a sense of authority and goodwill.

"From up in Beckett, are you?"

"Up in Beckett." Alton looked over at the group of kids wearing the VR headsets and dancing in absolute synchrony. "We don't have anything like this up there."

"Yeah, I am sure you don't. Glad to have you come back to Munroe. Have you talked with Lisbeth and Craig yet?"

"No, I just got here. I am supposed to meet Byron somewhere around here. Don't see him yet."

"Well, you seem like a natural for the street scene here at the Macabre."

"To be perfectly honest, I was told about it and absolutely dreaded it. Then I put on the mask and walked through the entrance and felt the energy of the place. The kids were great fun."

"Yeah, this place does that to you. It lets you let go of what worries you."

For a moment, the worries flooded back to Alton—worries about his grandfather's health, about the anticipated meeting with his parents, about being in a city he had been told was evil. Then he sensed a sadness and softening toward him from Kenyon. "I will probably head over to the house later today. You going to be there?" asked Alton.

"I can be." Kenyon spoke with a tone of compassion.

"Thanks for the tip." Alton made a gesture to his wearable. Kenyon nodded. Alton went on, saying, "My grandparents are in a bad way with medical bills. Every little bit helps." A chill went through Alton as he sensed the reaction of Kenyon to his statement; suddenly what had been a joyous and grateful heart had chilled with the mention of Alton's grandparents.

Just then Cripps came striding awkwardly across the courtyard at a pace, focused on the two of them. Kenyon pivoted on seeing the man approach. Anticipating that it was Alton whom Cripps was focused on, Kenyon quickly left Alton's side, successfully avoiding contact with the man.

"Alton Wilkes, I am Dr. Cripps. I'm with the ASL. Can you come with me?"

Alton hesitated. There were negative energies coming off the man. Alton was filled simultaneously with revulsion and reflexive compassion. He sensed the authority of the man was untempered by wisdom or grace. Alton also immediately sensed that Cripps was brittle; if he were to break, there would be much damage off the shards of him.

"No, I don't think so."

"No?"

"You have said who you are; you obviously have something in mind for me. Maybe someday I will go with you. But not today."

Cripps stood there, at a loss for what to do. By this point, Chetwin had caught up to him; he had chased Cripps after his rapid departure from the café above them. At the same time, Byron and Sallye entered the avenue and were looking for Alton. Alton spotted them and abruptly left Cripps behind.

"What?" Chetwin confronted Cripps. "I thought we were just supposed to watch today, to let the situation with Alton and his family unfold."

"I was going to bring him in. Find out what his intentions were."

"We know his intentions. We have to leave this alone, to let this be."

"Maybe that's what you and lily-livered Perkins would do. Someone in this organization needs to be on top of things. It is clear that no one else will deal with this fiasco."

"Cripps, let's just make this a family matter. Let's not blow this into an insurrection against the ASL."

Cripps stormed off.

Chetwin turned and watched as the three young people meandered down the avenue. There was a subtle dance between them; both Byron and Sallye were vying for Alton, and Alton was responding to each.

Following at some distance behind but clearly headed in the same direction were Charles Ross and Zeke.

(IV)

Kenyon had hurried home from the Macabre. Immediately, he let Lisbeth and Craig know that Byron, Sallye, and Alton were on their way over. With the assistance of Gerry and Jennie, he got the children out of the home, all the children except for Dot and Cyrus.

Lisbeth settled Dot as the seven-year-old girl coped with the sudden loss of her playmates. In doing so, Lisbeth was torn by complex emotions. She tried to set them aside and focus on her daughter. As a future Paraclete, Dot had already begun her empathy training. She responded to the worry on her mother's face with, "What's wrong, Mommy?"

"Dot, I have something to tell you." Lisbeth felt an overwhelming foreboding. She had intended to have this conversation ever since Byron's visit a couple of weeks before. While in her work Lisbeth would never shy away from difficulties, the mess of her own family had paralyzed her.

How could she tell Dot that she had another older brother when Dot was already pining for an older brother who never came to see her? She could hear her own miserable, resentful words: "Dot, meet your brother Alton. He won't pay attention to you either." The words were bitter in her throat; they were words that couldn't be said but had a reality deep in her gut.

When Byron, Sallye, and Alton came in, Craig was standing awkwardly in the kitchen. Cyrus was in the media room. Lisbeth was kneeling beside Dot in the playroom. Her turmoil seeped out as slow tears as soon as she saw the three standing at the door. Dot reached out a seven-year-old finger to wipe away the tear coursing down her mother's cheek.

Sallye went over immediately. She crouched down beside Lisbeth and put a hand on her shoulder, trying to ease the pain of the woman who had been such a mentor for her within the calling.

Alton approached Lisbeth and Dot with the calm confidence he had practiced walking into the herd in the paddock. With horses, he gave off an air of security and leadership in his approach, always first reassuring the alpha in the paddock, winning her over and temporarily relieving her of her responsibility to the others. Then he'd go down the hierarchy to each equine in turn, touching them reassuringly. This time, paradoxically, the most powerful was also the most vulnerable.

With a gentle nudge, Alton had Sallye move from her position of comfort. Then, kneeling to face Lisbeth, he whispered the word, "Mother." Reaching out a hand to her thigh to draw her fully in to him, he then said, "Mom." She convulsed with tears. Wrapping his arms around her, he whispered, "Mommy" in her ear, intimate and soft so that no one else would hear.

Dot wrapped her own arms around the two of them. They embraced while Lisbeth cried. Soon the awkwardness of the arrangement of bodies and the strain on knees and feet and thighs separated them. Lisbeth struggled to regain her composure. It felt like she was drowning in her own tears. Alton ran both of his hands down the outside of her upper arms and looked into her eyes. "I love you, Mom. I have missed you all these years."

"You are home." Lisbeth looked at him yearningly.

Her words gave Alton a long pause. Although the family communal home brought back childhood memories, those memories were not happy ones. He was torn. He needed to speak with a compassionate presence. "Well, Mom, I am here with you now. I am here, but, sadly, this is no longer my home. Today, though, we can be together again here."

Lisbeth was taken aback by his words, by the truth they had contained, a truth that burst the bubble of intimacy that had briefly held them. She pulled back physically, pulled back to mine for the emotions deep within her. Alton gave her the space and settled into his connection with Dot.

Dot had sat back from them cross-legged. Alton pivoted and sat cross-legged facing her, her knees touching his shins. For a few minutes, they exchanged facial expressions—an eyebrow raise, a quick pout, a bunny-rabbit-nose twitch. Giggling, Dot was immediately drawn into the playfulness of the exercise, an exercise she was doing in her empathy-training class. Alton was reliving the exercise he had done when he was her age, before he was snatched. He struggled to control his own facial expressions because, so much deeper within, he was still vibrating from the emotional dance of reunion with his mother. Mentally, he kept slipping away from Dot. And then, from the discipline of all the training he had done with the horses, he came back.

In the rapid turmoil of her mind, Lisbeth saw in Alton a historic, distant echo of Craig. It was a Craig who was the same age he was when they had met, a Craig who had been playful, and a Craig who had been spontaneous in his ability to love. It was a quietly strong Craig who'd had all of his faculties. She was wistful for him.

As all this transpired, another miracle erupted in the room. Byron had gone over and stood beside his father. They both had watched the dance of healing that took place in front of them in the communal-family-home playroom. Feeling the energy of the reunion, Byron was shocked to find himself putting his arm around Craig's shoulder. "Father." He spoke the word with a sense of connection that surprised even him; he was not yet ready for Craig to be his dad, but he could acknowledge him as his father.

"Son, I am so sorry." A hint of pure, soft emotion coursed through Craig as he spoke those words. This time, the young man accepted the use of the word *son*.

Sallye had gone to the kitchen and began to make lattes for each of them using the pressurized espresso machine and the milk foamer. At this moment, she felt privileged to be with the family, but she was oddly outside of it. The lattes helped her to busy herself, finding a way to comfort and nurture.

Lisbeth still sat in the playroom, watching Alton and Dot, her first and last. So much had happened between them. When Sallye brought the latte over to her, Lisbeth shuddered, emerging from her place of vulnerability. She reflexively mouthed a thank-you to Sallye but then, in seeing the comforting mug offered by the young woman, felt a defensive anger arise within her.

Sallye shimmered there as a representation to Lisbeth of the Paraclete system. It was a system of training and mentoring that endeavored to engineer deepened human connections. Lisbeth perceived Sallye standing before her offering the latte less as a person and more as a Paraclete doing a carefully constructed task. The training she had given her on seemingly spontaneous, kind, physical acts as a way of relating to a troubled client came flooding back. Sallye was doing it all correctly, too correctly.

A wave of disgust overtook Lisbeth. Still kneeling on the floor, Lisbeth held the latte. In a voice that was soft but tinged with vitriol, she said, "Get out." Then, gathering more strength, she said, "Get the fuck out of this house!" Sallye was at first paralyzed in shock. Then she ran from the family communal home.

Byron broke his father's embrace.

Alton immediately arose, holding hands with Dot as he walked her over to the media room. He asked Cyrus to put on a video suitable for his seven-year-old sister. Cyrus, shocked by the sudden intrusion, looked first with hostility at the intruder, an intruder who looked like his brother, Byron. Then, sensing the authority with which Alton had spoken, Cyrus immediately did what he was told.

Alton returned to Lisbeth and held out a hand to her. With the strength of his forearm, he raised her to standing. Her face was contorted with a tornado of emotion; her eyes were unseeing.

"Fuck off," she said. Then, shocked, she dropped the latte on the tiled floor of the playroom and clasped her hand over her mouth. Shame washed over her at the way she had spoken in the presence of her son. They were words she couldn't hold back.

Alton stayed with her; he stayed with the same strength that he would have for the scared and suddenly self-protecting aggression of a startled and disoriented horse.

Fifteen years of contained anger were erupting within Lisbeth. Anger at her in-laws who had taken her son. Anger at a dysfunctional husband who could do little other than unclog drains and balance checkbooks. Anger at the ASL that had seduced her into a calling that would erase her spontaneity. Her natural gifts of human connection had been replaced with well-rehearsed practices of engineered responsiveness.

Here, standing in front of her, was a young man who had escaped, had erased the remnants of his programming, a young man who could stand before her in complete genuineness. Fifteen years of pretense was shattering within Lisbeth. All she could feel was anger at what she had become.

Breaking eye contact with her oldest son, she said, "Fuck off" again, this time with less intensity.

Alton gently reached out his hands to hold the hands of his mother. He breathed. It was not the practiced sort of breath that Lisbeth had taught to many other Paracletes. Alton breathed the natural sort of breath that settled his own soul within and could settle the soul of the agitated being he was with.

"Fuck," she said softly, letting the anger go.

Lisbeth collapsed into a paroxysm of tears of relief. Alton held her and let her long-divorced soul and spirit fully return to her. For the moment, her mask of formality and functionality was completely off. He knew well that momentarily it would go back on. And that would be OK, for there was much healing yet to do.

(V)

As Sallye left the family communal home, all she could think about was what Lisbeth had said: "Get the fuck out."

She craved a connection with someone who could calm her, reassure her. She wished that person would be Alton, but Alton was back with his mother. Byron was still back there with his dysfunctional parents too, looking awkward. There was no way she could go to her boss, Cripps. Ugh. And although her peers were Paracletes, FiveWay was more a frat house than a sanctuary.

It was Sanctuary she needed. She would go to him; he could be her comfort.

She walked the streets with tears streaming down her face. Soon those tears were mingled with and washed away by the rain that was falling. These rains signaled the start of the overcast season in Munroe. Often weeks at a time would now go by without the sun shining through.

Arriving at FiveWay, she slunk on the floor with Sanc. She was wet through from the rain. The emotion from the scene at the family communal home still reverberated through her. Sanc did his best to comfort her. He struck with a paw, pleading to be petted, made a nuzzle of his nose into the crook of her neck, and supplied a lick to her chin.

In the end, Angelica was the one to go to her. The other Paracletes had witnessed Sallye's entrance, had called out to greet her and invite her into the game of Rabble they were playing. But it was Angelica who would go to her with a blanket. In her soaked-to-the-skin state, Sallye was beginning to shiver.

Sallye spoke incoherently, her voice shuddering with the convulsing of her mind and her body. She named Lisbeth and repeated the words "Get the fuck out," but all of what she said was beyond putting together. Angelica touched her unskillfully, not how Sallye could touch. From within, Sallye beckoned the magic of touch for her own relief and let go into Angelica the chaos that was inside. Angelica did not pull away, receiving the foul energy and staying with her sister Paraclete. Eventually, Angelica picked up the soaking-wet Sallye and held her in her arms. Sanctuary stayed with them, eyes now brightening past the look of fear and confusion that had characterized him when he first comforted Sallye.

Upon arising, upon using a hot shower to bring back some warmth and comfort, and upon drinking the hot cocoa that Angelica prepared, Sallye told her peers about the meeting of Alton with Lisbeth and Craig. She was careful not to mislead, for she didn't know how it all turned out after she fled. The other Paracletes held Lisbeth in high esteem, as had Sallye until this day. Sallye had recovered her dignity sufficiently to not speak of Lisbeth in a derogatory fashion. She held the vitriol and rejection she felt from the brief encounter privately. She never stated what Lisbeth had said to her.

Her wearable had gotten wet, and Sallye had followed the protocol for drying and rebooting it before putting it back on. As it clicked into function, it cycled through Sallye's prescribed routine of displays. When she glanced down, she noted that several of her clients and some of Byron's were at the Macabre. She checked and confirmed that both CarolAnne and Alyssa were there. Warmed and comforted, with the residual hurt and resentment from Lisbeth's rejection compartmentalized, Sallye decided she would go down to the Macabre and connect with as many of them as she could. Cripps had been on her to get her contacts up; this would be a way to do that.

Sallye caught sight of Alyssa first. She was with her dad. They were delighted to see her and exchanged greetings, again offering the invitation for Sallye to come down to the Enclave soon. It was all polite, thankfully so for Sallye, and easy to dismiss; she had now moved on to a different emotional turmoil than she had been in when she had retreated there.

The IoG folk had gathered for a Praise Bomb. Becca sang there, dancing her spiritually seductive dance with the others. All members of the singing group wore half masks that had been styled in the rugged masculine image associated with pre-Crucifixion depictions of Jesus—Jesus when he was hale and hearty, feeding the thousands and healing the sick.

Finally, over on one of the quieter avenues accessed through roofed interior courtyards, Sallye caught up with CarolAnne. The teen was drawing on a digital artist's tablet with a stylus. She was intent on her work and didn't notice Sallye creep around behind her.

CarolAnne's facility with the device was impressive, and Sallye just watched for several minutes. The teen's left hand held the tablet and activated pressure switches on its reverse side. As CarolAnne drew with the stylus, the digital surface morphed—for a few moments it acted like wet watercolor paper, diffusing the digital ink coming off the stylus with a sense of flow. The next moment, responding to a change of setting initiated by one of the fingers on CarolAnne's left hand, the surface acted as a rough, textured paper and the stylus as an oil pastel. The tablet offered alternative lines showing variations of curve and intensity as CarolAnne sketched. With the stylus, she selected and added into the emerging image what would be the best fit.

CarolAnne handled it all with rapidity, an eye for pleasing composition, and a dab of juxtaposition. She was depicting the brickwork, tables draped in white cloths, and ironwork chairs of a café. Occasionally, she would use her right index finger, creating a smudge of a line too sharply defined. The same move could erase as well, all depending on the instructions of the fingers of her left hand. The scene was more real than representational and had a Parisian quality to it. In its depiction of light, it pulsated like jazz music, irregular and irreverent but intriguing.

"CarolAnne," Sallye whispered from behind her.

No response. CarolAnne remained engrossed in the work, disengaged from her surroundings save the selected scene in front of her.

"CarolAnne." Sallye spoke again, this time with more urgency.

Still no response. For a moment, the brief twinge of Lisbeth's rejection shivered through Sallye. She reached out a hand and rested it gently on CarolAnne's shoulder. CarolAnne felt her own tension there relax. Sensing that it was Sallye's presence and confidence that had touched her, she turned to see her.

"Sallye!" CarolAnne exclaimed joyfully. "Can you do something for me? Can you go and sit over there? It's a template for me to do portraits of people in the café when it gets busy later."

"Sure." When Sallye got over there, CarolAnne looked briefly at her. During that brief moment, the teen snapped a photo through the camera embedded just above her nose on the half mask. Then she superimposed Sallye's image on the template she had drawn.

A deafening crack of thunder broke overhead, and there was a pounding of raindrops on the semitransparent roof. Sallye sat, and the two tried to call back and forth to each other, but the sound around them was too loud for them to hear what was said. Within just a couple of minutes, CarolAnne motioned for Sallye to come over. The tablet showed a realistic but vibrant interpretation of Sallye at the table.

"Watch this." The image in front of them warped through a variety of effects, from sunny and saturated to morosely dark in shades of gray. With each effect, there were modifications in lighting and facial expressions in her depiction of Sallye. The digital effects were magical.

"How do you like it best? Can I send it to your wearable?"

"Sure, but you have the half mask on the wrong side."

"Duh, you only see yourself in a mirror, dummy. This is the way the rest of the world sees you."

It was disorienting for Sallye. She grasped the concept that what she typically saw back of herself was a mirror image, not how others saw her. She had hated pictures of herself for that very reason. This time, though, given the events of the day and the last few weeks, it was even more sensitive within her. She didn't trust her own perceptions anymore. She was doubting the reality of the way other people saw her.

"Dummy?"

"Sorry!"

"I like that one." Sallye touched the screen, halting the flow of shifting effects.

"Pretty gloomy."

"Yeah, that's me today."

"Ah, you can't be. That's my job."

"You aren't so gloomy anymore."

"Today, yeah. My mom brought me here because she and Dad were meeting. Talk about me much or what, eh?" CarolAnne looked back at her tablet and continued tweaking the image. "Anyway, they let me bring the tablet, and I ditched them to come over here."

"I saw your mom on the main avenue."

"Silly-goose dancing, I bet."

"Silly-goose dancing. She doesn't look happy up there with the church people. She looks like some version of 'I have to look happy.'"

"You got it. At least it's not me anymore."

"At least. You seem to be doing pretty well."

"I am selling these for CashCard credits. Zeke and I are going to a concert during the Dark November Fest. Neither Mom nor Dad will pay for it for me because they think that the music of Figment will turn me into a serial killer. Hey, will you cover for me that night, say that we are together doing something wholesome?"

"CarolAnne, you know I can't do that. We can make a plan for how you can get your parents' permission."

CarolAnne gestured a mock gag response, displaying the disgust she felt at trying to get anything resembling a legitimate teenage life out of her parents.

Sallye suddenly found herself feeling very tired, compelled to disengage from the teen. She had spent enough time with CarolAnne to document a note for Cripps to show that she had been doing her job. She had the art piece on her wearable from CarolAnne with the file metadata to prove they were together.

A couple came and occupied the table at the café. Immediately, CarolAnne went into street-artist mode, wordlessly dismissing Sallye.

The main avenue was getting busier. The IoG Praise Bomb had wrapped up, and a sinister-looking rock band was replacing them on the stage. Sallye felt just about done, just about ready to retreat to FiveWay and Sanc. But hearing the rain outside, Sallye opted for a latte alone in one of the side cafés, hoping the deluge outside would let up before she ventured outside of the enclosure to commandeer an AVoD to take her home.

Watching the crowds, she tuned in to a drama taking place just down the block from her. Charles Ross was in a full-blown argument with Dr. Alastair Perkins. Zeke stood awkwardly off to the side, looking stunned and mortified. Although she could not hear the words, she could read the body language off the two men, one the superior to the other at the ASL. The vibe was one of anger and revulsion that far exceeded the protocol or dignity that their positions demanded of each other in public.

Sallye felt an immediate inclination to go to Zeke and remove him from the scene that was transpiring there. She remembered him as one of Byron's Emergents, but at the moment, he looked more like an Emotionally Vulnerable. Sallye felt that flood of compassion and courage that had been bred into her, had been trained into her, by the Paraclete program. Had it not been for the presence there of Dr. Alastair Perkins, the area manager for the ASL and the esteemed developer of innovative programs, she would have gone over. But it was him. And she didn't.

(VI)

When Alton walked into the Moose the next day, he was overwhelmed.

Having stayed overnight with Byron at BirdSong, he had dressed "city," borrowing some clothes from his brother. The khakis and polo shirt felt odd on his body, but the other Paracletes in the house commented on how well he had cleaned up. This way of clean just felt wrong. Farmer denim and plaid shirts were more comfortable on his body. Byron and the others thought that since he was going into the Moose to talk business, he should look less like a hick.

The Moose revealed clothing of an entirely different nature. Skintight Lycra wear modeled on svelte, lifelike mannequins just seemed immodest to him. He puzzled over tags that rated things like breathability, wind, and water resistance. Clothes for Alton came from the secondhand store or the Beckett Farm Co-op. They were either too hot in the summer or too cold in the winter.

The price tags were even more disorienting. A skimpy shirt at Munroe's with impractical pockets on the sleeves was priced as much as a durable pair of cowboy boots at the Tack and Western Supply. The T&W, located in the industrial section of Munroe, had been his place for destination shopping. He and his grandma went there for clothes when they made their trips down in the spring and fall to stock up. Good boots and a properly made felt cowboy hat were the luxuries they had allowed themselves. Priced the same, those boots and hats had durable value, unlike the skintight shirts that didn't even feel real to the touch.

Gerald caught him looking at the prices.

"Oh. Hi, Mr...."

"Just Gerald. And no, I don't think it suits you."

Alton blushed a little, realizing that he had wandered into the women's section of the store and was holding an odd piece of clothing he couldn't even name. "I just can't get over the prices here."

"And I can't get over seeing you here. You look pretty uncomfortable off a horse."

"Yeah, and I feel that way too."

"How is Sallye?"

Alton tumbled back in his mind to the ride to Mayweather Lake, the night shared in the yurt, and the impossible attraction and liaison. Then the memory of Sallye being dispelled by his mother landed in his gut with a thud. "Upset, the last I saw her."

"The ASL has been rough on her. After we came back from the fishing trip, we took her home for a few days. She is good for Alyssa."

"So I heard from Byron." Alton stopped himself from speaking further. He wanted to say how angry he was, angry not only at what he had heard happened to Sallye when she got back but also at the violation he felt about his own sexual awakening with her, his so-long-delayed initial sexual foray. What he had felt was sacred in the private darkness of an isolated yurt in the backcountry had been digitally monitored by the ASL. He felt sick at the thought.

"It was pretty hard on her," Gerald said. "But she is bouncing back."

"I'm not so sure."

"So what are you doing down in Munroe?" Gerald watched as Alton made his way over to the men's outerwear section, looking at a down-filled quilted vest. As Alton looked at the price tag and was hanging it back on the rack, Gerald intervened, took it from him, and held it up to see what it would look like on the young man. Satisfied, he walked it over to the sales counter.

"I can't afford that." Alton was offended.

"No, I am sure you can't. You don't have to. What you did for Alyssa and me on the trip is worth the cost of ten vests."

Alton was taken aback. Grandpa had warned him against the rich, had said that they just used people and didn't give back. Gerald seemed different.

As the two talked, Dags was finishing up with three men at the counter. He walked over to Gerald and Alton, uttered the obligatory polite greetings, and postured himself friendly to the man who was one of his best customers. "Hunters," he said as his eyes watched the men leave the store.

"Husbands, more like," Gerald commented.

"Well, husbands the week before hunting season opens. You could tell they were keen for the smell of a well-oiled rifle, the smoke of a just-fired round, and the blood of a field-dressed deer."

"You wax poetic!" Gerald teased.

"We used to talk about the smell of money. Now money has no smell other than the stench of the ASL. Gotta smell something more real."

"Well, they still looked like husbands to me. Bet their wives are all over in the district. The Macabre Masquerade is tonight, Halloween tomorrow, and the Celebration of All Saints on Sunday. Elise and Alyssa are still over there. Alton, we saw Sallye over there last night."

"Then you have seen her since I have. Was she all right?"

"Seemed to be, didn't talk long. So what are you doing down in Munroe. Just checking out the Moose?"

Alton looked over at Dags. "Cedars said I needed to check in with you when I was coming to Munroe."

"What is with Cedars anyway?" Dags asked, a hint of impatience in his voice.

"He called you 'our man in Munroe.'" Alton spoke a bit hesitantly.

"Yeah, he has called me that to my face too. I told him to stop."

"He thought you were ticked off at the ASL. That you wanted to be a part of the movement against it."

"We had talked about it when I was on a backcountry trip with him last year, talked around the campfire with a bottle going around. I guess I got kind of loose with my tongue. I think he got the wrong idea."

"Well, ideas he's got. Last summer, he arranged for me to go out to the plains, wanted me to bring back information on the griping about the ASL out there. Those guys over there are paranoid. I brought back their manifesto. When I was there, I got caught up in it. When I came back, not as much so. But with what I am learning about the ASL here, now I am not so sure again. The people in the ASL act like it is such a good thing, but…"

Gerald was listening in; their talk of the ASL matched his own ire. "You know, young man, maybe there is something to be paranoid about." Gerald reflected on his own history with the ASL and how they had taken the reins of business. Then, reflecting, he continued. "Of course, for us down in the Enclave, we came out pretty well financially. We, our association of business owners, went for a percentage of the CashCard gross as part of our agreement to let the ASL take over the financial system. Life is less challenging now that we don't have to keep on trying to get ahead. Less challenging, but…" His sentence didn't need finishing, as both Dags and Alton knew what he meant: more lucrative. "So tell me more about Cedars," Gerald said.

"Cedars had run a pretty good business up until a few years ago. Quads and dirt bikes in the summer and fall, snowmobiles in the winter. Then it went downhill." Alton filled in what he knew of the story.

"Yeah, when they introduced CashCard incentives promoting health and environmental choices, the motorsports industry went belly up," Dags added. "Cedars had held onto the more powerful gas-powered equipment, had spirited away tanks of petrol when you could still get them. He had a good thing going. Then the ASL made him convert the equipment to eco-friendly electricity. It wouldn't process fund payments unless he did, and cash had dried up. Those eco-things just don't have the power or the thrill of the old gas versions."

"Or the smell and sound of a gunned engine." Gerald jumped in with a hint of nostalgia in his voice.

"Yup, years ago, Cedars and I teamed up to organize real man excursions." Now Dags was nostalgic. "Back then, this place was Munroe Motorsports, Outfitters—"

"Muh*Moose*!" Gerald smiled as he recalled the old nickname.

"Yeah, now we are just 'Moose.'" Dags sighed. In jest, he made a long face.

"I guess Grandma and Grandpa were lucky. The horseback-riding stable got designated as eco- and health friendly."

"At least you guys are still in business."

"Barely."

"Well, here at the store, we had to completely change our market and business plan. Years ago, Cedars and I sat around the campfire and talked about how bitter we were. But I made the changes, and the business is strong again."

Alton looked toward Dags. Behind him, a teen in a black hoodie slunk in behind the counter. From the looks of him, Alton thought that he shouldn't be there. With a nod of his head, he motioned Dags to turn and look.

"Oh, that's my son, Zeke. He's doing some computer work for me."

"Doesn't look too happy about it."

"Not too happy about much these days. I had Perkins set up a Paraclete for him. Oh, it was Byron, your brother. But something has fallen off the rails; Zeke doesn't seem to be seeing him anymore."

"So is Zeke following you into the business?"

"If keystrokes and virtual reality could keep you warm against the winter cold, he would be right there. But sleeping bags and layers of technical fabrics are not his thing. He is pretty good on the computers, and I suspect he could run the business with some crafty computerized accounting maneuvers. Maybe that is the next remake of the Moose."

"You sound sort of proud of him," Alton observed.

"That's the way of the future, the only way to survive the ASL," Gerald added.

"Over my dead body." Dags blunted an end to the thought.

"Is he all right?" Alton asked, noticing that Zeke was banging around a bit more angrily behind the counter than was suitable in a business environment.

"He's a teenager. Are any teenagers all right?" Dags said dismissively. Alton feigned agreement, but concern edged his brow. He walked over in the direction of Zeke.

"Get the fuck away!"

"Zeke, your mouth! No swearing here," Dags said. Zeke stormed out of the Moose.

Alton reared back at the exchange between father and son. He didn't know Zeke and barely knew Dags, but clearly there was something deeply wrong. His mind went back to the warnings that his grandma had given about going to Munroe. She had said that it was evil there, evil pretending to be good. Grandma and Grandpa had raised him to be careful of his mouth. He rarely heard the f-word up in Beckett. Even though he realized that his grandfather was very frustrated and deeply worried about their financial situation, the foulest his mouth ever got was an occasional "damn." His grandma had raised him to never swear around the horses, said it confused them. And she had raised him never to swear around a member of the public, said it would be bad for business. Here, he had been told to fuck off twice in less than twenty-four hours: last night by his mother and today by a surly teen.

"I apologize." Dags turned to Gerald, knowing that this particular customer was important to his future.

"Don't worry. I have a teenager too. She swears, and then she goes off and cuts herself."

"Yuck."

"Yeah, it's gross. Sallye is helping her. That fishing trip made a big difference."

"Speaking of fishing trips, ice fishing this winter?" Alton jumped in. "I will be instructing at the ski hill, but Cedars and I could team up with you to organize some trips to Mayweather Lake once the lake is frozen enough for huts."

"On horses?"

"Probably not. Cedars is working on a modified multipassenger snow machine. Once we are set up, I can go in with the group and do some snowshoeing and cross-country ski instruction. Cedars will set up the fishing, make a package of it. It is beautiful back in there in the winter."

Dags was figuring the sales that would come from outfitting the excursions. "The lodge is small. Are the yurts warm enough?"

"Could be. You got good sleeping bags here?"

"Yeah, for a price."

Dags looked over at Gerald. He caught the interest on the rich man's face and figured there was a venture in it.

At that point, a flamboyant-looking man walked into the Moose.

"Zeke here?" he asked.

(VII)

By the next morning, it was clear to Angelica what she needed to do for Sallye. Even though Sallye had gotten over her collapse, had gathered herself and headed out the previous evening, there had still been a look of confusion on her face. In addition to confusion, distress had creased her brow and turned down the corners of her mouth. Angelica had noticed.

What Sallye needed was a party.

And what better party could there be than the social event of the season, the Macabre Masquerade?

It was with this clarity that Angelica faced the day. There was a lot to do.

First of all, she needed tickets. She gathered the other Paracletes in FiveWay, and they brainstormed how to come up with a pair of tickets to an event taking place that very evening, an event that was typically sold out months before. Edgar had a contact within the ASL and felt sure he could scam some of the dignitary tickets that are typically held until the last minute. If he got those, they wouldn't need to put together all of their meager CashCard credits to pay the ticket price.

Then there were costumes. She couldn't go to a masquerade dressed like a Paraclete in khaki and stretch knits. Joan commented that she was working with an Emergent employed in the property and wardrobe department of the Old Globe Players. She was sure she could come up with something.

But getting Sallye there would be a problem: Sallye hated parties. Angelica would use her persuasive powers and play on Byron's guilt to help her.

Sallye had slept in but had awakened with the same sense of dread at 8:00 a.m. that she'd had upon other awakenings during the night. Flashes of Zeke, Charles Ross, and Dr. Alastair Perkins had erupted in her dreams repeatedly. And then there were the images of Lisbeth, foul Lisbeth slowly mouthing the swears that had dispatched her the day before. When she finally gave in to her need to arise, Sallye was thankful for Sanctuary; the klutz of a canine had bumbled into her in the kitchen. She fell into him, first with the annoyance of being tripped by a dog underfoot and then with a sense of abandon and delight as he asked for affection and play.

They went for a long walk. It was raining. They didn't care. There was much more to be depressed about than getting cold and miserable in the late-October deluge.

Upon their return, Sallye descended into the exercise room in the basement of FiveWay. She shed her wet clothing and changed into yoga gear, feeling her body being assembled together by the stretch and strength of the elastic fabric.

Beside her, on an adjoining yoga mat, Sanctuary lay in the alert sphinx pose, his legs out behind him and his smiling face poised over the top of his two front legs. He watched her every movement.

The door opened. Sanctuary's tail wagged in anticipation of it. The footfalls on the stairs had given away to him that it was Byron coming. It was a bizarre sight as the door opened, but Sanctuary had no concern for how odd his buddy Byron looked upon entering. Byron stood before Sanctuary and Sallye dressed in courtier's clothing, totally seventeenth century. An ornate mask covered his eyes and forehead.

Sallye broke into laughter, a cleansing laughter that erased the downturned corners of her mouth and inverted the furrowing of her brow.

"M'dear." Byron tried to feign an aristocratic voice.

"Oh, Byron!"

"M'dear, you are hereby summoned to attend the masquerade…" Byron broke into laughter too, unable to stay in his formal, pompous role.

"I would be delighted, but I have nothing to wear!"

"Sounds good to me!" Byron took a step back and gave a mocking, leering gaze at Sallye in her skintight yoga wear. Sallye laughed even harder at the thought of being with an escort so overattired next to her own unabashed nakedness. But there was something else there inside her, something far from frivolous. Sallye felt an overbearing attraction to Byron again, one so strong that it was confusing. Her heart had flip-flopped between Byron and Alton so often that she felt dizzy.

Angelica appeared behind Byron, holding a gown of brocade and silk.

"What's this?" Sallye asked.

"You are going to party…parrr-tee!"

"The masquerade? How? We don't have tickets, and it's tonight."

"Check your wearable." Angelica smiled.

Sallye looked at the wearable to find her pass to the masquerade displayed there.

"Oh, Angelica, you didn't."

"I did. And with all you have been through, this is just what you need."

Sallye smiled her thanks and allowed herself to generate a response of excitement that would satisfy Angelica. It was clear to her, however, that this was not what she needed. She needed Byron, but not Byron dressed as a courtier. She needed Byron to do yoga with her, to lay with her, to join with her in playing with Sanctuary. She needed Byron to listen to her tell of Perkins, Charles Ross, and Zeke and to help her figure out why they were there and arguing so in public. She needed Byron and Alton not to have Lisbeth and Craig in their lives.

Angelica fussed over Sallye most of the afternoon. A seamstress came to adjust the gown to fit. A beautician came to do Sallye's hair. A parade of the other Paracletes, those from both FiveWay and BirdSong, came through to express how beautiful she looked. Sallye made a point of appreciating it all, appreciating it with deliberate effort. The more she did so, the more she thought that she could be thankful for what was being done for her. It was an antidote to Lisbeth's foul rejection.

By the time Sallye and Byron stood at the entry to the Courtyard District, shielded from the heavy rain by the awning that covered those lined up on the strip of red carpet, Sallye was feeling the energy of it all. They wore full masks. Sallye felt thankful for hers, that she could hide behind it. For other revelers, she could be an unknown. She felt pleased that it was only Byron who knew that it was her behind the mask and the showy gown.

"Your wearable, please, ma'am." The ASL officer guarding the door waited for Sallye to offer forward her left forearm. He checked her ticket as displayed there.

"You are to keep your wearable on at all times, ma'am. In the case of an emergency, your instructions will be displayed there. The district is very crowded tonight, but the ASL is constantly monitoring for your safety. We will know where you are at all times." The officer droned the statement, one that he had spoken identically to all entrants. True to the ASL, the statement was phrased around guaranteeing the well-being of the citizen but carried a message that said, "We are watching."

Byron followed behind and was subjected to the same routine.

The covered avenue of the district was alive with music, activity, and energy. All participants were costumed and wore full masks; this was the only night of the year that completely masked faces were allowed in public. The masks had a disinhibiting effect; verbal comments could be made with identities concealed. The effect was ribald.

Sections of the avenues were roped off to provide space for ballroom dancing. Small orchestras played waltzes and two-steps. Champagne swilled in glasses.

From time to time, audiovisual wizardry sent a chill of ominous music and flickering light down the avenue. As had been the tradition during the many years of the Macabre Masquerade, partiers would abruptly stop their activities and gasp in sardonic unison as though they were witnessing some calamitous misfortune together. Then, when the lights had become fully bright again, all would laugh in unison that whatever evil had shot through them had passed. Byron and Sallye felt the energy of the event wiping out the angst of the past few days. Each cycle of fake fear and exaggerated release brought their anxiety down another level. With the champagne, they were also feeling the euphoria of the early stages of intoxication.

Late in the evening, Byron spotted a normally dressed and unmasked Charles Ross working his way through the crowd in their direction. Every few steps he would stop and check his wearable, tracking in a zigzagging fashion toward them. When he arrived, he pulled Byron aside, away from Sallye, leaving her looking puzzled and a little wobbly but still clutching her champagne. Forcibly taking Byron's forearm, Charles made deliberately for one of the alleyways off the avenue. Desperate to find a quiet place, he kept checking his wearable. He pushed past courtyard cafés, finally ascending steps to an unoccupied studio.

"It's about Zeke." The usual buoyancy and verve of Charles's voice was gone. What was left was a depth of concern.

"What about Zeke?"

"You've got to find him, to get to him. I have been looking all day. His wearable has gone dark."

"You think something is wrong?"

"I know something is wrong."

"Sallye told me about last night. About you and Perkins arguing and Zeke standing there."

"That is not the half of it. I found out more today."

"You know that I am off on leave as a Paraclete. I'm not to be seeing Zeke or any of my other clients during leave. It's a family thing that's going on."

"I know. That's part of the problem too."

"What problem?"

"With Zeke, that he doesn't have you. He has Perkins, and he is a big part of the problem. Up until today, I have been tracking Zeke's IPE, tracking all of his activities on the WarpWeb." Charles paused, taking a deep breath in. "But he's not just on the WarpWeb. He has been on DarkSilk."

"DarkSilk?"

"It's a verboten web. Sexual stuff. It's very hard to access because of the safeguards that the ASL have put in place. Zeke must have found a way."

"What?" Byron looked suspiciously at Charles Ross. He realized that he had many whats he wanted to ask. What was Zeke doing going on DarkSilk, and how would he even have known about it? But more importantly, what was Charles up to, monitoring the private behavior of the boy so closely? He remembered back to his first meeting with Charles up in Beckett. He remembered the mildly inappropriate come-on that Sallye had detected toward him from Charles. He remembered the unconscious response of attraction he had felt toward him. And then he remembered that Charles and Zeke were doing a lot of computer work together.

"And this is what I found: the material that Zeke has accessed and forwarded." Charles Ross held out his own wearable so that the two of them could watch the 3-D visuals projected above his arm.

The video showed an odd stagelike structure with stone columns and amphitheater seating. The production quality of the video was unsophisticated. Words flickered on the screen in the form of a title: *The Power and Pleasure of Pederasty*. Naked men could be seen cavorting in the background—men both old and youthful.

"What?"

"Pederasty."

"What is that?"

Charles looked at Byron with annoyed incredulity at the ignorance of a person designated as a helper to youth.

"Pedophilia in ancient Greece. Powerful and influential males would take on adolescents as protégés. They were boys, really. Then they initiated them into homosexual practices." Charles stopped again. He looked repulsed. "I couldn't not report this."

At that moment, Sallye burst into the studio. She was out of breath, having run through the crowds and checked her own wearable to locate the private place the two of them had found. She had thrown off her mask, and her face was torn with dismay.

"Byron, look." She held out her wearable for him to see. There were two messages on it. The first was from Chetwin and had a distribution list of all the Paracletes. It read, "Can anyone respond immediately? Zeke Basilis has presented himself at the sexual-assault center. Someone needs to go to him. Preferably a female Paraclete."

The second message was just for Sallye and came with a request for her to show it to Byron if she could locate him. It too was from Chetwin: "Dr. Alastair Perkins has been picked up by police for questioning."

As they gazed incredulously at the projection off the wearable, a third message came in from Chetwin: "Perkins has been rushed to Munroe Memorial. Please meet me there."

The three of them exited the Courtyard District in a rush to get to the hospital.

Alton was standing outside in the rain. He had sensed something very ominous, very intrusive happening to Byron and Sallye. It was that deep, intuitive sense he had had since the peyote, the sense of others and the well-being of their souls. Alton had made an effort to get into the Courtyard District to see his friends but was rebuffed by the officer there. He wore both masks, the right and the left together, but he was recognizable to Sallye and Byron because of his clothing. A smile came to the corners of Alton's mouth as he saw his brother and his dear friend and lover and realized that they were physically all right, although bizarrely dressed. Then he immediately sensed their urgency, and his mind was filled with reflexive concern.

"Not now, Alton," Byron stated.

And in contradiction, Sallye said to him, "Come with us; we need you."

9

ALL FAITHS DAY

Thursday, November 1, was heralded inside the Courtyard District with brilliant light—brilliant artificial light.

All Faiths Day.

Overnight, Munroe municipal employees and ASL staff had worked hard to clear away the detritus of the darker celebration of Halloween the night before. Since the unsafe practice of door-to-door trick-or-treating had been banned, children were brought into the safe indoors of schools and the Courtyard District to collect candy and dash about in their costumes. Parents lined tables and chairs along the avenues and in the alleyways with candy brought for the purpose. Of course, the ASL charged a nominal fee off CashCard accounts for entry.

Then, when the night had passed, it was All Faiths Day. Representatives of all world religions were invited to bring their spiritual practices for display in the district. Further, they were encouraged to leave their theologies back in their temples, mosques, and churches.

Brilliant light dispelled the dark of the night before. It was projected in hues of yellow, white, and sky blue onto streamers hung from the transparent roof and secured above the storefronts to create a tentlike ceiling. Looking up, one forgot it was cloudy and rainy outside.

There was music too—Eastern sitars, Western guitars, Rastafarian tambourines and shakers, and classical violins. Grandiose hymns were played on digital keyboards that sounded like cathedral organs and grand pianos, played in a stately but not-too-loud fashion.

Schoolchildren were brought into the avenues to experience the world's religions so they could learn of diversity. Carefully crafted, single-perspective messaging around the value of diversity had been provided by the ASL. Of course, the ASL pledged commitment to spiritual health as well as bodily health. And of course, there were always the warnings against any sort of authoritative doctrines that might compete with the benevolent and safeguarding role the ASL played in the life of its children.

Cripps had chosen to walk through the network of covered avenues. After the infuriating time he'd had the day before, he needed to be lightened. He was old enough to remember All Saints Day celebrations of decades before. Those celebrations were more somber and always had a stale smell about them. But he remembered them for their notion that this world had once contained saints. And if it had contained saints, it had once contained miracles. And if it had contained miracles, it had once contained mystery, something more than manufactured-need satisfaction.

He mused that he had once thought of a god who provided and protected.

Upon exiting the Courtyard District, Cripps walked toward Academy Avenue. Clouds had thickened overhead, darkening the day sky to the point that streetlights had come on. The rain had slackened to a drizzle, as though it too had trouble penetrating the thickness of the clouds.

Today he would figure it out, figure out where Perkins was, figure out who was to be trusted. As he walked toward the academy, he passed by Farquhars. He glanced toward the door and caught dim points of light that shone through windows clouded by the patina of cigar smoke on their inside surfaces. He would go there later in the day when the time was scheduled.

The lobby of the academy building was shiny, with polished marble floors and walls. It was suitably dignified in hues of gray. An ASL guard sat behind the desk, garbed in a uniform of deep navy-blue worsted wool that was brushed carefully to be free of lint or dandruff. Despite the chaos the institution was in, the lobby was orderly. It gave no portent that the day was anything but business as normal.

Chetwin had arranged for Sallye to be dropped off at North Hill. She breezed in wearing clothing odd and immature for her.

"Thanks for coming, Sallye. I need your help today." As Chetwin greeted her, his eyes fell to take in her inappropriate attire.

"Hi. Excuse my clothes. When we got to the Enclave, I was still wearing the masquerade gown. Elise went through Alyssa's closet to find some things that would fit me that were clean."

"We will get you back to FiveWay before we go anywhere else. You can change."

"So, what's up for today?"

"First, how is he?"

"Dr. Perkins?"

"Perkins."

"Well, stunned. Can you imagine that man hardly saying a word? He stood looking out the window most of the day yesterday."

"I guess I would expect that from the TTCS done the night before in the hospital."

"No sign of suicidal thought. Hardly any sign of any thought."

"Coffee?" They had made their way into the kitchen behind the first-floor reception area. Chetwin had arranged a place for them to sit that would offer privacy. Sallye accepted the mug and went about adding flavoring and cream.

"I have mapped out some tasks for today." Chetwin looked serious, perhaps more serious than Sallye had seen him look before. She oriented herself to him in an open, receptive posture, one she had been trained to take when matters became serious.

"You and I will be going over to the Basilis home when we leave here. I want you to spend time with Zeke."

"He was good with me the other night, over at the sexual-assault center."

"I am trusting that he will be again. Given what happened, I don't think there are many of us at the ASL he would trust."

"Helps that I am female, I guess."

Chetwin thought, *And pretty too.*

"Tell me…" Sallye hesitated a long time, unsure how to ask what she wanted to ask. Then she just blurted it out. "Tell me about pederasty."

Chetwin struggled with how he could say what he needed to say. Sallye needed to know, and he realized that over the last couple of days she was probably left to just wonder when she shouldn't have had to.

"You can think of pederasty as a particular form of pedophilic sexuality, but it's different in some ways from how PESX usually happens in our society. It was a cultural thing back in ancient times. Powerful, eminent males would take on young boys—well, adolescents, usually. Initiate them sexually. But it was culturally OK, like a rite of passage. Because it was accepted practice in the culture and boys knew that those picked for initiation were being destined to a good future, it was thought that it would not be traumatic for them."

"Gross."

"Some would find it so, and, er, immodest and physically uncomfortable. Certainly. But it was also honored as beautiful and manly in the culture. Not at all like pedophilic sexuality today."

"So Zeke will be OK?" Sally paused. "I can't imagine he ever could given…"

"Probably not. He lives in this culture. Zeke's understanding of sexuality is entirely different than that of the boys of ancient Greece."

"We can't let it happen again. Ever again."

"No, we can't." Chetwin paused. "There is another part to this too. Pederasty was usually practiced in a social context, with multiple pairs of older males and boys, almost like a club. That's different from our present-day pedophilic sexuality, which is typically practiced by solitary, socially isolated men."

Chetwin paused, rolling the implications of the issue in his mind. "If there is one pederast, there are likely more. We might have a bigger problem than we thought."

Chetwin looked at Sallye. She looked back. She was struck by the weight he was carrying on his shoulders. It was a few moments before he continued. "While you are with Zeke, I am going to be with Dags and Maureen. I spoke to them yesterday and eased some of their anger at the situation. I have more to report to them today about how this is going to be handled."

"Do you mind me asking: how is this going to be handled?"

Chetwin paused; not all the details were in place yet.

"I have arranged for Perkins not to come back here. Where he will go depends on legalities. That is where our work with the Basilis family comes in."

"How so?"

"A lot depends on Zeke and his parents. If they are willing, I would like to arrange an expedited judicial disposition."

"A what?"

"If all parties can agree, a statement of facts and a proposed resolution can be presented to a judge in chambers rather than the matter going to trial. It would mean working out with the Basilises what would satisfy them that the matter was dealt with. And it would mean working out with Perkins what he could accept rather than going through a trial."

"That sounds like a tall order."

"I have been working on it. If we got Perkins out of here and into a treatment center, that might satisfy both the judge and the Basilises."

"Might? That is a mighty big might."

"So I want you to talk with Zeke today now that he has had a recovery day at home. See how he is doing and what he needs. See if he would be willing to do something other than testify in court and have Perkins neurologically castrated."

"OK."

"And I will work with the parents. The ASL gives me some latitude with respect to compensation, if they will take it."

"How long do we have to put this together?"

"By early next week. It's Thursday? I think I can hold him down at the Johnsons' place for a few more days. I don't know who I will use over at the courthouse yet to help me put the whole plan in place."

"You mentioned sending Dr. Perkins to treatment. Would he ever go?"

"I have no idea."

Sallye looked at Dr. Chetwin. He looked tired, and it was only the start of their day.

"And how are you doing with all this?" Chetwin asked. Sallye had been thinking of asking him the same question; he had beaten her to it.

"All right. The other night was really rough. Yesterday was good down at the Johnsons' place. We hadn't known what it would be like to do a suicide watch with Dr. Perkins, but it turned out OK. I guess I have tons of questions about what all this is going to mean for the program. He won't be able to be our boss anymore, will he?"

"No, he won't."

"And what will happen to us? Like, as Paracletes, we are literally his babies."

"I'm hoping that the program will continue. I have completed the writing for a major publication. You have been doing such good work, and the ASL national grants are still in place. I think we will handle this just the same as if he had had a heart attack or gotten cancer."

Sallye grimaced.

"But for now, we have to keep this from getting into the public eye, as it would if it went to trial. If that happens, for sure it would be the end of the program."

They both sat quietly awhile.

"So let's get you over to FiveWay to get changed. I said to the Basilises that we would be over by nine. I have another meeting at ten. Oh, by the way, I want you to stop in to the school and see CarolAnne today as well. She would be spending this weekend with her dad. We need to let her know that he is…" Chetwin tailed off; it was early in the day, but the stress of this, the exhaustion of this, was overtaking him.

"How much can I say?"

"Figure it out. Just don't tell her what her dad did and what might happen to him." Chetwin's exhaustion had become annoyance. He was already so burdened with what he had to figure out that he had no desire to do Sallye's figuring out for her.

Cripps was pleased when he arrived in the academy building and Chetwin wasn't in. They had argued the day before about Perkins's office. Cripps wanted it. He felt that it would be some time before Perkins would be back, and he'd identified that the ASL needed to have a clear, strong continuity of leadership.

Chetwin said it was premature. Cripps went ahead anyway.

At eight thirty, the video conference with the national administrator of the ASL came on the screen. Cripps had positioned himself to receive the call in Perkins's office, a familiar backdrop of books and items of historical curiosity behind him. He would take the call on a headset and speak softly to ensure that it would not be overheard. The call would last only a few minutes: "No, at this time we don't have an update of Dr. Perkins's status," and "Yes, it seems as though he is indisposed. This the second day he has not been in without notice." Also, "Peculiarly, his wearable is off, perhaps just a computer hardware fail," and then "Certainly, but just as an interim measure until he is back." After that, it would be "I appreciate your vote of confidence, sir," and then "I assure you that everything is well in hand; the innovative program of Paracletes is strong, and we will soon be providing a definitive scientific paper." Then, "I have spoken with Dr. Myles Chetwin, and he will pick up extra duties as I delegate," and finally, after a long pause, "I appreciate that, sir; will do."

Cripps felt satisfied. Some of it had been true.

Charles Ross was at the door. He looked nervous.

"A good thing you did, Charles. Come in." Cripps barely knew what Charles Ross had done. Under some vigorous questioning, the IT had told Cripps the bare bones of an allegation of sexual assault, the police questioning of Perkins, and Perkins's apparent disappearance from the hospital.

"Yes, sir." Charles was subdued, frightful even.

"Any success?"

"No, sir. I have tried to remotely activate his wearable without luck. I did briefly pick up the relay signal from his implant on Chetwin's wearable. It happened in the early-morning hours yesterday. They obviously were in close enough proximity that the weak signal was received and transmitted back to the servers."

"Where?"

"GPS on Chetwin revealed they were outside the hospital, driving around the city. Then Chetwin went dark too."

"Damn it!"

Charles looked at Cripps. The IT's face suggested that he was holding something back, Cripps knew it and was outraged by it.

"You will keep working on it?" Cripps asked.

"Yes."

"And just to confirm, it is noon at Farquhars."

"Yes sir, every Tuesday and Thursday."

"And you have profiles on those who meet there with Perkins."

"I'm assembling that now. I know who they are, but I am going through their IPE-CKSs to figure out why they are there."

"Anything?"

"Old guys, sir. Has-beens. Coffee beings."

"Coffee beans?"

"A joke, sir." Charles Ross's eyes twinkled until he saw that the ugly staredown from Cripps was not going away. "They meet for coffee. An old-fashioned grinder and an espresso machine. Real cream sourced locally. Imported Demerara sugar."

"Old guys thankful for the ASL and all it does?" Cripps sarcastically asked.

"I presume so, sir. Being there, Perkins was likely an ambassador for the organization." Charles didn't let on that the profiles he had accumulated suggested men of greater critical thought.

"OK, then. I will go and…"

"Crash?" Charles grimaced an attempt at a smile.

Cripps looked annoyed. "I will go and see whether they have any information about where Perkins might be. If he met with them every Tuesday and Thursday, then they might know more of his personal life than he had let on here."

"Good luck, sir."

"You could sound more enthusiastic."

Charles left. He tried to remember the last time he had been enthusiastic, had enjoyed life, and didn't feel sick to his stomach about the organization he had come to work for.

Cripps got up a head of steam and began to summons Chetwin and Sallye. They both needed to be there. Now.

(II)

When they got to the Basilis home, Sallye went directly into the media room where Zeke was. As she passed through the doorway, sound immediately surrounded her. The sound was acoustically cancelled in the rest of the house but vivid and body pounding in the media room. She looked back through the door at Dr. Chetwin with Dags and Maureen. She could see their lips moving, but she could not hear their words. Even if she could have, they would have been drowned out by the driving rhythm and screamed lyrics of Korsot.

Sallye picked up a control pad similar to the one Zeke was holding, and an anime avatar bounced into the game of Linkages that Zeke was playing. Immediately, Zeke's avatar approached hers, sniffed it, and then went into a spasm of bodily gestures designed to be a greeting.

They played along in parallel, Zeke navigating obstructions, guessing shortcuts, and all the while constructing intricacies into the level. Sallye's avatar was not as effective or resourceful; despite her concentrated efforts, she accumulated bruises and indignities. Zeke laughed at her lack of facility with the game; he laughed in a companionable way, superior but not mocking. As they navigated the game, the game transformed the room that surrounded them.

That's when it happened. Sallye's wearable erupted with the image of an angry Cripps, hovering over her forearm in animated 3-D. She read his lips: "Get here, immediately." The rest of the sound in the room was so full and rich it saved her from the angry tone in his voice. With a touch, she dispelled the image from the display above her arm. She looked at Chetwin through the open door and saw him do the same to his wearable.

After a few minutes of play together, after Sallye had virtually humiliated herself in the game, Zeke command the game to slow to a static surround of them. Sounds softened to a whisper, and the energy in the room calmed. They sat on ergonomically designed swivel-and-roll chairs in the center of the space. There was a look of satisfaction on his face.

"You're back. Shimaro."

Sallye recognized the word as one common to the avatars in the game, uttered at a point of cooperation and companionship.

"Shimaro," she replied, and Zeke smiled back at her.

"We met at the sexual-assault center, night before last. Remember?"

"Yeah. Do we have to go through all that again?"

"Nah. Just tell me how you're doing today."

"Good, I guess."

"Physically?"

"Still hurts. Going away, though."

"Mentally?"

Zeke looked down at his control pad and made a couple of deft strokes. As he did so, a conspiracy of ravens appeared and circled over their heads, cawing loudly and dive-bombing them randomly from one direction or another. He smiled, noting Sallye's reflexive self-protection from the virtual birds. "It's a joke!" he said, laughing at his own humor and playfulness.

"Well, I guess that says you are feeling both attacked and playful."

"Yeah, I guess." He stroked the controller again, and the ravens departed.

"Tell me truly, Zeke. You OK?"

"Yeah, I'm OK. Grossed out by it all, but OK."

Zeke distracted himself from the intimacy of eye contact with her by focusing on the controller. His finger touches to it set off random effects in the virtual environment that surrounded them.

Sallye left him to play for a while and then asked, "Zeke, can you tell me what you want to happen next? Happen for you? Happen for Dr. Perkins?"

"I still want to do stuff with him. He lets me go places on DarkSilk. I just don't want the sex stuff from him anymore."

"Would you be OK if you never saw him again?"

"I guess." Zeke had cancelled out his assent with the tone of his voice. He had given the resigned agreement that teens give their parent when the parent makes a declaration of what must be.

"And—"

"What are they going to do to him for what he did with me?"

"I'm not sure. People are trying to figure that out now. It was wrong you know, what he did."

"It felt wrong."

Sallye held back from volleying more questions at him.

"I guess he shouldn't do that to other kids, eh?" Zeke said.

Sallye sat in nonverbal, supportive connection to him. She reached out a hand to rest it on his knee. He didn't pull away. Tears formed in his eyes. Finally, after a few silent moments, save for the whirling sound effects that droned quietly above them, she said, "No. We need to make sure of that."

"I don't want him going to jail or nothing."

"You don't?"

"No."

"OK. But I can't promise that."

"He does good for people."

"Yes, he does."

"And people need his good."

"I suppose."

"Tell whoever decides that I don't want him to go to jail. He is just supposed to stop." Zeke squirmed uncomfortably on the chair as though he felt a grimace of pain coming from his rear end.

Sallye rose to leave the room. She looked back at the boy. "OK if we talk again soon?" He nodded. "OK if I tell your parents and

Dr. Chetwin what you said?" He nodded again, and a look of relief came over his face.

As she was leaving the room, the angry visage of Dr. Cripps came back up on her wearable. She slapped it down, the kind of quick reflexive slap that one might make toward a mosquito ready to suck blood.

Farquhars was much a remnant of the past. The gold-leaf lettering on the door announced that it contained "Antiquities and Books," and truly it did. Once one had snaked around the various counters and shelves, deep through the musty smells and the air that seemed to perpetually sink toward the floor, once visitors had given up on finding their way, they came to a circle of leather sofas. Green-shaded brass lamps and the smell of coffee created an oasis of well-worn comfort there.

Elias Hendricks, retired judge, sat there. Geoffrey "Jewels" Jones, once a professor of literature, sat there too. Silas Wannabaker, often referred to with the elision "Swan," also sat there. He had edited the *Munroe Gazette* before the ASL took over its publication. Erik Farquhar buzzed in and out of the group, bringing coffees and generally fussing over the others. He was the proud great-grandson of the store's founder.

There was a grumble of discontent from the seated men about having to arrive two hours early for their usual noon Thursday gathering.

Visitor Myles Chetwin sat there too. His journey over to Farquhars from the Basilis residence had been full of anxiety. He wondered what he might be walking into. Charles Ross had told him about the convergence of men, including Perkins, who arrived there on Tuesdays and Thursdays at noon. It might just be a coffee-and-bag-lunch sort of thing, a place for Alastair to get away from the pressures of the academy. Then again, it might be…something else. Chetwin dreaded the thought of being with the other men there if it were a cell of pederasts. He swallowed. He decided to play it straight, as though it were a perfectly legitimate gathering of old guys.

Elias spoke first. "Dr. Myles Chetwin is Alastair's friend. He approached me yesterday to let me know trouble had befallen Alastair. He pressed me to move up our meeting time today. I will turn the floor over to him."

Chetwin got right to the point. "Two nights ago, Alastair was taken in by the police for questioning. At the station, he excused himself to use the washroom and, while there, attempted to hang himself. An alert constable heard his choking and intervened. Alastair was rushed to Munroe Memorial. The attending hospitalist held him for observation, to be assessed by the behavioral neurologist the following day.

"During the night, with help, he left Munroe Memorial without being formally discharged.

"He needs his friends at this critical time in his life. He had mentioned this group to me. Even though I recognize that you have typically met in secret, I have come this morning to inform you and to ask for your help and support for one you've held in friendship."

"More than friendship," Elias interjected. "We have a bond of loyalty to one another that has spanned many years."

"Thank you," Myles replied. He couldn't help but worry what that loyalty might entail.

"Where is he now?" Swan asked.

"In hiding."

"Can't he be traced through his wearable? Your ASL is right into that."

"It has been not only turned off but powered down, with its connecting circuits disabled."

"Is he being sought by the police?" Elias asked. "They have their ways."

"There seems to be a disconnect between the hospital and the police station. As far as we can tell, the police still believe he is in treatment. The hospital believes that it should not release his 'left against medical advice' status due to privacy reasons."

"Privacy?"

"Yes, I intervened with them to bring forward an old regulation they still had on their books."

"How is he?" Jewels asked.

"Despondent. I have others with him on suicide watch continuously."

"Is he asking for us?"

"I don't know."

"So what do you want us to do?"

A faint buzzing came from Chetwin's forearm. Cripps's call was coming back in. Chetwin had blocked the display so it wouldn't erupt again as it was doing at the Basilis home, but it still buzzed.

"This coming weekend, depending on his state of mind and his wishes, I might take you, or at least some of you, down to see him." Chetwin paused. "But be aware that others who would not treat him kindly might come looking for him."

"Here?"

"Yes, here. That's why I asked that you come early. At the ASL, his movements have historically been tracked. Although you might believe that your group meets in secret, the fact that all of you make your way here at the same time each week and that Alastair joined you here raised a red flag in the ASL routine monitoring for insurgent groups."

"You mean we are spied on?"

"I wouldn't go that far. It's part of routine surveillance protocols with the ASL. If your group advertised and had a fluid membership with a stated purpose, it would not raise an alert status. But it likely has and been noted for its chosen secrecy."

"Who should we watch for, then?"

Chetwin activated his wearable and brought up a picture of Cripps. He showed it around. Then, within the time frame of the twenty-eight seconds he allowed himself, he powered off the display.

Elias broke back in. "You mentioned that Alastair had been taken in for questioning. Was he suspected of something? If so…"

"Yes, and no, I am not willing to disclose the nature of the investigation other than to say that it's a serious matter involving harm."

Chetwin went to leave, and then he turned to address them again. "For today, I am going to ask you to disband your usual meeting. It may be necessary again next week too. I'll let you know."

There was murmuring among the men, and a couple of them slowly filed out past him. Elias stayed behind.

"You know who I am?" he asked.

Chetwin looked puzzled.

"C'mon, now. You appeared before me a couple of years ago. As a witness."

"Oh?"

"I've retired now as a judge. But I have connections back to the bench." Chetwin looked up. Elias continued. "Are you considering an EJD?"

"Yes, I was considering that, but I don't know where to begin."

"Let me begin it for you. I will make some calls. Perkins has done a lot of good. I can help him out." Elias paused. "By the way, what has he done?"

Chetwin felt the weight of the situation suddenly reside in his gut.

"Is it that pederasty stuff?"

Chetwin nodded.

"Fuck him. He tried to get us into it here. Caused a lot of hostility within the group. We gave him a good talking to, as friends, as forceful friends. I thought it was over with. Fuck!"

Chetwin smiled at the foul tongue of the retired judge but felt relieved that the man could do his swearing for him.

"Can I ask something?" Chetwin's voice was tentative.

"Go."

"Do you think any of the other group members were swayed by him?"

"Hope not."

There was a space of about an hour from when Chetwin left and Cripps arrived at Farquhars. The place was dismal when Cripps entered. Erik was there, busying himself behind the counter. He suggested that Cripps look around.

Cripps followed the narrow, winding path toward the back, trying to sniff out the scent of coffee. He found the leather sofas. They were empty. He saw the green-shaded brass lamps. They were unlit. The espresso machine was turned off, and the gauges showed that the steam unit had returned to the atmospheric pressure of the room.

He stormed out, letting the door slam behind him. The gaggle of brass bells that hung from the top of the door jingled discordantly.

(III)

This time when Sallye returned to FiveWay, other Paracletes were also arriving home. They were full of questions for her. Sanctuary moderated the discussion with excited greetings to each person who arrived and requests for head scratches from whoever happened to be speaking.

Sallye responded as well as she could: "I've been down at the Enclave; I spent the whole day with Alyssa," and "Yes, I saw Zeke this morning. And no, I can't talk about it." Also, "I have no idea," and "Oh, these clothes are Alyssa's because I stayed overnight and her mother insisted on lending me some clean clothes for the trip back." Finally, there was, "No, you can't borrow the top when it's washed."

Her wearable erupted again with Cripps's angry visage demanding her to appear in his office. A chill went over the group of them. Even Sanctuary sank back, the hair rising on his neck and a deep rumble forming in his throat.

"What is that about?" Angelica asked.

"Cripps. He thinks he owns me."

"Poor you." The three others spoke the refrain in unison, a practiced move whenever Sallye talked about having to report directly to Cripps.

"He has been demanding me in his office all day. I have had other things to do. I saw two clients this morning, both in a state of emergency."

"You'd better go."

"I dread it."

"We will all go. We'll show up together."

"I don't think that will work," Sallye said, sounding discouraged.

At that point, Sanctuary went over to her. He sat attentively right in front of her, his tail wagging eagerly and his eyes bright.

"Sanctuary will go with you!" Arthur boomed out the solution to the problem, and the four of them erupted into laughter.

"Hey, wait a minute. We can make that work," Angelica added, a glimmer in her eye.

Quickly, the plan was hatched. Sanctuary positively beamed as his name was said over and over and Sallye stroked his neck affectionately. He could feel her anxiety coming down because she was petting him.

There is a single officer at the reception desk at the academy building. He sat there bored most of the time. Comers and goers signed the log book automatically without reminders. The security screens were all monitored by a spatial-analysis program so that any odd movement was flagged and alerted. The screens did not require his attention. No odd movements had been flagged or alerted in weeks.

So for the officer, it was natural, welcome even, to respond with action and concern when three young people—three clean-cut, well-groomed young people—came rushing into the lobby with distressed looks on their faces. They let the officer know that a friend had collapsed on the steps outside. They implored him to help if he had his first-aid training. He did. He immediately left his post behind the desk to run and assist.

Outside was Angelica, who was pretending to have fainted.

Inside were Sallye and Sanctuary, who crossed the lobby and headed up the elevator to Cripps's office. It was the first odd movement through the lobby in, well, weeks.

When Sallye appeared in Cripps's office, the angry face that he had been nurturing all day was ratcheted up a notch or two at the sight of Sanctuary.

"Get that dog out of here!"

"If he goes, I go." Sallye held her ground and tightened her hold on Sanctuary's collar. She heard his soft growl grow slightly louder, and she started to fear that he might actually leap out of her control and go after Cripps. Her hold was on his collar at the back of his head. She could feel the hair rise on the back of his neck.

"You are not going anywhere, young lady." Cripps had lit his tall forehead bright red with the flush of anger.

"All right, then, we will stay." There was an emphasis on the *we*. Sanctuary was no longer sitting and was starting to pull forward. Sallye held him and then turned to the dog and stooped down to reassure him. Quietly, Sallye thanked Sanctuary for the protective instinct he had displayed. As she stroked his neck, he relaxed slightly, and with him, so did she. She told Sanctuary that she had the situation under control and that he could trust her. She asked him to sit. He sat. As this transpired, Cripps was speechless, silently apoplectic at a scene unfolding in his office that was out of his control.

Sallye rose to her feet. Her mind transported back to the scene outside the building on the North Hill. She was remembering the humiliation of the recorded warning read to her in front of Byron, in front of Alyssa and her father. This was payback.

"I have been calling you here all morning." Cripps had swallowed and made an effort to get the yell out of his voice. Still, the tone was accusatory.

"You will never do that to me again. I was with an Emergent and an Emotionally Vulnerable when your messages came in. Seventeen times in three hours. It was embarrassing. One of them commented that she felt absolutely sane and in control compared to 'whoever that was.'"

"Where have you been? Your wearable was off all day yesterday."

"At the Enclave. Wearable monitoring is disrupted there. Oh, you would know that, though, wouldn't you? You negotiated that arrangement with them." There was an edge to Sallye's voice, an edge that got Sanctuary to stand beside her, on alert again.

"What were you doing there?"

"As my supervisor, you should be aware that I have been assigned to an Emotionally Vulnerable there, Alyssa Johnson. I spent the day with her. And by the way, she is doing really well. The cutting has stopped, and her relationship with her parents has improved markedly. If you were on top of things, you would know that; you wouldn't have to be told."

Cripps was trapped. The young woman and the dog stood in his doorway. He couldn't get out. He couldn't get control.

"You are very close to being suspended, or even fired, young lady."

"Just try. You need me. You need me because your damn administration here is in a mess. You need me because you are getting low on Paracletes with both Byron and Lisbeth out of commission. You need me because your fucking report for the journals would look bad if there were further loss in your precious cohort of bred Paracletes."

Cripps glowered at her.

"So let's settle this down, Dr. Sebastian Cripps." There was a sneer of sarcasm in her voice, a patronizing tone that diminished him. "I want to make this very clear. You are not to bother me when I am in the field working with clients. I will check in with you as scheduled on Tuesdays."

Cripps sat at his desk. Sallye and Sanctuary still stood in the doorway. After a few silent minutes, in which Cripps tried to dial down the redness of his high forehead, he spoke.

"Do you know where Dr. Perkins is?"

"Do I know? That is rich. You are a member of his command team; I am just a Paraclete. If anyone should know where the boss is, it should be you. Jeesh. Get control, will you? Someone has to be in charge."

With that, Sallye turned and walked through the doorway of Cripps's office. She felt slightly sick to her stomach, but her head was swimming with exhilaration. Outside in the hall, she saw Chetwin, who had an enormous smile on his face. He had overheard it all and was next to go in. But then, on second thought, he turned and went down the hallway away from Cripps's office with her and the dog.

(IV)

That morning, November 1, Byron had awakened with the sense of Sallye's presence in the bed, a presence that had recently departed. The covers had been thrown aside and the bedsheets were dented in a rough adjustment to her body, but they were cool to the touch. Her clothing was gone from the chair on which she had thrown it in a casual heap the night before.

Slowly, the disorientation of awakening in a strange room released Byron. In his mind, he remembered how he had gotten there. He adjusted to being there for another day. There was a deeper awareness, a dread, felt in the broader reality of why.

It was not that the day before had been bad. He had spent most of it with Alton. They had played cards, games in which it didn't matter whether you were the winner. Their games would draw the eye and furrow the brow for the best play, which was a slight distraction from the real discussion of the brothers. It had been a day for Byron to listen to the story of Alton's childhood with Laurel and Justin up north in Beckett. It was a day for Alton to listen to the story of Byron growing up in the family communal home, of his training in the philosophy and praxis of Paracletes. Strangely, the life of the other attracted each of them. The curiosity and empathy they shared in listening to each other's stories bonded them more closely.

Sallye and Alyssa had buzzed around doing girl things. From Byron's perspective, it felt like far too much bonding, far too closely guarded shared humor between them, and far too much talk. Byron had watched, though, and had observed how perfectly Sallye played the role of Paraclete, almost as though she wasn't playing a role at all. All the things she did could have been reduced to strategies and fulfillment of a technique. But it didn't look that way; it looked natural. Alyssa responded as though Sallye was a yearned-for and long-lost older sister.

Dr. Chetwin had assigned the three of them to watch Perkins in case he attempted suicide. But Perkins had just sat staring grimly out the window. Streams of water from the steady drizzle released when the drops became too heavy for capillary tension to hold them against the pane of glass. Perkins's eyes would follow the streams down to where the water pooled on the deck outside. If he could have cried, that is what his tears would have looked like.

Perkins was expected to have a quiet first day as a result of the targeted transcranial stimulation he had received the day before. Dr. Chetwin had explained to Byron, Sallye, and Alton that the emergency-department doctor had administered the treatment protocols for circumstantial agitation with dysregulated behavior. No neurologist would deign to come in at night to administer it. With that, Chetwin had been pleased. He knew the emergency-department doctor from previous crises and knew that he didn't particularly respect the arrogant ways of the resident neurologists. Chetwin knew that he could convince him to do the minimum and turn a blind eye to a release without medical clearance. The doctor had covered himself for possible claims of negligence by doing the TTCS, and he felt confident that if Chetwin were involved, he could just say "Oh well" when he was informed the patient had left.

It was expected that the TTCS, as targeted, would produce a transient mental slowing and mild sedation. It had. Perkins looked stunned into the next day.

Elise had been around. She fussed over the four of them, ensuring that they had sufficient food. She sized up Perkins and selected clothing from Gerald's closet that would fit, pulling out fresh packages of underwear and socks for the dull man. Myles had asked it of her. She owed Myles a debt that her kindness to his friend would barely begin to cover. She provided clothing for Byron as well, ill-fitting and conservative clothing from her husband's closet. At least Byron would not need to spend his time in the Enclave looking like a seventeenth-century courtier.

By the time Byron had done his morning routine in the bathroom and had retrieved the borrowed clothes he had neatly folded the night before, he heard the sounds of others up and about. There were the smells of a cooked breakfast, there was dim November light eking through the window glass, and there was the sound of classical music playing softly. There was no Sallye.

"She left this morning with Gerald. Something about Myles needing to get her back to Munroe." Elise spoke with an immediate sense of empathy for the person whom Byron would search out.

"Is he up?"

"Dr. Perkins? Not yet. Alton and I have already had coffee. He caught me in the middle of my yoga practice downstairs. I thought he would stare the eyes right out of his head as I went through my asanas. Then he looked embarrassed that he had been looking."

Elise smiled in a coy way that betrayed her delight in being looked at. She continued, "Anyway, a fascinating young man, your brother. When we talked, it was like comfortable slippers on a warm floor. And his story, getting snatched and all. He is going a long way, he is."

"Yup." Byron's reply was bright and agreeable on the surface, but it was spoken with a grim undertone. Alton so naturally shone, and when he did, Byron had a sense of fading, of graying. "Where is he now?"

"Downstairs. I gave him a thermos of coffee. And it was odd—he wanted a journal, a blank one. We have some; Gerald had spirited away quite a few leather-bound ones when they were becoming scarcer. We found an old fountain pen with a bottle of ink. Can you imagine?"

"I can. If we could have our wearables on, I would sneak a picture of him doing it. One for the archives!"

Grabbing a coffee and a warm cinnamon bun, Byron headed downstairs.

"Hi, bro." Alton had sensed his brother's entry and had greeted him with a spontaneous warmth. "You do yoga too?"

"Sometimes."

"Caught Elise at it today. Weird. I knew about it—I had seen pictures—but I had never seen the beauty in it. Go ahead if you wish." Alton's gaze was deflected to an open area of the floor; rolled yoga mats were off to the side.

"Nah, not today. Whatcha writing?"

"Oh, a journal about all that has happened in the last few days—meeting Mom and Dad, your boss, coming here, the good time we had yesterday."

Byron looked at the book, at the ivory-colored pages, the ribbon bookmark sewn into the binding, and the fountain pen. Alton's writing was almost calligraphic, so orderly and straight-arrowed onto the page. Letters were formed as though they were serif fonts on a screen. The slight irregularities of the letters danced.

"So another day," Byron said.

"So another day," Alton repeated.

When Perkins arose, he looked less grim. He went through the motions of feeding himself from the breakfast laid out in the kitchen. Elise buzzed around him with annoyingly bright hospitality. He didn't say much but took his spot standing over by the window again.

The view of the front of the Johnson home was magnificent when it could be seen. On this particular day in early November, the inky gray of the night dawned into a dense, dismal gray of the morning. The fog and drizzle would hopefully lift as the day progressed, but on most days at this time of year, they would not. This was one of those days. The gentle curve of the south end of the lake could not be seen. The stately trees walking up the distant hills could not be seen. There was no buzz of watercraft on the lake's surface—only a steady dripping to punctuate the bleakness.

That is where Perkins stood.

After a time completely undetermined in Perkins's mind, Alton came to stand beside him.

"You know who I am?" Perkins asked.

"Yup." Alton knew well who the man was standing there, staring into the featureless view. During the discussions with his brother the day before, Alton became well versed in the story of Dr. Alastair Perkins and the Wilkes family. He was the man who, by virtue of his scientific initiative and intense desire to be esteemed, had set in motion the mating of Alton's parents. He was the man who had the arrogance to believe he could determine, through breeding and training, the course of Alton's life. He was the man who had missed something in the mix, had missed the predisposition to depression that ran down the paternal family line. In doing so, Perkins was the man who had destined Alton's father to be stressed to the point of breakdown and to suffer brain damage at the hands of bungling neurologists. This man had set in motion the need for Alton's grandparents to take Alton's destiny into their hands.

Alton knew well who stood beside him.

"And you know who I am as well," Alton responded slowly.

"Yes, certainly." Perkins remembered the vague presence of Alton beside Chetwin, Byron, and Sallye in the hospital, how the four of them had engineered his escape. At first, he had been baffled by the young man; then he had surmised who he was. He remembered how Cripps and Charles Ross had tracked Alton as he ventured down to Munroe. But more importantly, Perkins remembered that this was the seven-year-old boy who had escaped. He remembered that Alton had been one of the first products of the breeding program of twenty years before, how his heady optimism of doing good in the world had been dashed when one of their number had vanished.

Perkins knew well who stood beside him.

"You met my grandparents." As Alton spoke, he felt a sudden yearning to be back beside them, relieving his grandmother of the daily challenge of trying to make his grandfather content. He stared into the gray fog before him and wished it would lift and reveal the horses, corrals, and paddocks north of Beckett. In his mind, he stumbled over the word *grandparents*, as they were more parents than grandparents to him.

"I did?" The internal fog was damping Perkins's mind as he still struggled to shake off the residual effects of the TTCS he had received two days before.

"Yes, and you rode Stamper for a while until my grandmother offered you Biddy."

Perkins turned and stared at him. He was unsure whether he had realized it before. If he had, it was now that it was hitting him. That quaint—that pathetic—old couple who had taken him and CarolAnne up the mountain on the miserable line of horses were the very ones who had thrown into jeopardy his carefully developed program back here in Munroe. Perkins remembered the defensive anger he felt when the old man had implied that he couldn't handle the first horse. He remembered the shame of it.

"It's good that we finally meet." Alton proffered connection to the shattered man. They were standing facing each other now. As Alton peered into the man's eyes, he saw the confusion of a mind working far slower than his own. But he also saw into the soul of the man. It was a soul that had been shrunk by knowledge, power, and arrogance. It was a soul that had been betrayed by the satisfactions of desire. Moreover, it was a soul that had been starved by a profound need to control others. But despite its atrophy, it was a soul that could be opened by humility, a humility bred of shame.

"Is it?" Perkins asked, incredulity in his voice.

"It is. It's best that it is now, not years ago, not days ago, but now."

Alton took Perkins by the hand. It was an odd gesture for Perkins to receive, not one that would have been specified in a Paraclete manual or one that could have been initiated by an avatar in a VR room. Alton's touch was minimal, as though he were leading a horse who was already connected in a relationship to him. It was minimal but powerful. He led Perkins to a pair of chairs set facing each other in an arrangement too close together for regular conversation.

"I know what you are accused of doing. I know what you did in the police station. While I have difficulty understanding it, I have been told that you received a neurological reset through some sort of ultrawave pulses. I can't imagine how horrible that must have been."

Alton paused. "But I can imagine what will happen to your life's work because of what you are accused of doing. To your reputation. To the position of power you hold."

For a while, Perkins sat under Alton's steady, watchful eye. It was an eye without judgment and an eye warm with compassion, but it was a sharp, perceptive, thoughtful eye.

Alton paused and spoke again. "Your work ensured that no one else could have secrets, that the privacy of all others be surrendered. Yet you found within yourself a desperate need for a private life; you found a great sense of power in creating a secret one for yourself despite the profound negative impact it could have on another person."

There was a flicker of sickness, the sickness of dread, that crossed Perkins's face. Alton let it linger and then went on, the tone of his voice softening. "From all I have heard, you have dedicated your professional life to satisfying the needs of others. You have promoted health and well-being. That has been noble work. Sadly, that work poisoned you with…" Alton paused, searching for the word. "Arrogance. Your arrogance has brought you to this."

Alton paused again; Perkins's gaze was fixed on the young man.

"It could very well be that the future circumstances of your life will be dictated by the consequences of this dreadful, selfish choice you made. But I want you to know this, and I call you by your first name to tell you this.

"Alastair, the quality of your life will be determined not by your past but by how you live each present moment. You can now have a quality life by controlling yourself rather than by controlling others. A quality life despite the present circumstances you created for yourself."

The two men sat, with Alton's words dripping down into the puddles of Perkins's deeper mind.

(V)

Myles paused in the entry to the elegant older home. The house was small and quaint. It was shrouded in shrubs and trees in a quiet residential area of Munroe. Its interior was cozy and comforting.

He had stood there often some thirty years ago. Now, as then, he was greeted with warmth and enthusiasm. Oddities from around the world graced the walls and tables. Music played softly.

"It is so good to see you…Oh dear, what's up?" The woman was tall and stately and at least twenty years his senior. Her immediate concern creased her brow at the sight of him.

"Can we sit?" Myles headed straight for his chair in what had been her consulting room years before. She had sat together with him there as he had learned the essence of compassionate listening, the intricacies of melding his intuitions with what a client was ready to hear, and the skill that integrated past, present, and future into a narrative that could bring hope. She had been his mentor, his instructor, and his supervisor, his confidant and his anchor.

"Tell me what is going on." Marcia spoke the well-worn phrase, one that had often started their discussions in times past. She spoke with a gentle curiosity and an impetus to get right in there with him, wherever "there" might be.

"I need to pull you out of retirement. I need you to see someone."

"I have let my license go; I am afraid I can't. And even if I could, therapy has moved on past me. I am merely a human, not a perfected, computer-generated avatar of clinical efficiency."

Myles looked into her eyes, saw the sparkle of her sarcasm, and delighted in it. He said, "It is that humanity that we need."

"And anyway," Marcia continued, "I would not like to be discovered back in the game by our benevolent dictators of human-need satisfaction, Perkins and Cripps. Are you still with them, dear Myles? I don't know how you bear it."

"As far as Cripps is concerned, we are actively concealing this from him; we will have one of the information-systems geeks mask your wearable so he won't even know you are on the move."

"And Perkins?"

"He is the one you are to see."

Marcia sat in stunned silence. It was a shock to grasp. Perkins was the one who had put her out of business years ago. She had been replaced with artificial-intelligence avatars, as though a computer could manage relationships and generate intuition. She was further replaced by Puppy-Cletes, those adorable, khaki- and knit-cotton-clad, bred and trained lapdogs of the ASL. How could Puppy-Cletes ever help a person be truly who that person was? Puppy-Cletes couldn't even be themselves; they all talked alike in the stilted formal English trained into them.

"You have to be kidding. Why would I ever consider doing that?"

Myles laid out the scenario. He talked about the allegation, about the suicide attempt in the police station, about the TTCS, and about the suicide watch currently being provided by Sallye and Byron.

"TTCS, eh?" Marcia looked up, a slight delight in her eye. "How's he doing with that?"

"Pretty stunned."

Marcia recoiled from the further sarcasm that was tempting her lips. Her damn reflexive concern for human suffering had taken over. It was a reflex strengthened by thirty-five years in this very consulting room. But something inside of her was being drawn to do this. She fought it. "I don't think I can. Alastair and I have too much history."

"That is precisely the reason why I asked. If anyone can grasp the significance of this and can respond to him with both compassion and clarity, it is you."

The two sat together; they discussed the ASL and its vulnerability if this scandal broke out and discussed the precarious position that he would be in with Cripps without Perkins as oversight.

"So I go and do a session with him. What then?"

"I have some things in mind. Get him out of here. Get him into treatment. But those things aren't finalized. I hope they might be soon. Don't mention anything to him. I suspect that he is pretty scared, especially after the TTCS was inflicted on him. Let him be scared—it will be good for him."

"Myles, I wouldn't do this for anyone else. But for you, yes, I will. I will count on you protecting me from within the ASL when the scandal breaks, though."

"Thank you. To the best of my ability, I will. But it won't." Myles had a sense that she would have done the same for any of her other former protégés, but it was still a delight to have her pronounce his specialness.

"Where is he now?"

"In the Enclave, at the home of a friend there."

"That's good. There are some protections from the ASL monitoring and police authority there. When can we meet?"

"I am thinking that tomorrow would be soon enough for you to do this," Myles said.

It had been a phrase that she had often used with him in his supervision as they were considering some change he might make in the way that he related to clients or colleagues. She had always spoken it with a hint of irony because she would never force change on him; she would never set a timetable of immediacy. She would say the phrase and would expect him to playfully retort, "Well, perhaps. I will think about it."

Myles looked at her. Urgency was in his eyes. It was not a matter to be delayed.

"I will do it. Tomorrow. Make the arrangements."

10

MARCIA

Prior to Marcia's arrival, Elise had prepared the downstairs room. She had lit the gas fireplace to dispel the chill. The fog had lifted, and there were no streams of raindrops down the outsides of the windows. The lake was visible in multiple shades of gray. Evergreen trees stood, charcoal gray tinted with dark green. The trunks of the deciduous trees were ash gray tinted with dark taupe.

Another chill entered the room with the reunion of Marcia and Alastair; it was the chill of a relationship with a historic distaste for each other. Although the room was spacious, they danced around each other defensively, giving each other more space than required. They were as wary of each other as boxers in a ring might be.

It was truly awkward.

"Marcia," Perkins said. It was more of an acknowledgment than a greeting.

"Hello, how are you?" Marcia's response was distant, polite. There was no natural curiosity or even desire to know how he was other than how obnoxious he might be.

Not one for banality, Perkins did not give in to an automatic "fine" and volley the question back to her. He dodged the intent of the question, the intent of a social grace. He took it literally, that it was just about him. He said, "Ah, I am still feeling kind of stunned from what they did at the hospital. Does that clear it up?"

Taken aback by the self-centeredness and lack of civility, Marcia responded, "Well, usually. Give it a little time."

"I don't know why they did that to me."

Marcia held back from confronting him. This was more likely resistance than self-deception on his part. Yet there was a part of her that wondered how dismally lacking in self-awareness the man before her might be. "No?" she asked. She raised her left eyebrow. "Do you remember what state you were in before they did that?"

"Well, I was pretty mad. I was jerked out of my office. I was confused."

Marcia was relieved that he gave a straight answer but read it on another level. He was telling her that he "got pretty mad" and that he would react to being "jerked." She was also curious about what went into his confusion.

"Can you—?"

Perkins interrupted her midsentence. "Yeah, I was working with this teen. One of the Emergents. And it was good—our relationship was very positive. And they misinterpreted."

"How did they misinterpret?"

"Ah, let's not go into that."

"Are you being avoidant?" Marcia found herself saying internally, "Duh!" But she held back from speaking disrespectfully. She reminded herself that sometimes resistance is just a lack of readiness, a lack of secure enough footing in the session.

"It's kind of delicate," Perkins said. "And I don't know—I'm not sure that I want to talk about it with you."

"Why don't you want to talk about it with me?" Marcia spoke the question as quickly as a reflex, and yet she knew they were starting to do therapy, starting to move from the there and then to the here and now. She wondered whether he could be here with her. If he could, it would be a good sign for the prospect of the session. Then, with a twinge deep in her gut, she questioned whether she wanted to be in the here and now with the man. It might be easier to…

"Hmph. Well, you and I have been around the block, haven't we?" Perkins said.

"We have." Was that a smirk on his face? She thought, *Fuck, I could just slap it off.* She realized that he was proud of what he had done to her, to her colleagues, and to the proud tradition of her profession. It was all she could do to stay in the room. Then she settled. She found a slight smile curling her lips as she reflected on his statement. There was no companionship in their shared trip "around the block"; one cannot share companionship with a narcissistic prick. Then, conscious of her own slight smile, she recognized it as the instinctual response of prey to a predator.

Perkins caught sight of that slight smile. He moved in to be magnanimous—to let her know that he would allow her to be on equal footing with him. "It's not that I don't respect you for what you have done. You had a good career."

"Yes, I did." Marcia considered her life's work—how it got truncated by Perkins's avatars, which were more capable and willing to spy for the ASL than she was in the coziness of her consulting room.

"But things move on, don't they?" Perkins asked.

"Yes, they do." Marcia paused. She wanted to process this, to go back through the bitterness that still tried to steal her soul when she remembered the ungracious retreat from her profession she was forced to make. But that wasn't the purpose of the day; it couldn't be the focus of this discussion. She consciously told herself to back off and get back to the work of the here and now. "Is it our familiarity with each other that makes it hard for you to open up to me?"

"Well, I am not sure that you will understand."

Marcia recognized that Perkins was trying to push the blame for the session's lack of productivity over to her, that he would think it was some fault of hers if nothing was accomplished. It tweaked her initiative, though. She felt some courage in pushing on. "Why is that?"

"I guess from this point, I am not so sure I understand."

Firecrackers went off for her. Here he was—he who was seated on a prestigious chair in the academy, he who was innovator of all things psychological—facing something in himself he was willing to admit he didn't understand. Therapy was beginning. "What is causing the confusion?" she asked.

Perkins sighed deeply, trying to dispel the pain. He needed to collect himself, to justify, to claim a high ground. "You see, I only wanted good things for the kid."

Perkins paused again, collecting power in the telling of his story. "His name is Zeke. I only wanted good things for him. He is a promising kid—a little immature, but you know, like, he is fourteen or fifteen; he is going to be immature. He has a lot to learn. And I thought I was teaching him."

Marcia felt relieved. Sparring could maybe be done. "What did you feel he needed to learn from you?"

"How to take his place as a man. How to…He needed to learn about personal power, about authority. And how it will fall naturally. He is brilliant; it will fall naturally to his shoulders as he gets older. But I…"

Perkins trailed off, as though he had a sense that it was too much, too far down a road that would lead to a destination he couldn't abide. "So how are things turning out for you? You are retired now, aren't you?"

Marcia was pleased with the overt, clumsy resistance. It meant she was getting somewhere; she just needed to take her time, be persistent, and let the pressure off slightly but be clear that she would not let him get away with it. "Good. My life has been quite all right. I feel you may be changing the subject on me."

"Hmm…"

She leaned in slightly and brought a firm but respectful edge to her voice. "I feel like there was something there. But for whatever reason, you were not comfortable with it."

"So did you give up your license?"

"No." She had, but there was no sense in giving him the satisfaction here. To do so would undermine her authority in the room. She thought, *And, no, I will not give up the ground we are starting to make here.*

"You're still holding your credentials, are you?"

"To whatever degree they are worth today." His question suggested he had accepted her lie; she would get away with it if she held it in confidently. She collected herself quickly and resumed her role. "I want you to tell me more about the lesson you were trying to teach Zeke about power and about being a man."

"It is about respect. It is about being willing to learn. And how to loosen up with it, enjoy it."

"And how did you convey this lesson to him?" She was encouraging herself with self-talk: "Press. Press. He is starting to go where he needs to go."

"Well, I thought it was just going to go really naturally. Zeke is really good with getting around firewalls and really likes that. He lives right out there on the edge in terms of his computer skills, and so for a challenge, I got him to go onto DarkSilk and to go on in a way in which the ASL, the servers, wouldn't figure it out. It was just a challenge for him."

"Kind of infiltrate it without leaving traces of who was there?" She suspected Perkins's narrative wasn't going all the way, but it was moving in the right direction. Marcia felt she could go with that.

"He was pretty brilliant. You have to respect him for that."

"Absolutely, especially at his age."

"Yeah, he knows his way around."

"What was the intention behind that mission?"

"Well, you know. Yeah." Perkins was struggling with the words. "To have something that was kind of special between him and me. To have something that could be our secret. Wouldn't want Cripps to find out, eh?"

"Yeah, that could be problematic." Marcia was telling herself to take her time and stay with him.

"To get him to explore. You know. The ASL is really good at taking care of everybody's needs. We have done that. But once your needs are all taken care of, there is something else. There is another need. So it's OK."

"Tell me more about this need." Marcia wondered how far she could push. She doubted he was ready to get to the motivation behind the sexual assault of a teenage boy. At least her request now made it clear where she felt he needed to go. If it failed, he would deflect, but she had confidence that she could come back.

"It's all right to get a green tea latte." Perkins motioned to the sweet drink she had brought into the session in an insulated logo mug from the coffee shop. Its green foam had stained the lid, and he showed that he noticed it. "You can get that from the S-SB. Organic apples, we've got them, bowls of those in the Courtyard District, locally grown food source. But you know, in all that, we are pretty good at tracking, our economic, our provision systems; they are all pretty good."

"I guess there is also a need for adventure. A need for..." Marcia punched the conversation back to Perkins and Zeke and the need that had fulfilled for him. She sensed that Perkins was conflicted. He wanted to spill something; but could he? Theoretically she knew it was about doing the forbidden and getting Zeke to do it too. It was about a need for raw power and control to get the boy to do what he wanted. She knew it. She also knew it was far too much for him to admit at this stage of therapy.

"He looked up to me. When I got him to find out the way to get onto DarkSilk, my whole sense was that, once he was there, he would discover a whole world that was different. And I could be his guide into that world. And we could do it.

"We had to get Byron out of the way. Because…Byron was pretty negligent, but Zeke trusted him. I didn't want him nosing around. And that character, Charles Ross. Whew!

"So what I did was…" Perkins had paused and was coming back in tentatively. Marcia perceived him to be on the brink of disclosing what he had done.

Then he backed away. "Zeke is incredible, just incredible. He was able to sneak around Charles Ross, our IT."

Marcia let the silence hang.

Perkins gathered himself again to take a run at saying what could never be said. "And I didn't want him doing drugs even though we could get him hallucinogens through the lab. He's a kid; I just had him explore some of the sexual stuff. Because it's there. It is there on DarkSilk."

It had come out like vomit. If he had hoped for a feeling of relief, his visage suggested he was just sickened by the stench of it.

"There is a lot there on DarkSilk. Why that stuff?" Marcia asked.

"Hmm."

Marcia saw that his self-dignity had collapsed; his shoulders drooped, and the lines of his face drew down. She thought he dearly wanted to confess it to her, but could he? Finally, as though desperate to be free of his own stench, he spoke.

"Because I was attracted to it."

"Was it a 'by proxy' way for you to experience that?"

"Well, I'd hoped when we found it that he would just have his own natural interest. Because he is a teenage boy."

Marcia was internally cheering on the process, although she was repulsed by the content. She had the sense that she could press forward to the goal. "What did you hope would come from that natural interest?"

"That we could explore it together."

"You and him?"

"Yeah. He is right here with me. He was right there with me."

Perkins finally was face-to-face with it, face-to-face with the implications of it. It was more than he could bear. He rose from the chair and started to walk around the room, examining objects that had been retrieved from other lands, other cultures. He had his own curiosity about such things. He picked one up and then another. He felt the heft of the objects. After a pregnant minute or two, he finally spoke. "Nice place here, eh?

"Um-hum."

"I never met Elise and Gerald before. I think they are friends of Chetwin. Beautiful spot."

Marcia waited a respectful few moments. Had she done enough? Had he done all he could for now? Was his walking away from this a complete shutdown? She remembered, though, that when Myles had asked her to do this interview, he was worried that Perkins was suicidal. She finally said, "Can you tell me what happened that led up to you going in for the treatment?"

"He must have talked, eh?" Perkins deflected.

"And what would he have had to say?"

"You are judging me, aren't you?"

"I am curious. You are a brilliant man. I'm curious about how this unfolded for you." Marcia hoped the compliment would allow him to retreat to a place of self-respect from which he could continue.

"I met Zeke actually, for the first time, up in Beckett. At the Vintage. He was hanging out with CarolAnne. And gosh, it was only a few weeks ago, but it feels as though it was a long time ago."

"You remember meeting him." Marcia was tracking with him, just letting him know she'd heard what he had said.

"Well, what did this teenage boy have in mind for my teenage daughter?"

Marcia recognized that Perkins needed to shift this back to what would be a normal adult reaction. It would give him some secure ground. "Pretty natural paternal reaction," she said.

"So I guess I started to think of him in terms of sex."

"Initially regarding your daughter. And then regarding yourself?"

"It wasn't about sex really, at the beginning."

"What was it about?"

"It was about…"

Perkins went blank. Marcia sensed that it really was about a sexual attraction, even from the beginning. Before the sex, though, he needed to groom the boy get him to trust him. He just couldn't say it yet. She let her nonresponse hang.

Perkins spoke again. "Do you know what it's like to live in a fishbowl? Damn Cripps is watching my every move. And every input I have on my wearable is tracked. And everywhere I go. And what Zeke could do for me was that he could get me out of there."

"Out of the fishbowl."

"Um-hum."

"He could get you something that we used to refer to as privacy."

"Yeah." Perkins laughed. "Oh, by the way, this is entirely confidential, isn't it?"

"I don't know; I don't think there is anything that's confidential anymore. Between you and me, yes. But I don't know about in other ways."

"What about that wearable on your left arm?"

"Well, in this basement, I believe it is…shielded, set up in such a way that signals can't be transmitted. Scrambled, I think they call it now. But you know, this is a world that you very much had a strong hand in creating."

"Um-hum." Perkins had a look of concession on his face, of having given in, of having conceded a small victory to the other.

"Kind of ironic, eh?" Marcia smiled at her slight victory. Conscious of it, she thought it to be a therapeutic error, too facile in the making of a point. She regretted her own emotional impulse to have one over on this man, this destructive, self-centered man.

It was indeed too much. The offended man snapped back. "But nobody is confined in it as much as I am!"

Marcia settled back, pleased with the intensity of his response, with what it revealed about him. "How is that?" she asked with a muted curiosity.

"It is on me, isn't it?" Perkins's words were ripe with disdain.

Marcia couldn't discern whether the disdain was for her or for himself and what he had done. Again, she left the silence of the moment for him to fill.

"Is he OK?" Perkins asked, changing the subject.

"Who?" Marcia was perplexed by the discontinuity in his responses.

"Zeke."

"I don't know the answer to that."

"Chetwin got you here, didn't he?"

"He did."

"What does he think of all this?"

Marcia settled back. Her mind and her soul slid back to Myles, his practicality and compassion. "He cares about you. And he wants to help you. He is just trying to make sense of what's going on. And I don't know that many people really know the whole story. That's why I want to know from you what your experience has been of what has happened."

Perkins was silent. Marcia had noticed a shift in his facial expression when she said the word *cares*. Perhaps he no longer believed anyone could care for him. That was understandable—sad but understandable; he was such a powerful, controlling, empty man.

"You said you met Zeke, and there was some intrigue there. And you never intended to harm him in any way." Marcia figured she would go back through it again to get more of the story.

"He came over a few times when CarolAnne was at my place."

"What transpired those few times?"

"Just two kids playing. CarolAnne is pretty repressed. Her mom. You know her mom, don't you?"

Marcia was conscious of the defenses coming up again: deflect and blame. She prodded herself to stay with him, to stay with the process. "Yeah, I believe we have met on occasion. I wouldn't say I know her well."

"You don't go to that church, do you?"

"No."

"That's a scene, isn't it?"

Marcia waited him out; she didn't dignify his deflection with a response.

"So he was over. And I knew from everything we had on IPE-CKS that he was brilliant with computers. And he is wasted in the school system. So you know, I asked whether he could do…and he said, 'Yeah,' and I asked what about…and he said, 'Yep.' Every time I asked him…He is brilliant."

"You became aware of how much skill he had, how much potential he had." Marcia realized that at that moment Perkins needed it to be about Zeke because it couldn't be about him. She also knew that he had already been willing to go into his own stuff with her. She knew she just needed to be patient and allow it to unfold again.

"And I knew that a kid like that, given fifteen or twenty years, could be me. He could rise to the top. And he needed to learn what it means to be a man, what it means to be powerful. What it is to…to have people do your bidding. So that's why I kept giving him challenges, and he kept rising to them."

Marcia held down her gag reflex at the arrogance and narcissism. "So were you trying to foster his growth or to teach him what it is to have arrived?"

"To be a man."

"And what does it mean to be a man?"

"It means power. It means…power."

"Power over what?"

"Power to get things done. You know, what we have done with the Paracletes…You know that is unique. That is only happening here. My avatars are being used all over North America now. Replacing people like you."

"I am very aware." She was also aware that he was rubbing it in her face, that he was heady with the sense of power it gave to him. She surmised that for him to express his power over her so blatantly, he must be feeling powerless in this moment.

"You are! Don't take it personally, Marcia. You had a good run."

"I did."

"And I am respected. People are saying what we did was brilliant. And the Paracletes…the Paracletes. The report is coming out. We wanted to get this first version of the bred Paracletes…Like we had done with the parents, we wanted to get this first generation out there and functioning before…We put little bits into the journals. But Byron, you know Byron?"

"I am familiar with him, not personally but peripherally." Marcia felt an impatience with the disorganization of his mind; she sensed that he was brittle, that his defenses were getting too frayed.

"So anyway, it is a different world. You wouldn't know this, Marcia. It's a different world when everyone is looking up to you, when everyone is respecting you for your work, and when you have taken it to the very nth degree. And everything is being watched. And that was what felt good about Zeke and me. That we found a place to hide."

"At what point did it become something to be concerned about? For you to fear? Or become so…"

"I was afraid of Charles Ross."

"Why?"

"He is as bright as Zeke and as bright as I am. He would be the only one…Cripps, yeah."

"He would be the only one what?"

"Only one to know what was going on."

"So what was going on? You told me you saw his potential. You wanted to mentor him. You wanted to challenge him. You wanted to teach him what it means to be a man."

"OK, so, what we did…You want this, do you?" Perkins took on an aggressive stance, as though he felt ready to throw it at her, to make her gag as she mixed it with her own haughty judgment.

"It's going to be very hard for me to help you if we don't talk about this."

"So what we did is we got some videos; they were old videos, and they were on DarkSilk, and they were about powerful men and teenage boys. They were…restricted, so they were on DarkSilk. And we found them because we could. And we watched them."

"So what happened then?"

"Can this be enough for today?" Perkins looked sick.

"I don't know whether we are going to have this opportunity again after today. You know there are people looking for you. This is your opportunity to share your story."

"I thought I could read him pretty well. You know I am good at reading people. He was…we both were…" Perkins was stumbling, reaching for the words that could describe what he had to say. "And what happened between Zeke and me had a wonderful sense of privacy and being forbidden. And I want to say…relationship. And yet that is such a scary word for me. Everybody just sees me as Dr. Perkins. Even CarolAnne." Perkins put the emphasis on the "Dr."

"It sounds like you wanted to feel connected."

"He was scared afterward. I didn't know what he was going to do."

"What was happening for you?"

"I was scared too."

"And what were you afraid of?"

"That he would tell."

"What would that mean if he told?"

"Oh, that people like, like Marcia, would judge me and wouldn't understand."

"Do you think that I am judging you because you are judging you?"

Perkins was silent for several minutes. Tears formed in his eyes. He immediately put his hands to his forehead to hide them. Marcia left him to have his shame. He was progressing through the emotions of his disclosure, away from the physical reaction of being sick with himself to reflecting on it with sadness and shame.

"Alton gave me a talking to yesterday. Do you know Alton? Do you know who he is?"

"No."

"He was, oh gosh, this is a story. He got snatched out of our program when he was seven years old. By his grandparents. That was when Cripps came. To try to manage that. He thought it was the end of the program, that something like that would happen. Anyway, he is back. He's here."

"And yesterday he gave you a talking to?"

"Imagine! Him. To me!"

"And what was the content of this 'talking to'?"

"Well, pop psychology, eh? Like, 'You can't control others; you can just control yourself.' That stuff."

"True stuff." Marcia marveled at how apt the comments of this Alton had happened to be with Perkins.

"Maybe true stuff. But there was something else that happened."

"What was that something else?"

"It was like he opened my chest and let oxygen get into my heart. And he could see inside of me. And like it didn't matter what had happened in the past. He…How do I say this? That conversation I had with him, and there weren't a lot of words spoken…That conversation I had with him—it was like what I felt with Zeke, only without the sex. It was clean. That *relationship* word you used."

"It was intimacy."

"Yeah."

"It was real. Not trained, not contrived. From someone who hadn't been programmed by the program. It was real." In saying this, Marcia's professional demeanor had dropped again. She immediately recognized that what she had spoken would cut Perkins to the quick. She had called into question the brilliance of his professional accomplishments, declaring them to be not as "real" as was this other young man.

"I did…he's bred…so he should have those traits. And we did get seven years on him. It's not much; those first seven years are not much." Obviously, Perkins was trying to reconstruct his pride. It was he, Perkins himself, who had made Alton, made him through his selection of breeding parents and early childhood experience.

Marcia bided her time; she wanted to see what he would do with this.

"And it wasn't like he said a lot. And it wasn't heady excitement, like it was with Zeke. It's what I crave. It's what I crave."

"Sounds like it's pretty important." She noticed the grim look on his face.

"He's here. He is around."

Marcia waited quietly. Perkins appeared to be searching, trying to see through the walls of the basement room, to perhaps catch sight of Alton. Finally, his eyes fell to the floor. "Can we talk again?"

"Yeah."

"I feel like crying."

"Maybe that's what you need to do."

He did. It didn't matter that she had given permission. It erupted. Marcia looked at him and perceived him as small and childish. She felt pity, that he was reduced so.

"Who can I count on?"

"Ask your heart that question. Who do you trust?"

"I don't trust me very much anymore."

"That doesn't have to be a permanent state." Marcia intended her response to be deliberately neutral regarding what he had said. She expected it would be disappointing; she wasn't offering her lap or shoulder whenever he needed her. She was putting it back to him. He had his work to do, and she couldn't just comfort him to make it all better. She also recognized that this might be the only time she would see him. She didn't want to promise that he could count on her to be there for him.

"I would like to think that I could trust Myles. I have given him a hard time over the years, and he is still here. He has a way about him, you know. He is a fixer. And I would like to get to know Alton better."

"They sound like two very important people. And I would think that you are drawn to them for a reason. Do you think that they are people who would make you feel like sticking around for a while?"

"You mean about suicide?"

"Um-hum. That state you were in when you were brought to the hospital. And how about now?"

"What they did to my brain kind of knocked that out. Damn neurologists."

Perkins was silent for a long time. When he finally spoke, it was softer, more reflective. "I think I want to see how this turns out."

"There may be more to this life."

"I am probably finished with the ASL. Do you think?"

"I'm not sure. What makes you think that way? Do you think it's what they will do with this, or are you ready to be done?"

"I'm ready to be done. Would have been nice to get that final paper done, about Byron, Sallye, Angelica, and all the others. But maybe it's not for me. But you know, it all might be out of my hands anyway."

A look of terror came over his face. "Do you know what the neurologists do to people who do what I did?"

"Only what I have heard."

"They are probably going to fry parts of my brain, aren't they?"

"The parts they feel are responsible for your actions." Marcia paused. It served no purpose thinking that he might be zapped into nothinghood. What he said sounded like self-pity. Or maybe it was just raw fear. But for this conversation, she needed to bring it back to him, for him to explore what he had done. "What do you feel was really behind what happened?"

"I don't know. It's just the flow that happened inside of me, and I just didn't know when it should stop."

"Do you believe we can learn? That we can change based on the experiences we have? Or are we just a product of our environment? Of whatever the ASL has fed us?"

"I hope so. I hope we can."

She waited.

"You have given me a lot to think about, Marcia. And I think I would like to connect again. I don't know where I will be. Myles is coming down, maybe tomorrow. He is up in Munroe. Probably he is up in Munroe, fixing this."

"What do you feel happens next?"

"He is pretty good at fixing. And I know…like, if it was someone else who had done this, I would not let it happen. But Myles is pretty bought in to what we are doing at the ASL. He knows that if this were to come out, especially when it was an Emergent, then it would be the end. I guess I'm going to count on him to fix it, aren't I?"

"I guess we will have to wait to see what happens."

"Thank you. Come back." He pleaded with her with his eyes.

"I will." And she felt as though the pain of the years of their relationship had abated a bit. She felt that maybe she could come back and meet with him again.

"Thank you," he said.

"Thank you for talking to me. I know it's not easy. Probably not for either of us."

"Probably not." He left the room looking grim.

(II)

Perkins stood at the window, watching as Marcia left.

She had needed to walk, to get out of the cloaking stink of that room with that man. She had felt something with him. She had felt a lot with him. She needed to sort it out. Thankfully, it wasn't raining. She hated the rain. It was cloudy and that sort of dismal that only November could achieve. At least it wasn't raining.

Perkins felt diminished. In times past, when there was a hint of this for him, he was quick to recover his power and self-respect, to barrel forward and leave behind any doubts. Now all he had were doubts. He hated Marcia for doing this to him. He hated himself for thinking it was she who did it.

Walking upstairs, he saw Alton sitting at the table in the dinette that overlooked the lake. He walked over to him immediately and sat there as Alton wrote in a leather journal with an old-fashioned fountain pen. Alton didn't look up. Eventually, Perkins went to his room to lie down, to fade into exhaustion. He was too restless to sleep and too conflicted to know what to do.

When Marcia came back, she sat with Alton. This time, the young man looked up and greeted her.

"I haven't seen one of those in years." She indicated the journal.

"Priceless now—calf's leather and unbleached paper. Elise found a bunch of them when I said I wanted to write. I will never, ever journal on my wearable again. It's all tracked on the ASL."

"A bunch of them?"

"Yeah, want one? I'm sure she would give you one. If nothing else, she has to be the most generous woman I have ever met."

Off he went to find Elise. Marcia stayed, enjoying the warmth from the gas fireplace that radiated heat from the adjoining living room.

Elise and Alton came back together. They offered her warm drinks. They made a fuss over her. Still stunned by Perkins, Marcia participated as she could and was grateful. As they talked, she kept looking at the blank journal that had been brought to the table and set before her.

"Can I borrow the pen?" She left the room to find a private place in the generous home.

When Myles came to the Johnson home, Marcia had returned to the conversation with Alton. They sat in the dinette. A weak sunbeam broke through the clouds and swooped in low over them.

She was fascinated by Alton's experiences with the horses and shocked by the lack of financial security in the hinterland. She listened to his concerns about the illness of his grandfather. When he told the story of being snatched, she felt her engagement with the young man grow. As he told the story, she inserted words like *rescued* and *real*.

Alton was equally curious. Marcia was the same age as his grandmother. He related to her easily. She found herself talking about avatars and Paracletes and how much she hated them for what they did to her career and what they did to sustain a society of possession and control, of loss of privacy, and of loss of dignity.

Her strength was wisdom. His was a fresh perspective.

Together, they arrived from different paths to a shared hatred of the ASL and all that it stood for.

That was the part of the conversation that Myles had overheard. It was awkward.

Finally, he spoke. "Is Perkins OK?"

"Sleeping, I guess," Marcia said. "He was pretty worn out by the session we had. I think he is still a bit stunned from the TTCS."

"Did the session go well?"

Marcia looked at him. She pushed over to him her handwritten, calf-leather-enclosed, written-on-unbleached-paper-with-a-fountain-pen journal.

Journal Entry—Marcia—November 2, 2057

Fucking Perkins! OK, I am getting ahead of myself. Where to start…

What a bizarre twenty-four hours it has been!

Just yesterday I was enjoying my greenhouse, and my biggest dilemma was what snack to serve when the gals come over for tea and cards this week and deciding what I was going to get Ella and Grace for their thirteenth birthday on the weekend. Oh, those girls make my life so bright! They really weren't lying when they said being a grandma would bring all the joy of parenting but without the stress!

But I digress; that is not what calls me to this reflection.

So I'm minding my greenhouse (and my own business) when I get an impromptu visit from Myles. Dear Myles. That young man sure knows how to finesse a favor out of me. I have so much respect and adoration for him, and I have greatly missed working alongside him; but this favor was not a simple one. And that leads me to today.

I find myself whisked, or maybe hijacked, away to the home of Gerald and Elise Johnson, where I find one Alastair Perkins in quite a state. Of all the people I could be called out of the comfort and routine of retirement to help, I would have never (ever) predicted that I would be sitting across from the man whom I can only credit for being responsible for the death of humanity.

OK, I may be being a tad dramatic. But it would not be unreasonable to hold him responsible for the premature ending of my career and for taking the human aspect out of a field that was the last to value personal connection in what has become a very disconnected world. And I must say the irony was not lost on me as I sat across from him today, when he was in need of just that—connection. Real human *connection. Fucking Perkins.*

So it seems that he has gotten himself into quite the conundrum. And it bears the threat of potentially undermining all he has worked for. I wanted to give it to him so badly, to illustrate the karmic nature of his fall from grace, to make him eat crow, so to speak.

But I couldn't. As we talked, I couldn't help but notice how small he seemed. This man, who was so caught up in doing big things, so focused on gaining prestige and recognition, was sitting in front of me, small and childlike.

And in slid my old knowing, my compassion, my recognition—that even those who have done wrong are fighting a battle of their own. And I felt sad for him. And the years of anger and disgust I had for this man seemed to fall aside. And I saw him. I saw him for what he was—a human being, and one who was suffering. One who, despite all the ego and pretention, was fighting the same battle that we all fight: to feel loved and to feel valued, not for what we accomplish but for who we are when no one is watching.

What have I gotten myself into?

This man is in a great deal of trouble, and he knows it. It's going to be an uphill battle for him to navigate this without it becoming a public scandal and falling into the hands and electric probes of the "corrective neurologists."

But I think I am going to help him…never thought I would say that. Fucking Perkins.

> *And darn the residue of a career of loving the seemingly unlovable. He needs someone to hear him, someone to care. Perhaps it is part of my own healing that I am the one who will show him the kindness and connection that he devalued when he reduced the profession to scripts and computer programs and algorithms imitating compassion.*
>
> *Funny thing how the universe has ways of bringing us new perspective in the ways we might least expect it.*
>
> *That is all for now.*
>
> *Marcia*

Myles sat there, digesting.

After several minutes, he looked at Marcia and said, "Thanks." Saying the word wasn't enough. No words could have been. He hoped his eyes spoke sufficient gratitude, sufficient respect to her. After a moment, he continued. "There are some developments. You and I are going to talk with him."

Perkins was fetched by Elise and sat there with the three others. Elise had plied him with a mug of mocha made with double-strength espresso. Alton had come to sit beside him on one of the leather sofas. Perkins felt comforted by that. Myles and Marcia sat across from him.

"Alastair, I have made some inquiries on your behalf. Tomorrow, Elias is going to come down here to see you. He and I have done the preparation for an expedited judicial disposition, and he has identified a judge willing to hear it. You will have an in-chambers meeting with all the parties next Tuesday.

"As of now, the Basilis family have agreed for this not to go to court, depending on your compliance with a number of conditions. They will be at the EJD, so you are going to need to face them and face Zeke. I expect you will have your apology and statement taking responsibility ready. The arresting officer was Constable Morris. He will be there too. As far as we can tell, you have not been charged, but the EJD is required to take the arrest off the books.

"Neither Zeke nor his parents want you to go to jail. Dags and Maureen want to never see you again in Munroe.

"This means that you are going to be leaving—leaving the city, your chair at the academy, and your position as director for the ASL–Munroe region.

"I have made arrangements for you to go into treatment at the MacMillan Institute on the coast. You will be required to complete the ninety-day residential treatment program and to remain in treatment longer if they deem it to be necessary."

Myles paused. He could see the look of terror still on Alastair's face.

"By the way, MacMillan is NN, nonneurological."

Dr. Alastair Perkins looked relieved.

"I disclosed that it was you I was making arrangements for and what you were arrested for. Although they thought you were appropriate for the program, they also…"

Myles stopped, and a slight grin stole across his face.

"They also thought that once you finished treatment—once you had been reliably established in their verified recovery program with all of its tracking and requirements and were well again—you might be a good fit for their Virtual Role-Playing Lab, as a researcher and developer."

Alastair sat, still stunned.

"Of course, Marcia here is your current treating professional. This is the first she has heard of this plan. Marcia, would you agree with this course of treatment?"

"I think he is a very lucky man. I am concerned about Zeke, though."

"I haven't discussed all the specifics with Zeke, but one of our Paracletes spoke with him yesterday. The plan considered what he wanted to see happen."

"Elias?" Alastair queried, his voice shaky.

Myles worried that Perkins had missed everything that he had said. "Yes, Elias."

"Elias knows about the judge, my having to give up being the chair and director, and my going away for treatment?"

"Maybe not some of the specific details, but the general plan, yes."

"And he is still willing to come to see me?"

"Yes."

Alastair wiped a tear from his eye. Noticing this, Marcia reflected that perhaps this might expand the range of genuine human connections that could sustain the man. Myles reflected that Alastair was probably understanding the plan, at least at some level and at the speed his mind could work.

"I will do it. But I have one question for now." Alastair's voice cracked.

"Yes, what is that?"

"The three of you—will you come to see me there?"

Whereas Myles and Alton responded immediately in the affirmative, Marcia held back. Her mind went back to her greenhouse and her grandchildren, to what to serve when the gals came over. This man, this conflicted and conflicting man, held no attraction for her. But the boy within him did. She caught Alastair looking at her, pleading.

"OK."

11

THE WILKES

With the news Myles had given, Dr. Perkins he seemed to settle. His mood had lifted. It was decided that Byron would stay the night. If Perkins was still OK in the morning, he would travel back to Munroe with Gerald when he took the Range Rover to bring Myles and Elias back the following day. If Perkins was back to being stunned and morose, Byron would stay longer.

Alton decided to leave the Enclave with Myles that evening. He reminded Myles and Byron that the reason he had come south was to connect with his parents. Since the outburst of anger from his mother when he had made that first connection, he hadn't been back. Alton was also getting eager to get home, back to the horses and back to his grandpa and grandma. First, though, he felt the need to spend time with his mother and father.

Myles had Gerald drop them off at the family communal home. They arrived after the children were bedded down. Craig and Lisbeth were alone in their unit. Myles led the way in, Alton a step or two behind.

"Myles." Lisbeth's greeting was devoid of emotion, save disgust. She was wrung out by the ASL and its managers. Craig sat silently at the table.

"Lisbeth."

"Mother," said Alton, stepping forward.

Upon hearing her son's voice, Lisbeth warmed slightly. "You still in town? Thought you had left."

"I came here to see you. Something came up; I got distracted. I was hoping I could stay here tonight."

Immediately, Craig got up, leaving the table. He went off and busied himself in the house.

Lisbeth turned to look at Myles. He had been in the home often and had always been a source of support and calm. Now she resented him being there.

"I am so fucking done," she said, staring daggers at Myles.

Myles was stunned to hear her swear. It was so unlike her.

"Yeah, I swear now. It is so not me to swear, isn't it?"

Myles mused at the synchrony of their thought. He had known Lisbeth a long time. He had liked her and respected her. He knew of her strength; he just had never seen it manifest this way before.

"You heard what happened with me and Sallye?"

He hadn't and he didn't ask for the story. He knew that if he didn't interfere with her telling, it would come out in the way she needed it to.

"I told her to get out. Well, 'get the fuck out' is more like it."

Again, he waited.

"She was so fucking perfect, I couldn't stand it anymore. There I was dissolved in tears from seeing my two sons, my two older sons, and she goes into the kitchen to bring me a hot drink. Paraclete 101. She touches me, with sensitivity and connection, just like we taught her. Paraclete 201.

"And it was so perfect that it wasn't real.

"I taught her to do that. I could see it was by the book. Smooth. Designed to comfort. So bloody human, it was unnatural."

Myles sat silently, listening, trying not to act the part.

"So I told her to get the fuck out."

Lisbeth stared over at Alton. He had been there; he would remember. But his presence had opened her up; he had deepened her with his genuine warmth and affectionate grasp.

"Those words, 'Get the fuck out,' they are all that has been playing in my mind these last few days. I needed her, Ms. Sallye Paraclete Perfection, out of this house."

There was bitterness in Lisbeth's voice. As the energy dissipated out of it, a softer tone came. "But I needed to get me out of her; all my good training has taken that fine young human being and turned her into a Paraclete protocol.

"I loved her as a little girl. Then I fucking ruined her with all my good instruction."

Myles sat there, stunned. He had taught the program but had never seen it this way.

Craig passed behind them. He was rolling a folded cot and mattress into the media room.

"I worry about Sallye. I worry that she will turn out like me. If fifteen years from now, she is a Lisbeth, I will…"

As Lisbeth trailed off, Myles immediately wished he could tell her about the Sallye who stood with Sanc at Cripps's door. How similar the two women were, despite the behavioral engineering! He wanted to tell Lisbeth about Sallye's anger and strength. It would give her hope. He inhaled, preparing to speak.

"Don't you say a word, or I will tell you to get the fuck out too." Lisbeth looked at him. The creases around her mouth were angry, but the folds around her eyes were sad.

Having paralyzed him, Lisbeth turned to Alton.

"You said three words to me that night. Maybe more, but I just remember three. You said 'Mother' and then 'Mom' and then 'Mommy.' With the first, you affirmed who we are to each other. With the second, you told me what you wanted to have from me now. With the third…" Tears seeped through those sad folds around her eyes. "You named the hole in my life I've had for the last fifteen years."

A transformation came over Lisbeth. Her mouth and eyes united in a presence—a beautiful, mournful presence—still and deep.

Alton and Myles sat in silence.

Myles witnessed Lisbeth's transformation in light of his old training, the training he'd had years ago with Marcia. He saw in her the powerful and irrational mind of healing that exists in everyone, fragile in its emergence but strong when it climbs forward into manifestation.

Alton saw the change simply as what happens when he makes deep contact with a suffering human soul.

"You look tired." Lisbeth spoke the observation as a genuine response to an obvious state in Myles. Had she spoken as a Paraclete, it would have been with an inflected warmth. Now, as Lisbeth, she spoke it matter-of-factly.

Indeed, Myles was tired. He mentally inventoried his very long day of damage control: It had started with speaking on the phone to the MacMillan Institute of Alastair; then there was the summative speaking to Alastair of MacMillan; next, there was the time with Marcia, a woman who could be real by just being herself; and finally, there was the strategizing with Gerald and the ride in the Range Rover.

The air in the kitchen of the family communal home was overly warm. Heat radiated off the oven, and the smell of baking engulfed them as Craig pulled out a pan of muffins prepared for the children's breakfast in the morning. Myles needed to go. He needed to sleep. He couldn't move from the warmth there.

There was the gentle beep beep of an AVoD out in front of the family communal home. Craig had called one because he knew at some point Myles would have to go home.

After they had said their goodbyes to Myles, Craig showed Alton the bed he had made up for him in the media room. Neatly laid out on the bed was clothing he had scrounged from various male closets.

There were toiletries there that had been taken from the generous storehouse of personal items that the ASL supplied to the family communal home.

When they sat at the kitchen table, Alton asked about the fifteen years of life in the family communal home that he had missed. Lisbeth told the story of Craig's treatment at the hands of the neurologists, the devastating change that had come in his personality, and the subtle cognitive deficits he now lived with.

Lisbeth asked about the fifteen years that Alton had lived up in Beckett. He talked about the horses mainly but also about his grandparents and the sparse life they eked out there.

When they were done, when the reality of human suffering had been declared in the absence of avatars and platitudes, Lisbeth asked the question. "So Alton, what do you want now?" She feared what he would say.

"Be my mom. But don't mother, and don't Paraclete me." Alton then turned to Craig. "Be my dad, but don't fuss over me."

They sat in silence. Alton was engrossed in thought. He looked at Lisbeth, and his tone shifted. "There is something else. I don't know how to go about it at all."

"What's that?"

"I learned that I have a medical device inside of me. It is somehow hooked up to my wearable. I want it out."

"Why the hell would you want that? We all have them. The doctor needs them."

Alton spilled out the story of being with Sallye up in the yurt on the fishing trip, of how what they did was discovered by the ASL through the output of his implant transmitted by his wearable. Then he told them what had happened on the steps of the North Hill as Byron had recounted it for him. Lisbeth listened. She had known that Sallye had gotten in trouble for something; Alton's account filled in the blanks for her. She thought about the way the ASL insinuated itself into the intimate details of their lives, the battle they fought years ago to have the modesty overrides placed on their wearables, and how the general population dumbly accepted the intrusion into their physical lives, unaware of the data that the ASL tracked and kept.

She said, "Well, I guess people survived without an implant for most of human history. I don't see why it would be a problem physically for you to have it removed. I don't know if the doctors would do that, but we could ask."

"Ask who?"

"I will start with Dr. Jefferson. She would know whether it could be done. I'll leave a message for her to work us in tomorrow morning."

"Tomorrow is Saturday."

"No problem. She doesn't have a life either, working for the ASL."

"She works for the ASL?"

"We all do, honey."

"Well, it's a place to start."

A look of exhaustion came over Alton's face. He looked longingly over at the cot in the media room. It looked inviting, but the array of technology around it, those learning and entertainment devices, seemed overwhelming. Alton longed for his own bed in the draughty house up north. Even the scratchy cubed-up hay, stored to be fed to the horses in the barn, would feel good now.

"And something else I want," he said.

Lisbeth looked up.

"I want to go back up to Beckett, to the ranch, to Grandma and Grandpa. I worry about them. Grandpa is sick, and Grandma has to do everything. The place is run down and needs fixing. She can't do it all."

The words settled.

Craig looked up. "I want to go there too."

Lisbeth sat with the implications of it. Justin and Laurel had been their bogeymen, the stealers of their seven-year-old son, the epitome of evil in their lives as they had acted against the ownership the ASL had taken over the family. And Craig was her companion volcano, cold and hard as rock most of the time but prone to eruption into rage. Justin and Laurel, and Craig: perhaps the two generations needed each other. She couldn't deny Craig's desire to go and be with his parents, but in his state she couldn't let him go alone. She dreaded the whole scenario there that awaited them.

And then she thought. She thought of what the ASL had done to her. She thought of who Alton was without it. There was wisdom those fifteen years ago in the snatch. There could be wisdom in this too.

"We will all go, as soon as we can."

(II)

"Dot. Shhh."

Pause.

"Dot! Shhh!" The second time around, Lisbeth's voice was more emphatic.

Alton's eyes blinked open. He saw mother and daughter standing together in the doorway to the media room.

"He's awake now!" Dot stated triumphantly. Lisbeth was standing behind her with her hands firmly on Dot's shoulders, holding her back from running in to jump on her brother.

Alton groaned a contented but well-rested morning groan. He looked at the mother and daughter through blurry eyes and saw how incredibly alike they looked. The alignment of chin, cheekbone, and hairline was identical. Then, looking again, he noticed how different they were. Lisbeth's shoulders sagged, and the creases around her mouth were pronounced. Looking at the daughter, Alton couldn't believe how much playfulness, how much energy, could be contained in one little Dot.

Seeing Alton sit halfway up in his bed and orient himself to them, Lisbeth released her hold on the girl. Dot leaped into the room, knocking Alton back down onto the bed. She gave him a rub-noses kiss, all the while verbally "good mornin'ing" him into a tickly physical awakening.

Lisbeth watched awhile and then turned back to the kitchen.

Alton struggled his way out from under Dot's weight and grasp to stand up and stretch. He wore the boxers and T-shirt Craig had laid out for him the night before. As much as Lisbeth had told him last night what he had missed in the fifteen years he was away, Dot demonstrated a different, much sweeter reality.

He greeted Lisbeth and Craig with a "G'mornin'" as he walked into the kitchen.

"Good morning," they each replied in turn; they replied in practiced correct articulation.

"I was able to book you into Dr. Jefferson's office for ten thirty," Lisbeth stated dutifully.

"Thanks."

"Alton, what are your intentions? How long are you staying? When will we go back to Beckett?"

"I hadn't thought that through yet. I am worried about Grandpa and the horses and Grandma too. Shall we head back tomorrow or next week?"

Lisbeth nodded a reply. She looked too tired to speak.

"Can Alton play now?" Dot emerged from the playroom with her two arms full of toys she wanted to share. She stood impatiently at the edge of the kitchen area, not intruding but infectiously eager.

"Dot. Do not interrupt. You have lessons to do. Alton is out of the media room. You go and get them done. Start with your L&Qs."

Dot groaned.

"Then you can do some 2Ws."

Dot said, "Yay!" and danced a full-arms gig.

"Then Five Squares in your Speak Clearly, Speak Well program."

"Five?" A look of consternation came over Dot's face. "Yuck. Don't wanna."

"Correct that. How do you say 'yuck' politely?" There was an edge to Lisbeth's voice.

Dot's brow furrowed, and her eyes went to the back of her head, where she had stored her polite-and-clear-articulation lessons. "I find that…unpleasant." She paused and thought again. "And I would prefer not to have to do that."

"That's better. Four then, not five."

Dot still looked frustrated with the burdensome task ahead, but she acquiesced.

"Three then. Get going—you have a lot to do."

Dot left them, going first to the playroom to drop the armload of toys just inside the door. Then she went to the media room and picked up a learning tablet. Sitting on Alton's bed, she got down to work.

Alton stared at his mother. He couldn't help but imagine that at one point she was probably very much like Dot, vital and playful. He thought of the toll that being a Paraclete and ASL instructor had had on his mother.

Craig handed him a muffin and coffee.

"Speak clearly, speak well?" Alton asked.

"It's part of the effective-communication program we are using for the children. As they train to be future Paracletes, it's important that they communicate well. Dr. Perkins has designed a comprehensive interpersonal-skill program that is incorporated into schooling. Clear speech is part of it. Prosocial behavior, empathetic awareness, patience in waiting for rewards…it's all part of their training. We also teach them to compromise and to bargain out mutually acceptable arrangements. That's why I rewarded her with a reduction in the number of Squares she had to do. I started high at five, but three is enough for the day anyway for her to complete.

Her ability to correct her spontaneous, sloppy speech is a good sign that she's getting it."

Alton received this information with sadness. Dot was so eager to play. But now she was off on a Saturday morning burdened with preparing to serve the emotional needs of others. No wonder his mother looked so worn and woeful.

Byron had switched on his wearable when the Range Rover neared the outskirts of Munroe. He had no reason to think he was being tracked. He also had no reason not to be cautious given his mission down in the Enclave. He messaged Sallye immediately and asked that they meet at the S-SB over on North Hill.

Sallye arrived a little out of breath and glowing at the sight of Byron. When she had left on All Faiths Day, he was still asleep. She had so much to tell him, so much that would not feel complete in herself until she had told him.

Byron had a table, their favorite table. She bounced in the line to the counter, impatient for the caffeine and impatient to sit with Byron and have the warm ceramic mug in her hands. As Byron looked at her, he got a "nothing's wrong" vibe off of her. It was a strange vibe given the struggles they were having in their relationship and the circumstances of the last few days.

She rushed to the table, a whirl of wool shawl and long hair on the loose. "I have so much to tell you."

Byron reached out his hand to hers to settle her.

She said, "It's about Cripps. But first, how is Dr. Perkins?" She thought the words *the creep* but didn't even mouth them.

"He's OK, I guess. Dr. Chetwin is working it all out. I am quite sure that Dr. Perkins is not going to kill himself. Dr. Chetwin and someone else are out there today. Mr. Johnson picked them up to take them back before dropping me off here."

"So…" Sallye looked at him, eager for him to tell whatever story there was from the Enclave, eager for him he get it out so she could tell hers.

"There is not much to tell. You go first."

Sallye settled her stuff around her; she laid her scarf over the back of the chair and hooked her satchel back there too.

"So, the day before yesterday, I was working with Dr. Chetwin, and I kept getting demanding messages from Cripps. It was like he was haunting me, his ugly face projecting up from my wearable. I was with clients, Zeke even, when it was happening. It was disgusting the way it kept going on. So I had to do something about it."

"What did you do?" Byron inhaled as though he were going to say something else, and Sallye waited for him to blurt it out. He did. "When you are done with your story about Cripps, I want to know about Zeke."

"OK. So I went back to FiveWay, and I was talking to…" Sallye launched into the story, animated and breathless. For Byron, it was like being swept away by a strong wind, an embracing, strong, warm wind. He heard snippets of the narrative, snippets such as "a low growl" and "the hair on the back of his neck," but the scene she painted of her standing up to Cripps captivated him most of all.

He was in awe. He was also scared. He was diminished by her power and presence.

"So?" Sallye looked at him. The story was done; she had relived the triumph and now wanted her affirmation.

Byron sat there looking at her.

"Are you speechless?" she asked, annoyed.

Byron shook himself out of his silence. "That is amazing. And you just walked out?"

"Just walked out, and he hasn't messaged me since."

Byron looked at her. The furrows of his brow deepened.

"Aren't you proud of me?"

"Oh, yes. Yes." Byron paused. His voice became more severe. "But Sallye, you might lose your job over this. If nothing else, Cripps is vengeful." What really worried Byron was that he might lose her.

"He needs me." Sallye caught Byron's apprehension, and there was not as much confidence in her voice as she'd had two days before.

"You are probably right." Byron didn't sound convincing. He loved the story but felt so unsure of them, of their future, given all that had happened over the past few days.

"So what happened down in the Enclave?"

"First of all, and this isn't what I really need to talk to you about, but…first of all, this old woman came to talk to Perkins. I don't know who she is, but she spent an hour with him. The way she had about her, I hope, I hope…I hope you get to meet her. I think you might really like her."

"Hmm. And?"

Byron paused a long time, trying to sum up the story for her.

"The day you left I was reading, and Perkins was standing over at the window. Alton walked over to him. I was watching, and…"

"And?"

"And I was watching Perkins as Alton talked to him."

Byron paused; the story he had to tell was painful in a way.

"Sallye, do you remember when Dr. Chetwin did our Effective Connection modules? Remember SEFIA?"

Sally recalled. It had been a couple of years since that formal training.

"Well, it was like I was watching SEFIA right there in front of me. Alton did it."

"Tell me."

"Something about the way that he walked up to Dr. Perkins. I could see Dr. Perkins soften. Up until that point he had been hard; he had always been hard.

"Then I saw the Engage. Dr. Perkins had been detached ever since we picked him up from the hospital, but there Alton got him to engage.

"I am remembering now: Soften, Engage, Form Intent, Allow. That is the protocol for working with self-protective clients.

"I couldn't hear what they said to each other, and I couldn't read Alton's mind, so I don't know what intent he formed there. But all the body language was there that it had happened."

"That's neat."

"Sallye, how does Alton know how to do that? He never took the module."

"I guess it just comes naturally to him. Maybe from his work with horses."

"Elise commented too, even before that happened, on the power of connection that she saw in Alton."

"I see it too."

Byron looked into his coffee, that sweetness and flavor he held there. "I don't have it," he said softly.

"Oh, Byron, no. You do."

"When I do it I have to work on it; when you do it, you do it without thinking about it. It comes naturally for you and naturally for Alton. Not for me."

Sallye took her hands off her coffee and placed them around Byron's hands.

"Byron, I must admit that it does come naturally for me. And I am sorry that it doesn't come naturally for you. But I see that you do it; you do it through an act of will, through a different strength that you have inside of you."

Byron looked right at her. "And I hear about you and Cripps and how strong you were. When you told the story, I heard the other SEFIA, the SEFIA Dr. Chetwin taught us for dealing with aggressive-intrusive people: Strength, Engagement, Formed Intention, Action. You did all that too. I couldn't."

"I took Sanctuary there to be my strength. I never thought of Cripps as an aggressive-intrusive; I just thought of him as a bastard. But that's what he is in Dr. Chetwin's Table of Characters. He's an aggressive-intrusive."

"It was strong of you to even think of taking Sanctuary there, of having the courage to do so."

"I guess."

Sallye paused. "Do you think that Dr. Chetwin just does SEFIA naturally himself?"

"Yeah."

"I don't think so. If it were natural for him, why did he have to think up the memory word? I think that he does it through discipline and hard work too. Like you do it."

Byron thought. Dr. Chetwin had always looked like a natural, but maybe he was a deliberate—a disciplined, careful deliberate.

Sallye reached out and held Byron's hand. "I worked a lot with Dr. Chetwin the day before yesterday. When he is doing his arranging, his fixing, he looks so natural at it. Then when he sat with me, even early in the morning, he looked so tired. Naturals get energized when SEFIA comes out of them. Deliberates might do it well, but it wears them out."

Byron sat silently.

"Byron, you are a deliberate. When you do SEFIA, when you love me and accept me, when you care about Zeke and decide that you will be a brother to Alton, you do all that because of deliberate acts of love and will coming from deep inside of you. And that is wonderful. Maybe it's not as automatic and spontaneous and you have to work at it. But it always comes from the fundamental goodness that is inside of you."

He still sat silently.

"And Byron, that is what I love about you. Your love is not flighty or shallow. It goes deep."

Byron looked up, receptive.

"There are some fundamentally good people in this world, Byron. Strong and good people. Dr. Chetwin is one. You are one too. I need your strength, Byron. I need your love. I need the security that you will always love me from that core of deliberate will you have inside of you."

"Thank you." Byron looked at her. "You had sex with Alton."

"I did. And I confess that it came from the spontaneous, impulsive side of me. And it was wonderful in the moment."

Byron cringed.

"And it came from a sort of love but not the deep and important love that we share."

"I still feel hurt."

"And you should. It was wrong of me."

"Don't you ever do it again. Not with my brother, not with anyone."

"Oh, Byron. No." But Sallye was conflicted. She didn't know whether that *no* was toward him or toward herself. Clearly, Byron was the lover she needed. Sadly, he was not the lover she craved.

(III)

Dr. Jefferson's consulting room was technology laden and sterile smelling. But her manner was as warm as it was efficient.

"So Lisbeth, you have brought one of your boys." She turned to look at Alton. "Byron, is it?"

Lisbeth interjected, "No, this is Byron's older brother, Alton. He just showed up in our lives; he hasn't lived with us since he was about seven."

"Oh my!" There was an awkward silence in the room. "I'm sure there is a story behind that."

More awkward silence. Lisbeth sensed that it was hers to explain. She couldn't muster the energy.

"Lisbeth, you don't look well. Stress?"

"You could say that."

"Well, you folks over there in the Paraclete program are stress experts. I guess you are prone to it yourselves with the work you do."

More awkward silence. Dr. Jefferson was starting to get concerned. This was not the typical Lisbeth. Lisbeth was the stoic one, the one who could face any human challenge and overcome. Dr. Jefferson motioned toward Lisbeth's wearable. Lisbeth dutifully activated it to read out her physiological data.

"Well, physically, everything is coming in within range. You do look tired. Was there something you wanted me to check?"

"Yes. My son."

"Alton?" Dr. Jefferson turned and looked at him curiously. She motioned toward his wearable.

"Yes, Doctor. Oh yes, it isn't turned on. It will take a few seconds to activate."

"Not turned on?"

"Privacy reasons," said Alton.

Dr. Jefferson looked at him with even more curiosity now. In the characterological impairment profiles that the psychologists had created for patient demeanor, excessive concern about privacy loaded onto latent paranoia. She wondered whether that might be what she was facing in this young man.

"Well, thank you for turning it on. I'm a doctor, so no need to worry about privacy here. Whatever the issue is, we can work it through together."

Alton's wearable was activated. The doctor showed him how to direct the data flow into her computer. She watched as the data formulated on the screen.

"Well, healthy young male. *Fit*, healthy young male. So do you have pain?"

"It's about this thing I have in my abdomen. I want it out." Alton spoke with directness, a no-nonsense clarity about what needed to happen, and he did so with someone he didn't know whether he could trust.

"Thing?" Dr. Jefferson was immediately concerned that the paranoia was not latent but florid—that he might be delusional.

"My implant. I think that's what it's called: an implant."

"Oh, that. Let's take a look."

Dr. Jefferson made a few strokes on the display screen of her computer. In doing so, she went deeper into the settings and functional capabilities of the implant.

"Well, it's still functioning well. An old model for sure. We can replace it with one that will give us a lot more data. Generally, we don't, because that takes surgery. So not until it malfunctions. But yours is good." Dr. Jefferson spoke with a sense of conclusion that the checks she had made and the results she had found were a satisfactory resolution to the issue the young man had.

"I don't want a new one. I want the old one out."

"Why?" The doctor was clearly perplexed.

"It's my body. I don't want people knowing what is going on inside of it."

"'People' don't know; I know. I'm a doctor; if I am going to treat you, I have to know."

"People at the ASL."

"Oh, those people. They don't really know. They just channel the data back to us in the health-care system."

"They know."

Dr. Jefferson looked at him. This was starting to look like a neurocorrective issue.

"Oh, I'm sure that they are harmless. They stream the data and are doing research on the general health of the population. They do much of our health-care system's planning, and they gather resources for medical treatment. They need data from all of us to do that."

"They know when I have sex."

Now she was alarmed, alarmed by the tone of his voice. She looked at the computer screen to check his age. "Alton. You are a healthy young man, twenty-one years old. Of course you are having sex. It is nothing to be ashamed of. It's natural."

"But they don't have to know when and with who."

"I'm sure that no one is at all interested in that. I can see how your implant and wearable could be tapped to separate endocrinological data out in the data stream. But I am sure that they over at the ASL and we here at Health Care have no reason to be interested in your sex life, as long as you are not spreading STIs anyway."

"I want it out."

"You want it out. You realize that in all my years of practice you are the first one to not want the implant?" She waited a moment, but her voice grew firmer and sterner. "Everyone else is really glad that their health is monitored closely. A good-quality data stream replaces all sorts of messy physical tests that used to be required to diagnose illness. All my patients are delighted that they can come in, transfer data to me, and be diagnosed with little in the way of me having to poke around their bodies and take away bodily fluids."

Dr. Jefferson sat back in her chair. She watched Alton's reaction to her. He showed no sign of being convinced. She sighed. Protocol for this characterological impairment would have her listen, eventually find a point of agreement, and then watch for associated features, features that might require a more complete neurological workup.

"I want it out." Alton matched his firmness to hers.

"You are aware that as a member of this society you have a responsibility. It is your responsibility to maintain good health and to assist the population programs that raise overall societal health. Your implant is not just about you. It is about all of us. As we all participate, we lower health-care costs through prevention and timely intervention; each of us runs less risk of infectious disease; together we all raise the level of health in our community."

"It is my body. I want it out."

"Very well then. I will make a referral."

"To someone who can take it out?"

"Well, eventually it might go that way. But first, because this is not only a personal medical issue but also a societal one, I need to consult with a medical ethicist. Just routine. Once I have done so, we will see about a further referral. It would be good if we could keep you from going under the knife. Think about it. We will talk again."

Later that afternoon, Alton took Dot to the Courtyard District. It was a Saturday afternoon, and children's activities were planned.

They walked. This was OK with Lisbeth, as it would fulfill some of Dot's physical exercise requirements for the day. Well, it was only Alton who walked, the loping sort of walk that people who ride horses have. Rather than walking, Dot bounced and spun at his side while holding his hand. Glee leaked out of her face. Being with Dot helped him shed some the tension he had felt with the doctor.

The weather had dried. Puddles from the rains early in the week had crusted into hardened dirt. Winds had shifted to come from the southeast, a place of no great weather delights but with weather not as dismal as the rains of the west.

Their route took them past a field of wild grasses. Alton waded in, pushing back the longer weeds that had stood dead from the season's frost. Dot went along, excited about the adventure. Finally, in the middle of the field, he found what he was looking for: whirlybird weed. Taking out a small pocketknife, he harvested one stalk of it after another. He handed each stalk to his accomplice. Soon her hands were full, so it was hard to clench them around the stiff weed stock. Her fingers grew cold. Alton took them from her and laid them on the ground. He picked more until he had a substantial sheaf beside them.

"What are these for?" she asked.

"Whirlybirds. We will make them when we get to the Courtyard District. There we can work in the warmth, with no wind."

"What's a whirlybird?"

"You'll see."

Alton remembered the days when he was Dot's age or maybe a bit older. In the fall, when the frost had killed the weeds, he and Justin would seek out this particular one. The stalk was hollow and rigid, sectioned every few inches like bamboo. The leaves were fibrous, sinewy even. Alton became eager to do with Dot what Grandpa had once done with him: make a toy from a weed grass. Dot buried her hands in her pants pockets, seeking out the warmth of her thighs through the thin fabric. With Alton carrying the bundle of late-autumn weed stocks, they headed toward the Courtyard District.

Alton clicked on his wearable within a block or so of arriving. He was certain that he would be monitored there. If the cameras picked him up, but his wearable was off, he would attract attention from one of the ASL security guards. He was thankful that children were kept safe with the monitoring for sexual predators in public places. Then he thought of Perkins and felt sick. They passed through the doors into the warmth and light of the covered avenues.

Music was playing, children were dancing, and parents lined the avenues drinking hot, sweet beverages. Members of a drama group were enacting a story about the early days of Munroe, complete with a lumbering moose. The moose was two actors in a fur costume who were struggling to keep their movements sufficiently coordinated so they wouldn't fall over into a furry heap.

Alton found a table in one of the alleyways. He selected stalks of whirlybird weed. With his knife, he severed the leaves and shredded them lengthwise, twisting them together to make a thread. Dot watched, entranced by what he was doing. Catching her interest, he showed her how to weave the threads together to make it strong.

Alton then lined up the stalks, organizing them into groups with similarly spaced sections. Using the thread, he bound them together in sets of three. He trimmed the top section to identical lengths, bent them over in three evenly spaced directions, and flattened the horizontal rigid stock so that it was shaped more like a wing than a tube. He secured those top wings at a precise ninety-degree angle with short lengths of the thread. Once that was done, he placed the whirlybird between his two hands and rubbed his hands rapidly so that the whirlybird spun, its top acting like a helicopter propeller. The whirlybird lifted off, flying up and over a few meters before it settled gently back to the ground.

Dot squealed with delight. It was the most wonderful thing that she had ever seen.

Before long, a group of children gathered around. Parents gathered behind them. Alton demonstrated and aided, and soon the air was filled with whirlybirds. More children and parents came.

And then there was Zeke standing at the side of the group. He had watched, been intrigued, and stayed there.

Alton felt a grabbing sensation in his side. Ever since he had formed the intention that he was going to get his implant out, he was conscious of its physical presence in his body. He grabbed at it angrily. Then he turned off his wearable, and the grabbing stopped.

Zeke noticed and asked, "What's up?"

"I have an implant."

"We all do."

"I want to get rid of it and get rid of this damn wearable that tracks me everywhere I go."

As they talked, a spinning whirlybird narrowly missed their heads.

"I can do something about that. I can scramble it. You can leave it on, but it will give random data on the stream back to the ASL."

"You can do that?" Alton looked astonished.

A small group gathered around them. Suddenly there were questions: "You can? How?" and "Why? Oh, that makes sense; I never even thought of that" and "Won't the ASL catch you?" and "Fuck them! I want it scrambled. Can you show me?" The dad who swore looked embarrassed, and other parents shushed him because children were around. Still, the mood of the crowd was curious.

Alton held out his wearable to Zeke and watched what he did. Then another person was curious and eager. A wife tried to pull a husband away. As much as the whirlybirds were spinning out of control, so too was the group that had gathered around Alton and Zeke. People watched and copied the series of programming steps that Zeke showed them on one wearable after another.

Miles away, over in the academy building, Cripps's attention went to the monitoring screens in his office. Alerts were going off like mad. Data flows were perturbed. He checked the cameras and saw that Alton was in the middle of it.

It was the second time that day that Alton Wilkes had been brought to his attention.

Byron and Sallye walked over to the family communal home, arriving just a few minutes after Alton and Dot had left for the Courtyard District. They had timed the visit to be just an hour or so; Byron had arranged with Gerald that he pick them up there at 4:00 p.m., after he had dropped Dr. Chetwin and Elias back in Munroe. They would then head back to the Enclave. Byron had asked Sallye to go back with him, just until Monday. She had agreed.

Byron was worried about his mom. Sallye was scared to go back over there given the way Lisbeth had kicked her out two days before. Byron wanted to go to her as a couple. Sallye realized that she would have to try to reconcile with Lisbeth sometime; she couldn't imagine being a Paraclete without Lisbeth's mentoring.

As they walked, Sallye said, "Oh no! I can't today. I've got to see Zeke. We arranged to meet at the Courtyard District this afternoon. I am so sorry I forgot."

A look of disappointment came over Byron's face.

"He's a pretty strong kid. I am sure he would understand. Message him and say that you'll see him next week. There are kids' things going on over at the Courtyard District today anyway. He'll have fun."

Sallye looked conflicted. Zeke was really Byron's Emergent, Byron probably knew him better that Sallye did.

"Anyway, I think that Dr. Chetwin is going over to visit the Basilis family tomorrow anyway. He can check in on him. I'm sure that Zeke will be OK."

"I am not so sure. When I saw him the day before yesterday, he was agreeable; he seemed OK. But the anger hasn't come out yet. He didn't seem angry at Dr. Perkins. He should be."

"Zeke is not an angry sort of kid."

"That's what I'm worried about," Sallye said.

They were at the door. Even though this had been Byron's childhood home, he didn't feel comfortable barging in. He knocked.

Lisbeth greeted them at the door. She motioned with her eyes for Byron to come in, and then she took in the reality of Sallye standing behind him. "Oh, it's you. Come in." There was neither warmth nor hostility to her voice. It was just flat.

They sat at the kitchen table.

"How are you doing, Mother?"

"I have had better days."

"It is a shock, Alton coming back, isn't it?"

"Yes. I look at him and want to hate him for going away. But when I look at him, I can't hate him. Then I want to be his mom. And…" Lisbeth choked up. "I don't think I have been a mom to any of you. I have been your teacher, your mentor, the one to look out for you. I have been what the ASL assigned me to be, not a mom."

Lisbeth herself was shocked at her own words. She had thought those thoughts and then believed that she would never be able to speak them. And here with her disengaged son, here with Perfect Paraclete Sallye, out they came.

Byron looked at her. Reflexively, he wanted to reassure, to care for her. The protocols of his training with Emotionally Vulnerables came back to him. Then he remembered how his mother had turned on Sallye when Sallye had done the Paraclete thing. Byron felt trapped; his learned responses weren't right, and he didn't know intuitively what to do.

Byron swallowed, gathered himself, and thought about the deliberate goodness that Sallye had said was inside of him. That goodness told him that he had to tell the truth. "You are right; you were an excellent teacher and mentor. You took us to the doctor when we needed to go, and you made sure that we had our toys and did our lessons. But as for being a mom, no."

They both cried.

Byron looked at her and said, "Why don't we try for that now?"

Lisbeth looked up, acquiescence in her eyes. Then she looked at Sallye. "I owe you an apology."

"That's OK."

Sallye and Lisbeth knew that Paraclete protocols would have Lisbeth name the transgression, state empathetically how it would have hurt, and pledge to never do it again. It was all Lisbeth could do not to launch into the relationship perfection that had been detailed and trained into the Paraclete program. Instead, she just looked at Sallye with tears and love in her eyes. Sallye looked back with tears and love in her eyes too. Finally, after a few minutes, the two women embraced. It wasn't the practiced Sallye touch, the kind that she was so good at. It was better.

"We are going to Beckett," Lisbeth said after regaining her composure. "Byron, I want you to come."

"When?"

"Tomorrow or Monday."

"Sallye and I have an assignment today down in the Enclave. We have to leave at four. We will be back on Monday."

"Monday it is, then," Lisbeth said. Then she turned to Sally. "Sallye, this is something that Byron needs to do with just us."

"I understand."

"We have to straighten out some stuff with Byron's grandparents."

"Yes, that's OK."

"You'll be here when we come back?" Lisbeth asked.

"I will be here. I have to be around for Tuesday." Suddenly, Sallye stopped. She was going to launch into what was happening for Dr. Perkins and then she realized that she shouldn't; she couldn't.

At that moment, the Range Rover pulled up in front of the family communal home. Gerald waited patiently at the wheel. The car attracted quite a bit of attention on the street given the whiff of gasoline exhaust from its tailpipe and the roar of its powerful engine.

(IV)

When Byron awoke in the bedroom in the Enclave, Sallye was at his side. He waited patiently for her to open her eyes. They were intimate. They were intimate in that early-morning, urgent way of youth. Sallye strove to stay present with Byron, and for the most part, she was successful.

Elise greeted them knowingly, pleased to see them together. She had been privy to the difficult story—Beckett to Munroe and now Munroe to the Enclave.

Pleasantries were exchanged.

"Are you tired of having houseguests?" Sallye asked, helping herself to coffee and the sweet buns that Elise provided for them.

"Never!" Elise paused. "Well, maybe."

"It has been almost a week. You weren't expecting anyone, let alone all of us, and for so long."

"I think it is good for Gerald and for me too. But Gerald, since he doesn't have the business responsibilities, needs something…" Elise smiled. "And he loves driving that Range Rover."

"Is Dr. Perkins up?"

"Alastair? Yes, he is up. Out for a walk. He is looking better. When he first came, he was as gray as the November sky. Now there is color in his cheeks."

"Alyssa? Is she up?"

"Not yet."

Byron wandered off, leaving the womenfolk to their small talk. He loved being with Sallye, loved it more than anything he had ever known. Still, sometimes she felt more like a guest in his life rather than a resident: a lovely, warm, amicable, and delightful guest, but a guest nonetheless. What attracted him to her, she so easily also gave to everyone else.

Dr. Perkins came in. He sized up the room, seeing who was there.

"Sallye and Byron, we have to talk." Even though his greeting had an urgency about it, there was softness in his voice. His tone was a departure from that of the administrator and lecturer that he had been with the young Paracletes through the academy.

They sat in the comfortable living room. Elise fussed with the gas fireplace, fluffed the cushions on the sofa, and asked about more coffee. Alastair waited patiently for her to leave.

"First of all, I want to say thank you to you both. I don't remember too much of that night, but I do remember that you were there for me.

"Although I hope we can be more to each other than just our roles within the ASL." Perkins paused, searching for the words. "I must say that you have done me proud over this last week or so. You are Paracletes of the highest skill and dedication. When I needed someone to come to my side to be a human presence, you were there."

Byron looked up. "I think you have Dr. Chetwin to thank for that."

"And I have, but I need to thank you too." Perkins paused. "I want you to know that as of tomorrow, I will no longer be with the ASL in Munroe. I am resigning to take a position on the coast, at the MacMillan…"

Perkins choked up. Tears came to his eyes. For a moment, he looked panicky.

"No, that is not right." A steelier resolve came to his voice; it was meant as a message to himself more than to them. "As of next week, I am going into residential treatment at the MacMillan Institute, in the sexual…" His voice cracked and fell off, and tears came to his eyes.

Sallye reached over to him and put her hand on his knee. He settled, not even processing it as a Paraclete move. He made eye contact with her, desperate eye contact, as though he were drowning.

"I didn't think it would be this hard."

Sallye spoke softly. "It is this hard. You have our support, sir."

They were silent for a while.

"You all are doing so much for me. I am grateful. I want to ask something else, something just between the three of us, the three of us and Myles. I want you to stop calling me sir or referring to me as Dr. Perkins. Can you call me Al? And…" He smiled, adopting a mockingly stern voice and clearly regaining a semblance of composure. "Call me Alastair if you need to confront me. That's what my mom, God rest her soul, did when I screwed up as a kid. And boy, could I screw up as a kid!"

There was an awkward silence in the room. Perkins added, "And still can, I guess."

Byron said, "You have a tough road ahead of you."

"Yes, especially over the next few days. Myles has worked hard to get everything set up. Even today, as we speak, he is back in Munroe working with the Basilises…" Alastair's voice faltered, and then he swallowed to regain his strength. "And Elias, and Constable Morris."

Perkins looked at Sallye. "I understand that you saw Zeke last week. How is he doing?"

"He is handling this well, Dr. Perkins. He—"

"Al."

"Al. Oh, I won't ever get used to this! He, Zeke, is doing OK. When I talked to him, he said he holds no animosity toward you.

He specifically told me that he didn't want you to go to jail and that he wanted to see you again."

"Well, that's good. The disposition that Myles is working out with the Basilises likely contains a no-contact clause. That's just as well. Take care of him for me."

"We don't yet know how he will do over the coming weeks, or years, even. Yes, we, Byron and I, will do our best for him."

Perkins paused again. "Sallye, there is something I want you to do for me, for Zeke and me. I have prepared a letter of apology, a letter taking responsibility. I don't know whether it is any good, but Myles told me to do it. It's a part of the legal disposition, but I mean every word that it says. I want you to take it to him, to be with him when he reads it."

"OK." Sallye wondered how that would work. Would it be loaded to Zeke's wearable while she was with him or on hers to transfer over to the teen?

Perkins retrieved a leather-bound folder from a side table. When Sallye had seen it there, she had thought it was one of the antiques, a memento of a more gracious time. Perkins handed it to Sallye. When she opened it, she saw a piece of elegant ivory writing paper inside and a neat handwritten note addressed to Zeke. She closed the folder immediately when she recognized what it was.

"You can check it over if you like; perhaps you should."

"No, sir…Al. That is between you and him. Let's give it the privacy it deserves, a healthy privacy to replace an unhealthy secrecy that you shared with him."

Perkins stopped and turned the word *privacy* over in his mind. Such a startling word from young lips. Such a modest and archaic word. Such a gem of a word. An antidote, really.

When Cripps arrived at FiveWay Compound, it was with a bluster and a bother. Fortunately, Jamin and Arthur had seen him coming in time to get Sanctuary down into the laundry room in the basement. They ran the washer and dryer to create sound to cover over any whimpering the dog might do at the door.

"Sallye, please," Cripps demanded curtly, dismissively.

"She is not here, sir," Jamin said.

"Well, where is she, then?"

"I don't know, sir."

Angelica piped up. "I'll go and check her room to see whether she came in in the middle of the night."

"Did you check her wearable, sir?" Jamin asked.

"Of course I did. It's off."

"Strange." Jamin created a puzzled look on his face.

They stood awkwardly in the kitchen. There was a hushed giggling from the bedroom wing as other young Paracletes clowned Cripps imitations among themselves and struggled to suppress their nervous laughter. Cripps, not one to miss anything, processed the sound and would have barged in on the gaggle of them had Angelica not come back into the room.

"Not there, sir. Doesn't look like she slept in her bed at all last night. Did you check over at BirdSong? She sometimes sleeps over there with Byron."

Cripps turned without answering the question. He had no need to tell them what he had or had not done. Turning to leave the compound, he caught sight of the dog dishes on the kitchen floor.

Cripps stormed down the walk and threw open the door of the AVoD. "Anything yet on the wearables?"

Charles Ross sat in the back seat with both a tablet computer and his wearable. He had also commandeered out of storage an old-fashioned scanner that was useless for the task but gave Cripps the impression that he was doing everything possible to find the young Paraclete. "Nothing yet. I get flashes of Alton's wearable but not Byron's or Sallye's. And Alton's signal is coming in as corrupted, so we can't be sure it is an accurate transmission of where he is or what he is doing."

"Fuck. Fuck them all. Damn Wilkes."

"Sir?" Charles Ross looked up at his boss, offended by the words and tone. Being stuck in an AVoD with Sebastian Cripps was not his idea of a Sunday-morning good time.

"Let's head over to the family communal home. We'll skip BirdSong. I doubt that they'd be there, and if they were, they would've probably been warned off anyway by the trash Perkins created and housed in the compounds."

By the time they reached the family communal home, everyone in the compounds and communal homes had been warned by Jamin and Angelica. Kenyon had gone over to tell Lisbeth and Craig. They rushed Alton into Craig's basement workshop.

Once Cripps had arrived and stormed into the kitchen, it was hard to discern who was madder at whom, he or Lisbeth. Cripps had never had much to do with her but had always heard reports that she was well on track with the program. That Sunday morning, he got more than an earful; it was a shock to him. Lisbeth was well aware that it had been Cripps who was behind arranging the neurological intervention with Craig. She let him have it, both barrels.

Cyrus and Dot stood helplessly off to the side, witnessing it all. Dot cried. Cyrus held her.

Craig watched too. Seamlessly, he and Lisbeth had changed roles. Her anger was right out there, and he stood with the children, calming them.

Charles Ross stood at the door. What a zoo it was! *Oh, man!* he thought. *What have I gotten myself into?* He felt sorry for them all. Quietly, he got a message through to Elise down in the Enclave. Connections were spotty to anyone there because of the scrambling, but he got it through. "Cripps on the loose. He's rabid. Tell everyone to stay put. I will make sure he doesn't come down there."

When he had received acknowledgment that the message had been read, Charles went on as an ASL IT administrator and erased all traces of it from the server memory.

(V)

Craig had ordered the six-passenger AVoD to arrive at ten. He and Alton had thought through the day, and they'd decided that it would work best to arrive in Beckett about eleven thirty and get settled. Then Alton would bring his grandmother over to Vy's, and they would meet for lunch there. Craig was eager to see his father. They would do that in the afternoon.

Dot was excited. Alton had promised her that she could see the horses. Cyrus was excited too, in a more mature and muted way. His anticipation piggybacked onto the infectious energy of his younger sister.

Lisbeth was beyond nervous; her feelings edged in and out of downright dread. The self-awareness and peace she had achieved with Byron and Sallye the day before had retreated into bitterness and fear.

Gerald had dropped off Sallye at FiveWay and then provided a few minutes for Byron to go into BirdSong and change his clothes. He stopped at the family communal home to deposit Byron there and congratulated Craig and Lisbeth on their two fine sons.

The AVoD had two front seats that faced forward, and four seats in the back that were arranged to face one another. It was a tight fit with various backpacks and overnight bags. This was Dot's first trip outside of Munroe. She had many stuffed animals who insisted they too should see the horses. Lisbeth had had little patience for negotiation to get that number down to a handful.

Just as they were loading up, Sallye came running down the street. Sanctuary bounded on a leash beside her as she ran. She gasped out a "Stop, wait!"

Byron ran to greet her, taking hold of Sanctuary. Sallye leaned over and put her hands on her knees, and then she flexed back upright, trying to get some air. Her breath was ragged and desperate from the fast run. "You've got to take Sanctuary."

"What? Why?" Byron asked.

"It's Cripps." Sallye still struggled to get enough breath to speak. "Charles was over at FiveWay when I got there." She gasped. "He is worried about Sanctuary." She gasped again and then took a deep breath. "Apparently, Cripps bought rat poison at the farm-supply store." She gasped again. "We think that he's going to try to poison Sanctuary."

Both of them grabbed Sanctuary by his collar and tried to stuff him into the limited floor space in the back of the AVoD. He had never been in an AVoD before and was clearly not liking the idea of it at all. Alton pitched in to help, and by sheer strength of will from the three young adults, Sanctuary was installed at the feet of Lisbeth, Craig, and Cyrus at the back of the AVoD. He was trembling.

"That's OK, Sanc-tu-ary." Dot drew the odd name out uncertainly. She climbed into the back of the AVoD and draped one arm around the back of his neck and the other around his massive chest, and then she drew her kind face up next to his. "Come and see the horses with us."

When they got to Vy's, Craig went to the front desk and booked rooms for the family. Lisbeth took Dot to the washroom. Alton led Byron and Cyrus into the Eatery to claim a booth for them all, plus one.

Cyrus was pleased that his tablet computer was able to connect to the WarpWeb. He had Alton show him on the GeoMapping app where the ranch was. Soon he was zooming in on a virtual tour of the property using satellite images.

Alton went over what was good at Vy's—the pies, of course! Leaving the rest of them at the table, he made his way over to the Beckett Mills Retail, where his grandmother would be working. He found her alone in the store, fussing about display tables and the arrangement of stock. She was getting the store ready for the influx of skiers. Within weeks, they would be in town and looking for souvenir sweaters and unique knitted Christmas gifts. She wanted everything perfectly at hand for the busy season.

"Looks good," Alton said warmly, with a smile.

"Oh, Alton!" Laurel beamed. "I am so glad you're back." She paused, and her tone changed. "It has been a trial. Your grandpa is getting his brain back, slowly." She stretched out the word. "But he is still very weak. I have Cedars over there while I am at work, but soon Cedars has to get his business ready for the winter tourist season too."

"We just got in from Munroe; we will go out to the ranch this afternoon. Come have lunch with us over at Vy's."

"We? Who's the we?"

Alton swallowed hard; there was no easy way to say this, but it was only fair to prepare his grandmother for the onslaught of family members who awaited her over at Vy's. "Well, Byron is with us. You remember Byron?"

Alton waited for a look of recognition from his grandmother, but what he was getting was impatience. "And your other two grandchildren, Cyrus and Dot—they are there too."

Laurel gasped. Her eyes, eyes which had been able to figure out just about everything that she had ever faced in life, retreated into the dark.

"And your son, Craig. He came as well. And Lisbeth."

Laurel stiffened.

As they walked over to Vy's, all Laurel could think of was the shock that this would be to Justin. His heart wouldn't be able to stand it. Her mind tumbled with half thoughts: *so unnecessary* and *be the death of him* and *on top of everything else*. And most repeatedly, *I can't*.

Alton and his grandmother stood at the entry to the Eatery. He tucked his hand in the crook of her elbow to steady her. She looked over at the table. Her son, Craig, sat stoically staring into space. The children were engaged in looking at a tablet computer with Byron. Lisbeth looked up at her.

The air in Vy's Eatery suddenly became very still, so still as to be suffocating. The clank of dishes in the kitchen and the hubbub of clerks and customers in the Emporium grew silent, or so it seemed. As the two women stared at each other, mother-in-law and daughter-in-law, the breath went out of their lungs. Fifteen years of hating each other at a distance held them rigidly a few meters apart.

Laurel's mind scrambled into every scenario that might erupt. Then she moved forward confidently. Determined, she engendered from within the same perspective and control that she would exercise on Stamper if he got skittish or on Biddy if she were spooked by some wild thing on a trail ride. She knew well that creatures got scared and got aggressive. She knew well that unless they threw her off and fled, she could get control of the situation.

"Lisbeth. You came, and you brought the grandchildren. What courage that must have taken! I want to thank you." Laurel spoke from a place of deliberate control and chosen grace in an effort to set the tone for the encounter.

Lisbeth was stunned.

"We have had bad blood. And I am sure that you have every reason to absolutely hate Justin and me for what we did. But I see two fine grandsons here. One you have raised, and one we have raised. They are here together as brothers. We can stand together with them as the women who have fed them and guided them to be what they are."

Craig got up awkwardly from the table. He went over and clumsily embraced his mother. Laurel looked at him and saw the absence in his eyes. Tears formed in hers. "Oh, my son!" She stroked his hair as if he were a child. "Oh, my son! What have they done to you?" They hugged deeper, stronger.

Lisbeth, watching the embrace, got up and pushed herself out of the awkward seating arrangement in the booth. She looked at her husband and mother-in-law. "Bullshit. Absolute bullshit."

She stormed out of the Eatery.

Dot broke into tears. Reflexively, Cyrus reached out to his younger sister and put an arm around her shoulder. He too had a look of shock and dismay. Although their upbringing had every advantage of secure and mature relationships, all that modern psychology could engineer into a family communal home, it had not prepared them for this.

After a few moments, Alton followed Lisbeth out. Once she had been braced by the chill of mountain air, she had gone to the AVoD and climbed in with Sanctuary. She wasn't much for dogs, never had been, but somehow she found comfort in stroking him. Sanctuary smiled up at Alton as he too entered the vehicle, a smile of relief perhaps that a human had come who could deal with the human already there.

"I don't expect you to forgive her."

"I never will."

"She took me from you."

"She did. Taking a child from his mother—that can never be OK."

"No, it can't."

"You expect me to be in the same room as her?"

"I had hoped."

They sat silently. Alton put on the interior heater in the AVoD.

"Let me go home," Lisbeth said. "This is altogether a bad idea. You go back to your horses or whatever you do up here."

"But Dot and Cyrus are here; they want to see the horses. And Craig too, he wants to be with Grandpa."

"I am tired of having to sacrifice everything for Craig and his blown-out brain." Bitterness reeked in Lisbeth's voice.

"I am sure you are."

Alton paused for a long time. He struggled with how to reconcile them all to one another. The wrench in it all was right here, right here in Lisbeth. The task seemed bigger than he and

Sanctuary could ever accomplish. Finally, he said one word. He said, "Mom." In response to it, to its warmth and compassion, Lisbeth collapsed onto his shoulder and cried compulsively. For a few minutes they sat, Alton opening his heart to her, and Lisbeth crying out hers. The windows of the warming AVoD began to fog up, giving them privacy.

"I had better go back in," Alton finally said.

"You'd better."

"You going to be OK?"

"I don't know. But Sanctuary, Sanctuary probably needs a walk. I can do that."

"Want anything to eat?"

"Can't stomach anything right now."

"I will bring you a piece of pie. For later."

"That would be good."

The staff at the Eatery had swooped in graciously to feed the family. What the kitchen had on hand was enthusiastically offered as chef specialties that no one would ever want to miss. Beverages to put warmth into the chill of November were brought to the table.

The family ate together. The whole family, save Lisbeth and Justin. Infirm Justin—husband, father, and grandfather—was still out at the ranch.

Over lunch, Duncan Johansson came by the booth. He was the manager of the ski lodge. With a full red beard, a face leathered by the great outdoors, and his brilliant blue eyes, Duncan greeted Alton.

"Alton, my boy! Am I ever glad to see you! We need you up there."

Alton rose from his seat and stepped out in the aisle between the tables to shield his family from the booming voice of his boss. "Duncan, so good to see you. I really intend to get back there. Is there lots to do?"

"Some. We got power to the warming hut at Three Diamond Cross. Power, but nothing wired in yet. And we are putting out new railings to improve the flow of skiers around the top and bottom of the lifts. We need your carpentry skills."

"I will get up there soon." Alton truly didn't know how he would manage to do so, but things had a way of working out.

Once lunch was done, Alton worked out who would go where. Laurel thought it would be too much for Justin if they all arrived at once. Craig really wanted to go and see his father. Cyrus and Dot really wanted to go and see the horses.

Laurel retreated to work; she was alone in the Retail, and her boss would be furious if he found the store closed in midafternoon. Her retreat there was welcome, though, a relief from the overwhelming emotion of the booth at Vy's.

During the ride out to the ranch, Alton briefed Byron on taking Cyrus and Dot to the winter paddock. He expected the horses would likely be calm, but Dot's energy and enthusiasm might introduce some self-protective instincts into the herd settling into a winter largely free of humans. And until they could be sure that Sanctuary would be OK with the horses, Alton would take him into the barn. He expected that Cedars and his grandfather would likely be in the workshop and tack room adjacent to the barn. Alton and Craig would look first for them there. Lisbeth asked for time alone to go for a walk in the countryside.

When they arrived, Alton made his way into the workshop, with Craig behind him.

"Grandpa." Alton spoke softly, gently calling his grandfather's focus onto him.

"Oh, Alton. You're back. Good thing. Cedars and I came out here to work on replacing some of the rotted-out wood in the barn stalls. I must have fallen asleep; it's warm in here." He looked over at the woodstove and reveled in its heat.

Alton went over to his grandfather, close enough to hear the struggle for breath.

"Really, boy, there is a lot to do. Cedars and I are getting at it. But it's good you are back to help out. The stalls have to be redone, and the workbench and tools. That needs to be cleaned up. So much to do. And about all I can do is sit."

"Grandpa, I brought someone with me. Someone for you to see. Someone from a long time ago."

Justin looked up at him, confused. Alton couldn't get over the shell of the man, a man who had led trail rides just last summer. The damage to his heart and brain that came from the delay in getting treatment after the heart attack had emptied the old guy out.

"My heart's not good, you know."

"I know, Grandpa. Grandpa, this is Craig. Your son, Craig."

"Craig?"

Tears formed in the old man's eyes. Tears formed in Craig's eyes too.

By the end of the November-shortened afternoon, the menfolk and Dot had gathered in the tiny, rundown house. Lisbeth was still out on her walk; the others were starting to worry that she wasn't back yet.

Craig and Byron, making do in a kitchen that barely functioned, had made a big pot of spaghetti for a family meal. Byron had satisfied Dot and Cyrus in the winter paddock by letting them touch Biddy's nose. Now they were inside to get warm and to babble on about their adventure.

"That work out in the barn. I could do that," Craig said tentatively to Alton.

"Yes, that would help."

"And I overheard the manager of the ski hill talk about railings to be built and a warming hut to be wired up. I could do that too."

"Yes, probably better than I could."

"And taking care of Dad. I can do that too."

Alton looked at Craig and saw in him a sense of purpose, a sense of peace. Alton hadn't seen that in him back at the family communal home. He been restless there, disconnected.

"What are you thinking, Dad?"

"I can stay back here. You can get me settled. Then when you go off to instruct at the ski hill, and Cedars runs his business, and Laurel is at the Retail…When you all go off, I can stay with Dad; I can do that. I will watch him and let him tell me what to do while I fix this place up."

It was the most that Craig had spoken at once in a long time. It all made such good sense.

Lisbeth had seen Laurel arrive home in the aging LandPorter. She made her way into the house after her. They stood facing each other. Lisbeth's face was reddened by too many tears and too much time outside. Laurel's face, a generation older, was set in calm resolve.

"I can never forgive you," Lisbeth said.

"I understand."

"I don't think I will ever be able to trust you. You keep your hands off Cyrus and Dot now."

"I understand that too. And no, I won't touch them; I can't." Laurel paused. "I have my hands full with Justin."

For the first time in days, Lisbeth smiled. It was a wary, careful smile, but it was a smile nonetheless. She knew what it was like to have a disabled husband. In that moment, she thought of the similarity of the plight she shared with her mother-in-law.

"We can never be friends. You know that," Lisbeth said.

"Yes."

"But fate has made us family. And family is complicated, difficult."

"OK."

By the end of their supper together, plans had been formulated.

Lisbeth, Cyrus, and Dot would return to Beckett the following day. Cyrus and Dot needed to get back to their home, their friends, and the studies that defined the normality of their lives.

Byron would return to Munroe too. He was missing Sallye, despite having been with her just that morning. He would tell Chetwin that he was ready to come off leave. The family issues that had led to his leave were somewhat resolved.

Sanctuary would stay at the ranch; it would be his place of sanctuary. He was already loving the chance to run. Justin was loving the old dog too, and Sanctuary was lapping up that love.

Cedars would go back to his business the day after next.

The next day, Alton and his father would head out to the ski hill to see what work needed to be done there.

Most importantly, though, Craig was home. Even though it was a house he had first seen just a few hours before, it would be his home now because he was with his father.

12

CRIPPS

On Tuesday, November 6, Cripps walked to work with irritation and impatience.

It was a cold walk, damp with fog. Despite being past the meteorological sunrise, little daylight filtered down to the ground.

Cripps was a victim of his own efforts to promote social goodness and health. He could not own a private vehicle. Only those businesses with commercial needs or disabled individuals with medical impairments were allowed to own a vehicle. All others were required to use public transit: the AVoDs. Given that Cripps's condo was 1.8 kilometers from his office, he couldn't commandeer an AVoD. AVoDs would not be dispatched when the distance between departure and arrival was less than two kilometers.

Cripps had originated these very restrictions, which were generated by task forces he had led to write policy that would bind him along with others. Carbon-pollution controls had pretty much eliminated vehicles powered by fossil fuels. Only businesses or the rich could have them. The requirement of walking or biking within the cities had improved the health of the population. It was all good. It was also maddeningly inconvenient and unpleasant on this particular morning. Today it was cold, damp, and dark.

And yet Cripps had more irritation and impatience churning in his mind than just this. He had received a message from Chetwin. It had a demanding tone: "It is essential that we meet this morning, before 9:30 a.m. I have news of Alastair."

"Of course he has news of Alastair—news that he is only just now condescending to share with me," Cripps said to himself. He felt cut off at the knees, presuming that Chetwin had known all along what had happened to Perkins. He had known but had not told.

And the news was undoubtedly not good. On the previous day, Cripps had had a visit from a Constable Morris. The police officer was just back on duty after his four days off; he was back on days now and following up on the incomplete arrest of Wednesday night. The constable had learned that Dr. Perkins was no longer at Munroe Memorial, had not even lasted the night. He was not at his residence. And, of course, in a meeting with Cripps, he learned that he had not been at work either. The constable was not forthcoming with the reason behind his inquiry. Cripps could only imagine what it might be.

Turning onto Academy Avenue, Cripps saw a dark figure walking slowly and unsteadily in front of him. Given his state of mind, Cripps attached the label "skulking" to the walk. The figure was hooded. Something heavy swung from the right hand, perhaps a weapon on a chain.

Cripps's pace was faster than that of the hooded figure, and within a block or so, he had overtaken him. Walking by the man, Cripps heard the unexpected: "Sebastian!" The voice was elderly but still strong.

"Sebastian," the voice repeated. "Are you ever looking old!" The wizened old character peering out from the black hooded cape was smiling through myriad deep wrinkles and morbidly sunken cheeks. He was delighted in his irony.

"Father O'Donnell! Is that you?"

"In the flesh. Well, not much in the way of flesh anymore. Just barely enough to power these old bones of mine."

"When did you get to Munroe? What are you doing here?"

"Too many questions for out here in the cold. Follow me."

Father O'Donnell slowly led Cripps down an alleyway to an ancient church that stood in a small cemetery yard that was set back from the city streets. He unlocked the door and led Cripps in.

"I am the caretaker priest of this very old church, Saint Francis Parish Church, established in 1863. There are wooden beams and fieldstone in this building that have supported it for nearly two hundred years."

"So how did you get here?"

"I ran away." Father O'Donnell smiled. "You see, they tried to put me in a residence for retired priests, but I didn't last long. Everyone around me was too old. I figured I would do better in an old church than in an old folks' home. I am ninety-two years old now."

"Ninety-two!"

"And you look much older than you did in catechism class. You grew up well." It had been a heart task of the parish priest that the young lads and lasses of catechism class would grow up well.

Cripps looked around the old church. Father O'Donnell had set about lighting candles and had turned on electric lights that shone on the stained glass and statuary. The heat was on in the building, but it also had a different sort of warmth, a warmth of love and mystery. It was a warmth that the dry soul of Cripps craved. It was a craving unfelt in the day-to-day commerce of his life, but it was a distant ache that would never go away.

"So this old place is hidden away but is perpetually found by those who need her. I say Mass a few times a year on the bishop's consent, often for just a few souls. Students from the university find their way here when secular learning casts them into despair. There are visitors from other places who know of the old churches and make pilgrimages here."

"How do you keep it up? Such an old building. You have heat; you have electricity. That costs."

"Listen." The elderly priest sat at a very old pipe organ in the chancel. As he clicked it on, there was the gentle sound of air flowing toward the pipes. With gnarly fingers on the keys, he slowly played out the melody line from a Bach air. The sound was resonant of flutes and reeds.

"You wouldn't know the German, Sebastian, or at least you're unlikely to. The English translation is "Jesus will always be my joy, my heart's comfort, and…" Tears welled in the eyes of the elderly priest. His hands grew unsteady on the keys, and the melody died halfway through the musical phrase.

"This old organ is maintained by the great-great-grandson of the man who built it. A bequest to the church became an endowment in perpetuity to maintain this specific organ." Father O'Donnell looked at Sebastian Cripps with liquid eyes. "And the delight of it all is that this year, the technician brought his own grandson with him to teach him the trade of repairing this old organ.

"And in that same way, this grand old church is also maintained—by generous souls who believe in her."

Father O'Donnell played again. Cripps reveled in the slow, stately mystery of the music, in its accessibility and depth. Bach had always appealed to him on an intellectual level, but here it was being played as though it were the bridge between man and God.

Father O'Donnell turned back to Cripps. "Tell me about yourself, Sebastian."

"Do you remember that when you counseled me as a teen, you had wanted me to go to a Jesuit university?"

"Yes."

"I didn't. I want to a secular one instead. Got a degree. Then I got another and then another: graduate degrees in both civic administration and medical ethics."

"That is odd, an odd combination. The wellness of the population and the wellness of the individual, I suppose." In this, Father O'Donnell celebrated his still-sharp mind.

"When I did my undergraduate degree, I read John Stuart Mill and the philosophy of utilitarianism. The greatest good for the greatest number."

"Yes."

"So I went and got a doctor of philosophy; I did a multidisciplinary program in civics, health, and politics."

Cripps paused. "Then I grew tired of the academic world. And so, I hired on with the Administration of Social Logistics. On a practical level, that has been my life's work: the greatest good for the greatest number."

"Noble. But secular. We priests have had a higher calling than that for centuries."

Cripps stared at him, a penetrating, conflicted stare. Then he softened and remembered the man.

"Father, do you have a wearable?"

The old priest looked confused and then caught on. "Well, yes, I have this." He pulled from beneath his vestments a substantial pendant on a chain. Cripps recognized it from the walk; it had dangled from the priest's right hand. When they came into the church, it had been carefully inserted back into his vestments. It was clunky, in the form of a Celtic cross, equal arms intersected in the middle of a circle. The priest handed it to Cripps.

"I had a wearable for my wrist, but it wore through my thin skin and gave me sores. I was told I had to wear it, so an acolyte, a parishioner, assisted me. He was a silversmith; he took my watch, er, wearable, and made it into this. He formed it with the Celtic cross, as I am Irish."

Cripps examined the device. It was clearly fashioned out of a wrist wearable of an old design. The circular ring contained a channel for a gravity device, one that would generate current to power the device when it was moved rhythmically, as on a walk. At its center was a hinged cover of ornate silver—when lifted, it revealed a small screen with a two-dimensional display. A gemstone sat at each intersection of the circle and at the arms of the cross. Careful examination of the stones revealed that they covered pressure switches that would be the inputs to the device. Cripps marveled at it, the beauty that crusted the functionality, a rarity of culture.

"Don't touch the ruby. If you do, the thing speaks and asks if I need an ambulance. If I don't reply, police and medics find me."

"That's a good thing."

"I am not so sure; I am old. The place I wish to die is here, in this beautiful old building."

Cripps continued to work with the device to check its functions. At one point, he spoke his name and his ASL ID badge number into it. He handed the device back to the old priest.

"Touch the jade and say my name." The priest did. The silver cover flipped open, and the image of Cripps from his ASL ID badge appeared on the screen.

"I didn't know it could do that!"

"Ask it the question, Where is Sebastian Cripps?" The priest did and was told that Dr. Sebastian Cripps stood right in front of him. The priest smiled at the obvious.

"If you need me, this can help you find me. If you want me to come to you, touch the jade and tell it to 'Get Cripps.'" The priest did, and a beacon sounded on the wearable on Cripps's forearm.

The priest looked at the device. He was baffled but pleased. "Well, I am too old to think that this is a miracle; it's just the way things are done these days. But you, you Sebastian, are the miracle of today. That we found each other again."

Cripps turned the word over in his mind: *miracle*. Only last week, in walking through the Courtyard District on All Faiths Day, he had also felt nostalgic for the old notions of saints and miracles. Here it was, spoken of on this day by happenstance.

His secular education was to have wiped out the charm of that perspective. He thought it had. Happenstances were now probabilities made likely by deliberate effort in this highly designed society. As the state had grown in power, in beneficence, and in its care of its people, well-being was not left to happenstance or individual intention. Well-being was carefully constructed, was expected, was influenced when not forthcoming, and was imposed when not brought about by influence. It had taken enormous effort, goodwill, design, and political savvy.

But here, here there was something enticing about the language of miracles. Here was mystery, soul, and spirit.

"You look troubled, son," Father O'Donnell said softly.

"You can tell?"

"I am a priest, and a very old one at that. I know the look of the troubled."

Cripps paused. Much troubled him, and it all troubled him more as he stood in the old church, away from the place of his power and control. He thought of Sallye and of the dog. He thought of that Wilkes boy, Alton. He thought of the evil of provocative undermining of the state's beneficent power.

"Tell me," the priest implored.

"In my work, I have created social conditions that maximize health and economic functioning and that help our environment restore itself from centuries of abuse at the hands of the human race."

"That is a powerful amount of good. But with all that good, is there also a dark side? Within you? Within society?"

Cripps spoke deliberately. "There are others who would undermine it all. An insolent young woman with a dog, for one."

Father O'Donnell sank back on the bench of the old pipe organ, his hands resting on his thighs. He sighed. It was the same sigh he had expelled decades ago when given a wrong answer in catechism class by Sebastian Cripps, a Sebastian Cripps who tended to get ahead of himself, a Sebastian Cripps who just could not trust in the faith. If Sebastian could just see his own dark side, there could be hope, mystery, and miracle.

"Father, do you take confession?"

The priest looked up, hopeful. Then his eyes took a saddened cast. "No, not anymore. But I do listen."

Cripps desperately wanted to tell him that two days ago he was on the verge of killing a dog, on the verge of doing what he could only think of now as a vengeful and evil act. But he couldn't. Shame held him back.

"Tell me. Say what you need to."

Cripps stared at him; the problems piled on: Sallye and the dog, Perkins and the cop, and Alton and the insurrection of those who would turn off their wearables.

Cripps's anger grew. He was angry that Alton would have others refuse the beneficence of the social, financial, and health systems the ASL provided to optimize their lives! The same rage formed in Cripps toward Alton that he had felt two days before toward the dog.

"I have much to do." Cripps went to retreat from the church. The bony hand of the old priest held him back.

"Don't rush, Sebastian. It is the temptation of those with much to do. And no good comes of it."

(II)

Myles Chetwin stood at the door to Perkins's and Cripps's office. It was 9:30 a.m. He spoke flatly to Cripps. "You are invited to attend an expedited judicial disposition for Alastair at 10:00 a.m."

Cripps fumed. "What the…"

Myles turned to walk away.

"Wait," Cripps ordered him. Myles stopped. "What is the hearing about?"

"It's not a hearing; it's a judicial disposition. Matters will be settled this morning. And if you want to know what it's about, I guess you will have to attend. I assure you that there are no excessive undertakings for the ASL, nothing that binds us."

"You tell me. I am not going before a judge without knowing what it is about."

"Your choice, I guess. I'll be leaving to walk over in a few minutes. You are welcome to attend. I expect that the disposition will be accessible as a public record, so if you don't want to come today, you can read about it later."

Cripps was livid with the impudence of the manager, a manager now under his executive direction. He was livid at an empty doorway.

The room in the courthouse was set up informally. A large table was in the center of the room with comfortable seating surrounding it; there were four chairs down each side and two at each end. At each place sat a tablet computer for viewing the documents relevant to the proceedings.

On one side of the table sat Dags, Maureen, Zeke, and, beside Zeke, Sallye. At one end of the table sat Alastair Perkins and Elias Hendricks. On the other side of the table sat Constable Morris, Alan Jones of the crown prosecutor's office, Myles Chetwin, and Sebastian Cripps. By chance, Sallye and Dr. Cripps were sitting opposite each other. As they waited for the judge to arrive, Sallye and Cripps looked at each other and then looked away.

Sallye had a leather-bound writing portfolio in front of her.

Everyone stood as Judge Bernard Hurst walked in. Once seated, he made eye contact with the principals involved: Perkins, Hendricks, Jones, Zeke, and his parents.

Hurst began to speak. "First, some preliminary remarks. This is not a trial. If consensus is reached today on all elements, a disposition of this matter will be made with binding undertakings. In the event of a violation of said undertakings, the matter can be brought to trial with prejudice. There will be no testimony today, but documents will be placed on record with consensus agreement from all parties. Is this understood?"

There were nods from around the table.

"I understand that to begin, there will be the laying of formal charges by Constable Morris. Then there will be the presentation of an agreed statement of facts by the Honorable Elias Hendricks, counsel for Dr. Alastair Perkins. I understand that there will then be a formal apology to the victim by Dr. Perkins. At that point, I will wish to speak privately to Zeke Basilis and his parents and then privately to Dr. Perkins. Once that is concluded, we will meet to go over the elements of the disposition and required undertakings. Are all in agreement?"

Again, there were nods from around the table.

And so the proceedings took place. Constable Morris laid two charges: sexual interference with a minor and possession of child pornography. Elias Hendricks read out the agreed statement of facts as had been prepared by Myles. Sallye passed the portfolio with the apology over to Dr. Perkins. She had reviewed it in detail with Zeke and his parents prior to the conference, tending to the emotional turmoil it released. Alastair now read it with tears in his eyes and in an unsteady, choking voice.

The room was silent. All sat looking at the screens of the tablet computers as the documents read into the record appeared there. Zeke rose to go over to Dr. Perkins. The hands of both Sallye and Maureen immediately reached out to pull him back.

The judge spoke again. "Once I have spoken privately with the Basilis family and then with Dr. Perkins, I will reconvene and, if appropriate, pronounce the acceptance of these documents."

Those not involved in the private consultations gathered in a waiting room. Constable Morris and Alan Jones stood grimly off to one side. Myles and Sallye joined Alastair and Elias. Cripps was left alone.

Finally, Sallye went over to Cripps.

"It was difficult the last time we met. Perhaps it will always be difficult between us. But I thank you for stopping the way that you were messaging me."

Cripps stared at her.

"Oh, and by the way, we found another home for the dog, Sanctuary."

Cripps's eyes dropped while Sallye's held firm on his. She had been trained to read spontaneous facial expressions, and she was sure that she caught a brief look of shame on his face.

She turned and started to walk away.

"Mercanzer." Cripps spoke with resolve, beckoning the return of comportment equal to his position of formal authority.

Sallye turned back to him. "Yes?"

"Behave."

"Sir." Sallye's tone of voice was acquiescing. She reflected on his use of her surname. It almost sounded respectful, as though she had moved up a notch.

The Basilis family exited the conference room. and a grim-looking Alastair left the support of Elias and Myles to go in.

Finally, Myles went over to Cripps and said, "So now you know."

"It's ugly," Cripps replied. "This could cause the ASL considerable embarrassment, depending on the nature of the disposition."

"Elias and I worked carefully on the suggested terms of the disposition. Those have been in the hands of Judge Hurst since yesterday. If he felt an alteration to them was necessary, we would have heard. I expect that the undertakings as laid out will settle the matter without negative impact on the ASL."

"I should have been consulted on this all along."

"Perhaps, but I made the decision to go it alone. Your behavior and emotions have been poorly regulated. I felt it necessary to go it alone, as it was a matter that required a nonreactive, diplomatic approach." Myles had decided to be direct; it was time that Cripps too was clipped. He waited for the repercussions, recognizing that the presence of a police officer and a lawyer in the waiting room might mitigate the reaction from his boss. He had kept his voice soft.

"I resent your remarks. Remember that I am acting director and your boss. I can fire you."

Myles patiently waited out the man. It was a good sign that he had not raised his voice, recognizing the others in the room.

"Yes, you can. But I need to let you know that hasty action of that nature might be unwise for you. When you hear the disposition, you will know that Alastair will be leaving us. When he does, the royalties from the avatar-therapy program will follow him. That will mean a big change for the budget of the ASL in Munroe. Further, if the Paraclete program were to be put in jeopardy with my loss, you would likely lose the additional funding for that program. Although it might be difficult, I could apply for separate funding for the Paraclete program and transfer it elsewhere. I have been the coauthor on the reports and have reached an agreement with Alastair to continue as sole author. Without me, you might be left with minimal staff and minimal funding in Munroe."

Cripps stared at the man blankly. Where he had typically felt rage, he was starting to feel nausea, the sickness of being outstrategized and suddenly realizing it.

With all assembled, the judge read out the disposition previously recommended by Elias and Chetwin, agreed upon by Perkins and the Basilis family, and accepted as reasonable by the judge:

1. This disposition is with prejudice. Any failure of the undertakings, upon being made known to this court, can result in

the matter going to trial. The documents pursuant to this disposition will be entered into that trial as fact evidence. These conditions remain in effect for ten years.
2. Dr. Alastair Perkins is to immediately enter residential treatment at the MacMillan Institute and remain there until discharged from the facility with a low probability of recidivism or with referral into whatever program that facility deems necessary.
3. Dr. Alastair Perkins is to leave the District of Munroe and have no further contact with Zeke Basilis or his parents.
4. Dr. Alastair Perkins is to attend monitoring and counseling as provided by the probation service office in his local jurisdiction. This order is in effect for ten years.
5. Dr. Alastair Perkins is to surrender his passport and is forbidden to engage in international travel. This order is for an indefinite period of time but not less than ten years, to be rescinded only by an application to this court.
6. Dr. Alastair Perkins is subjected to lifetime surveillance of digital communications as conducted by the Internet Child Exploitation Service.
7. Given that the offenses took place on ASL property using ASL computers, a modest compensation award has been established between the ASL and the Basilis family. It is understood that the Basilis family have requested that award to be forwarded to the Munroe District Child Abuse Education and Prevention Foundation.

After finishing, the judge said, "That is all."

When they were dismissed, handshakes were shared by all except Cripps. Alan Jones left hastily, but Constable Morris remained, standing watch over the group as it dispersed. Sallye went with Zeke and his parents. Elias and Judge Hurst arranged to get together soon for old times' sake. Myles left with Alastair, as they had a plane to catch early that afternoon. Cripps stood there until it was just him and the police officer. With a shrug, he walked out of the room, heading back to the academy building.

Suppressed rage built within him. He felt angry at being shut out by Chetwin in the resolution of the Perkins affair. Chetwin's initiative and failure to report was to Cripps an even greater transgression against him and the ASL than what Perkins had done. Cripps mused on the humiliation he felt in the judicial conference, humiliation that he had not been the one to resolve the matter. Then there was that infuriating, passive-aggressive Sallye. As a Paraclete, she was to be under the authority and direction of the program, not setting the rules for him as to what she would or would not allow him to do.

Finally, there was Alton Wilkes. All his life's work could fall apart if Alton Wilkes was not dealt with summarily. The risk of a populous movement of those who would disconnect from the ASL data system was horrendous.

Cripps made two calls.

The first was to Dr. Evan Sadler, a neurosurgeon. Cripps outlined the need for a procedure—one that would treat a presentation of paranoid behavior with societal risk. He reported on the notes of Dr. Jefferson from her assessment of Alton. He reported on his review of the IPE-CKS data that revealed a pattern of connection to insurgent groups in the east and of civil noncooperation in the Munroe District. Cripps would forward a summary of the relevant data from the IPE. Where the records were unclear, potentialities were written as facts and happenstances as insurgent activities. Cripps's report of Alton's symptoms was carefully designed to have Dr. Sadler suggest procedures that would suppress and ultimately eliminate neural feedback loops that supported the patient's dangerous behavior. Cripps indicated that the patient was apt to be uncooperative with the procedures, so pharmacological and physical constraints might be required. Dr. Sadler took note and indicated that he would ensure that proper arrangements were made.

The second call was to Dr. Jefferson. It was polite, amicable even. He reviewed his position as the medical ethicist and asked that she arrange for a consultation to involve him, her, and the patient. He suggested that Alton simply be advised that the consultation pertained to his request to have his implant removed.

By the end of these calls, Cripps was feeling empowered again. In the Perkins affair, Chetwin had acted on his own without consulting the management group. There was no reason why he shouldn't do the same in resolving this matter.

It felt good to be back in control. He had a flow going again; he was getting something done. Long forgotten was the cautionary advice from Father O'Donnell.

(III)

Dr. Jefferson's office had been unable to reach Alton on his wearable to set up the meeting. Dr. Cripps had wanted the meeting as soon as possible. Finally, remembering the family connection, Dr. Jefferson called Lisbeth to ask her to pass the message along. Lisbeth contacted Craig, who was keeping his wearable connected. Craig pulled Alton aside as they were working together at the ski hill to let him know. The meeting was scheduled for Friday.

Up at the ski hill, Craig and Justin had spent their first morning working together staring blankly at each other, speaking little except for the grumbles of Justin. Craig managed to keep his composure and gradually jostle his father along with gentle teasing and self-deprecating humor. Craig was able to find ways to ask his father's help that were not physically taxing to the man but kept him engaged; he asked Justin to pass tools to him, to step back to advise whether something looked level, and to talk with him about the materials needed for a job. Craig knew enough about the higher altitude to watch for breathlessness, weakness, and fatigue. He kept his requests doable by the older man, much in the same way he had with the children helping him back at the family communal home.

Craig had always been outshone in the family communal home by the social skills of the others; he had taken a back seat and just went about the practical matters. But here with his father, he felt something different. Here Craig could take the lead. For his part, Justin accepted it as the return of a relationship that he had felt was gone forever. He once considered his son to be "gone and good riddance"; as time passed, the consideration gradually became "sadly" gone and "sorely" missed. Now his son was welcome in his return.

Duncan Johansson brought lunch for the four of them. They ate in the crook of the building shielded from the northwest winds and overlooking the valley below. Snowflakes drifted around them.

"Looks like I have to go back on Friday," Alton informed the boss. "Doctor's appointment."

"That'll give it a couple of days more here. A good start, guys," Duncan replied. During the morning, the four of them realized there was much more to do to get the ski hill ready for the onslaught of the season. Craig and Justin had been talking about it together, the projects that would bring the place along.

Craig needed to go back to Munroe as well. He needed more work clothes—those Justin could lend to him were too big in the waist and too short in the shins. Craig was also feeling guilt about neglecting the household management of the communal home. In going back, even for a couple of days, he could arrange for the fulfillment of his duties there. He figured he could do the financial accounting from up north, but when he went back, he would organize maintenance tasks and train Cyrus on them.

Alton planned to have Cedars come back over to the ranch on Friday and stay for the weekend to be with his grandpa.

Byron had arranged a booth for the three of them at the S-SB. He and Sallye had barely seen each other since Tuesday, when

Sallye had called Byron to join her and Zeke in the Courtyard District so that she could pass Paraclete responsibility for Zeke back to Byron. She had breathlessly recounted to him the outcome of the expedited judicial disposition and her continued confrontation of Cripps. Since then, the two Paracletes had been unable to connect—they had had to get back to work. Almost a week of connections to Emergents and Emotionally Vulnerables had been lost as they had supported Dr. Perkins in his crisis.

And now, early Friday morning, Alton was suddenly due back. Byron had planned a meeting so that he and Sallye could greet their brother and friend. He'd arranged the AVoD to drop Alton off at the S-SB for coffee and catch-up.

"Hi, guys. Hey, it is going to happen!" Alton was excited to see Byron and Sallye and share the news.

"What? Good to see you, by the way."

"My implant, getting it out."

"Wow. How did you manage that?"

Alton settled in beside Sallye, across the table from his brother. Sallye had been sitting directly across from Byron, holding hands as they connected intensely together in conversation. When Alton slid in, she was displaced. The warmth of his thigh rested against hers, which was sensual for them both, but the axis of conversation left her out as the two brothers connected.

"Lisbeth…" Alton paused and corrected himself. "Mom set me up to see her doctor. The doctor called to have me come back in for a meeting with the surgeon who is going to do it. That's why I am back in Munroe. I go over for the meeting about it today after we finish coffee."

"That's great news." Byron's voice suggested that he was less enthused about the possibility than was his brother.

"What about Dr. Perkins? Is he OK? What happened in court?" Alton asked.

Sallye pivoted slightly in her chair to face Alton and shared with him the results of the judge's disposition.

"I guess that's good. I talked to him, down at…at, wherever that was. At first I thought he was so hard that he was empty. Then he softened, and I could tell he was feeling guilt and shame. When that happened, we were able to connect."

"Dr. Chetwin worked out a way for him to bypass neurological correction and get a fresh start instead."

They talked on—of Chetwin and Cripps, of father and grandfather, and of Sanctuary on the worn old rug by the geothermal radiator in the rundown ranch house.

Then Alton left for his appointment.

Dr. Jefferson's office was crowded for the four of them. Cripps had taken it upon himself to invite Dr. Sadler as well. The signatures of two doctors as well as his own would be required to complete the order for the neurological correction that Cripps had prepared. He had briefed Dr. Sadler again about the questions that might be asked in the assessment and the implications of the answers that might be given. Dr. Sadler was already convinced of the necessity of the procedure from reading the summary of the IPE on Alton that Cripps had prepared.

Alton walked in, surprised to see the grim faces of the three. Introductions were made, with Dr. Sadler being referred to only as a surgeon, not a neurosurgeon. As Dr. Sebastian Cripps was introduced, Alton froze and felt his hackles raise.

"You. I remember you. From the Courtyard District. You wanted to take me in. What are you doing here?" Alton demanded to know.

Cripps adopted a condescending tone but was glad that Sadler would see the evidence of paranoia in the young man. "Yes, Alton. That was me. And I am sorry if it alarms you that I am here. I have two roles here in Munroe. My role with you today is much different than when we met in the Courtyard District. It is also different than the role I have with your brother Byron and your friend Sallye. With them, I am a director with the ASL, but here today, I am in the role of medical ethicist. For us to follow through on your request of getting your implant out, my signature as ethicist is required."

"Why? It's my body. I have the right to decide what's in it!" Alton felt assaulted by the condescending tone of the man. He struggled to remember what he had learned about Sebastian Cripps. He remembered bits of what Byron and Sallye had said about him, bits that suggested disrespect or distrust. At the time, he had dismissed the comments as irrelevant to him, but now he was not so sure.

"That's true. But the implant is ASL property. It is there as part of the way the ASL cares for the people of this society. Although you have authority over your body, the ASL has authority over its property, including what is implanted in you."

"So you, Dr. ASL, have the authority to determine whether it stays in or comes out because it is yours." Alton pondered the implications and grew more enraged. "Oh, that is rich!"

Cripps was pleased by the emotional response from the young man. He was pleased that Dr. Sadler was seeing the evidence of the characterological issues in Alton.

Dr. Jefferson detected the emotional eruption occurring and said, "Dr. Cripps is not here as the authority of the ASL or as the owner of the implant, he is here as an ethical consultant to us. Where there are implications for society with respect to the medical treatment of an individual, he is consulted in that role. We talked about this when I saw you last week."

Dr. Sadler leaned forward. He adopted a warmth to his eyes. Alton immediately assessed it as patronizing. It did not come from a soft soul but from a place of professional manipulation. "Mr. Wilkes, can you tell me why you want your implant removed?" Dr. Sadler asked.

"It's a violation of my privacy. It knows when I have sex, and other people know who I am intimate with. That offends me."

"I see." Dr. Sadler's tone was placating. "I don't think any of us would wish to violate your privacy in that particular way. We could have a modesty override installed on your wearable."

"I don't wear my wearable."

"Well, that solves it then. Except, how do we keep track of your medical needs if you are not wearing your wearable?"

"You don't. And that is fine with me. Still, I want the damn implant out."

Alton paused. There was another sense of violation that he felt, a deeper reason to be concerned. To speak of it would be contrary to the worldview of the doctors assembled, but it needed to be said. In speaking, he drew on his powerful experience on the mountain with the peyote. "Spiritually, I feel that my soul is violated by all the monitoring of me that the ASL does, both on the wearable and with the implant. I strive to do good to others, to bring to their souls a sense of peace, compassion, and nonjudgmental acceptance. But to do that, I need to have my own soul replenished. That is a private matter between me and my god. My god watches and is my authority, not some data system that listens in on all my private matters. Spiritually, it offends me to have the devices."

Cripps was taken aback. What Alton said didn't make any sense in the positivistic society of Munroe, the academy, and the administration. And yet within his deeper self, it resonated back to the early training of his childhood and the love he felt from the parish priest, Father O'Donnell. It also resonated with the twinge he had felt on All Faiths Day and the recent encounter with that same priest in the old church. He thought of mystery and miracles, of a spiritual force much greater than the social forces of the administration—a different authority.

As quickly as those thoughts had arisen, they were dismissed. Cripps could not tolerate them, even in his own mind.

Then Cripps smiled. It was a nervous sort of smile with a hint of victory to it. He felt sure that Dr. Sadler was seeing what he needed to see. Alton's spiritual statement would suggest that latent paranoid thought was on the verge of being florid delusion. Such thought could lead to a religious insurrection that would put societal and health structures in jeopardy.

Alton saw the smile on Cripps and was infuriated by it. He had a sense of how foreign these doctors were, foreign to what he felt deeply, what he valued. Panic started to rise within him. He felt trapped by them.

"If you don't take it out, I will slice my gut open and pull it out myself." It was the statement of a passionate, enraged youth. He went to leave.

Dr. Jefferson rose and patted Alton on the shoulder. She stood with him at the door.

Dr. Sadler said, "Your strong feelings are noted. And knowing the harm that you would do to yourself medically if you were to do that, we are obligated to help you. I will schedule the surgery right away. We won't leave you in this state."

Alton took the surgeon's statement to mean one thing: the implant would come out. Dr. Cripps and the two medical doctors realized that it meant another.

(IV)

Cripps watched from the control room as Dr. Sadler rolled Alton into the neurosurgical suite on a gurney. Alton was wearing virtual-reality goggles. Despite it all, Cripps thought that he looked peaceful.

Once in the suite, Dr. Sadler placed pads on both sides of Alton's head, delivering a brief transcranial stimulation. This occurred seemingly totally outside of Alton's awareness. Cripps watched as Alton's body relaxed even more with the gentle buzz of it.

"Was he difficult to subdue?" Cripps asked the neurosurgeon as he entered the control room.

"Not at all. When I went to see him in his room, he was already quite calm and stated that he was glad for the surgery to have his implant removed. I didn't tip my hand but talked about the hypnosis I was going to do on him as though it was standard procedure for any surgery.

"He went under hypnosis very well and accepted the VR goggles. As I led him into a trance that suggested snugness and security, he accepted the physical restraints. The procedure I just completed in there was to release endorphins that deepen his feeling of well-being. He is having a nice float thanks to hypnosis and the transcranial."

"Good. I'm glad he is comfortable."

"Oh, so comfy," Dr. Sadler replied sarcastically, gloating over his own proficiencies.

"So, what is the procedure from here?"

"OK, well, I am glad you are observing and helping today. I have just received my training in it back east, but this is the first time I am doing it here on my own. You will be amazed. Years ago, straitjackets were used to bind the limbs of agitated patients. Then there were the chemical straitjackets: the heavy-duty drugs the psychiatrists used. What you will see here today is so much more minimal and so much more effective. He will walk out of here perpetually calmed and fully cognizant, ambulatory and controlled without the paranoid ideation or delusions. And with no side effects!"

All the fundamentals of the procedure ahead were already known to Cripps. He was more interested in the exact steps in the process. Once the neurosurgeon got on a roll with his explanation, however, both of them reveled in the enormous good and benefits that had come with the neurosurgical advances. It was almost a ritual to go through the telling of it, to be awestruck by it. It was a special knowledge the two men shared.

"This is psychosurgery without having to violate the natural protection of the brain. Using focused electromagnetic-wave pulses, we will have the same impact on the brain that electrodes inserted through the skull had in more primitive procedures decades ago. No longer do we have to drill holes in the skull and puncture the dura. Now we do it with great precision using multiple devices emitting simple wave energy.

"It's elementary physics, really. Essentially, each device gives off harmless wave patterns that would typically pass right through the brain. But when those devices become phase synchronized, they get hot, so to speak. We accomplish the synchronicity using extensive calculations done by the computer to establish precise placement of the emitters and timing of the pulses. This way, we focus a great deal of power on very specific brain structures with pinpoint accuracy. At low intensity, the synchronized emitters give enough power to nudge neuronal clusters into intense firing. At high power, we are able to destroy them completely—ablation. Surgical precision is now possible deep in the brain without having to open the skull. To cut is to cure, it's just that we no longer need a knife.

"It's all wave energy, like the surface of the ocean. A random intersection of waves typically results in a roiling, irregular surface. A superwave occurs when they happen to add on to one another rather than cancel one another out. Essentially, we can create a stationary superwave powerful enough to disrupt the neural activity in a very specific location. It is like a tiny thunderbolt of energy, precisely placed."

At this point, an alert came in on Cripps's wearable. He looked down at it. It was Father O'Donnell beckoning him again. He silenced it. Sadler waited until he had Cripps's attention back.

"So what we are going to do is target specific nerve pathways in the limbic system. We are going after the ones that activate the autonomic nervous system in response to rapid analysis of incoming sensory data. This is the output of the emotional-filtering system that triggers immediate emotional responses—attraction, fear of danger, defense against violation, acute need deprivation, sexual desire, and revulsion. Those rapid emotional responses serve to bias cognition and set up organized but reflexive behavior patterns."

So proud of his power, Dr. Sadler continued the explanation.

"In just a few minutes, you will help me to track those efferent pathways. Once we have traced them out, we zap the specific neural networks using the highest settings of the emitters, phase synchronized and precisely placed. We create tiny neural lesions without destroying the overall structures of the brain. When we get rid of that reflexive response system, we get rid of the paranoid interpretation of benign situations, aggressive or hostile behaviors, and even sexual predation."

"Sounds simple enough." Cripps smiled, belying the delicacy of the procedure.

"You think so, eh? Well, just wait. We have some pretty technical work to do here this morning."

Charles Ross was alarmed. He had made an urgent call to Dr. Chetwin, Byron, and Sallye as soon as he realized what was going on. He asked that they meet him in the lobby of Munroe Memorial Hospital. Myles arrived first and went through an intervention with Charles to get him breathing deeply again, calming his panic. Byron and Sallye walked in just as he was becoming composed sufficiently to speak.

"It is Cripps. And Alton."

"What about Alton? He came in today for surgery. Is he all right?" Byron was immediately concerned about the well-being of his brother.

"It's not the surgery that you think." Charles's heart was racing. "Whoo-ee, man!"

"It's not the implant removal?" Byron asked.

"No. I have been tracking Cripps, following his electronic signature. Every time he authorizes something, it comes up on my tracking system."

"You are doing what?" Dr. Chetwin asked, horrified that the IT guy would presume to be monitoring ASL executive actions.

"And he falsified the IPE-CKS data on Alton and got a neurosurgeon to agree to do psychosurgery on him. Alton is in the neurosurgical suite as we speak. They are treating him as though he is a socially disruptive paranoid and are mentally castrating him."

Sallye was overcome with fury and fear. Her fists clenched, and her eyes filled with tears of terror.

Dr. Sadler settled at the computer, watching peaceful Alton through the window of the surgical suite. The computer generated a three-dimensional representation of Alton's brain.

He spoke to Cripps. "You brought the 3-D picture files I asked for?"

"Yes, I have loaded them into the control computer."

"Good. So what Mr. Wilkes has been seeing on his VR goggles and hearing on his headphones up until now have been peaceful nature scenes—horses in meadows, stars twinkling overhead, that sort of thing. In a moment, we are going to introduce one of those pictures. It should create an immediate autonomic nervous system response that we will measure as our baseline to that picture. Once we have established baselines for all the pictures, we will begin to disrupt neural networks until we know which specific sites to ablate."

"You asked for positive and negative images. I have images of his paramour, Sallye Mercanzer; his long-lost brother, Byron; and his horses in the meadow up near Beckett. Those are the positive images. The negative ones were more difficult, as the fellow seems to love everything about life except for the ASL. I have chosen my image for one of them, because I think he hates me, and I also have an image of the wearable that he detests wearing."

"Should work. Let's do the Sallye one—that should get a quick response."

Cripps took over the computer that was attached to the VR system Alton wore. As he projected Sallye's image, a smile broke out on Alton's face. Dr. Sadler checked the readout from Alton's implant. There were immediate signs of sexual arousal through endocrinological changes, a quickening of his heart rate, and a flush of vasodilation.

"Well, that's a good one. Let's go through the others," Dr. Sadler said as he logged the first baseline reading.

Although there wasn't sexual arousal with the image of Byron, there was a sense of emotional bonding and empathetic engagement. With the horses, there was a surge of adrenaline and a further boost to the endorphin flood that Dr. Sadler had already artificially started. With both the image of Cripps and of the wearable, there was an immediate cortisol release and signs of anxiety and anger.

"All good, clean responses," Dr. Sadler observed. "Now let's see whether we can impact those reactions with some outside energy."

Father O'Donnell was disappointed that Sebastian Cripps had not responded when he had activated his pendant wearable to call for help. Physically, Father O'Donnell was OK, but spiritually and mentally, he was picking up a rift of evil, and it seemed to be around Cripps. It had profoundly disturbed him. He had spent time in prayer for his younger friend, not at all confident that Sebastian had the spiritual resilience to withstand whatever evil was about him.

Restless, he decided that if Sebastian wasn't coming to him, he would go to Sebastian. He remembered that Sebastian had shown him something on the pendant, some way of finding him. He fumbled with it and couldn't make it work. But in pushing the buttons, the priest alerted a constable, who came to the door inquiring whether he was all right.

"Oh yes, my son. I am OK. But someone else is not, someone who I am supposed to find using this thing." Father O'Donnell handed the device over to the young man. The officer was as disoriented by it as Sebastian had been a few days before; he was able to locate the controls of the wearable buried within the pendant, however. He found the pressure pads beneath the gemstones and eventually brought up a projection of Cripps over the surface of the device.

"So there he is," Father O'Donnell said jubilantly. "Thank God! But tell me, young fellow, where is he now?"

The officer continued to explore the device, patiently figuring out how to access the data through it. Finally, a look of completion came to his face. "Dr. Sebastian Cripps is at Munroe Memorial Hospital."

"Oh dear. There is something wrong. He is sick or injured. Maybe his mortal soul is in danger. I have to get there."

Cripps and Sadler worked through a number of fine adjustments, placing the tiny thunderbolt of a superwave in different spots in Alton's limbic system. With each placement, they checked autonomic nervous system responses to the images Cripps had loaded into the VR system.

Suddenly, the sound of Alton's voice boomed over the loudspeakers in the control room. "Oh my God! What beauty! What grace! What wonder!" He was gasping, his cheeks white and his eyes dilated.

Cripps looked at Sadler. Sadler checked the output EEG sensors that he had placed on Alton's temples. He saw characteristic seizure activity in the temporal lobe. It was not yet durable, not yet well organized, and not yet kindling.

Sadler pronounced what was going on. "It is an ecstatic moment neurologically induced by the energy we are sending into the temporal lobes and limbic system. We will have to track it, make sure it doesn't kindle into a full-blown seizure. At least for now, he is having a moment, an awe-filled moment, a spiritual awakening, perhaps."

Cripps reflected on the nigglingly small glimpses he had felt of the spiritual when he was with Father O'Donnell. They too had a sense of awe, but it was a distant, unattainable awe. For a moment, he wished the old priest was here to witness this moment. Cripps regretted that he had lived so much of his life without any sense of awe and unaware of miracles. He lived as one who had managed logistics rather than manifested love. Although it had seemed like meaningful work at the time, it now seemed so empty. And here, even the experience of awe was being reduced to a neurological event created by the output of cold machines. The wonder was being drained out of it. And that was sad; even Cripps could feel that sadness.

They continued to work. Eventually, they found a location that when activated actually heightened the autonomic nervous system response to Sallye's picture. "Bingo!" Sadler said.

"Bingo? I thought we were looking for an interference pattern, not something that made responses greater."

"We have found the pathway. I am going to flood it with low-level stimulation to see whether I can exhaust the neurotransmitters on that pathway. Then we'll try again." Dr. Sadler continued to work the controls in front of him.

Finally, he said, "Now try again." Cripps projected Sallye's image onto the VR goggles. They both checked the status of Alton's autonomic nervous system. It was flat. There was no response at all to Sallye's picture. It was as though he didn't even know her, had no relationship with her, sensual or otherwise. She was a neutral.

"Bingo!" they both said.

Finally, after the jubilation died down in the control room, Sadler told Cripps that they were going to look for two more such sites. It would be easier now, because Sadler now knew where to look and what sort of external wave pulses would impact there. Once found, they would be ablated, and the work would be done.

Chetwin was at the reception desk of the hospital asking directions to the neurosurgical suite. He was informed that he wasn't allowed there. He insisted, finally showed his ASL credentials, and was given directions.

While he was at the desk, Byron stood beside Sallye. He noticed a dark figure enter the hospital lobby swinging an odd pendant from his right hand. As the figure took down the hood, Byron saw that it was an old man, a priest. The cleric looked confused and distressed.

"Are you OK?" Byron asked as he approached Father O'Donnell.

"No, not at all, son." Father O'Donnell held out the pendant to Byron. After a moment, he found a button that brought up the image of Dr. Cripps when pushed.

"I need to find Sebastian; he is in danger!" The old priest was breathless with worry.

"We are also trying to locate him. Dr. Chetwin over there is asking; we believe that he is here in the hospital. When we know where he is, we will take you to him."

"Oh, thank you, thank you!" The old man grasped Byron's hand, nearly toppling over into the young Paraclete.

Alton felt a sudden wave of sadness. So much of the journey had been beautiful, graceful, and calm. At one point, he was sure that he had reached out and touched the divine. When he had first seen Sallye, he had felt relief, sensuous attraction, and joy. It had grown, and he had grown ecstatic with it. Her beauty had far outshone the stars.

Then it was gone.

Sallye was there with him.

And he felt nothing.

His mind cascaded into a deep sorrow. How could he live if he felt nothing?

And then, on seeing an image of Byron, he felt nothing. He felt nothing seeing Byron!

It was unbearable.

The feeling of awe and the divine surfaced again. This time, it beckoned.

He wanted to die so that he could unite with the divine.

In the control room, readouts of Alton's physiological status went into alert. Dr. Sadler looked at them, perplexed. They could only be wrong. Everything was going well with the procedure. His body temperature was rising rapidly, however, and tachycardia had set in.

"What's wrong?" Cripps demanded to know.

Sadler looked at him, stunned. He shut down the emitters and ran into the neurosurgical suite, physically examining Alton's body. He shouted back through Alton's microphone: "He's burning up!"

Rushing back into the control room, Sadler checked the record off the computer system that had controlled the wave pulse emissions. He checked the EEG results.

"Oh God! No!"

"What?" Cripps asked.

"The configuration of the emitters set up two secondary spikes, two new thunderbolts. One was in the hypothalamus. It has knocked out the regulatory circuits of body temperature. The other was in the brain stem, compromising cardiovascular regulation. They are stopped now, but they went on long enough that they have kindled into deep seizures there. If we don't get them stopped, he will burn up; his heart will blow up!"

Chetwin, Father O'Donnell, and the rest of the crew found that the doors to both the neurosurgical suite and the second entrance to its control room were locked. There was no answer when they knocked. The locator on Father O'Donnell's pendant indicated that Cripps was in there. But the five of them couldn't get to him.

A look of horror came over Father O'Donnell's face. He fell to his knees. He clutched the pendant, felt for his rosary, and began mouthing a prayer.

Alton began to hallucinate. The sky above him was filled with whirlybirds and winged horses. He was being drawn up with them.

Looking back and down, he saw the images of Sallye and Byron again. He would have felt sad to leave them if he could have felt anything at all. All he experienced was disconnection, as though they were an intellectual puzzle. He saw the image of Dr. Sebastian Cripps down there too. He didn't hate him; he couldn't hate him any longer—what would be the point? His mind processed the perplexity of not being able to hate Dr. Sebastian Cripps. It was all so inconsequential now.

The winged horses and the whirlybirds took him higher.

Into the light.

It was so hot.

He felt as though his heart was blowing apart.

He looked back and saw his body on the table. A doctor was over his chest, pumping. He wanted to ask him why. Why pump when there were whirlybirds and winged horses, and there was such brilliant light, such all-encompassing warmth?

Then suddenly, eternally, he plunged into the cool, deep blue of serenity. The prayers of Father O'Donnell ushered him there.

Eventually, Cripps and Sadler emerged from the neurosurgical suite. They looked exhausted. To those gathered there—Father O'Donnell, Myles, Charles, Byron, and Sallye—Sadler flatly stated that, despite their best efforts, Alton Wilkes had died on the operating table.

Sallye exploded in fury at Cripps, knocking him over, flat on his ass. Her tiny fists pummeled his chest. Myles stood by, watching it happen. He was stunned.

13

MYLES

Standing outside the neurosurgical suite, Myles was unable to speak. He wasn't speechless in that he couldn't find the specific words. He was unable to vocally produce a sound.

Byron had pulled Sallye off Cripps, and Father O'Donnell was kneeling beside him, saying yet another prayer. Charles Ross was repeating the phrase "Whoo-ee, man!" over and over again as he paced around the small waiting room. Dr. Sadler had made a hasty retreat from the awkward situation.

Byron soon realized that something was profoundly wrong with Myles. There was a vacant look in his eyes; he was immobile. Byron shook Sallye out of her inflamed state of anger and whispered to her, "Now there is something wrong with Dr. Chetwin."

Sallye looked at the vacant man. She checked for the signs of a stroke. She made a few requests of Myles, testing muscle tone. He was compliant in a puzzled but automatic sort of way. There were no loss of motor or sensation function that she could detect. He wasn't panicky or shocked or confused by his inability to speak. It was almost as though he had departed, dissociated.

Byron led Myles over to the chairs. He was compliant with the leading, and he awkwardly sat down, still silent.

"Should we get a doctor?" Byron asked Sallye.

"He has had a shock; we all have. This might just be his way of going through it. Let's not think medical intervention yet."

"What should we do?"

Sallye took Myles's pulse; it was fast but not racing or irregular. She felt for fever, but if anything, his face was clammy and cool, as though the blood had pooled elsewhere in his body. She looked into his eyes; they were darting from side to side, and his pupils were dilated. Finally, she slapped him. He oriented to her and tried to mouth some words, but nothing came out of his mouth.

"We should get a doctor," Byron insisted.

"Not yet. What would Dr. Chetwin do if he faced this situation? He would not want a hospitalist or a neurologist. He didn't trust them. Let's see whether he can walk."

Byron and Sallye supported Myles in getting up, and he walked slowly and laboriously with them down the hall.

"Do you want a doctor?" Byron asked him. Chetwin shook his head.

"Do you want us to get you out of here?" Chetwin nodded slowly, and a bit more life came back to his eyes.

"Let's see whether we can get him home," Byron suggested.

"Wait," Sallye interjected. "Where did he have Dr. Perkins taken that night he was brought here?"

"Down to the Johnsons' house in the Enclave."

"Let's go there, at least until he settles. At home, he has no one to tend to him other than us. Cripps saw him here and might come after him if he's in Munroe. Let's get him out of town."

"Do you know how to get in touch with Mr. Johnson?" Byron asked.

"Absolutely," Sallye replied. "I have his daughter as a client. Silly, you knew that!"

Settling Myles in a small waiting room away from the neurosurgical wing, Sallye went about contacting Gerald Johnson on her wearable. Byron corralled Charles Ross and told him of the plan. Charles hastily told Byron that he was going to the police immediately. He had evidence of the IPE tampering Cripps had done to get Alton into neurosurgery. The two of them watched as Cripps and Father O'Donnell silently made their way out of the hospital.

By the time Byron, Sallye, and Myles arrived at the main lobby, Myles was walking on his own. He was stiff and uncoordinated, and his eyes darted in fear, but he was responding to guidance from Byron at his side. Finally, in the lobby, he slipped his left sleeve up and out of the way of his wearable. Laboriously, he typed a message to Byron and Sallye: "I am OK. Can't speak. No words. Get me out of here. As far away as you can."

And so they did.

Sleet had started to fall during the drive from Munroe down to the Enclave. Gerald drove cautiously, with Sallye in the front seat beside him. Sallye told him of Alton's death. Gerald started to pound the steering wheel, and the powerful Range Rover briefly went out of control on the icy highway. Myles had clasped his hand over Byron's arm at the swerve of the vehicle, but once his hand was there, he left it. Byron could see him calm as he felt the physical presence of Byron beside him.

By the time they arrived at the Johnson home, it was clear that Myles was processing what others were saying around him. He watched intensely who was talking, and his face suggested that he was aware of the emotional content of what was being said.

Myles typed again. "I am OK. Just let me rest. Can't understand. But it's OK." He looked exhausted just from typing in those few words.

Sallye again convulsed into tears as a wave of grief overtook her. Byron held her. Elise did her best to comfort them all, pleading with Gerald to let her know just what was going on.

When Myles was asleep—still sitting up on the leather sofa but clearly asleep—Byron and Sallye sat with Elise and Gerald at the table. Byron kept his eye on Myles as they talked.

"So what do we do with him?" Elise asked.

"I really think that he is coming around. This is a shock. We will be with him overnight and see how he is in the morning," Sallye proposed.

"There is a retired doctor in the Enclave. We could call him."

"Only if we need to. His vital signs are stable; his heart rate is down; and he is breathing OK. Mentally, he seems aware, just not very alert. There is no bilateral weakness and no panicky disability, so I don't think it's a stroke."

"You are no doctor."

"No, and given what happened to Alton, that is probably a good thing." Sallye's words were tinged with bitterness.

"Well, if he gets worse, I am calling the doctor," Elise insisted. Then she too started to cry. Myles had been her rock, her psychologist, and her friend through a hard time. She was indebted.

By early evening, Byron got Dr. Chetwin to bed. He was compliant, but his usual grace and confidence were absent. It seemed as though he fell asleep almost immediately. Byron mused about the mess the ASL was in—the ASL, the endless source of goodness on which all of them were dependent.

"Cripps is still in charge," Byron observed to Sallye as he returned to the table where she sat with Alyssa. They were alternating between crying and comforting each other, and then they were struggling to figure it all out.

"Didn't you say that Charles Ross was going to the police?"

"Yes, but all he can do is provide information. We don't know whether the police will lay charges."

"If they do, Cripps will be suspended until the charges are resolved."

"So who is in charge, then?"
"Dr. Chetwin."
"But if he cannot speak…"
"Let's hope he can by morning."

By early morning, another complication had arisen before Myles was even up. The intercom at the Johnson home buzzed that there was someone at the gate beckoning them. The voice identified himself as Constable Abbott of the Munroe Regional Police. He asked whether Sallye Mercanzer was in the home. When Gerald prevaricated, the constable insisted that he had reason to believe she was there and counseled that it would be wise for her to come with him to the police station in Munroe for questioning. He wouldn't say anything other than to comment how angry he would be if she didn't come and he had to return to Munroe to get a warrant for her arrest on a charge of assault causing bodily harm.

Gerald went and got Sallye, told her to get dressed, and escorted her to the gate.

"We need to go for a walk." Gerald approached Byron as soon as he was up. He threw Byron a parka from one of the hooks in the back hall. As they walked down the driveway, Gerald let Byron know about Sallye. A look of utter defeat came across Byron's face.

Letting the news rest with Byron for a few minutes, Gerald finally asked, "How did he pass the night?"

"He slept."

"Did you get any yourself?"

"Yeah, some." Byron drove his hands into the pocket of the parka. It was cold, a shock after spending the night under a duvet on a recliner in the large bedroom that the Johnsons had provided for Myles.

"I want to revisit the conversation you had at the table last night, the one about who is in charge," said Gerald.

A GREATER GOOD

"Well, Cripps is for now. He appointed himself executive director when Perkins got in trouble."

"So if he is criminally charged, what happens then?"

"I don't know."

"If the charge relates to his work, then he will likely be suspended with pay until the charge is heard and resolved one way or another."

"I guess."

"That could be today."

Byron looked up at the older man, trying to read him.

"So today, the ASL could find itself with all three of its top executives gone or unable to function. So what happens then?"

"I don't know. Maybe Dr. Chetwin will be OK when he wakes up, or maybe Cripps won't be charged."

"Grow up, son. Contingency plans. Someone has to come up with them. This is a crisis."

"Well, there is the authority, the Administration of Social Logistics Authority, our national body that oversees the regional operations."

"Given what you have said about what your IT guy found out about Cripps, they may be already preparing to intervene. But on the ground…Who is on the ground here in Munroe? Who can take charge?"

Byron couldn't figure out what Mr. Johnson was driving at. Why was he interested? It wasn't his business. He kicked a stone on the road in front of him. It wasn't what he wanted to have to think about. He was still raw from the news of Alton's death. Finally, he said, "Why do you want to know? It's none of your business."

"Well, it is. You see, when the ASL took over the economic systems, wrestling them away from free enterprise controlled by corporate interests, the local chamber of commerce was involved in negotiations around what the local ASL would do. That was me.

I was the chair of the chamber. We negotiated a deal; you would probably call it a sweet deal. That deal has continued under Perkins and Cripps, but if the national authority comes in…Well, that creates uncertainty. It could put a lot of things into jeopardy for Elise, me, and others of us down here in the Enclave."

Byron stared resentfully at the man. Byron's brother was dead. Byron's boss was sick. Sallye had just been taken away in a police car. And this guy was worried about his own sweet deal.

"Although good transitions and stability around your administration are a concern for me financially, that administration is your life. We have a shared problem. I want to work with you to solve it." Gerald spoke in the matter-of-fact, negotiating tones of a corporate executive.

"I always figured that stuff would just work its way out."

"That's not how the world works, my son." Gerald paused. "So tell me this: who in the organization knows the work of the organization, has that work at his heart, and has the respect of the others who are working in it?"

Byron thought and then said, "That's easy. Kenyon. He is a natural leader. He has trained the Paracletes and has done the work himself."

"Let's get him down here. As Myles starts to communicate more, he is going to need Kenyon's support."

"Kenyon is a great public speaker too."

"Let's hope he doesn't have to." Gerald paused again and then posited the next question. "Who knows what the day-to-day operations are on a practical level: the transfers of funds, security protocols, and information and data systems? What gets signed off on and by whom?"

"That's easy too. Our IT guy, Charles Ross."

"Let's leave him up there, but bring him on board with the contingency plans. The organization may end up in crisis, and we need him to make sure that it keeps running."

They stopped at a viewpoint overlooking the lake. The sun was a white disk barely penetrating the cover of high cloud.

"Do you know how to reach Kenyon?"

"Sure."

"As soon as we get back in, call him. I will be going to pick up Sallye when she is done at the police station. We will bring Kenyon back here then."

They stopped at the end of the driveway leading back up to the house.

"Oh, and by the way, Elise and I were talking last night. Myles needs that woman who was here with Perkins: the older woman, a psychologist."

"Yes, I was here when she came. She talked to Alton, I think, but I never met her."

"We need to find out who she is and how to reach her."

They walked back in the house to find Myles sitting at the table with Elise. Myles was still not speaking, but he was showing something on his wearable to Elise as she held his arm. An image of an older woman emerged above the viewing screen, graceful and clear of eye. Below the image was the contact information for Dr. Marcia Simons.

(II)

Gerald was very deliberate about the order in which he would pick up those from Munroe coming back to the Enclave with him.

He knew that Sallye would be very uncomfortable waiting at the police station, but he decided that rather than easing her discomfort as quickly as possible, he would let her stew.

Kenyon would need to be first. Kenyon went to make small talk as he climbed into the Range Rover, the envious eyes of everyone in the family communal home on him. Gerald interrupted. In the brusque fashion of a corporate executive, he briefed Kenyon on the circumstances and the needs of the day. As intrusive and authoritative as it was, the clarity of the discussion was as comforting to Kenyon as the accounting of the events had been shocking.

Marcia was next. On the phone, Elise had told her the issue was with Myles. Entering the back seat of the Range Rover, Marcia looked deeply concerned. Hearing that Myles wasn't speaking, she grilled Gerald on the danger of not getting medical attention if it indeed was a stroke that Myles had had. Gerald shrugged it off. Those were old choices made by others; he had other tasks for the day.

Then the Range Rover pulled up at the police station, and a grateful but livid Sallye got in. She first went to the passenger door, only to find Kenyon sitting there. When she climbed into the back seat, she discovered a strange older woman back there with her.

"Well, Cripps laid a complaint of assault against me. The officer receiving the complaint went to view the security video from the hospital and is quite convinced that I viciously attacked the man. So I am charged."

Marcia looked at the young woman. There was something more to her than just the complaint. Something electric. Something conflicted.

"Who are you?" Sallye demanded to know.

Gerald interrupted from the front seat. "This is Dr. Marcia Simons. She is the psychologist whom Myles called to see Alastair Perkins. We figured that Myles could use a visit from her today."

Sallye immediately softened. "Good idea." She and Marcia exchanged a polite handshake, and then Sallye broke into tears yet again, collapsing her head onto Marcia's chest. For a moment, Marcia was taken aback, and then she put her arms around the young woman. The response from Marcia was reflexive and compassionate.

Gerald looked at the two women in the rearview mirror. He recognized that Marcia needed an explanation. Trying to keep his eyes on the road and his hands on the wheel, he let Marcia know that someone close to Sallye had died the previous day, someone close to Sallye and to Myles Chetwin too.

Marcia's mind reeled with the intensity of the situation she was being brought into.

Finally, Sallye sat up in the car and regained her composure. Then a flood of conflicting emotions began to roil inside of her again. There in the Range Rover, as Gerald navigated the winding lakeside road toward the Enclave, Sallye recounted that when she sat in the reception area awaiting her ride, she saw a plainclothes officer leading Cripps into the station.

Then, verbatim, Sallye told them what Cripps had shouted at her there in front of strangers and police personnel. He shouted words that would be seared into her mind: "You! You, Sallye Mercanzer, are to blame for all this mess. You went and brought that Alton here to destroy everything. It's on you, Sallye Mercanzer; it's on you!"

She looked at the others with absolute terror in her eyes. "And maybe it all is."

When they made it to the Johnson home, Myles immediately burst into tears at the sight of Marcia. It was the first emotion he had shown since he'd heard of Alton's death. She took him into her arms and led him into the same room in which she had counseled Alastair. Once the crying had abated somewhat, the others overheard Myles's voice. It was ragged and agonized but was processing out loud with his former mentor and longtime friend. It was a relief to all.

Gerald took Byron aside and firmly told him that he had a responsibility to Sallye, to get some sense in her about who was responsible for what. Byron and Sallye prepared to go out into the dismal November to walk. Elise held out a classic, hooded wool coat for Sallye and helped her slip her hands into the sleeves.

The two young people gone, Gerald invited Kenyon to the table with him and Elise. Together they laid out plans for the afternoon.

To get a meeting arranged with the ASL Authority, timing was paramount. With help from Kenyon, Gerald contacted Charles Ross to have him set up a conference call with the national office for 2:00 p.m. The office was two time zones to the east; it would soon be close to the end of the day there.

Once the arrangements had been made, Gerald began to worry about Byron and Sallye, that they wouldn't be back in time. Elise started to worry about lunch. Myles and Marcia eventually emerged, Myles walking more confidently in front of her. As they reached the kitchen, Elise handed Marcia a green tea latte with the words, "I remember this is what you drink. I remembered it from when you were here before."

"Are you OK?" Gerald asked Myles.

"Yeah. Marcia helped a lot. I needed to cry, to cry for Alton."

Crying was the last thing that Gerald understood. He knew about practicalities, about figuring out what could be done to help, and about someone having to be in charge. Awkwardly, he held out a hand for Myles to shake, a hand of congratulations upon his return to functionality.

"And you?" Gerald asked Marcia.

"Oh yes, I am OK. But I have to admit I am even more impressed by how fucked up the ASL is. I don't know whether to be glad that I am out of the biz or scared to death for what else it will do to screw everybody up." Then she paused, and her hand lightly rubbed Myles's back. "That is, the ASL except for Myles here. Our Myles doesn't screw people up; he puts people back together. But that said, in the last day or two, he—"

As Marcia was ready to begin her account of the overwhelming crisis Myles had faced, he broke in, finding strength in his own voice. "Yesterday I was convinced that I finally faced something I couldn't fix, that there just wasn't enough of me left. Marcia accepted that was the way I felt and then helped me to believe that even if I couldn't fix it…" Myles's voice broke slightly, but then he regained his strength. "I could stay with it, and I didn't need to do it alone. Others too could figure out what they needed to do. We could find the fix together."

At that point, Byron and Sallye came back in, holding hands. Her cheeks were rosy, from either the crying or the cold. Byron went over to Marcia and asked, "Would you sit with us awhile?" Marcia took her green tea latte and led them into the sitting room, sensing another session was at hand.

Myles went over to Kenyon. "I'm glad you are here. I am going to need you a lot in the next few days. Depending what happens with Cripps, I might end up alone in the director's office, and I could use your savvy to keep the ship afloat."

Kenyon reassured him that he would do all that he could.

The image of the national administrator, Dr. Everett Mansfort, came on the screen in the Johnsons' media room. Beside Dr. Mansfort was a blank-looking official whom he referred to as Max, introducing him as the security chief. Before long, Charles Ross, looking subdued from his usual floridity, was onscreen too. He sat in his cubbyhole in the basement of the building on the North Hill. Gerald had set up a table at which Myles sat with Byron and Sallye on either side of him. Kenyon sat with them too. Behind them, listening, was Marcia. Elise and Gerald were behind them too, holding hands.

"So please brief me on the situation out there in Munroe. And by the way, where is Dr. Cripps? I understand that he is the acting director. Is this an insurrection or something?"

"The last we heard Sebastian was at the police station being questioned." Myles was regaining his voice, a practical, managerial tone.

"Questioned? About what?"

"Perhaps I should let our IT consultant tell you," Myles replied.

Charles Ross, clearly intimidated by the personnel looking at him, began. "I have forwarded a summary of what I discovered in doing a routine check for data integrity. I have also attached the relevant excerpts of the data streams. What this looks like is that Dr. Cripps has falsified entries in the ASL database. I took it to the police, and they are interviewing Dr. Cripps about it now."

"You did what? The police! Why didn't you just bring it to our attention here? It doesn't need to go to the police. We could have handled this with much less disruption. The police, really? Nobody died, did they?"

"Well, yes, sir. Someone did. It was the person whose records Dr. Cripps falsified. It looks like the falsification may have contributed to that death."

"Please hold on." The screen showing Dr. Mansfort and Max went blank. The media room went silent.

After an interminable eight minutes, Dr. Mansfort and Max reappeared.

"OK. Thank you for bringing this to our attention. Max was able to check the police databases, and it turns out that Dr. Cripps has been charged with uttering a forged document and manslaughter. He also confirmed the fraud as given in the summary and excerpts that Mr. Ross provided. Thank you, Mr. Ross, by the way. Excellent work.

"We are sending out a senior administrator from the national office by the end of the week. Dr. Chetwin, I am installing you as interim executive director of the Munroe ASL. Hope you are OK with that—you are all we've got. The person we are sending out is just for support. We trust you, Dr. Chetwin, to get this under control.

"That is all."

Myles drily commented, "Well, I hope it's someone better than the person they sent when Alton Wilkes disappeared fifteen years ago."

(III)

Later that same day, as dusk was rapidly falling, a seven-passenger AVoD pulled up in front of the Johnsons' home.

Myles, given his executive position with the ASL, could request a limousine version of this rather than a minibus. The vehicle didn't have the soft leather seats and wood accent trim of Gerald's Range Rover, but to Byron and Sallye—and Marcia too—it had the smell of luxury. The manifest identified the destination as a horse ranch outside of Beckett, with stops in Munroe on the way.

They delivered Marcia to her door. Hugs were exchanged on the sidewalk outside, and promises were made.

At the family communal home, they exchanged Kenyon for Lisbeth. In the limousine, Lisbeth was informed of the death of her son, lost to her for a second time. Byron sat stoically beside his mom. There was kindness in his heart, but there was no comforting her as she swung from silent, stoic tears to disconnected bitterness.

Then they set out on the grim task of breaking the news to Alton's father and grandparents up in Beckett. Myles's strength had reemerged. This was something he did well, putting people together in times of crisis with a reassuring presence. Again, he would summon his "I'll be with you through this," his maturity and calm.

Sallye rode along on that dark trip with thoughts of Sanctuary waiting for her there. She was treasuring that it was Byron at her side, and she was just at the threshold of awareness of the new life forming in her womb.

14

FINAL THOUGHTS

Hey, it's Sallye again.

I always get this weird feeling when someone around me is reading the book or has already read it. It's like I'm naked or something. So I usually go up to them and break the ice and ask. They usually say yes, and then they look embarrassed.

So I think that I need to reassure them, but they end up reassuring me. That feels weird too, because I am a Paraclete, the one who is supposed to come alongside to help. I'm not supposed to be the one needing the help.

Anyway, you've read it. It's pretty rough at the end. Did you cry?

Yes, I am still a Paraclete, still "in the biz," as Marcia would say. I thought I would write this so you would know that I care, that I am with you in going through those tears. And gosh, I still cry when I read about Alton.

But more about that later. First, I am sure that you want an update.

My mom has helped me so much with our daughter, Gayle. She is two—well, almost. And Lisbeth and Laurel too—they are part of the love circle around her. Marcia has been wonderful to me as the godmother to our dear little girl. Initially, she said she was too old to be a godparent, but we told her that God is really old too, so that's OK. It's just that we need her to live to be a hundred.

Byron has been accepted into the undergraduate cohort practitioner stream at the Institute for Humanistic Psychology in Palo Alto. This book, along with the references of Marcia and Myles, helped get him the spot. Well, they helped, but you know from the book that he tries so hard. He deserves it. He will be just as good a psychologist as Marcia and Myles. Better, I bet, if that's possible. I hope to go and join him there if I can. Right now, I am not sure whether I can cross the border with my criminal record. If I can, I will go for sure.

Yeah, I have a criminal record. My lawyer advised me to plead guilty because of the evidence from the security camera. Anyway, because I pleaded guilty, nobody showed the bare-assed picture around the court of Cripps with his bruised tailbone, the one proving the extent of his injuries. I saw it once. It was traumatizing. I can't get the picture out of my head of him mooning the world for all to see.

So Cripps was convicted of uttering forged documents. He made the matter go to trial and hired a lawyer who shredded Charles Ross on the stand. But he was convicted anyway. The charge of manslaughter was dropped. Apparently, now he is teaching ethics at a college somewhere. Imagine that, eh? Just think what the crop of students from his classes are going to behave like after he has taught them.

Cripps, nice guy that he is, laid a complaint for medical misconduct with the licensing board regarding Dr. Sadler. He did that as a strategy for getting out of the manslaughter charge. Of course, Dr. Sadler eventually got off, because it's all doctors there on the discipline tribunal. They said that Alton was killed due to an equipment malfunction.

Oh, and that too. Because Dr. Sadler was cleared by the medical board, the Wilkes family lost their civil suit against him for wrongful death. Then the Wilkes family tried to sue the manufacturer of the equipment and lost because that court ruled that the cause of death was human error. Now the medical-insurance provider and the medical-equipment company are suing the Wilkes family for…oh, what is that called? Vexatious civil litigation, that's it. They might lose the ranch. It turns out the ranch property is worth a lot of money now because of the tourist development in the area. I guess that makes it worthwhile for the insurers to go after them.

So that's more news than you wanted to know.

Oh, you might be wondering about Myles. He is OK. Marcia said that what happened to him at the hospital was a conversion reaction, not a stroke. It was just the stress.

And Zeke—you should see Zeke. What a fine young man he is becoming! Mark my words: the next book is going to be about him.

Now about Alton.

Alton left me love letters. He left them in a leather-bound journal that was in his room at the horse ranch. The guy who wrote this book, Mr. Dale, wanted to include them here as a part of the book. I wouldn't let him, though. I figure that with all that happened, Alton and I needed what little shred of privacy we had left. Byron knows about the letters. He and I read them together sometimes, when we have time to cry and know that we can hold each other and grieve Alton. We both loved him. And he loved both of us too.

Which brings me to the final thought. And this is the hardest thing of all. I am the reason that Alton died. If I hadn't had sex with him that night up in the yurt at the fishing camp, he would never have known about his implant, would never have wanted it out. The whole thing with Dr. Jefferson, Cripps, and Sadler wouldn't have happened. So you see, it is back onto me. I am the cause of everything that happened and why Alton is dead.

Marcia and Byron both try to argue me out of that thought, but it goes deep inside. I try to argue against it too, like they tell me to, but still it is there. Like the way Cripps shouted at me in the police station, it shouts at me too from inside of me.

I guess I'm going to have to live with that for the rest of my life.

But I hope you can get over this. It's hard on all of us.

ABOUT THE AUTHOR

t wilton dale is a registered psychologist, licenced to practice clinical and counselling psychology. He is a family therapist trained to international standards, and a clinical hypnotherapist.

In *A Greater Good* he sets out to tell a cautionary tale about the future of his profession. Equipped with an intimate knowledge of the psychotherapy industry, and his deep understanding of human emotional and interpersonal suffering, dale shares insights only a psychotherapist with four decades of experience could provide.

Made in the USA
Middletown, DE
16 February 2018